Most !

A novel of Edwardian Espionage

By

Jon Wakeham

To
Maureen & Bill
best regards

Jon Wakeham

CHELONIST

First Published in Great Britain in 2013 by Chelonist

Chelonist Publications
www.chelonist.com

A CIP catalogue record for this book is available
from the British Library.

ISBN 978-0-9573921-1-3

Typeset by Chelonist.com
Printed by Lightning Source

Chelonist Ltd
Knapp View
Westhope
Hereford
HR4 8BL
United Kingdom

Email: Mark@chelonist.com

There are endless great stories in history.

Please enjoy this book as a story and, if you are interested, read the history, which should be close to the truth.

When reading history always ask the question, 'What axe does this person have to grind?'

This book would not exist but for the support and help of Hazel Maidman. While she has not provided endless tea and sympathy she has kicked me into publishing it, helping with the editing and proofing and giving boundless support and encouragement in the manner of tough love.

There are many others who have helped with the book, friends who have reviewed parts and suggested changes. I include among these Liz Hirstle, James Errington and Katie and Tom Davies.

If I have neglected to mention the others who have made this possible, complaints should be addressed to the author.

JW

TUESDAY 21st SEPTEMBER 1909

Sergeant Alfred Murphy was very drunk. He often drank seven or eight pints of weak bitter beer during the course of an evening session. His local pub was the Drum and Eagle, an East End drinking den where the beer was cheap and the company anonymous. He boasted that he could drink a gallon of beer with most of the effect being on his belly and bladder. The stranger had kept buying him large whiskies and pints of the strongest old ale available behind the bar and Murphy was not used to drinking whisky. He had even tipped a few extra scotches in the beer when Murphy was looking the other way or had gone out of the public bar to empty his bladder in the outside urinal. Now they had left the pub, though Murphy could not remember doing that. He was incapable of walking in a straight line and had to be guided by the stranger. His senses had been dulled by the alcohol to a state where he was barely more than conscious. Murphy was vaguely aware that he was not being guided home, though he had no idea where he was. After passing along some ill lit and unfamiliar streets they stopped by a large double door in an otherwise blank wall plastered in posters. The stranger found a large key in a waistcoat pocket and opened it while Murphy was propped against the door-frame. There was just sufficient strength in Murphy's legs to prevent him sliding down to the pavement. The stranger supported Murphy around the waist and together they went into some kind of abandoned building site. Murphy had a vague memory of walking down a long flight of concrete steps. After this descent into the dark Murphy passed out, waking sometime later to find himself in a long, narrow, brick-built store room. Other than the dull glow of some distant lamp he was in almost total darkness. There were smells of damp and brick dust, and also of electric motors and hot oil. Every few minutes there was the rumble of a nearby electric train and the change of air pressure caused by the movement of the train in a tunnel.

Murphy attempted to stand but was unable to. His ankles were bound together with thin, strong cord fastened to a ring cemented into a wall. His hands were tied with a similar length of cord which was tightly wrapped in a figure of eight around his wrists and also to a chain which dangled from somewhere above. The chain ran up most of the height of the room and through a pulley wheel fixed to a steel beam on rollers. The room had been used to store lengths of rail and sleepers but was now empty. The movement of the beam had been arrested by a pair of wedges and the chain had been shortened so that Murphy could not move his hands down to the level of his feet. There was a smell of strong tobacco smoke from somewhere near. He turned his head as much as he could to try and discover its source. The stranger was squatting in the entrance to the store room, smoking a pipe of some aromatic foreign mixture. He was illuminated by a single candle.

'Welcome back to the world, Sergeant,' the stranger said quietly, in slightly accented English. He stood up and sauntered over to Murphy, carrying the candle.

'What the hell do you want?' demanded the sergeant, tugging at the chain and kicking his legs uselessly.

'Well, what the hell I want is for you to die, Sergeant. And I want you to die knowing what real suffering is,' the stranger said in a dull but relentless tone. He puffed reflectively on his pipe.

'Just let me out of here now, or you'll really regret it,' the sergeant blustered.

The stranger blew out a cloud of smoke before replying 'Oh, I don't think so, at least not yet.' He laughed in a soft and mirthless manner.

'I don't understand, what have you got against me? I mean, I don't think we've even met before. So, just let me go now, and we'll say no more about it,' Murphy said, trying to sound reasonable.

'It's true that we have never met before tonight, my friend. But I know that you met my mother and my sisters,' the stranger said coldly, 'and besides, I've gone to a good deal of trouble to find you and bring you here. Then there was the trouble I went to finding this place'

'And just where am I supposed to have met your mother and sisters?' The sergeant asked, and he rattled the chain again. He was beginning to sense the remorseless determination of the stranger.

'Oh, it would have been nine or ten years ago when you met them. Now, do you remember what you were doing ten years ago?' The stranger stood, walked over carrying the candle and looked down at Murphy, who struggled again, more weakly this time.

'Well, ten years ago I was in South Africa, so I can't have met 'em can I?' The sergeant replied, breathing heavily from the futile effort.

'Perhaps you met them in South Africa, then. What were you doing in South Africa, Sergeant?' the stranger asked, and Murphy now recognised the guttural rasp of a South African accent.

'I was in the bloody army of course. How do you think I'd gotten to be a sergeant?' Murphy asked in return.

'And what part of South Africa were you posted to, Sergeant?' the stranger demanded in a soft, slow voice.

'God knows! Some camp in the Veldt somewhere. Middle of bloody nowhere it was. Some hell-hole in a stinking swamp. What's it got to do with you anyway?' The sergeant demanded.

'The British army, in their wisdom, rounded up the families of us Boers in an effort to control us. They put my family into what they called a concentration camp. Your army took my mother and my two younger sisters, and locked them up in a camp in a malaria ridden swamp by the Orange River. They died there of hunger and fever. And you, Sergeant, were the man charged with distributing the food and medicines for this camp. Only you didn't distribute most of those supplies, you sold them instead, and many of the prisoners, the ones who could not afford to pay, in one way or another, died of disease and hunger. And that is your army record, Sergeant. No real active service or honest fighting, just a prison warder responsible for many of the deaths of the women and children and old men who were locked in that camp. With a service record like that you must feel like a real hero.' The stranger knocked out his pipe against a wall, inspected the bowl to ensure that the tobacco was extinguished and put it in his pocket.

'Look, lots of people died. You're not the only one to have suffered. I 'ad mates who were killed out there, on the Spion Kop, and other who died of disease. What makes you so special?' The sergeant tried to stand up again, but the cord tying his feet was too short. He collapsed back against the wall of the chamber, the fall knocking the breath from his body.

'What makes me special is that I've tracked you down. I found out about what you did in that camp from some people who survived. Then I came to London and found you. I learned your routines and I tracked and trapped you. And I've locked you in your own little concentration camp, one I made especially for you,' the stranger said calmly. 'I'm going to leave you now, sergeant. You'll find some food and water on the packing case in front of you. I've made sure that you will be able to reach that far. The water is foul and the food not fit to eat, just as it was in the camp. Of course someone might find you in a few days, or you might just die here. So I suggest that you pray to your God for help. I don't suppose that we will meet again.'

'But I was only obeying orders, Sir,' Murphy said, as though talking to an officer, trying desperately to change the tone of the conversation.

'Don't be ridiculous, Sergeant. You are corrupt and without proper human feelings. You really deserve everything that will come to you,' the stranger said, smiling nastily.

'I'll tell you anything you want to know, Sir,' Murphy said, his voice breaking with fear.

'But you don't know anything I want to know, Sergeant. I already know all I need to know about you. You are not the only person I want to meet. There is another man I'm looking for who had something to do with concentration camps. In fact, he helped to implement the policy. I'm going to enjoy meeting him, though he will not enjoy the experience. Well, I don't think we have anything more to say to one another, so I'll bid you goodnight, Sergeant. It wasn't good to meet you, but it has given me a good deal of satisfaction. Now, be a good fellow and do something for me,' said the stranger.

'What's that, Sir?' Murphy asked, suddenly anxious to please.

'Go to hell,' the stranger said, simply.

The stranger turned and walked slowly to the entrance to the store room. He closed the crude plank door to the room and fastened it from the outside with a heavy padlock. Murphy was aware of the echoing footsteps of the stranger as he walked at a measured pace away from the chamber, the noise becoming gradually fainter until it could no longer be heard.

'For God's sake, come back, don't leave me here,' Murphy wailed. He was enveloped in a deep silence as well as in the velvety blackness. There was no reply.

WEDNESDAY 22nd SEPTEMBER 1909

It was not quite what was generally referred to as a 'Pea-souper', one of those thick London smogs, where cold, heavy air descending on the city trapped the smoke from three million domestic fires of cheap, sulphurous coal. Banks of smoky autumn fog rolled lazily down the roads and between the buildings. The smoke bore the odour of the exhaust fumes of taxis, motor busses, trucks and cars as well as the ripe smell of horse shit. Two men were strolling in the lower end of the Inns of Court, where it butts up to the Thames embankment. The fog surrounding them muffled the bustle of the great city, almost turning it into a tranquil village setting. Elegant Georgian buildings were arranged tastefully across airy squares. The soot stains of the bricks were the only hint that their position was close to the centre of London. It was late in the afternoon.

They were tall young men, obviously members of the ruling class, and they were well wrapped against the weather. And though both wore expensive overcoats, there was something more flamboyant about the coat of the taller of the two men, with its collar of Persian lamb. It was not just his coat, but also his movement which marked him out. He walked lightly on the balls of his feet, like a gymnast or dancer, while the other man planted his feet firmly on the greasy York stone paving, the crunch of his boots sounding louder than the subdued tones of their conversation.

'This is a delicate matter' said the shorter man in a hushed voice. 'I trust that I can rely on your complete discretion in this'. He looked into the face of the other man with pale, watery eyes.

'That would depend on what was involved in the matter,' said the taller of the two with a slight sigh, 'I don't like to commit myself if I don't know what I am getting into'. A fog-horn sounded distantly in the estuary.

'That is a very reasonable comment. Let us just say that it concerns the honour of a lady, and one who is well known to you,' the shorter man said, pausing for effect. 'There is also the question of our national interest, but I do not expect you to be so impressed with that argument. If you accept my explanation then you must do so on the understanding that it is on the basis of information passed from one gentleman to another'.

'Really, Scrivener, you do not have to be so melodramatic about this,' said the taller man, testily, 'We could easily have discussed it in your office. And I have no idea what you mean by "a lady's honour". Why don't you just tell me whatever it is you have to say to in plain English. I'm happier speaking in that language'. They stopped by a nearly leafless lime tree whose top branches almost disappeared into the fog.

'Offices have walls, and they sometimes have unwanted ears', said Scrivener lifting his cane and touching the silver top to his lower lip in a gesture suggesting secrecy. 'This is as good a place to meet as any. Halfway between where I work and where you live. And, please remind me, just what are you working at these days?'

'Oh, please stop! I have enough lectures on my general uselessness from my father. Just tell me what it is you want of me. After that I will refuse. Then we can part on the same terms as we met. I don't think you can call on any friendship. We never were friends,' the taller man said with a slight sigh of remembrance.

'Yes, I seem to remember some incidents when we were at Harrow. You were a bumptious little prig then, and you don't seem to have changed much, Mansell-Lacey minor,' the shorter man said with barely suppressed anger.

'Well, you were two years ahead of me. And you didn't dare to bully me because of my big brother, who was in your form. What I distinctly remember is that you tried to bully my friend Gurney-Stewart. And if my memory is not playing me false I recall giving you a damn good thrashing because of that. Please do not insult me again. The Laceys won their honours on the battlefields, not in the banks and law courts, like some did. We have never taken insults lightly, Scrivener, so don't forget it'. Mansell-Lacey drew breath, took a Turkish cigarette out of a silver case and lit it with an exquisite silver lighter. As he exhaled he added to the density of the fog. He made no move to offer one to Scrivener. The smoke scarcely rose from the glowing tip of the cigarette.

'I never realised that you were so keen to uphold family traditions,' said Scrivener, with a distinct note of sarcasm. 'Before you were asked to this meeting we did some checking up on you and your background. You were supposed to go into the cavalry as second son. And that is one family tradition that you have singularly failed to carry out. I believe your father is refusing to pay any more of your debts until you accept a commission. Personally, I regard you as completely useless. You dabble at painting pictures and hang around with a bunch of useless artists and bohemian types. But someone has looked at what you did at Oxford, but not your academic record. It seems that your feats at rugger and rowing count for more than my opinion. Tell me, do you still play any rugby or row?'

'If you were checking up on me you will know that I no longer play rugby, but I still do some sculling. All this sounds like you've been spying on me. But then, you always were a sneak. Now will you please just tell me what it is that you want,' Mansell-Lacey said with a tone of strained patience.

'It seems to me that family connections are more important than talent, these days,' Scrivener sniffed, 'It really is beyond my comprehension that you are allowing your life to go to waste in this way'.

'You had better have a damn good reason for spying on me. Because I have never had any respect for you or your opinions, and

I think that you have wasted enough of my time,' Mansell-Lacey said with a snort, 'Now, if you please, just tell me what it is that you want, and let me get on my way. If I wanted to get insulted, I know of many people who can do it with considerably more wit than you could ever have. So don't strain what little brain you have trying to think up witticisms, Scrivener'. The ash from his cigarette now formed a long grey trunk, and it was a tribute to the steadiness of his hand that it did not fall.

'Alright then, I shall tell you,' said Scrivener with a twisted little smile, 'It concerns your friend Gurney-Stewart, or rather it concerns his wife'.

'What about Em?' asked Mansell-Lacey, at last flicking the ash away.

'It seems that Lady Emily has been holding company with a man who has connections with a…. well let us say a foreign embassy'. Scrivener paused for effect, but achieved very little. He continued, 'With Sir Charles being a junior minister in the Ministry of War, and party to the great decisions of state, we are concerned that his wife might be involved with a foreign agent. And this agent may be working for our enemies. Even if there is no direct danger, we cannot be too relaxed in matters that might influence the very security of our nation. So, you see, we are concerned that certain information may be passed to those who do not wish us well. We want to know what the relationship between Lady Emily and this man really is, and if we need to be concerned about this entanglement'.

'I don't see what this has to do with me,' said Mansell-Lacey, frowning slightly. 'And I can't believe that Emily is involved in anything that might damage her marriage to Charles. They are, I believe, the only truly happy married couple that I know. And who the hell are "We", in any case?'

'Well, let us just say that I represent a department concerned with keeping an eye on people who wish England no good,' Scrivener explained, 'As to your friends' marriage, I can't comment. The reason that you have been approached is because you are a childhood friend of Lady Emily and were close to Sir Charles at school. As you may guess, it is not easy for us to discretely question either an MP or his wife about such matters. There is more at stake here than mere social etiquette. There is also the question of Parliamentary privilege, not to mention the damage that might be done to the government. You can, as a friend, ask questions that would not be possible for us to ask. Discrete questions that require an answer'. Two clerks wandered by holding an animated conversation. There were several seconds silence before they passed out of earshot.

'You still haven't told me who you are working for,' said Mansell-Lacey, testily, 'Last that I heard is that you were due to join the Navy after getting a second in Law. I don't see any sign of a ship around here, or of a naval uniform, for that matter'.

'Suffice it say that I am attached to the Admiralty, and hold the rank of commander. And it is not necessary to sail the seven seas in order to serve your country. There are many other tasks that must be performed,' Scrivener said, puffing out his chest in pride.

'So, you really are a spy. Well, they got it a bit wrong, sending you to see me. Didn't they know that we can't stand each other's company? What is more, I think the reason you dislike me quite so much is that I was better at games than you were,' Mansell-Lacey said with a grim smile.

'The powers that be knew we were at school together, and at Oxford, though not the same college or the same year. I presume they thought that there was some kind of connection between us. And, anyway, I've found a game I can play better than you'. Scrivener trailed off into silence.

'What on earth leads you to believe that I would be willing to spy on my friends for you? I mean, that is not the way that a gentleman behaves, is it?' Mansell-Lacey said in a slightly louder voice.

'You misunderstand. We don't wish to find guilt, only innocence. It would be much more convenient for all the parties involved if there were no awkward consequences, and much easier for us. But we need to know, we need to have the proof to find them innocent. It's not like the law courts. In politics and diplomacy you are always guilty until proven innocent. And the wife of a man in government must, like Caesar's wife, be above suspicion'.

'You always did talk in clichés, and legalistic gobbledygook. No wonder that you trained in the law, you have a natural bent for it, probably inherited. And you still haven't said anything to make me want to work for you'. Mansell-Lacey turned away and walked a few paces before turning back. Scrivener pursued him and raised his voice above a whisper. Two riverboats hooted a conversation or warning.

'Well, there's no use in appealing to your patriotism, as you claim to be a socialist, despite being the third son of a Duke, nor, I think, of appealing to your religion, as we have reports that you claim to be an atheist, despite still attending church. I am just appealing to your better nature, or what there is of it, and a duty of friendship to help clear this lady's name. Oh, yes,' here a pause and a sneer, 'and we are willing to pay some reasonable expenses. With the size of your tailor's bill, you could use the money, right now,' Scrivener snorted in triumph.

'Didn't you know that it is very vulgar talking about money like that? And anyway, I have funds I can use and friends I can turn to. Just because I believe in social justice doesn't mean that I don't love my country. I am not that stupid that I don't know that we have enemies', Mansell-Lacey said, thoughtfully. He dropped his cigarette butt onto the damp flagstones where if fizzled briefly before being extinguished. 'It's the Germans, I suppose. I have no illusions as to their ambitions, knowing that country as I do. I mean, my dear mother is German. I'm sure you know that. Mind you, I haven't spoken to her for five years. She has the most ghastly, rapacious Junkers family, you know. Every time I visited Germany I realised just how much I loved England. So if it is the Germans, please tell me.'

'I can't tell you that,' Scrivener said flatly. Mansell–Lacey considered his next words.

'If it is someone other than the Germans, just nod your head'. Scrivener's head remained steady.

'Very well then,' said Mansell-Lacey, 'I agree, in principle, to do your dirty work. But I must be told a little more before I accept formally. Just where is this alleged assignation supposed to have taken place?'

Scrivener turned and walked slowly towards the embankment while considering his answer. Mansell-Lacey followed. 'In the strictest confidence, and to go no further than ourselves. This is most secret, do you understand?' Scrivener glanced questioningly at Mansell-Lacey, who gave a brief nod in return. 'It took place at the Palatine Hotel, last Tuesday, room 247, at eleven thirty in the morning. You see, we are watching the man involved'.

'Well,' considered Mansell-Lacey, 'The Palatine is certainly a place where I have met ladies, so it seems a likely enough venue. In fact I have arranged a meeting there for tomorrow afternoon. But I can't believe that anyone would have an assignation at such a time. Early morning, lunch-time, mid afternoon or evening are all common, but not the middle of the morning. It just doesn't sound right. And who is this fellow Lady Emily is supposed to have met, anyway?'

'You don't need to know that, so I shall not tell you. All I will say is that he is a foreigner who has diplomatic status. As for meeting ladies at hotels for assignations, you are, I believe, an expert in these matters,' said Scrivener, with scorn in his voice, 'Your dalliances are well enough known to us, legion though they may be,' Scrivener said, the note of sarcasm reappearing in his voice.

'A man has to have a hobby,' said Mansell-Lacey, trying to sound wittier than he was, 'Though I have never thought that Lady Emily would indulge in such activities, and I have known her since we were very small children. Our fathers share their politics, what they have of it, being Tories. And they share a common passion for hunting. Their houses are only a few miles apart. There is hardly a beast or bird or fish in all the country around that is safe from them'.

'Well, as you were speaking of Lady Emily's father, it is a good point to tell you of the arrangements which have been made. Lord Randall will be holding a house party at the end of next week, and Sir Charles and Lady Emily will be present. I have made sure that you will receive an invitation, and I suggest that you accept in the most enthusiastic terms. It would be a good place to ask questions' Scrivener said, meaningfully.

'Well, I suppose I could get some amusement from a house party,' said Mansell-Lacey. 'So who else will be there? I ride to hounds but I don't think there is any hunting planned. And I don't shoot, at least not pheasant, so other diversions would be welcome'.

'There is a meeting of some eminent people discussing some matters before the weekend proper. They might stay on. The writer, Doyle will be there,' said Scrivener,

'Conan Doyle?' asked Walter.

'Yes, do you know him?' Scrivener asked.

'You probably already know that we aren't acquainted,' said Mansell-Lacey, 'we move in rather different social circles, but I should like to meet him.'

'And I believe that Mr Baden-Powell will be present, and some kind of diplomat, a Mr Buchan,' continued Scrivener, 'and Lady Caroline and her husband have just returned from the United States and will be there. I hear that you were once very friendly with Lady Caroline. And there will be other guests, including at least one gentleman of my acquaintance who, for some reason, wishes to meet you. So, you see, there should be more than enough going on to keep you amused'.

'Yes,' I shall look forward to seeing Caroline again. I haven't seen her for over a year. The social scene in New York may be fine, but, money apart, it surely can't compare with our season'.

'It's autumn already,' Scrivener pointed out, 'The season has finished. There is only the hunting, shooting and fishing until next spring. You might as well enjoy it. Either that, or head for warmer climes. And, talking of warmer climes, that reminds me, how is Mehmet?'

'Well, I'm surprised that you don't know that,' Mansell-Lacey said testily, 'or were you just making conversation? Anyway, Mehmet's off to South Africa, or some other god-forsaken outpost of empire, with the MCC. The fellow is a positive martyr to the cause of cricket. You'd think with all the money his father has he could find more amusing ways to spend his time'.

'How about you? I'm surprised you never considered the colonial service. There are some choice postings if you have the right connections, and the climate and workload need not be too onerous' Scrivener suggested.

'Never, said Mansell-Lacey with a note of finality, 'I rather object to the principle of the Empire. And as for meting out justice to some savage race, well, no thank you!'

'I see it as our duty to spread a bit of civilisation,' Scrivener said haughtily, 'and we make a much better fist or it than anyone else. What we do only benefits the lesser races of the empire'.

'Children of a lesser God, eh? I'll let Mehmet know that when he gets back, it will amuse him so much' Mansell-Lacey said with a slight laugh.

'Well Mehmet's the exception to the rule. He is more British than we are, despite having a brown face. Why else would he play for the MCC?' Scrivener said.

'Because he's the best number five bat in the country, of course. And being the son of a mogul prince, he can be classed as a gentleman, which is always an advantage. I'll send him your regards anyway, when I see him,' Mansell-Lacey said with a touch of sarcasm.

'Before you go, I just want to remind you of how important it is to act with discretion in this matter. The very last thing we want is for the press, especially the foreign press, to be involved, or even any untoward gossip. There must not be the slightest whiff of scandal. I hope I make myself clear,' said Scrivener, looking intently into Mansell-Lacey's face.

'Perfectly,' replied Mansell-Lacey, 'And how, precisely, do I go about claiming these expenses you were talking about?'

'See my clerk. Admiralty Office G346. And please make an appointment before turning up'. Scrivener turned up his collar and walked away.

'Goodbye, Scrivener major,' Mansell-Lacey called into the fog.

◊

Walter Mansell-Lacey shared a first floor flat in Belgravia with his schoolboy friend, Mehmet, who was away for the winter. It was a large, expensively-furnished apartment in a block owned by the Duke of Westminster which opened onto one of those London squares that surround a little park that is there for the sole enjoyment of the residents. Those without the key to the gates cannot enjoy the gardens, nor can they afford the exorbitant rents that are charged for such properties. Outside the flat a Leyland truck was parked. Walter slipped slightly on a patch of oil which was dripping from its sump.

The stairway leading to the apartment was blocked by a pair of men struggling to carry a large and very heavy trunk to one of the flats. Walter wondered whether someone new might be moving in upstairs, and who it might be. He waited patiently for the stairway to be cleared before making his way up. It was with some surprise that he found the trunk resting outside his door. One of the men was standing by the trunk, whilst the other was inside the flat. He was being given instructions by a lady with a commanding voice. It was a voice that Walter recognised, belonging, as it did, to his friend, Miss Godiva Williams. The man by the trunk removed his cap as Walter passed by, and Walter made a curt nod of acknowledgement as he entered his apartment.

'Ah, hello Walter,' said Godiva, before he had time to speak, 'I wasn't expecting you back quite yet'.

Walter was left speechless for a few seconds. 'How did you get in?' he asked.

'The usual way, with a key,' Godiva replied, 'The one you gave me'.

'But I never gave you a key,' Walter managed to blurt out.

'Well maybe Mehmet did. Anyone, I've got one, so I let myself in'.

'But what are you doing here, with that trunk and everything?' Walter asked, even more puzzled than before.

'Oh, you see I've left home. I had a massive row with my father, so I've come to stay with you for a while. Just until I get a place of my own. I hope you don't mind'.

'But you can't stay here. It's not proper. I mean, what would your father say?' Walter protested.

'Oh, he won't mind,' replied Godiva reassuringly, 'In fact he'll be relieved that I have a friend I can stay with. And it's not too far away, so I can still do some work for him. Anyway, if he suddenly gets overprotective and demands satisfaction of you, which he wouldn't do, I'll just have to remind him of all his talk of open sexual relationships that he goes on about. He's not a complete hypocrite, you know. And you needn't worry about your privacy, I shall stay in Mehmet's room, just while he's away. I won't bother you at all. You'll hardly know that I'm here. If you want to bring a lady back here I will completely disappear'.

'My bringing ladies back here has nothing to do with it. I don't do that anyway. It's just not done, an unmarried girl moving in with a bachelor. I mean, what about your reputation?' asked Walter, getting irritated.

'My reputation is already fast and loose, coming from the family that I do. And I hardly think that it will damage your reputation. In fact it might improve it. Also, if you knew anything about the working classes you would realise that cohabitation is a most common condition'. The delivery man coughed in a sort of disgusted way at this moment, attempting to gain some attention. 'Oh, yes, could you pay this delightful gentleman who was kind enough to help me, I am a little short of ready cash at the moment'.

Walter fished in his pockets and found a ten shilling note. He placed it in the outstretched hand of the man, and when the hand was not withdrawn he added a half crown, which seemed sufficient to close the transaction. 'Look, I'm not exactly flush myself at the moment. In fact I am having to take on some work myself'.

'Poor Walter, fancy you having to work for a living. How the mighty are fallen. Has your father cut off your allowance again?' said Godiva, with only the faintest trace of sarcasm in her voice.

'Seems like we are both having problems with our fathers. You shall have to live on what I earn while I'm staying. It may not be much, but it will be an honest wage'.

'I still insist that you can't live here,' said Walter.

'Where else am I supposed to go, Walter? I thought you were supposed to help a friend in need, and I am in need right at this moment. And you needn't think you can crawl into my bed or expect me to get into bed with you. The one thing that has kept our friendship going is that we have always resisted that particular temptation. Frankly, it is one temptation that I find very easy to resist. So you need have no worries on that score. I am no blushing virgin, and your virtue is perfectly safe with me. Now be an absolute darling, and help me get this trunk into Mehmet's room'.

Godiva was of more than average height, well-shaped, red haired, bespectacled when reading or typing, with a fondness for bright, showy clothes quite at odds with her Suffragette sympathies and was a one woman tornado in all her interests. Her father was a well known socialist with advanced views on freedom in sexual relationships. There was no possibility of Walter's father ever approving of Godiva as a suitable marriage partner.

'So what was the cause of this argument you had with your father?' Walter asked.

'Much the usual, I suppose,' Godiva said, 'He wants me to put aside my feelings about women's suffrage until the other goals he sees as more important have been achieved. You know, for such a convinced socialist he has a very limited idea as to what social justice actually is.'

'Do you mean to tell me that he is against women's suffrage?' Walter asked in surprise.

'No, not really. He's in favour of it. Well, in principle at least. But I don't think he really appreciates women that much. He likes to use them and to talk about freedom, but when it comes to treating them equally, he really doesn't like the idea much. You know, he expects me to do all his secretarial work and most of his research for him, at virtually no pay, just because I am a woman. He may preach equality, but when it comes to the realities for most of us, he doesn't believe in what he preaches. I'm not saying that he's entirely a humbug, but I don't think he really understands his own prejudices,' she said indignantly.

'And I suppose that you told him your opinions in a strong but reasonably argued way,' Walter said, with a trace of irony appearing in his voice. Godiva did not appear to notice.

'I made my position on women's suffrage abundantly clear to him, and I told him several other home truths. I was really annoyed by him,' she said.

'So, is he likely to come round here sometime, or are you going to visit him?' Walter asked.

'Oh, I never gave him this address, nor told him who I was going to be staying with. He'll presume it's one of my suffragist friends, and he'll never guess that I'm here. But I suppose I'll go over in a few day's time, if only to see mother and to collect my post,' Godiva replied.

The trunk was largely full of books and proved to be almost immovable. Most of the contents had to be emptied before it could be manoeuvred into the bedroom. The piles of books and notebooks were stacked in tottering piles in the living room. It took Godiva only a few minutes to put away the few changes of clothes she had brought with her. Walter reflected that this might mean only a short stay. He liked Godiva a great deal, and found her attractive, but had little wish to be in such proximity to her for an extended period. This was typical of Godiva, assuming so much, and stretching the duties of friendship to breaking point. As one of the first women to gain a university degree, and in a science subject at that, she would have been regarded as one of the most notable examples of a blue-stocking in the country had she not been a vivacious and popular young woman with a stream of bright young things as suitors. But it seemed that she was only interested in their minds. In that respect, they usually fell well short of the required mark. She had only small regard for Walter's mental capacity, but thought him well favoured with a good nature and capable of improvement. Walter liked her because she had never fallen at his feet, as most women seemed to do, and she could safely be regarded as a friend, so this platonic relationship suited them both very well. However, meeting her socially was very different to sharing a flat with her, and he was most concerned that this new intimacy would ruin what was a beautiful friendship. They had met through mutual friends at some meetings of radicals in Bloomsbury, and though their backgrounds could hardly be more different, and their fathers would surely be the fiercest of class enemies they found that they had a good deal in common. It was a relationship in which the differences more than the similarities were the attractions. Walter knew from his school days that the sort of people you can live comfortably with are rarely your closest friends, and that visitors, like fish, begin to stink after a few days. He was too gentlemanly, or too weak, to refuse Godiva's request, and her moving in became a *fait accomplis* within a very few minutes.

'Now tell me all about this job of yours', said Godiva. She had made them a cup of tea, and they were now standing in the lounge, by a sulky fire that refused to draw properly, despite a great height of chimney.

'I'm afraid that I can't. It's all very hush-hush you know,' said Walter, trying not to sound too devious, but Godiva's attention had been well and truly grabbed by this revelation.

'Oh-ho, you mean intelligence stuff', she said, enthusiastically, 'They approached me at Birmingham, thought I might help them out with something to do with a chemical plant on the Rhine, but I told them I wasn't interested in going out to Germany. I'm surprised that they asked you!'

'Thank you for that vote of confidence,' said Walter, a little sheepishly, 'It wasn't a career I had ever considered, but this is a personal matter, and it must remain a secret'.

'I'll get it out of you one way or another, you know I will,' said Godiva.

'Please don't try,' said Walter, 'It's not something I'm proud of, or something that I want to talk about'.

'Well, we shall see,' said Godiva, with the air of an inquisitor.

Dorkins, the manservant who nominally attended to Mehmet, but worked for Walter when his master was away, arrived while Godiva was still unpacking. He remained tight lipped and disapproving, as she bustled around. He said almost nothing to Walter and disappeared into the kitchen to perform his duties. An hour later he served them a modest dinner, made the more modest as it only been prepared with the ingredients for one. His manner was a little unfortunate, in that he always seemed sarcastic, but what was more unusual, in a flat of two very active heterosexuals, was that Dorkins was an effeminate homosexual with a startling line in innuendo, the complete master of the single entendre.

While he was in washing up in the kitchen Godiva questioned Walter about Dorkins.

'Why do you keep him on? He's a dreadful cook and far from being the best housekeeper. He doesn't seem to keep time and he won't stop gossiping,' she hissed.

'Well, I suppose it amuses Mehmet to keep him on. He refers to Dorkins as his eunuch,' Walter replied, 'and besides, he is very good with all my clothes and gives an absolutely excellent shave.' Dorkins poked his head around the kitchen door and called Walter into the kitchen to speak to him. Walter sighed and walked towards the kitchen.

'What is it, Dorkins?' Walter asked.

'It's about the young lady, Sir. Is she intending to stay?' Dorkins enquired.

'She seems to have invited herself. She has had some kind of argument with her father and has moved out. Please don't think that there is any other motivation to her stay.' Walter had a good idea about what Dorkins was getting around to asking.

'That is as maybe, Sir, but I hope you are not expecting me to perform any additional duties. If I might remind you, it is Prince Mehmet who employs me, not you,' said Dorkins. Walter sighed.

'How much extra do you require to perform all these onerous new duties?' Walter asked.

'It's not the money, Sir, it is just the presumption that I will fit in with all these changes. And the young lady is a very untidy person. She has scattered clothes and books all over the room. I have never seen anything like it. I have many other duties in my life, other than cleaning up after her,' Dorkins said in a whining tone.

'How much?' Walter continued.

'Fifteen shillings more a week should cover it,' Dorkins said, smiling.

'Ten shillings is my final offer,' said Walter

'Agreed,' Dorkins confirmed. They returned to the living room.

Dorkins lost little time in insinuating a sexual motive to Godiva's stay, if only in a way that could be interpreted as nothing else to anyone with an ear for speech. But Godiva refused to rise to the bait, and she began to make sly, coquettish sideways glances at Dorkins instead. One time when he was passing her chair she caressed his buttock as he passed and blew a kiss as he looked round in surprise. These actions seemed to unsettle him a good deal.

Dorkins did not reside at the flat, having digs in a shabby house near Drury Lane with a moveable feast of theatrical chums. After noisily clearing the dishes and making a token attempt to put things away in the correct place he returned to his home, a little after nine at night. He was due to return again at nine o'clock the following morning, and could be counted on to arrive by ten most days.

Walter, still hungry after the frugal meal, went to his club and dined again there. When he returned at eleven o'clock, Godiva had already gone to bed. Whilst at the club, Walter had determined to make inquiries next day at the Palatine Hotel, and try to confirm that it had indeed been Lady Emily Gurney-Stewart who had been to that establishment on an assignation.

Walter knew the manager of the Palatine hotel reasonably well, and was not hopeful of gaining any information from him. However, he found a photograph that included a good likeness of Emily, and stowed it in his overcoat pocket for use tomorrow.

◊

The young man hurried down the darkened street, almost running. He could hear his footsteps loud on the greasy cobbled surface, echoing off the soot-stained brick of the closed warehouses and yards. Behind him, or perhaps in front of him, were his pursuers, and he hoped that they were as lost and confused as he was, among these anonymous streets. He was sweating with the effort and shivering with fear. Out in the open he felt vulnerable, even his breathing sounding loud in his ears. He ducked down a passageway leading to a yard half filled with stacked, empty barrels that smelling of stale beer. On the other side of the yard was another stack, this one of steel drums which reeked of oil. He hid behind the barrels, trying to stand as still as possible. He peeked through a small gap to view the entrance to the yard.

For some minutes there was no noise. Then came the soft pattering of rubber soled shoes. Those wearing these soft shoes were barely hurrying. Then there was the sound of a low growl from a large dog. Four men, one of them with a hound on a leash, came down the passageway, not talking. The near silence was menacing. He could hear the urgent breathing of the dog, straining at the leash, and he tried to find another hiding place, within the stack. His foot met with an unseen strip of iron which lay on the cobbled yard. The iron strip struck a barrel with a dull thud and rebounded onto the ground with a ringing noise. Within a few moments he was surrounded, with no escape to hand.

Three of the men were in jackets with mufflers to guard against the cold and cloth caps; the fourth was dressed in a long, dark overcoat, with the collar turned up and an elegant grey homburg on his head. One of the men was patting the head of the dog, who sat quiet and content, tongue lolling to the right of his mouth. Two men held him fast by his shoulders and arms. The man in the homburg approached within a few feet, reached in a pocket and pulled out a cigar case. He extracted a cigar and found a cutter to remove the wrapped tip before lighting it with a match. He let the flame grow along half the length of the match before holding the wide flame to the tip of the cigar. The match illuminated the man's face with a sinister light. He was smoothly shaved with thick curly hair onto which oil of Macassar had been heavily applied. A silver rimmed monocle was screwed into his left eye. There was nothing unpleasant about his expression or features, or, rather, there was almost no expression or individual features. He exhaled the smoke, in a steady stream, and spoke in a smooth, well modulated baritone voice.

'I am disappointed in you, Tommy. I thought that we had come to an arrangement,' He drew on his cigar again. 'I am a very busy man, Tommy, and I don't want you interfering in my business deals any more. You should have taken that boat when you could. In a very short time you are going to feel some pain. But this will be nothing compared to what I shall do to you if I find you still in this country tomorrow. And if you attempt to make contact with him again, you know who I mean, I shall kill you. Nod if you understand'.

Tommy nodded dumbly. Then the beating started. The smooth man stood back and watched with considerable and indecent pleasure.

THURSDAY 23RD SEPTEMBER 1909

Walter returned from riding on the gallops around Hyde Park and Rotten Row. Strictly speaking the tall, handsome chestnut gelding he rode belonged to Mehmet, who also paid for the stabling of the animal. But it was a spirited beast and needed exercise as much as Walter did, and while Mehmet was away it did good to both man and horse. Riding was just one element of Walter's exercise routine, along with training at the gymnasium, playing squash rackets, rowing and fencing. He also had lessons in pugilism in a boxing gymnasium on the Old Kent Road. As in all physical activities, Walter excelled. That he rose early every morning to maintain his fitness and figure might have been a surprise to those who believed in his contrived air of distain for such physical activity. He also ate carefully and had an ability to sleep at any convenient moment. The total effect of this way of life was the development of an all-round athlete.

Still warm and dusty from his riding, he returned the horse to the stables and made his way back to the flat on foot. As he came through the front door, he caught sight of Godiva, who had risen not long after him. She was sitting at the writing desk, and had begun to make notes and time-plans for some enterprise. Walter went to his room and washed. After drying his face he spent some time arranging his dark blonde hair and admiring his even profile with its' slim, straight nose, in a mirror. His complexion was quite dark, and was in contrast to the bright blue of his eyes. Dorkins did not arrive until half past nine.

After Dorkins had served breakfast, an entirely more substantial repast than provided the previous night, Walter bathed, was shaved by Dorkins, dressed in the clothes laid out for him and made ready to go out. Godiva was sitting on the hall chair, ready to leave herself, when Walter made a surprising suggestion.

'If you have nothing better to do this afternoon, why not come with me to a den of iniquity that I sometimes frequent, and learn how the other half loves'.

'But why would you want me to come?' Godiva asked.

'Because, old thing, I need to have someone who is observant and analytical with me. And, I suppose, I have been known to take young ladies when I go there. The manager might be a little suspicious if I were to arrive unaccompanied. I can introduce you to him. It would be an education for you, for he is a most discrete and interesting man'.

'And is this part of your job?' asked Godiva, quite intrigued by the prospect.

'It could be,' said Walter, mysteriously, 'So, if you could be at the Palatine Hotel at two-thirty, I shall see you there. You do know where the hotel is?'

'I know it perfectly. But why are you going to this hotel?' Godiva asked.

'Because that is where the dirty deed is supposed to have taken place,' Walter answered.

'Right,' said Godiva, 'then I can make an educated guess that this is to do with some assignation at this hotel, probably an affair. And I suppose that you know the hotel staff a little. But the people you are working for wouldn't expect you to investigate a stranger, so I must think that someone you know is involved. How am I doing so far?'

'Not bad, but I really will not tell you everything. No doubt you will pick it up as you go along,' said Walter.

'Of course I will. You can't hide anything from me,' said Godiva.

'So are you coming to the hotel or not?' Walter asked, a little peevishly.

'I suppose I might. It sounds like it might be amusing,' Godiva answered.

◊

Walter worked on his paintings in a small hired studio in Pimlico, close to the embankment. He walked there briskly and found a client waiting for him. She was a lady of about thirty, not as slim as she had been, and with a pale complexion and fair hair. She was expensively dressed beneath her overcoat and seemed a little anxious and excited. Walter could not remember arranging a meeting with her but still ushered her through the door before speaking.

'Agnes, my dear, how very wonderful to see you, and looking so delicious too.'

'Walter, darling,' she started, 'I wondered if we could do a little more work on that portrait you are doing of me. That is, if you have the time. It is just that my husband is anxious to see it, and seems to be wondering why it is taking so long to finish.'

'Well, actually I have another commission to finish first, one that pays rather better, but perhaps I can do just a little more to your eyes, just to show that sparkle they have. I'll go and fetch the canvas now.' He wandered into the back room, emerging with an unfinished canvas, which he fixed on an easel in front of Agnes. She had taken off her overcoat and hat and was sitting on the gilded French armchair that Walter used as a prop. She was leaning slightly forward, with her right forearm under her bust in a provocative pose. In this position she was revealing a good degree of décolletage. Walter walked to the window. He opened a shutter and allowed some of the weak autumn sunshine to crawl in.

'I'll just get the paints ready,' said Walter. He found the palette on the rack in which it was stored and the tubes of paint in their meticulously labelled and arranged box. When he looked up again he noticed that Agnes had contrived to loosen her dress a little to reveal even more of her breasts. Walter gave a crooked smile before arranging Agnes into the more modest position she had adopted for the painting. He squeezed white, red and blue paint onto a palette. The oil had partly separated from the blue and needed to be mixed in with a pallet knife. After selecting a few small brushes he added some small daubs of red to her cheeks. Then he started on the finer work around her eyes, trying to turn their blue-grey paleness into a more positive blue with the use of highlights. When satisfied that he had improved the image sufficiently he put the brush down, walked over to Agnes, placed his hand behind her neck and kissed her long but softly on the lips. She responded enthusiastically, and was soon divested of her outer clothes. The sofa was amply big enough for amorous adventures, and was regularly put to such use. After she had dressed and left for another appointment, Walter put the portrait away and continued on the canvas he had meant to work on for a good hour. Afterwards he cleaned all his equipment most meticulously and placed it back into the various containers and racks.

As he was locking the studio he was approached by a sturdy, well-dressed man of middle height with a bushy military moustache. This man had his hands folded behind his back.

'You, Sir!' the man called. Walter turned to face the man.

'Did you wish to attract my attention?' Walter drawled. A number of people passing stopped to observe the scene and to get whatever entertainment they could from the threatened conflict between these toffs.

'By God I do!' the man shouted. He stretched his hands forward. In his right hand was a riding crop.

'You seem to have the advantage of me, Sir,' Walter said, 'Perhaps you could tell me your name and what you consider your business might be with me.'

'I, Sir, am Major William Simmons of the Buffs. And my business with you concerns your seduction of my wife. By God I am not a man to be trifled with! Prepare for a beating.'

'Please stop calling me "Sir", it makes me sound like a prep school master. If you wish to address me correctly you can call me "My Lord". I presume that you are Honoria's husband. She said you were a bore and a bully, and that is exactly what you seem to be,' Walter said in a bored tone.

'I don't care who or what you damn well are. I am here to give you a beating, one which you richly deserve.' Simmons advanced towards Walter, brandishing the whip. When he came within range he raised his arm to strike. Walter backed away a little, drawing him in, then took a half pace forward and administered a simple straight left to Simmons jaw before the riding crop even began to descend. The Major crashed to the ground insensible, a trickle of blood seeping from the corner of his mouth. Walter gave him a kick in the ribs for good measure, then, rubbing the knuckles of his left hand he turned and went on his way without a backwards glance. The entire confrontation had taken only a few seconds. No-one in the crowd attempted to stop him, to complain of his conduct or even to cheer. All in all it had been a very disappointing fight.

Taking a motor taxi from the embankment, Walter made his way via some of the lesser known thoroughfares of West London, to a tall edifice of brick with stone pilasters. The embossed gold leaf lettering on the tympanum above the pilaster bore the two simple words, "Palatine Hotel". Next to the hotel was a millinery store that was well known throughout the kingdom, and many society ladies were known to shop there. The exit from the rear of the shop led to a passage way which, after a very few yards, entered the rear lobby of the hotel. This convenient connection was known to a select set of independent minded ladies intent on adultery. It was also well known to the private detectives of London.

Five floors high, the Palatine was one of many hotels that had developed in London in the last thirty years, crowing the virtues of trade and solid British hard work. It had only the most conventional taste with little or no imagination or originality, but was as safe as the Bank of England. A respectable façade for a building with a respectable purpose but a less than respectable use. The doorman was an Indian Army veteran who wore an immaculate yet colourful uniform and sported a ferocious moustache. His salute was as sharp as the creases in his trousers.

It was a little after two thirty when the taxi drew up to the steps of the hotel. Walter waved cheerily at the doorman as he entered through the swing doors and into the lobby. Godiva was seated on a armchair, reading a small red book. He walked over, tapped her on the shoulder and smiled. She rose and gave him a chaste peck on the cheek. After she had replaced the book in her bag they made for the reception desk. A grey clerk in greyer clothes fluttered behind the desk like an obsequious moth. Walter asked to see the manager and Godiva wandered off to explore the corridor which led from the reception desk.

Alfredo Borsellini, the day manager was an Italian immigrant, originally from Milan, who spoke English that was more than perfect. His demeanour was grave and dignified, his figure lithe and slim and his suit exquisitely cut from the finest dark grey cloth, all of which gave him the look of a dandified undertaker. But his manner was friendly and his smile, though slight, was genuine and helpful.

Walter produced the photograph from an inside pocket and indicated where Emily was pictured.

'Look, Alf, I wonder if you could look at this photograph. It's of a friend of mine, I believe that she was here last week, and I am anxious to trace her. Her husband is also a friend, and, well, I am acting as a sort of go-between, if you understand'.

Alf studied the photograph closely, looked up, sighed and shrugged. 'I do not recognise the lady, Sir. You must understand that in an establishment such as this people come and go all the time, and I am not always on duty as I am now'.

'Were you on duty a fortnight ago?' Walter asked.

'I could check my business diary, but I don't know what that would show. And, as you know, I am not always stationed at the front desk,' Alf said in a neutral tone.

'Perhaps you have some record concerning the visit in the register that I might see,' suggested Walter.

'That would not be possible, for reasons of privacy, and even if it were, I doubt that you would learn very much. That much I think you understand very well. You see, for private transactions we do not enter the details of who booked the room, but merely allocate the room number and the date. As our clients generally pay in cash there is no way of tracing who booked any room. This is, of course to ensure our discretion, and the privacy of our customers. It is arranged so that it is not possible to trace anything back to the client'.

'And you wouldn't remember who it might have been?' asked Walter.

'I am very sorry to say that even if I did breach my own rules I could not remember. You see, I have studied hard to forget names and faces. I naturally have a retentive mind, so it was difficult but necessary for me to learn the technique. You see advertisements in the newspapers which attempt to sell techniques to improve the memory. Well I have had to do the opposite. Genuinely, I am unable to help you'. Had he been French, he might have muttered '*Je suis desolé*', with an elegant accompanying shrug. As it was, he looked gravely down at his shoes, and his shoulders slumped.

While Walter was talking to Alf, Godiva was walking around the lobby of the hotel trying to understand how the booking system at the hotel worked. In the corridor which led to the kitchens she found a notice board. A discrete postcard advertised a job vacancy for a typist with some experience of accounts, on a temporary basis. Taking her memorandum book and pencil from her bag she copied out the details. By the time she found her way back to the reception desk Walter had completed his conversation and was ready to leave.

'Any joy?' she asked.

'Not a great deal. Alf is, as always, the very model of discretion and refuses to remember', Walter grumbled.

'Well I have had an idea, a way of getting to look at the books,' Godiva said mischievously.

'So what is this great idea?' Walter asked.

'Now it is my turn to be mysterious. Mind if I use your telephone when I get back?' she said, smiling conspiratorially.

'Be my guest,' Walter replied.

'I already am,' said Godiva.

'Good-oh,' said Walter. 'Mind if you find your own way back? You see I have a lady waiting for me, and I don't want to be too late, as that would be rude.'

'Of course not, Walter. You do what you have to do,' said Godiva. She gave him a brisk kiss of goodbye on the cheek and walked out of the hotel with a most determined expression on her face.

◊

Walter made sure he was in the room before his visitor arrived. He had a bottle of good champagne in an ice bucket, some cocaine and a small syringe in a Harrods pack waiting by the bed. There was a discrete tap at the door and Walter opened it to find his latest conquest waiting for him in the doorway. He stood back, allowing her to enter. The woman was small and quite dark with sharp features. She would make an excellent model if he ever had to paint a Madonna in the cod medieval style. At this moment she seemed very nervous, her hands shaking a little.

'My dearest Alexandra, it is almost impossible for me to tell you how much I have been looking forward to this moment.' Walter said, opening his arms for a conventional embrace.

'I'm not sure that I can go through with this,' she said in soft tones in a surprisingly deep voice, ignoring the invitation.

'But, Alexandra, you have already risked so much,' said Walter, 'please stay for a little while and let me down a little gently. The door is not locked, and I can assure you that I have no intention of forcing myself on you. You and your honour are quite safe. So, please sit down on this little chair and talk a while.'

He motioned towards a delicate little mahogany bedroom chair. Alexandra sighed quietly and sat down stiffly on the chair, still wearing her hat. Walter poured champagne into two tulip glasses, one for each of them, and passed one to her. She took the glass in a still shaking hand, raised it to her lips and took a gulp. Her eyes remained downcast. Walter sat on the side of the bed and smiled gently at her until she raised her face.

'Oh, the games we play,' said Walter, with a slightly bitter little laugh, 'I can see that you must have screwed up your courage to come here to see me. My reputation is bad enough already, and it will do no damage to me, but you reputation is absolutely pure. Even coming here must be a danger to you. But it does seem a pity that, having come this far, you don't finish what was started. You are alone in a hotel bedroom with a man. Even if we stop here, and it became known that we were together, people would not believe that nothing had happened'.

'You mean that I might as well be hung for a sheep as a goat,' said Alexandra, bluntly.

'That's not quite as I would have said it, but I suppose the meaning is much the same. And I can understand your being a little nervous,' Walter said in a soothing tone.

'To be utterly frank, I am rather more than nervous. Terrified is more like it, and excited as well. I have never done anything like this before.' She raised her eyes to him and managed a thin smile.

'Well let me see if I can do anything to help you be a little less nervous, whilst still keeping the excitement. I have a little cocaine here. That usually seems to help. Do you know how to administer it?' Walter indicated the bottle and syringe which stood by the bed.

'Of course,' said Alexandra, 'but I will only use a little, as I don't wish to risk deadening any real sensation too much.' She rolled up her sleeve as she made her way to the bedside table. 'And of course, there is my husband's feelings to consider,' she continued.

'You told me that he was having a very indiscrete affair with a French chorus girl,' said Walter.

'Yes, I'm absolutely certain that he is. But this is really more of a moral question. I've just been asking myself if it is right to try to get my revenge in this way? The thing is, we are English, and we can't just separate our lives into little compartments and divide out the feelings. The French manage that much better than we do. So to use another cliché, is it really true that what is sauce for the goose is sauce for the gander?' She had placed the needle of the syringe into the narrow neck of the small bottle and extracted a little cocaine into the tube of the syringe. She then held it vertically and tapped it to remove any air bubbles.

'I never know how to answer rhetorical questions, so I usually don't try. As for your motives, unless I am very much mistaken, you came here entirely of your own free will.'

'Free will,' she said, laughing, 'Don't you think we're all just playing some silly game we don't really know the rules of?'

'I was always good at games,' said Walter with a smile. Alexandra found a vein in her forearm and injected herself with a steady action.

◊

Wearing a plain off-white dress with a green ribbon around her waist, and with a green hat, tied with a matching green ribbon beneath her chin Godiva marched out of the flat and made for a drafty Methodist Hall in Bow, her trusty umbrella rolled and ready for use. The meeting at the Hall was to be addressed by Marion Wallace Dunlop, a leading supporter of Woman's Suffrage, and the first woman to go on hunger strike to support her political views. As it turned out, Miss Dunlop was not an inspiring speaker, but being in the company of the sisterhood of the movement buoyed Godiva's spirits. Her determination to obtain the vote for women was reinforced, with the need for affirmative action firmly set in her mind.

There were piles of the WSPU newspaper at the back of the hall, and Godiva took a dozen copies to distribute on her way home. She proffered the copies to ladies on the streets as she walked. Her dress was a good forewarning of her political beliefs, and most women, especially those walking with men carefully avoided any eye contact with her. One woman failed to spot Godiva coming and was startled to be addressed by a striking red-haired woman who exhorted her to fight for women's suffrage, startled enough to be rendered speechless. Her husband, or lover, had a ready-made speech straight from the pages of the Daily Mail, and delivered it at considerable volume straight into Godiva's face from very close range. Having made his point in words the man became more physical. He tore the newspapers from Godiva's grasp, threw them on the pavement and then spat into her face. With the bigot's saliva running down her cheek, Godiva struck the man on the mouth with the handle of her umbrella, splitting his lip to some bloody effect. It was at this point that a policeman ran up to end the confrontation.

'I'm going to have to arrest you, Miss,' he said breathlessly while trying to restrain the man with the split lip who was attempting to strike Godiva. She ignored this verbal arrest as the officer was too occupied to lay hands on her. There was a struggle during which the bigot and the policeman ended up wrestling on the ground. The policeman's helmet had come off in the melee and Godiva kicked it under a passing motor bus before running at speed down the street, a grin of triumph on her face. At the scene of the crime the woman stooped to pick up one of the fallen newspapers and walked away from the policeman and her noisy, boorish husband who were still jostling with each other. Another woman had been converted to the cause of female suffrage.

By the time Godiva reached home she felt more invigorated than she had done for years, a veritable force of nature.

FRIDAY 24TH SEPTEMBER 1909

It really had been very simple. One telephone call, a partly imaginary description of her experience as an accountancy clerk and the offer of references from her father was all that was required. She had been taken on by the hotel to type out letters requesting outstanding payments from the businesses that made use of the account facilities available at the hotel.

Godiva had dressed herself in a plain and conventional way. She presented herself at the desk and explained why she had come. She was taken to the office behind Reception and was given the most cursory of interviews before being hired on the spot, to start work immediately. On the shelves around her were ledgers and piles of business booking forms, all neatly filed. There was also a brute of an Imperial typewriter that became her enemy the instant she tried using it. The office was not a busy place, and, other than her initial introduction to the filing system, she was left on her own. After typing a few bills and adding some entries in ledgers she felt sufficiently relaxed and secure to make her investigations, knowing that what she was doing would be indistinguishable from the duties she had been employed to perform, should her employer interrupt her.

Armed with the knowledge of the room number, supplied by Walter, Godiva was able to locate all the bookings for it for the previous month. She reasoned that she should be able to match the numerical entry in the register with the entry for payment in the cash book. In almost all private bookings the payment was marked as 'Cash', but, as luck would have it, for business bookings the counter entry in the ledger that matched the register number was almost always the details on the payment cheque. The entry in the ledger for room 247 on the day of the meeting was in the in the name of 'The Arthur Gregory Company' and she typed the payment demand in duplicate, placing one copy in the accounts receivable tray and the other in the post out tray. Godiva made a note of the details of the company name and address and bank account number in her memorandum book before she typed out some more letters. Out of professional pride she typed as many letters as she could before the end of the day, despite the best efforts of the typewriter to frustrate her. Before leaving she tidied everything thoroughly. The last thing she typed was her letter of resignation which she placed on the centre of the desk. She never attempted to collect her wages.

◊

The Harwich steamer untied from the dock and, with screws working in reverse, eased itself out into the channel, churning the water in the modest harbour into a muddy brown soup. The watching man in the grey overcoat and low-crowned bowler hat stood half-hidden by a pillar. He waited in the perishing cold until the ferry became small enough to have almost blended into the horizon, where the grey sea melted into the dull sky. The smoke from the funnel gave the only clue as to the ship's position. The watching man seemed to feel satisfied that his task had been completed. He stubbed out his cigarette against the brickwork of the pillar, then turned and walked away in the direction of the railway station. If he hurried, he would just have time to catch the next express to Liverpool Street. For some several minutes after he had gone nothing seemed to move other than the circling gulls with their sarcastic cries. Then a small blond-haired man emerged from behind a luggage trolley. He bore a set of livid bruises across his face and he moved gingerly, as though he had cracked ribs. After a minute's consideration he walked away from the dock heading south. By doing this he avoided the railway station and the quick way out of the town. Instead he headed along the road which led, though he didn't know it, to the next town along the coast, the genteel resort of Frinton. The walk would take him the greater part of the day, as he was unable to move fast. He stopped at a baker's shop and bought some buns for the journey. In a pub called the Anchor he bought a quart bottle of Bass. This he jammed into the capacious pocket of his new tweed jacket, stretching the fabric. Thus supplied he started walking in the persistent drizzle. His coat became increasingly sodden and began to smell of the urine which was used to fix the dyes to the yarn. Worse than this, his boots, which he had purchased as they were fashionable, proved to be less than practical. They hurt his feet and after a few more minutes of rain began to leak badly, adding to his already considerable discomfort.

◊

On the evening of the same day Walter and Godiva were seated opposite one another in the living room of the flat. A letter had arrived for Walter by the third post. It was a demand for money from his tailors, Anderson and Sheppard of Burlington Arcade, the street which runs parallel to Saville Row, near to The Royal Academy, just off Piccadilly. This was not one of the stuffier, long-established firms, but one which provided him with the fashionable and discretely flashy clothes which suited his self-image, if not his pocket. The note from Anderson and Sheppard was a second reminder and so was more terse and threatening than the first reminder that a payment was overdue. Walter tore the letter into four pieces which he dropped on the fire, then he turned to face Godiva.

'What's the name of this friend of yours who went to the Palatine? You see, I found several names in the accounts, and I might be able to identify the booking,' Godiva asked.

'Did you mean Emily or Charles. Either way their surname is Gurney-Stewart,' Walter answered with his mind still on the tailor's bill, 'Ah, I wasn't supposed to tell you that!'

'Aha! So now I know who you want to know about. Right, you can tell me the other details or I won't help you,' Godiva stated firmly.

'Alright, then, as you know that much I might as well tell you about them. I grew up with Emily, the Hon. Miss Emily Worthington, as was. She's the younger daughter of Lord Randall, who is a Viscount. A few years ago she married a school-friend of mine, Charles Gurney-Stewart, the Hon. Charles, as he is now, since his father was ennobled.'

'And Charles was at the hotel?' Godiva asked.

'No, it was Emily at the hotel, with someone who seems to be some kind of German spy. I'm supposed to ask her what it was all about,' Walter said wearily.

'Well, there isn't any reference to Gurney-Stewart, which means that Lady Emily didn't book the room,' said Godiva.

'Did you find any names for whoever it was who booked that room, then?' Walter asked.

'There was one booking that stood out. It was made in the name of The Arthur Gregory Company. Most of the others were just anonymous or completely respectable. I looked at every trade directory I could find in the central library, even the really old ones, and I can assure you that there is no record of any such thing as an Arthur Gregory Company, certainly not in England.' said Godiva.

'I suppose that if you've been through every trade directory for the last ten years, and we still haven't found any business owned by an Arthur Gregory then it probably means that it has never existed. It must be some kind of deception, some kind of deliberate diversion, possibly something to do with the hotel', said Walter, rubbing his eyes.

'You could be right, I suppose, unless the Arthur Gregory Company isn't a business,' said Godiva, a note of inspiration in her voice, 'A company, right. That could have another meaning'.

'What meaning would that be?' Walter asked, intrigued by her sudden enthusiasm, but puzzled as to her meaning.

'A theatrical company,' answered Godiva, 'you know, a company that puts on theatrical productions.'

'Please believe that I am not entirely stupid. I fully understand what you mean, but I still don't see what that could have to do with this business,' said Walter, moodily.

'Dorkins would know about theatrical things, wouldn't he?' said Godiva, with a rising note of excitement in her voice.

'About theatrical things, well, yes, I suppose he would' said Walter. Dorkins had trod the boards of various music halls as one of three young men in a dance turn. An injury to his left knee had forced him to stop dancing. He stayed on in the business for some years as dresser to several major artistes, though he never managed to retain any position for long as he was a very disrespectful and indiscrete servant. What wasn't generally realised by Walter, or by most of his acquaintances, was that Dorkins was a tough and experienced street-fighter, with considerable experience of using fists, feet, elbows and teeth on the thugs who considered him an easy target because of his size and manner. He had grown up in a rough area, and was well used to defending himself. It did not do to underestimate him in a fight.

'And Dorkins hasn't left for home yet?' Godiva asked.

'As far as I know he's still in the kitchen,' Walter answered, 'He certainly seems to be making a lot of noise'.

'Dorkins,' Godiva called in her best stentorian tones.

'Coming, Miss,' answered Dorkins voice from the kitchen. He entered the room at a fast but mincing shuffle, wearing the half apron he used whilst cooking and carrying a spatula that was dripping beaten egg onto the carpet. 'What can I do for you, Miss?'

'I want to learn something of the activities of a theatrical person, and wondered if you knew of him. This is a man called Arthur Gregory, some kind of actor-manager I believe'.

'Actor-manager he may have been, Miss, but if it is the person I think it is, then he doesn't do much acting anymore, and being an actor-manager isn't his only profession,' Dorkins said in a measured and formal tone.

'Then if he is not just an actor manager, would you kindly care to tell me what his other profession is?' asked Godiva, with a trace of irritation just noticeable in her voice.

'There is a Mr Arthur Gregory who runs a sort of club out West. And he still employs chorus girls, in a manner of speaking, and some chorus boys as well. Mind you, they have to be fairly desperate to take employment with our Mr Gregory, as he has a pretty bad reputation,' answered Dorkins, with a suggestive leer.

'Does he still put on shows, then?' asked Godiva.

'He does arrange entertainments that could be thought of as a er..., part of the entertainment business, Miss,' replied Dorkins, winking at Walter.

'From what I gather by his attitude, what Dorkins is suggesting,' interrupted Walter, 'Is that Gregory's club offers services of a sexual nature to his members or clients. Isn't that so, Dorkins?'

'Yes, Mr Walter. That is precisely what the club is entirely about'.

'Oh,' said Godiva, thoughtfully, 'And what parts of society would the members of this club come from?'

'Well that I wouldn't know, well, not exactly, but I do believe that the membership includes some very distinguished gentlemen. Persons of quality, so to speak,' Dorkins said in a lively tone.

'Persons of the highest quality?' asked Walter, sensing the note of gossip in Dorkins' voice, 'Leaders of industry, members of parliament perhaps?'

'Exactly, Sir, that is precisely what I mean,' replied Dorkins.

'Then, if this club is concerned with sexual antics and acts of a sexual nature, why don't you know about the existence of the place?' Godiva asked of Walter. Dorkins coughed politely and answered himself.

'They probably thought that Mr Walter would not need the services of such an establishment. It deals with more, how should I put it…., less common, more specialised tastes'.

'You mean sexual perversions, don't you, Dorkins?' said Godiva, fiercely, slightly shocked, despite her upbringing.

'Not to put too fine a point upon it, yes, Miss,' Dorkins replied.

'But what could that club have to do with the matter we are looking into?' Walter wondered. This was a most puzzling development, and his brain was not the quickest.

'We could always go there and try to find out,' Godiva suggested.

'My opinion is that it really isn't safe for you to go anywhere near to the club, Miss. I also believe that Mr Walter wouldn't be admitted unless he was accompanied by a member, and possibly not even then. And in order to apply for membership of the club Mr Walter would need to be nominated by an existing member of the club and be approved by the management, Miss,' said Dorkins patiently.

'So do you know of any of the members that might also be known to me, in some social capacity?' asked Walter.

'I wouldn't have a clue, Sir. Those are not the kind of circles that I move in. However, I might be able to ask one of the boys who I know has worked there,' said Dorkins, 'I have a friend, or more properly a friend of a friend, who knows all about the club. If you would like me to, I can have a word with my friend and see if the boy is willing to talk to you about Mr Gregory and his business.'

'Could you arrange some kind of a meeting, do you think?' asked Godiva.

'I shall endeavour to do just that,' replied Dorkins.

'Thank you, Dorkins,' said Walter, 'That could well prove to be useful. And where and when do you think that you might be able to arrange this event?'

'Well, I'll get in touch with this mutual friend and try to get him to come to a coffee shop, if he's willing to do it, and he's not too frightened. As to when any meeting might take place, I really couldn't tell. It entirely depends on my friends powers of persuasion. Of course, a little money can be very persuasive. If I manage to arrange a meeting I shall tell you immediately.'

'Thank you, Dorkins. Do you think a couple of pounds would be enough to help smooth the way?' said Walter.

'I think five pounds would be considerably more persuasive,' said Dorkins. He made a small but theatrical bow and minced back again to the kitchen.

'Actually, I think I may know someone else who could help us. And this person knows the theatre business inside out,' said Walter, mysteriously.

'Anyone I might know?' asked Godiva.

'Mary Henry,' answered Walter.

'The famous singer?' asked Godiva, 'You really know her?'

'We are old acquaintances,' answered Walter, 'and her husband is also her manager. He seems to know everybody in the business. It's him I'd really like to see'

'For once, Walter, you have genuinely surprised me,' Godiva said.

◊

Mary Henry lived in a large second floor apartment off Shaftesbury Avenue. It was much more elegant and spacious than Walter's but the address was not as good. It was extremely unlikely that Mary Henry would ever be allowed to take the lease on any property in Belgravia. For despite being hugely successful in her career, and a shrewd businesswoman in her own right, Mary was a music hall artiste. Known as the 'Blackburn Blackbird', Mary had headlined at the greatest Music Hall venues throughout the country, and had, unlike many other British artistes, toured the USA to great acclaim. She counted industrialists, generals and aristocrats among her lovers and was about as notorious as it was possible for her to be. Her audiences loved her for her public behaviour, and for her lavish spending. What was the use of success if you couldn't have your fun?

Mary was more striking than beautiful, with a slight hook to her nose and a high forehead. At forty years, there was a slightly thickening of her waist, but she still moved like a dancer. She had extravagant tastes and liked to dress in the richest silks. Even now, dressed in her robe, her dark auburn hair was beautifully arranged and her makeup perfect. At this hour of the evening she was still mostly sober, though there was the perfumed smell of gin on her breath as he kissed her. She slapped his hand away in a playful manner.

'Walter, you are a very naughty boy, I haven't seen you for months'. She had the soft rolling vowels of the Lancashire mill towns, but this was a trace of an accent rather than the full blown item spoken by a mill girl. She was reclining on a sofa, looking at the fashions in a copy of the Delineator Magazine. Walter was sat in a rather over-stuffed chair right next to her.

'Surely it has not been that long, Mary. You know how I adore you, and I couldn't stay away so long'.

'Well, now that you are here you can say hello properly'. She put the magazine down, leaned forward and gave him an open-mouthed kiss of some duration, then broke off, leaned back on the couch, opened her robe of blue silk, shot with gold, and pulled Walter's head down to her breasts. They were pale, quite large and not as firm as they had been, with brownish-pink nipples and aureoles. Walter nuzzled and kissed them without much real passion. This wasn't what he had come for. He knew from experience that her outrageous behaviour did not necessarily indicate that any uncontrollable passion was involved on her side. Mary liked to use her sexuality as a demonstration of her female strength and importance. Shocking people was her stock in trade, especially the Lord Chamberlain's Office. This office had insisted on several changes to her act, where they believed it might have offended public taste. Her response to these requests was to change the wording to something much less controversial. Not that this would make much difference. Mary could make nursery rhymes sound pornographic with the right leer in her voice and the swing of a hips. Her private life was an extension of her professional persona, but more concentrated. If she exposed her breasts it did not necessarily mean that she felt particularly lewd, or expected service in return. This was not the case on this occasion, however, as she slipped a ring encrusted hand to his crotch and began to knead gently but enthusiastically.

Mary moved her hand away and drew Walter to her. Placing her hands on his shoulders she pulled him down so that his face was on the level of her parted thighs and lay back on the couch. Walter took a deep breath, prepared his tongue, succumbing to his fate. He did the needful act, efficiently effectively and gently without hurrying. It was all part of the transaction. If he wanted some information from Mary, then she would demand suitable payment in kind.

'How is Stan?' Walter asked after she had rearranged her clothing and sat him next to her on the sofa. Stan was Mary's erstwhile husband. She had married him when she found herself pregnant. Stan was her agent, a small mousy man who actively pursued any likely young men at the theatre. Being married made him more respectable, and Mary gave him free reign to indulge his tastes in return for similar consideration on his part for her peccadilloes.

'Ooh, I haven't seen him recently. He sent me a card from somewhere in France. He's there with this dancer from the Royal. Is there something you wanted to know?' She took a good swig of neat gin.

'I wanted to ask him something. Perhaps you can help'. He looked at Mary and smiled. She looked sleepy and satisfied like a cat that has just been fed.

Walter waited until she had poured herself another drink before he asked the question he had been waiting to put to her.

'Do you happen to know anything about a Mr Arthur Gregory?' asked Walter. There was a delay of a few seconds before Mary answered.

'Oh I know Arthur, alright', said Mary, with a grim smile 'And I hope that you are not mixed up with him.'

'I thought I might like to talk to him,' said Walter.

'One of your friends in trouble, are they?' asked Mary. Walter considered his reply.

'Well, I suppose that might be the case,' he agreed.

'Then tell him to pay up, that's the best thing for him to do. You don't want to mess with Mr Gregory, he's not a nice person, and he knows people,' Mary said flatly.

'What sort of people?' asked Walter.

'People who know other people who can find out where you live. People who can hurt you,' said Mary, 'Hurt you really badly'.

'I still want to find him,' said Walter, with a note of determination in his voice.

'Well, you might want to find him, but I won't tell you anything more. You stay away from him. Arthur Gregory is poison, darling Walter, pure bloody poison. I don't want you hurt, I don't want your pretty face scarred. You stay away from him and keep yourself just as perfect and handsome as you are now. Make sure you take care of that pretty face, do it for me', Mary said, and she took another swig of gin.

◊

Three days had passed from the time when he had been entombed behind the rough wooden door. Sergeant Murphy was very nearly dead. It was the fluffers, the women who work nights clearing the tracks of the underground railway of accumulated dust and debris, who noticed the noise. They were cleaning this section of track as a part of their monthly rota. The moans from behind the old doorway were low but audible when the hum from the electrical transformers ceased after the power had been turned off. As the door was locked shut they were unable to get in. A maintenance team was sent for. It took them over an hour to arrive with their tools, but only a few seconds to break the hasp of the padlock with a cutter and jemmy the door open. Inside the narrow brick cell a man was near to death. He was positioned in a half sitting posture, his arms tied to a lifting hoist and chain. His ankles were tightly bound with strong narrow cord which had cut off the blood supply. The chain and cord proved much more difficult to deal with than the lock on the door. Every time they tried to move him he groaned in agony, and they needed to be both firm and gentle in order to cut his bonds. Every movement that attempted to free him seemed to threaten the man's life more. Although he was conscious he seemed unable to respond to the queries directed to him. An improvised stretcher was constructed from coats and poles and two strong men carried him from his improvised cell, along the edge of the track and from there to the surface. At the ground level of the station an ambulance was waiting to take him to the Royal London Hospital in Whitechapel.

At the hospital they made him comfortable. The duty doctor thought his legs might have to be amputated, but that would be the decision of the consultant surgeon who would visit the next day. At this stage the most important thing to do was to save his life, and no immediate attempt was made to find out who he was. It was not until the following morning that questions began to be asked about who this patient might be. The police were contacted and they were very interested in finding out how he had come to be locked in a closed store-room on the London Underground.

SATURDAY 25TH SEPTEMBER 1909

The police examined Murphy's clothes and possessions. They would have liked to question him, but he was still unable to communicate. He lay motionless in bed, eyes and mouth open. There were no details of anyone reported as missing who matched this man's description. In his pocket was a pawn ticket which had passed its redeem date some weeks before. The pawn shop had no records of the man's name, but still had the item to be redeemed. It was a medal from the South African campaign, the Queen's South Africa medal with a Zand River clasp. From the number stamped on the medal the police were able to find out from the War Office that it had been awarded to Sergeant Alfred Murphy of the Rifle Brigade in April 1901. Door-to-door enquiries in the area near to the pawn shop led them to a run-down boarding house owned by a Mrs Hillman, a middle-aged widow with a sharp face and wary eyes. She was Murphy's landlady and was owed three weeks rent. If Murphy had not left his few possessions in the room she would have presumed that he had done a midnight flit. They learned from her that Murphy drifted in and out of work and spent most of his money, when he had it, at a local pub.

At this pub, the Drum and Eagle, the Police identified a small group of heavy drinkers who were Murphy's regular companions. They knew he was named Arthur, a little about his military service and what his favourite drink was but nothing else. Murphy had mates, but no close friends. The Police detectives were able to glean some details about what had happened to the ex-sergeant on the night that he disappeared. Between them the drinkers were able to provide a description of a fairly tall man who had been buying him drinks throughout the evening. This man was not known to any of them, and he had a distinctly foreign accent. Quite where that accent came from the drinkers couldn't say. Some said he was

American, while others thought he was Australian, and one thought that he might have been German. None of the drinkers could provide an accurate description of the stranger; not his features or build or even if he had a moustache.

Using the information they had gathered Scotland Yard decided to release some details to the press, in the hope of learning more of the mysterious stranger. The Deputy Chief Constable had decided that it would be better to give details of Murphy's ordeal rather than to suppress them. The bigger the story in the press, the more publicity would be gained and the greater the likelihood of a useful response from the public.

Murphy's injuries were severe. Gangrene had set into both legs. It was not long before the consultant surgeon, Mr Darius O'Keefe, decided to amputate both legs below the knee, to prevent further spread of the infection. He was put through surgery the same afternoon. The delirium Murphy was suffering was put down to severe dehydration. Even when he had been re-hydrated with many cups of water Murphy still did not talk. The horror of his ordeal seemed to have disturbed his mind. You could talk to him, and though he could now turn his head to look at you and move his lips, no speech came out of his mouth.

◊

Walter, Godiva, Dorkins and Dorkins' friend of a friend, Gordon, sat around the table at the Lyons Corner House at 213 Piccadilly. Nippy waitresses flitted past delivering pots of tea and coffee and plates of cake slices. Gordon was a pale young man, tall and skinny, with a square forehead and cornflower blue eyes. He sat back in his chair with his arms folded, more surly than taciturn. His eyes were directed down to the table for most of the time. It was difficult to start any conversation with him without the sentences trailing off to embarrassing silences.

'I don't know why you brought me here,' Gordon complained.

'We just want to find out a bit more about the club. You know, Arthur Gregory's club' Walter coaxed, 'And we might be able to pay you some expenses.' Gordon visibly winced at the mention of Gregory's name.

'Well, expenses won't be much use to me if I've got two broken legs. Legs are quite important to a dancer, if you didn't know,' Gordon muttered. Across the restaurant a man in a nondescript grey suit who was facing their table folded his newspaper.

A Nippy in lace-trimmed cap and starched apron deftly placed a plate of buttered scones onto the small space in the centre of the table.

Godiva took a sip of tea and placed the cup and saucer back down on the table. 'You must be very fit, being a dancer,' she suggested.

'Look, I'm a chorus boy,' Gordon said, leaning away from Godiva, 'I don't know how simple you are, but if you are trying to chat me up, I'm afraid that you are wasting your time.'

'I'm not quite that naïve,' Godiva said, almost giggling, 'I was just trying to make conversation. What I meant was physically fit. Dancing is supposed to be one of the best forms of exercise.'

'And there's no need to be rude, Gordon. I mean, look at her she's a lovely girl,' said Dorkins.

'She's too big for me to lift. I wouldn't want to have her in a chorus line, but she seems nice enough. She's got bona riah and lallies' Gordon said sulkily.' Gordon indicated Walter with an upturned look of eyes and then whispered to Dorkins, 'I don't suppose that your friend there might be a homie-palone?'

'Not a chance. From what I know of this gentleman I can safely say that you would be wasting your time,' said Dorkins, 'He really doesn't go that way, in fact I think you'd better apologise to them both.'

'Sorry,' Gordon said without a hint of contrition, 'Look, as for other information, it's just that I don't want to get hurt. You don't know what he's like. He had this German boy beaten up just because he thought he was interfering, asking questions. Tommy his name was, pretty little blond boy. Mr Gregory's probably killed people or had them killed. Everyone's frightened of him. And they have every reason to be frightened.' The man in the grey suit turned another page of his newspaper.

'Has he hurt some of your friends?' Godiva asked.

'You don't know the half of it,' Gordon confided, 'You see, he actually enjoys hurting people, just for the sake of it. He gets some kind of pleasure out of it. It's not natural. And some of his friends are even worse. There's a Mr Crowley. He's a real wrong 'un. And there's some kind of vicar, the Rev. Davidson. He's completely barking mad.'

'Tell me more about this German boy,' Godiva probed. Walter started to eat the scones. He spread thick layers of clotted cream and strawberry jam on them before sitting forward with mouth above the plate so as to catch the crumbs. He used the opportunity to listen in to what was being said.

'Well,' said Gordon, leaning forward conspiratorially, 'it was quite funny in a way. Seems this German boy was put up to some kind of lark. It was something to do with a man in government. Mr Gregory was trying to blackmail him or something of the kind. Well, I don't really know all the details, but it turned out that the man they were trying to blackmail wasn't queer after all. But the boy fell head over heels in love with him, and you're not exactly supposed to do that if you're trying to do blackmail.' He nodded as though emphasising an important point, folded his arms and sat back in his chair.

'It's funny, but from what I've heard, I would have thought Mr Gregory would be a bit more efficient in his operation than that,' Godiva observed.

'Oh, it wasn't his plan at all. He was setting it up for someone else,' said Gordon, 'the gossip was, it all started out in Germany. Mr Gregory only got involved when the German boy came over to England. I think Tommy came over here to warn this man about what was happening, or maybe just to see him again; oh he was really smitten, poor dear.'

'Do you have any idea who might have organised this blackmail attempt?' Walter asked. Unlike the questions from Godiva, this one was met with silence, fidgeting and a look of blank hostility.

'What do you know about how Mr Gregory gets involved in this blackmail?' Godiva asked, 'And how does he make his money?' Gordon tipped his head up in thought before answering.

'He gets information, from the club mostly, but also hotels and other places. All kinds of gossip. Anything he can use. You know, blackmail stuff. About people with money or influence who do something naughty. He sells this information to anyone who is willing to pay; doesn't usually do the blackmail himself. And he sucks up to anyone who is rich or aristocratic who turns up at one of his shows. He keeps notes of everything, every little failing they have, every little peccadillo. Another thing he does is to takes photos when he can, with a hidden camera. As far as us boys are concerned, he's got the power over us because he'll report us to the police if we say or do anything. And he blackmails us into taking part, threatening to tell the police about us. We're not harming anyone in private, but you know what happened to poor old Oscar Wilde.' Gordon gazed wistfully at Walter.

'And does Mr Gregory entertain any foreign gentlemen, or have any business dealings with them?' Walter asked. This time Gordon answered quite quickly.

'All sorts of foreigners, I told you already about that German. I wouldn't know what kind they were, other than rich. You know, away from your own country you might feel like misbehaving a little bit, by going to a club,' said Gordon in a flat tone.

'You talked about this German boy, and what happened to him. Does Mr Gregory often arrange things for someone else? You know, a sort of go-between for someone setting something up that is not quite nice?' Godiva asked. Gordon nodded slowly.

'That's just the sort of thing he does, our Mr Gregory. And it's sometimes more complicated than that. He gets some kind of hold on some rich person, then gets them to use his services at a very high cost, so it doesn't exactly count as blackmail. It's all very clever, and very difficult to prove anything against him. And nothing ever goes to his office, or anywhere near. He's got some kind of arrangement with a newsagents shop in Whitechapel. That's where all the letters go.'

Two tables away the attentive but nondescript man continued to listen to their conversation from behind the early edition of the Evening Standard.

'Do you think you could arrange for me to meet with him? I have a number of questions that I should like to ask,' Walter asked in a pleasant voice.

'No, absolutely not. I don't work for him anymore, but that doesn't mean he can't get to me. I've told you far too much already. If he gets to hear that I have been talking to anyone he'll make an example of me. So you just leave me alone. And don't breathe a word of this to anyone.' Having said this, Gordon rose quickly from his seat, spilling the remnants of his cup of coffee, and rushed out of the cafe.

'Is it worthwhile our following him? Godiva asked.

'I shouldn't think so. Like he says, he doesn't really work for Gregory anymore, and we'll only get him more upset,' said Dorkins.

'And do you really think he's in any danger?' Godiva asked.

'Dunno,' answered Dorkins with a shrug.

'I wouldn't have thought so,' said Walter, 'like he said, he doesn't work for Gregory anymore, and I don't see how anyone could know that he's been talking to us.'

They finished their coffee in near silence before Walter paid the bill, leaving a generous tip of a half crown and they left. They were followed by that discrete gentleman who had been watching them. He left his newspaper on the table of the restaurant together with payment for his tea a minute after they left.

◊

They took a bus the relatively short distance to Holborn, where Godiva knew a restaurant where she was happy to eat. The restaurant was a pleasant, if slightly rustic looking place, with scrubbed wooden tables. The staff were mostly women in rational dress, with none of the corseting and frills which were to be seen on the Lyon's Nippy waitresses. They were cheerfully efficient and welcoming. This was Walter's first experience of a vegetarian eating place and he was pleasantly surprised by the informality and the quality of the food. In his club the meals were generally reminiscent of superior school dinners, but here the freshness of the ingredients and the efforts made to provide interesting flavours was much superior. All kinds of radical types were dining there as well as a selection of typists and clerks of both genders. The discussions were lively without being gossipy and the atmosphere was welcoming and tolerant.

They sat at a table near the back of the place, and a thin, bearded young man took their order. There seemed no hierarchy separating the male from the female workers. Godiva ordered a mushroom omelette with a seasonal salad, while Walter somewhat reluctantly took the waiter's recommendation for a nut cutlet. They talked as they ate, Walter wishing that he could be eating mutton chops instead, but not objecting too much to what he was given.

'How did you get to know of this place?' Walter inquired, just to make conversation.

'Well, lots of women in the suffrage movement are vegetarians. It seems to go together, somehow. I have a friend, Maud, who has been sent to Holloway. She always insists on a vegetarian diet when she is in prison. She says you always get much better food that way. But it's not just women or suffragists who eat here. Almost all people who want to change society seem to gravitate to vegetarianism. Besides, the people are very pleasant here and I enjoy the food,' Godiva said, as she took another mouthful of omelette.

'Yes, it's quite nice. Much better than I expected. Everything seems very, er.., nutritious,' Walter said, damning the food with faint praise.

'You know,' Godiva mused, 'If we could find out what your friend Charles is doing, I mean, what he is working on, then we might be able to make an educated guess as to what this business is all about. That way we could work out what is happening with his wife, or why it is happening at the very least. If she is as innocent as you say she is, then it seems to be that what happened at the hotel is some kind of indirect attempt to blackmail him'.

'I have known Emily almost all of my life and I am certain that she would never do anything improper. I'm sure of it.'

'Well, if she hasn't done anything, then is it possible that Charles has done something indiscrete?' Godiva asked.

'It wouldn't be like him, but a man is a man, you know. It's always possible he's had some kind of fling,' Walter mused, 'But one thing I'm certain of is that he would never get involved in anything like Gregory's club. He's far too discrete for that.'

'If he really had been indiscrete, perhaps whoever it was who met Emily was informing her about what he had done. That would be quite clever, really, threatening to expose him. Then she would be able to put pressure on Charles to do something against his conscience,' said Godiva.

'I think we ought to try to do is to find out who it was who met Emily at the Hotel. If we can find out who he is, then it might give us an idea what he's after,' Walter said.

'Didn't your friend Scrivener tell you it was to do with the Germans? Because if the man is German, then it couldn't have been Gregory trying to blackmail Emily,' Godiva suggested.

'You mean that Gregory is acting as some kind of go-between. Actually, Scrivener, and he's no friend of mine, he didn't actually say this man was German, but he didn't deny it. If he is German, then he is something to do with spying. There are two possibilities, either he is an agent, not very important, or he is some kind of spymaster attached to the German embassy. That seems to be the way it works. But Scrivener already knows who he is, and I know he won't tell me. He'd just say that I don't need to know, that it is not part of my job. So I don't think it would really be worthwhile for me to pursue that line of enquiry. Besides, if the room was booked in Gregory's company name, then he must be something to do with it,' Walter replied.

'There is another possibility. Given what happens in that hotel, I imagine that private detectives operate there. Perhaps one of them might have spotted who it was really hired the room,' Godiva suggested.

'Well, possibly, but I think those detectives are generally looking for a specific person, almost always a woman. Some of them would have known me by sight. But I don't think that any of them would take notice of an unknown man,' Walter said thoughtfully.

'Well, let's say that you are right. If that is the case, let's concentrate on Charles instead, then,' Godiva suggested, 'So is it possible that you can find a reason to pay him a visit?'

'Well of course it is. I'll visit him at his club this very evening,' Walter said, 'He's certain to be there if he is in town.'

'For some reason I thought you'd belong to the same club as Charles. Obviously you don't then?' said Godiva.

'Oh, no. His club is far too stuffy for me. The one I belong to is far more radical. His club is just the place for an ambitious young Liberal MP. But look, if I'm going to question Charles, what are you going to be doing?' Walter asked.

'I think I shall try to find out what the nature of Charles' work is. If I can find that out, I may have some idea as to the motive for a German spy trying to exert some influence on him. Perhaps I'll start by reading through Hansard to see if I can find anything,' said Godiva.

'And I have a prior arrangement this afternoon,' said Walter.

'Another of your ladies, I suppose,' sniffed Godiva.

'Yes and no,' said Walter, 'It is a lady, but a rather more mature one. I have to finish a portrait of her I've been commissioned to do. It's well paid work.'

◊

Sir Charles Gurney-Stewart stayed at the Reform Club on Pall Mall when he was in town. The appearance of the building was that of a Greek temple from the Age of Reason. This style was derived from renaissance Italy and contained some classical elements while not attempting to ape the pure classical style. Those that favoured this Palladian style tended to be progressive and liberal, while supporters of the pure classical design were more conservative, and were anxious to preserve the existing social order. The club was built for gentlemen who wished to make changes to society, but only those changes which would not directly affect their own position. The Liberal Party had been in power for some years now, and many of their Members of Parliament were also members of this club. The driving power of the Government and of new reforming legislation was a maverick Welsh lawyer, David Lloyd George, who would certainly not have been invited to become a member of the Reform Club. Walter had arranged to meet Charles Gurney-Stewart in the Smoking Room, which lead off from the Gallery.

'Walter, my good fellow, how d'you do?' Charles greeted Walter. He stood up from his armchair and shook Walter's hand enthusiastically.

'How d'you do,' came Walter's correct reply, 'Well, you certainly seem to be getting on well. Member of the Reform Club, no less, how splendid. Very kind of you to see me. I know that you must be busy at the moment.'

'Well, if you like it so much, maybe I can get you in as a member,' Charles suggested, 'In the meantime, do sit down.' They sat in deep green leather armchairs, and both started to smoke; Charles had a small Havana cigar and Walter one of his Turkish cigarettes. A uniformed club flunky brought them two generous glasses of very good brandy.

'Ah, thank you, for the suggestion about membership, but you know, I'd never join any club that would even consider having me as a member,' said Walter.

'Still using other men's words, Walter? Ah, well, never mind, don't suppose we'll ever cure you of that. And it's an amusing enough comment. It really isn't that stuffy here, you know. Plenty of lively discussion and you don't get shot for talking quietly in the Reading Room.' Charles sat back in his chair. 'Considering we're such old friends, and we are both in London most of the time, we don't see all that much of one another. You really ought to come round for dinner sometime soon.'

'But we do move in rather different circles, you rising up the ziggurat of government and me, well, I suppose I'm just a useless drone,' said Walter. Charles pretended to ignore this slightly barbed compliment, as though he hadn't heard.

'Are you still creating those awful daubs of yours?' Charles asked.

'Oh, yes, I have several commissions on at the moment and a couple more coming up. Mostly portraits of course. And I will be having a little exhibition, along with a sculptor friend, next spring. We've already booked the gallery and ordered the wine,' Walter replied.

'Actually, I rather like your paintings,' Charles admitted, 'in fact I've been meaning to ask for some time if you might paint a portrait of Emily and myself, sort of an Arnolfini wedding thing, only at home and updated, of course.'

'Hmm,' Walter mused, 'I'm not sure I have the technique for that kind of thing. It's not exactly my style. I'm more of a sort of Post-Impressionist, really. But if you are not expecting the exact Van Eyck style, I don't mind giving it a go. Maybe I can arrange you in a similar position and make a reference to that painting. Now, as we seem to have gotten onto the subject, how is Emily?'

'Oh, Emily is very well indeed, and I'm sure that she would love to see you. If you do that portrait, you'll have ample chance to catch up on all her news,' Charles said.

'So which of your houses did you have in mind as a backdrop?' Walter asked.

'The one in Leicestershire, I thought, in the withdrawing room. We'll be going up there as soon as this session of Parliament finishes,' Charles replied.

'I might be seeing you a little sooner than that. I have somehow managed to get myself an invitation to Blackleigh Court. Are you going up to Em's father's shoot next week?' Walter asked.

'Well, I'll try, but I'm very busy at the moment, so who knows what may happen. Mind you, I have promised to go, so I'd better make an appearance. I didn't know that you'd been invited as well, Emily never mentioned it to me. You know that Caroline and Gerald will be there?'

'Yes, I know,' said Walter, 'but what is it that is potentially stopping you from coming to the biggest shoot of the year?'

'Oh, it's all a bit hush-hush, but I suppose I can tell you that it's something to do with fuel supplies for the navy. For some reason it's landed on my desk, and there is an awful lot of organising to do. You wouldn't believe the complications arising out of it, despite the help of the various Empire departments. Then there is always the Foreign Office to deal with,' Charles said, guardedly.

'In that case I understand that you can't say too much. After all, I might be spying for some foreign country,' Walter said with a smile.

'No, no, I'm not bothered about that, after all, we were at school together,' said Charles with a confiding smile.

'Though I was recently approached by someone else from Harrow, asking me to do some work for our home security agency,' Walter said nonchalantly.

'That would be one of the new agencies, then,' said Charles, 'they split them recently between work over here and work abroad.'

'I wonder why that was?' Walter mused.

'Well, I suppose it is to separate out the people who look out for foreign spies from the people who do the spying for us. It's probably pure nonsense, of course, but it must have seemed like a good idea to someone at the ministry. I was supposed to be involved in the process, but nothing came of it. Anyhow, that business has nothing to do with me, and I've got more than enough on my plate as it is at the moment, without worrying about that sort of thing,' said Charles, with a sigh.

'I knew there was a reason that I didn't go into politics,' said Walter, shaking his head gently, 'let's hope you manage to get a bit of a break next week.'

'I really think I could do with a decent break, but the way things are, I'm not sure that that I will get one soon, or even this year,' Charles said wistfully.

'Where was it that you went last year?' Walter asked.

'Oh, I went off to some German spa,' said Charles, 'I'd been a bit under the weather and I took some time off for a bit of a rest cure.'

'What did Em do while you were there? I mean, I can't imagine her hanging around some provincial German town, drinking mineral water. The warm weather and the sea are much more her sort of thing.'

'I know what you mean. It wasn't really her kind of thing at all. She was with Caroline and Gerald down in Nice, which was much more to her taste,' said Charles, 'but we both came back refreshed, so in different ways the break must have done us both good.' He brushed some imaginary ash from his waistcoat and crossed his legs neatly.

'So what did you do for company while you were in that spa?' Walter asked, innocently, 'Presuming that you went there on your own.'

'Oh, the people there were friendly enough, and I chummed up with this German boy who was very intelligent, and friendly. He spoke very good English, and it seemed to be a bit of a meeting of minds. But I had to stop seeing him because he turned out to be a queer, and he tried something on with me. Being in politics, I can't afford any kind of scandal, especially that kind. Besides, I don't approve of that sort of thing. We both saw a good deal of it at Harrow. And for all I knew he might have been put up to it by some foreign power. If they'd tried that, then they would have been wasting their time. You know that I don't have those sort of tastes.'

'Well I never noticed you experimenting with those buggers at school, and, as you said, it certainly went on, so I believe you, of course. And as for politics and your reputation I can well understand that. In your position, you need to be blamelessly clean,' Walter said in a reassuring tone.

'I don't need to remind you to be discrete about all this. I'm sure that you won't repeat the story,' said Charles, leaning forward a little and looking into Walter's face, 'You know what the press are like, and all that business of no smoke without fire. That sort of scandal could ruin my career, even if there is no basis at all to it.'

'Of course not. I wouldn't dream of saying anything at all about it,' said Walter, but it occurred to him at that moment that he had never known Charles to show any sign of sexual interest, be it to man or woman, in all the years that they had known each other. He seemed to lack the sort of sexuality which is common to the vast majority of young men and women. Walter wondered at the state of Charles and Emily's marriage for the very first time. From their childhood contact Walter knew that Emily had a sexual nature, but one which was rigidly controlled by loyalty and convention.

'Well, I shall look forward to seeing you in Worcestershire, provided the pressures of work allow me to get there,' said Charles, with a wry smile.

'I am anticipating seeing you and Emily again with an almost indecent degree of pleasure. It's been a long time since I saw you together,' Walter answered, 'And I really hope that you do manage to find some free time.'

◊

It was after Dorkins had left and Godiva had gone to her bed that there was a loud knock at the door. Walter put out his cigarette and went to answer it. As he opened the door it was rudely pushed in at him, and a man stood in the doorway wearing a buttoned up overcoat with raised collar and a silk scarf across his lower face. More unusually, he was holding a revolver that was pointed towards Walter's chest. Walter could have identified any number of makes of shotgun, but handguns were a complete mystery to him. What he did know for certain was that they were made for killing people, and not for any other purpose.

'Get back in!' the man hissed. He was shorter and slimmer than Walter. Had it been a fist fight, Walter would have made short work of him. But the gun decided the matter in the intruder's favour and Walter moved backwards.

'What do you want?' Walter asked. They had edged through the entrance hall and into the centre of the living room in a slow and measured dance, perfectly co-ordinated. 'Look, I don't know whose husband you are, or which one of them is employing you, but it is hardly worth shooting me. You are bound to be caught,' Walter said rapidly and quietly.

'Shut up. Stop your gabbling and start listening,' said the man, 'Because I've got a message for you'.

'Who is this message from?' Walter asked.

'You'll work it out soon enough,' the man replied.

'What is the message, then?' asked Walter, playing for time and hoping to distract this man.

'The message is, don't interfere anymore in things that don't concern you, or you will really come to regret it,' the gunman hissed.

'I still don't know what you are talking about. Perhaps it would help if you told me who sent you on this fool's errand,' Walter said through gritted teeth. He was watching the man's movement, waiting for him to drop his guard.

'Well, I'll give you a clue. The warning doesn't come from any husband that I know of. It concerns another matter. Something you've been sticking your nose into recently.' The concentration in the man's eyes was fierce, and he didn't even seem to blink.

'I don't know what you mean. Will you kindly explain?' Walter asked, feigning puzzlement.

'You already know what this is about, so don't get bloody clever with me, or I might just decide to add a little more to what I was told to do to you!' The man moved the gun down so that it was aimed at Walter's knee. 'And this is a sort of aide-memoire for you'. He cocked the hammer with his thumb causing a loud click. Walter could see that Godiva had been tip-toeing across from her room in bare feet. The upturned collar of his coat had prevented the intruder from seeing the movement from the corner of his eye. She had taken the poker from the fireplace at the same moment that the gun was cocked, and this covered the sound. She held the poker by the shaft with the brass handle raised above her head.

'This is just business, mind. I hope you learn from it,' said the intruder. His hand was trembling slightly.

The sound which followed was a dull muffled thud and not the deafening crack of a pistol shot in a closed room. The man crumpled to the ground, blood pumping from a scalp wound. Behind him stood Godiva, still holding the poker by its shaft, the grim expression on her face turning to horror and concern.

'Is he dead?' asked Walter, not daring to look too closely. The man lay half turned on his side on an antique Persian rug, bleeding profusely. He appeared insensible, but there was some sign of shallow breathing.

Godiva knelt down and felt for a pulse on the man's neck. 'No, he's not dead yet, but I have a very good idea that he's got a depressed fracture of the skull. We need a doctor now, and the Police as well'.

'There's a doctor of some kind in Flat 6,' said Walter, 'I'll go and fetch him. You telephone for the Police'. He strode out of the doorway in the direction of the doctor's flat.

Godiva lifted the heavy handset of the telephone. She jiggled the cradle to attract the attention of an operator. After a few seconds a man with a slightly affected accent came on the line.

'Good evening, Sir. And h'what number to you require?' he asked.

'Please connect me to Whitehall 1212,' Godiva commanded.

'One minute please, madam. I h'am just connecting you,' the operator corrected himself. There was a few seconds silence before another voice came on the line.

'Scotland Yard. How may I help you?' The voice was deep, with a touch of a Welsh accent.

'Hello, yes,' Godiva began, 'There's been an err…, an incident here. A man broke in brandishing a pistol. I hit him over the head with a poker. My friend has just gone to fetch a doctor for this man. I think I might have killed him. He was threatening to shoot my friend, you see.'

'Now just calm down a little, Miss, and give me your address. We'll have someone round to see you in a very few minutes,' the Police operator said.

'The address is, Flat 4, 23, Russell Square,' Godiva said, concentrating on her breathing in order to remain calm.

'Thank you, Miss, and is there a separate door-bell for the flat, so you can let us in?' the operator said.

'Yes, just press the bell and someone will come down,' Godiva said.

'I'll arrange for an ambulance as well, as it sounds like you will need one,' the operator said.

'Thank you, thank you,' Godiva said. She put the telephone handset back into the cradle. Quite suddenly she began to shake uncontrollably.

The doctor in the neighbouring flat appeared in dressing gown and slippers after a great deal of knocking at his door. He hurried to Walter's flat with a small bag of medical equipment. This doctor turned out to be a pupil of Dr Freud of Vienna, and not to have practised as a physician for several years. His earlier training had taught him what to do in such situations, and he was able to staunch the flow of blood and perform some basic treatment to relieve the pressure on the intruder's brain due to the fracture of the skull. In a thick Austrian German accent that sounded very rustic to Walter's ears he enquired as to how the injury had occurred, tutting at the replies given my Walter and the still shivering Godiva. He was later able to accompany the ambulance crew who came to claim the injured man and take him to hospital, giving then instructions on how to carry him.

◊

Detective Sergeant Clift was a large, hairy man in a large hairy overcoat. He had pendulous mutton-chop whiskers and a ginger moustache like a yard broom. His eyebrows were bushy and mobile and almost met in the middle, but he had only a scant tonsure of hair on his head. As hair covered most of his face it was difficult to gauge his age or to read his expression. There was little enough expression in his voice, though it had a soft Hampshire burr lurking beneath the London accent. If anything, the uniformed constable who accompanied him was even bigger and more taciturn.

'Do you have any idea who this man might be?' asked Sergeant Clift.

'He didn't exactly formally announce himself,' replied Walter.

'And you never met him before?' The sergeant said.

'To the best of my knowledge I've never seen him before in my life.'

'Have you any idea why he may have wished to attack you?' the Sergeant persisted.

'I have been making some enquiries on behalf of ...' Walter started, 'Er, can I have a word in private, Sergeant?'

'And why might that be, Sir?' the Sergeant said in a bored tone.

'Because this is a delicate matter which has something to do with national security,' Walter explained. There was a brief silence.

'In that case, by all means, let us go somewhere a little more private,' the Sergeant agreed, sighing slightly.

In the privacy of his room Walter confided his mission to the Sergeant.

'I'm doing some work for people concerned with national security. Someone I knew at Oxford asked me to find something out,' Walter said, gnomically.

'And who might this personage be?' asked the sergeant with a heavier sigh.

'A Mr Henry Scrivener. He has an office in the Admiralty. I can give you a room number for him. Perhaps you can locate him through that. Of course, I can't tell you exactly what this about, but I am certain that it concerns the matters that are to do with national security, ones that I discussed with Mr Scrivener,' Walter explained in a low voice.

'In that case I had better get in touch with our Special Branch. This sort of thing is what they generally handle. I noticed that you have a telephone in the hallway. Do you mind if I make a telephone call to a colleague?'

'Of course not, Sergeant. Please feel free. But just one thing, is the injured man being guarded? I wouldn't want him regaining consciousness and running away,' Walter said in a serious tone.

'Have no fear of that, Sir. He won't be going anywhere for a day or two, and I'll make sure there is a constable always at hand, standing or sitting guard near his bed,' the Sergeant explained patiently.

'That's good, Sergeant,' said Walter, 'I imagine Mr Scrivener will also be wanting a word with him.'

'I imagine that he will, Sir,' said the Sergeant. 'Now, as it happens, us, the uniformed branch, well, we don't always see eye-to-eye with the Special Branch wallahs. They don't think we can do our job, and we don't trust them to do theirs. I really don't like to bring the Special Branch in. Are you sure that it is absolutely necessary?' He leaned forward and seemed to be pleading his case.

'Yes, Sergeant, unfortunately it is,' Walter admitted, wishing it wasn't so.

'Just one more thing, Sir, have you any idea how this intruder came to know where you live?' The Sergeant asked, cocking his head to one side.

'I can only assume that he followed me home. Perhaps it happened after a meeting I had today, with a potential witness. I am rather afraid that I may have put this man's life in danger,' Walter said, and he swallowed awkwardly.

'Do you have this other man's address, Sir?' the Sergeant asked. He took out a notebook and a stub of a pencil. He licked the tip of the pencil in preparation for the answer.

'No, but my man-servant does. I promise I'll get it to you in the morning, as soon as he comes in,' Walter said.

'And I'll put one of my best men onto it,' the Sergeant said.

'But before that, I probably need to inform Mr Scrivener about what has happened. Not that I'm looking forward to that very much, but I suppose it must be done,' Walter admitted, knowing the trouble he was likely to be in.

◊

The Police car dropped the Sergeant and Walter off at the Admiralty offices. An expressionless orderly led them through the seemingly endless corridors to a blank looking office on the second floor. There was no sign on the door to give the name of the occupant. The orderly knocked firmly on the door and ushered Walter and the Sergeant in before closing it and walking off back to his station.

Scrivener was still wearing an evening suit and had obviously been called in from some dinner engagement. He looked angry and impatient. There was a sharp-faced man with hooded eyes standing behind the desk. Walter was motioned to a hard chair and it was indicated that he should sit. He did so immediately. The sharp-faced man then had a whispered conversation with the Sergeant, who nodded gravely towards Walter and left the room.

Scrivener was furious, and moved in staccato bursts of motion around the room, talking in short, fast phrases. Walter sat and listened, wanting to smoke but unable to do so as he had left his cigarette case and Dunhill lighter back at the flat.

'All I asked was that you ask some private questions of Lady Emily, and you run around stirring up a hornets' nest. I have never known such irresponsibility, such utter imbecility. Don't you know anything about obeying instructions, about discretion? You may well have ruined everything. It will take a lot of effort to retrieve this situation. I mean, can't you understand the simplest instructions? Don't you know how necessary it is to be discrete in this kind of work? Have you the slightest idea of the sort of trouble this could lead to? I am now involved in briefing the Special Branch, who I distinctly did not want involved in this matter. And what is more, you seem to have involved Miss Williams in the matter, and with her family background she is definitely not considered to be trustworthy. I don't know how much you have confided in her, but you should not have said anything at all. Absolutely nothing at all. Can you not keep anything secret?'

Walter gave into temptation and took a cigarette from the case on the desk, lighting it with an available match before replying. 'I had to establish that there was something in your story, and, well, one thing led to another. As for Miss Williams, she knows very little, and I can assure you that she is completely trustworthy in every way. If I am going to do a job like this I feel that I must make my own little enquiries. As it is, I do seem to have stirred up a bit of a hornet's nest. There is some very dirty business going on, which you probably already know about, but which I didn't. By the by, do you know about a man called Arthur Gregory?' Walter added as an afterthought.

'Oh, we are very well aware of Mr Gregory and his activities. However, it is not that simple. Mr Gregory has, in the past, proved very useful to us, and he is not someone that I wish to anger, as he may prove useful to us again at some point in the future. You, on the other hand are no bloody use to anyone, especially to me!' Scrivener snorted in disgust.

'So you don't want me to go to the Shooting Party, then?' asked Walter.

'As for me, I'd be more than happy to see you die in agony right in front of me. But what has been put in place has to continue. You can at least go to Blackleigh Court and fulfil that job for us,' said Scrivener, and paused, taking a calming breath, 'Even if it is the very last thing you ever do in this life. But I don't want you charging around like a bull in a china shop anymore. This has to be absolutely discrete, and it has to be completely secret. No-one else must know any of this, any of it. Especially your dear friend, Miss Williams. Do I make myself utterly clear?'

'As day, Scrivener. Clear as day,' replied Walter, bored.

'Then you would oblige me by accepting the invitation, attending the party, asking only the right questions of the right person, at the right time and place and not getting me involved with any other shenanigans again until you have the answers. Until then I look forward to not hearing from you and not speaking to you, not ever again. And once again, I don't have to remind you, this meeting never took place!'

'Of course not,' said Walter, determined to make his point, 'But what are you going to do with Mr Gregory? He seems to have been responsible for that man coming to the flat with the gun. And I am worried that he might turn his attention to someone I was talking to, someone who used to work for him. I think this man may be in very grave danger.'

'Don't you concern yourself with Mr Gregory or any of his doings. I shall be having more than just a word with him. And I positively forbid you to go anywhere near him or ask anything more about his business, do you fully understand?' Scrivener said between clenched teeth.

'Well, I'll not bother him, provided he leaves me and my friends alone. But, if I find that he is threatening anyone I know, then I will make it my personal business to make sure he never does business again,' Walter said slowly.

'Just leave it to me, and I will ensure that he never bothers you again. So, kindly leave everything in my hands. Leave it to someone who knows just what is going on, and knows what to do. You can redeem yourself a little by doing your duty, and nothing more,' Scrivener took a breath to calm himself before continuing. 'And, despite your failings, you seem to have some friends in high places, so there is one more thing you can do.'

'And what might that be?' Walter asked.

'You are to go down to Blackleigh Court two days before the party officially starts. There are a number of gentlemen who will be present, discussing matters of state. Lord Randall has urged most strongly that you be allowed to attend, in fact he insisted on it. But be warned, this is another matter requiring the greatest discretion. It involves some detailed discussions, the results of which must be known only to the gentlemen involved,' Scrivener refused to make eye contact with Walter.

'How very mysterious,' said Walter, trying to look into Scrivener's watery eyes, without success, 'some intelligence matter, no doubt.'

'I have no further comment to make. You may leave now,' said Scrivener, with a good deal of finality.

'Aren't you going to introduce me to this gentleman?' Walter asked, indicating the sharp-faced man.

'No, I don't believe that I will,' Scrivener answered.

◊

Walter arrived back at the flat around midnight and had a very stiff brandy and soda before going to bed and a fruitless search for sleep. He was lying awake with eyes open when the bedroom door opened and Godiva entered wearing a very modest high-necked cotton nightdress. Her hair was unbound. Without saying anything she slipped into the bed beside him. Walter was very tired, but decided to make some kind of effort and placed an arm around her shoulders.

'Well, this is most unexpected. And I'm not really sure that this is quite the time or place for this,' Walter said sadly, 'Mind you, I'll do my best.'

'Don't get the wrong idea,' said Godiva, 'If you try anything unnecessary I will make it my business to circumcise you very artistically with a pair of pinking shears.'

Walter sighed deeply but continued his platonic comforting.

'Look, I'm not lusting after your body, Walter, it's just that for some reason, the act of nearly killing a man seems to have upset me a good deal,' said Godiva, and she shivered again.

'I can understand that,' Walter agreed, 'I'm not too good when it comes to facing men carrying revolvers, and just looking at all the blood spilt on that rug made me feel queasy. I do hope that Dorkins can get the stain out. The carpet belongs to Mehmet and I believe that it is quite valuable.'

'You don't think any other thug will come to get us, do you?'

'I don't think so. This particular thug is supposed to working on our side. Scrivener is going to have a word with him,' Walter answered.

'Oh, God, Walter, what if the man dies?' Godiva asked, tears appearing in her eyes.

'They think that he's going to be alright,' Walter said in a calculatedly calm voice, 'And, I haven't thanked you for saving me yet. If you hadn't bashed him with that poker, I'm sure he would have shot me in the leg. He was just about to shoot, you know.'

'Well do it then,' said Godiva, with a mock note of impatience.

'Do what?' Walter asked.

'Thank me, you silly goose,' said Godiva. Walter laughed.

'Of course. Thank you. Thank you for saving my life.'

'Do you know who this man is, or who set him on you?' Godiva asked, after a pause, placing an arm around Walter.

'The person who arranged it is a very unpleasant man indeed. But it seems that he has done some work for the intelligence people before,' Walter stated.

'Then he *was* sent by Arthur Gregory. I thought he might have been. Why would British Intelligence be employing such a terrible man?' Godiva asked, with a shake of her head.

'Precisely because he knows so many dirty little secrets, possibly even the secrets of those that employ him,' said Walter, kissing her chastely on the forehead, 'now please try to get some sleep.' Godiva turned her back and curled into a foetal position. Walter stroked her back for a while until her breathing became more relaxed. This action had the effect of calming him as well, and he soon dropped off to sleep.

After a largely sleepless start to the night they both fell into a deep and dreamless slumber and were only awakened by the noises made by the arrival of Dorkins around half-past nine. The servant smirked when he saw Godiva leave Walter's room garbed only in her nightdress and made some comments that could only be interpreted as lewd. He was much less happy, indeed nearly mutinous when Walter instructed him to wash the congealed blood from the antique Persian rug by the fireside.

'And what did your last slave die of?' Dorkins asked, rudely.

'He asked too many rhetorical questions,' Walter answered.

Sunday 26th September 1909

The story of the imprisonment of Sergeant Alfred Murphy and his subsequent fate appeared on the front page of every newspaper, except for 'The Times' which, as always, had only advertisements on the front. It was the most sensational tale to have come into the public domain for several months and the popular press spared none of the gory details of the case. Murphy's landlady had been exclusively interviewed by three newspapers. The 'Daily Mail' raged against the foreigner who had tortured a war hero. The hue and cry was set well in place, but no accurate description of the hunted man was available. This did not prevent 'The Daily Express' and 'The Daily Sketch' from printing line drawings of him, on no evidential basis whatsoever.

Murphy's fellow drinkers at the Drum and Eagle had also been interviewed. The journalists had misquoted or invented the words of these barely literate semi-alcoholics and some had just invented witnesses as well as words.

The less prestigious and more rabidly nationalistic press ran lurid stories about the nature of Murphy's imprisonment, vying with each other to print the most sensational, gory details and outrageous speculation about possible perpetrators and their motives. Even the respectable press covered the story in great detail, emphasizing the war service of Murphy, and speculating on why he may have been attacked and by whom. Despite this blanket publicity, no new witness came forward and there seemed to be little immediate progress on the case. Privately, the Police were disappointed by the lack of reaction and worried about possible revenge attacks on foreigners.

◊

Walter was toying with some bacon on his plate that somehow managed to be both overcooked and greasy. The fried tomatoes were burned on one side and raw on the other, and the mushrooms were spongy and tasteless. Godiva was tucking in to some toast and marmalade with slightly more enthusiasm.

'You, know,' she began, 'the person we really ought to ask about this is Emily.' She swallowed a mouthful toast and took a swig of sweet tea, supposedly good for shock.

'Oh, Godiva, we can't do that, Emily is already in the country, at her father's. Besides, I shall be seeing her at Blackleigh Court very shortly and will be able to speak to her then. After last night's escapade, I have been told in no uncertain terms that I am to restrict my work to just asking those questions, and nothing more. And another thing, I am not supposed to tell you anything more, either. It seems that you are not to be trusted,' Walter said, firmly with a trace of bitterness.

'Utter twaddle!' Godiva ejaculated. 'How are we to know what this is all about if you are unable to ask the right people the right questions?'

'That's not my problem,' said Walter, putting down his knife and fork and giving up on the breakfast, 'I've been given a very limited job to do, and after what happened last night I'll do that job to the letter and no more.' He took a long draught of coffee, bitter and black.

'You are hopeless, Walter, you know that. I mean, what did you manage to get out of Charles that we didn't already know?' Godiva protested.

'I'm not telling you that, you'd only go asking questions again, and it's me that will get into trouble,' said Walter, grumpily.

'Charles is the junior minister in the Ministry of War, isn't he?' Godiva asked.

'That's right,' Walter agreed, 'Sort of taking over from his father in law. Lord Randall had a senior position in the War Office before him. During the South African war, I think. Why do you ask?'

'Oh, no reason in particular,' said Godiva, in an easy conversational tone, 'It's just that I was looking through Hansard last night, and I was interested in what Charles had to say. It gave me some ideas about why someone would be trying to blackmail him. The sort of things he is dealing with really are quite important, vital in some ways. It's to do with the security of the fuel supply for the Navy. Then I suppose anything which threatens our naval power also threatens the Empire.'

'Just so long as you are not intending to carry on with this nonsense of asking questions,' Walter said, trying to give his words the full weight of his disapproval.

'Perish the very thought,' said Godiva, 'Still, what I don't tell you, you won't know.'

'I don't much like the sound of that,' Walter observed.

'Isn't it about time you were on your way to work?' Godiva asked.

◊

It was a dark little office at the back of the club. This was no purpose built palace of pleasure, but a converted furniture shop in an unfashionable part of north-west London. The only natural light for the office came from a slit window set high on the wall which itself faced into a small yard with high walls of soot-stained yellow brick. A bare light bulb offered a harsh addition to the weak sunshine. The furniture of the room consisted of three hard bent wood chairs, one leather-faced office chair, an ink-stained desk, four filing cabinets and a small safe in the wall. A smooth-faced man was sitting behind the desk, leaning back in his chair, a wreath of smoke from a cigar partly obscuring his face. A tall, gaunt man with a scar on his cheek sat ramrod straight on one of the chairs facing the first man, silently objecting to the perfumed stench of the cigar smoke.

'I do not appreciate being called here like this,' the tall man said angrily. The other man smiled and sat forward. His accent was too correct to be perfect English.

'I am sorry to have inconvenienced you, Herr Braun' said the smooth-faced man, 'but I have some urgent business to discuss.'

'It is not good for me to come here. I do not know if the club is being watched by British Intelligence,' said the tall man, and he crossed his legs at the ankle.

'Don't worry about that. I have an arrangement with some persons in Whitehall which is very similar to the arrangement that I have with you. They do not interfere with me, and I help them out when they need me. What is more, I get paid for my services. But what I would like to discuss today is rather different to the arrangement we have had so far. In fact, I would like you to provide me with a service this time,' said the smooth-faced man, and he blew more smoke at the ceiling where it swirled around the light bulb.

'Just what kind of service would this be?' Braun asked, suspiciously.

'Just a little job. There is a man who is proving to be a little awkward to me. And I don't want anyone directly connected to me involved in the business of dealing with him,' said the smooth-faced man.

'It sounds like you are in a bit of trouble yourself,' said Braun, and he gave a wolfish grin.

'Believe me, it is nothing that I can't deal with, just a temporary situation. However, there is a more pressing need for me to deal with this man, without seeming to be personally involved, and given the business arrangement between us, and the information which I hold about you, I was wondering whether you would like to help.' He sat forward in his chair and took another puff on the cigar before continuing. 'There must be people you use for all those little jobs we all need doing. Well, I'm sure that you could find someone who is suitable for such a job as I have in mind. All I need to do is provide you with the man's name and address and we speak no more of it. After the job is completed I shall give you all the original documents that I have been preserving for you, and we need never speak again.'

'But how can I trust your word on this, Gregory?' Braun asked, 'Because so far, it is I who have been in your debt. I have paid you for carrying out work on my behalf, and I have paid far more than you deserve. If I am to perform this service for you, it would mean involving myself in something the police would get involved in. In such circumstances, I do not suppose that my embassy would be very helpful in dealing with such a matter, should any problems arise. I would need better assurances from you about the return of those documents before I would consider taking such a risk.' He folded his arms and sat back in his chair.

'In that case, what I am willing to do is to provide you with half of the documents now, and the other half when the job is complete. You are, of course, free to do what you like with these documents. I imagine that you will wish to destroy them. The last thing you would wish to happen would be for them to fall into the hands of your ambassador, or into the hands of British Intelligence,' said the Gregory with a nasty smile. Braun seemed to wince slightly. Gregory removed a buff manila envelope from beneath his jotter and passed it across the desk. 'This is just to show my good will.'

Braun leaned forward and took the envelope, opening it to see the contents, then returning the papers into the envelope before putting it back into an inside pocket of his jacket. He looked up at Gregory.

'These are the original, are they not?' Braun asked in a suspicious tone.

'Of course they are,' Gregory lied.

'Very well, then. There is an operative in my pay who will perform this task for you. Give me the name and address of the person you wish to deal with and I will make sure that you achieve the result that you require. If I find that you have failed to keep your part of the bargain, I will set him onto you, do you understand?' Braun said, indicating that he understood the weakness of Gregory's position.

'Are you sure that this operative is trustworthy?' Gregory asked with simulated carelessness.

'I am utterly sure,' said Braun. 'This is because I have some information that I can supply to him which he wants very badly. He would, quite literally, kill to get this information.'

'What is this information?' Gregory asked hopefully.

'Come come, now, Mr Gregory. It is nothing that concerns your operations,' said Braun, in a slightly mocking voice.

Gregory sighed and passed over a sealed envelope, on the back of which, in neat block capitals, in blue ink, was written a name and address.

◊

The house of Offa Williams and his wife was a large Georgian yellow brick building in a good part of Islington. The social and family interactions within the house were complex. Offa was married to Gladwys, who was the mother of Godiva and her older full sister, Edith. Godiva had three younger half siblings, a brother, Harold, and two sisters, Maud and Anne, who were the results of her father's dalliances. There were other half siblings who resided with their mothers. All the children in the house were brought up together without apparent prejudice or favour. Offa was currently sharing a bed with the long-term housekeeper, Mrs Russell. Whether there had ever been a Mister Russell was open to doubt, but Albert, the second boy in the house was her son by a previous relationship. Gladwys was a retiring little woman who rarely offered an opinion, unlike Mrs Russell who had many opinions and expressed them frequently and loudly.

Offa Williams was a tall, stout, heavily bearded man with a bald pate who wore a grey frock coat and habitually smoked strong cigars. He was a well known author of decidedly left-wing leanings who wrote articles for various journals as well as books which were read for their provocative content. He was known to be friends with a variety of foreign émigrés and radicals.

Most notoriously, Offa Williams was a proponent of open sexual relationships and an enemy of marriage. He was castigated and mocked by the populist press and by bishops and social conservatives. This opposition served as the best form of publicity he could possibly have and he made a good deal of money from his writings. In recent years original ideas seemed to have largely deserted him, and he had become increasingly reliant on the energy and imagination of his second daughter.

Godiva, carrying a Gladstone bag, let herself in using her own front door key and was immediately surrounded by the cacophony of family life generated by a noisy and chaotic brood. Maud and Anne chased each other around her skirts, almost tripping her up, but uttering no word of greeting between them. They ran into the kitchen and were chased out by Mrs Russell who was brandishing a wooden spoon.

'Hello, Mrs Russell. Is my father in?' Godiva asked.

'He's in his study,' Mrs Russell replied, wiping her forehead with the back of a forearm. 'And I hope he can work through all this noise. Those girls are really playing up today. I've a good mind to take a slipper to their backsides if they don't calm down.'

'Thank you, Mrs Russell. I'll just go up to my room to fetch a few things. Then I'll go and see my father,' Godiva said in a polite and slightly formal way. She disapproved of corporal punishment.

'How are you keeping, Miss Godiva? In fact I don't know where you've been recently. I heard the argument when you left, and Offa's been in a frightful temper recently. He can't find where anything is, and he keeps saying he needs someone to do his typing. He's got to finish a book by the end of next month,' said Mrs Russell, without taking a breath.

'I'm keeping very well, thank you, and I'm staying with a friend, but I'm very busy at the moment,' Godiva said, and she mounted the stairs. Her room in this house was as tidy as her habits in the flat were messy. It was Gladwys who quietly maintained this level of order and cleanliness. It took Godiva very little time to locate the clothes she required and some notebooks and library cards. These were rapidly placed in the cavernous interior of the Gladstone bag. Having finished packing she walked to the window and gazed out into the back garden, her hands resting on the window ledge. She sighed softly in a form of goodbye to her room and turned to leave. Her mother was standing in the doorway.

'Hello, dear,' said Gladwys, with a sad smile, 'how are you?'

'Oh, very well, mother. I'm keeping very well. I'm staying with a friend,' Godiva answered.

'Oh, Goddy, I have been worried about you,' said Gladwys, and she came over and embraced her younger daughter.

'So how has everyone in the house been? How are you in particular?' Godiva asked, extricating herself from her mother's grasp.

'Oh, you know, I'm quite well. Everyone is quite well. But your father is in a dreadful temper. He didn't realise just how much he relied on you. There is this book he has to finish in a month, and I don't know how he will manage to finish with your help. Anyway, his temper is very bad, and there are lots of arguments. We really do need you here, to keep the peace,' said Gladwys, shaking her head.

'Then I had better see my father, then,' said Godiva, with a firm jut to her jaw, 'though I will not work for him under the same terms as before. There will have to be considerable changes if I am to work for him again.'

'He's in the study at the moment. Please promise me that you won't be too proud when you go in, or it will only make him angry,' Gladwys pleaded.

'If you mean that I am to go in humble and apologetic, then that is something I cannot promise. The cause for our argument was his lack of respect for my opinions and feelings. If he has not moved on those, then I cannot work with him,' Godiva stated in a firm tone.

'You are so very like your father in some ways,' Gladwys sighed.

'I'll go to see my father now,' said Godiva, 'But I will come to see you before I go.' She briefly embraced her mother, then went down the stairs to her father's study. She knocked once and walked in without waiting for a command or reply. Her father was sitting on an easy chair with his feet up, one hand behind his head, the other clasping a large, evil-smelling cigar.

'Good afternoon, father,' Godiva began.

'Oh, Godiva, good to see you. It's good to have you back. There is much work to do,' Offa said, getting to his feet.

'I'm not back, father. I only came to collect some more clothes and a few things. From what my mother and Mrs Russell have told me, I believe that you wanted me to help you with your work,' Godiva said, with absolute clarity.

'Oh, it doesn't matter to me where you are living, just as long as you can help me with this damned book,' said Offa.

'And what would the terms of this employment be?' Godiva asked, tilting her head quizzically.

'I don't understand you, Godiva. What I meant is that we return to the way we were before you stormed out like that. And I would certainly accept any apologies you have, so don't bother to say anything. I knew you'd come to your senses and be back, so least said, soonest mended, eh?' Offa said in a bluff, fatherly voice.

'No, father, I will not work for you in the way I did before. Either you pay me a proper wage for the work or you allow me to collaborate and give me full credit, an acknowledgement in print, and a proper proportion of the payment for that part of the work which is my own. Just because I am family does not mean that you can exploit my time and ideas without giving me what I am due. Try to remember what it was like for you when you first started to write, and then imagine how I feel when you tell me to set my ambitions aside and just to bask in your reflected glory,' Godiva said, walking around the room. Offa puffed on his cigar and considered what to say.

'Now, look here, Godiva, I fully agree with you about the need for women's suffrage, but there are so many other issues, so very much injustice to fight against. Just at the moment we have to work together to ensure that all these injustices are challenged. What I feel is that the campaign for women's votes is giving other campaigns for social justice a bad name. I realise that this is largely due to the right-wing press, but they do have a very real effect on public perception. If I were to come out in full support of the Pankhursts, what do you think it would do for the campaigns for miner's welfare, and all the other worthy causes? We must do what we can and get public support for the principles, and only then can we get real change,' Offa said. He flicked his cigar ash into the fireplace.

'So you mean that we, the suffragists, are to keep quiet and let our demands go until your idea of Utopia has been accepted. But I tell you this, father, if women do not get the vote then none of your other reforms will get put into legislation. Without the support and enthusiasm of the women of this country, none of the reforms you are so anxious to see will ever get enacted. You have to see that women can be the most important force for change that this country has ever seen. If women do not get the vote, then nothing else that you believe in will ever come to pass,' said Godiva, with triumphal logic.

'So, Godiva, are you coming back to work for me?' Offa asked after a pregnant silence of some seconds.

'No, father, I am not going to work for you, not ever. I have just offered to work with you, and that is a very different thing. Until you realise that I have my own opinions and my own ambitions, I do not believe that we can do that. Until you change your attitude towards me, I cannot consider working with you again,' Godiva said with great finality.

'Well, in that case, there seems little more for us to say,' said Offa, sadly.

'Goodbye father,' said Godiva, and she turned and walked out of the room. Her mother was waiting in the hallway.

'Oh, Goddy, that didn't go so very well, did it?' said Gladwys.

'I'm sorry, mother, but I really do have to stand up for myself. I hope that it doesn't cause you too many problems. Do send my love to the children, and do take good care of yourself. I must be going now. I will try to come to see you in a week or so,' Godiva said and she embraced her mother before picking up her bag and leaving the house.

◊

That morning Walter went to the Eucharist service at the church of St Clement Danes in The Strand. Walter regarded the process of religion and the ceremony of the service as part of his inheritance, a way of identifying the stratigraphy of society. In conversation with friends he professed to be an atheist, but he quite enjoyed the ritual and the music, finding it familiar and soothing. Perhaps he gained some comfort from familiarity of the words or maybe he was looking at the well dressed ladies taking communion with a judgemental eye. Going to church on a Sunday morning was what he had always done. And if you had to go to a church, it had to be the right sort of church, not too high or too evangelical. The church had to be middle Anglican, the real Church of England, as traditional as Barchester Towers. The officiating priest was a fellow Harrovian and Oxfordian, known socially to the best people of the city. And besides, the singing of the choir was divine, the peal of bells made a satisfying clarillion and the architecture, by Sir Christopher Wren, was just what it should have been, classical and clean in pristine Purbeck marble.

After the service Walter tipped his hat to a pair of young women who had taken his fancy and made his best self-deprecating introduction. He learned enough to judge where and when he might meet up with them again, making a mental note which he later entered into his pocket memo book. After committing this information to paper, Walter strolled to his club to read the Sunday newspapers and to enjoy the roast beef with Yorkshire pudding with some decent claret to wash it all down. Though not as good as at Simpson's it was well up to standard.

◊

Godiva arrived back to find a blond woman of about thirty standing by the door of the flat. She was carrying a large black handbag and pacing about in a nervous fashion. As she could not reach the door without speaking to the woman Godiva asked a question.

'Can I help you?'

'Who are you?' the woman asked.

'I'm Godiva Williams,' said Godiva, 'And you are...?'

'I'm Agnes. Is this Lord Walter Mansell-Lacey's flat?' Agnes asked, a little desperately.

'Well, I think the flat actually belongs to his friend, Mehmet, but Walter does live here,' Godiva answered.

'Why are you going in? You can't live here. Walter's not married,' Agnes said, tersely.

'No, he's not married, and I'm just staying here until I get my own flat. I'm a friend of Walter's,' Godiva explained in a patient tone. Agnes seemed increasingly agitated.

'But I've left my husband. I've come here. I've nowhere else to go,' she blurted.

'Oh, I see, you are one of Walter's conquests. Now I don't wish to be unkind, but I think it very unlikely that he will want you here. Look, I think it is a bit public out here. Let's go inside and I'll make you some tea. Just don't expect to stay when Walter returns,' said Godiva. She manoeuvred past Agnes and unlocked the door with her key.

Agnes entered the flat with her mouth slightly open and tears in her eyes. She put the bag down by the fireplace and gazed absently around the room.

'Please take a seat,' said Godiva and Agnes sat as though in shock.

Godiva took off her coat and hat and put them on the hall stand. She went into the kitchen, boiled a kettle and brought in a tray with cups, milk and sugar, as well as the teapot. After the tray had been placed on the side-table she sat down opposite Agnes and poured two cups of tea.

'Milk and sugar?' Godiva asked.

'Yes please. Two lumps, but not too much milk,' Agnes mumbled in automatic response. She took the cup. It shook slightly in her hands, but she did not raise it to her lips. There was a long silence before Agnes spoke again.

'I didn't realise that Walter had any permanent lady friends. I knew that there were other women, of course, but I didn't know he was spoken for. I wouldn't have come here otherwise. Then I come and find you here. You're not married to him are you?'

'No, I'm not married to Walter,' Godiva said patiently, 'And, just to make it clear to you, we have separate rooms, as I said. But I don't think that you ought to raise your hopes too much. I've known Walter for years, and he doesn't bring his lady friends back here. He always makes other arrangements for his pleasures.'

'But he loves me, I'm sure he does,' said Agnes.

'Has he told you directly that he loves you? And has he ever mentioned wanting to live with you?' Godiva asked.

'He never told me directly, but I could see it in every word and every gesture. Oh! I love him so much. I just want to be with him. I made up my mind last night, after I had a really serious argument with my husband. He's a complete beast and he made the ridiculous accusation that I was being unfaithful. So today I packed a bag and just came here,' Agnes confessed. 'Will Walter be here soon?'

'Walter will appear when you least expect him. I think he is due back this afternoon, but you never really know with him. Look, tell me, did you tell the servants or leave a note for your husband?' Godiva asked, with sincere interest.

'No, I didn't leave a note or anything. I didn't know what to say. I mean, what is there to say in such circumstances. I'll send a note around to John later, once I had settled in,' said Agnes.

'It's good that you didn't leave a note,' said Godiva, 'that means that you can go back without too many questions being asked. If he's still away from home, then your husband need never know what you did.'

'But I want to talk to Walter!' Agnes said bursting into floods of tears.

It was at this time that Walter walked into the room. He looked at the Gladstone bag and then looked at Agnes coldly.

'Walter, darling,' said Agnes, leaping up to embrace him around the neck, 'I've left my husband. I've come to live with you. I don't care about the scandal. I just love you so much.'

Walter unwound her arms and pushed her to a decent distance away before he answered. 'You may not care about the scandal, but you really ought to. If I had ever mentioned at any time during our dalliance that my intentions were in the least bit honourable, then you must have misheard me. Frankly, I have no intention of entertaining you here, nor ever did. Our relationship, such as it was, was solely concerned with mutual pleasure without being bound by convention or the social niceties. I will state now, without equivocation that I have no intention of living with you. I do not want you in my flat, and I never wish to see you ever again, so kindly take your bag and go on your way, either back to your husband or to hell!' Walter said grimly.

'But no-one ever made me feel the way you do!' Agnes insisted, pleadingly.

'Then you shouldn't have thought of trying to change the relationship, should you!' Walter said emphatically, 'Now kindly leave, Madam, and never come back again.' He took the bag, strode down the hall and threw it out, then returned and dragged a weeping Agnes out to join her possessions, slamming the door behind him.

'What in God's name did you let her in for?' Walter asked of Godiva in an angry tone.

'She was confused and upset. I told her it was no good; that you wouldn't want her here, but she just wouldn't listen.

'I do hate such scenes, they are just so common, like a cheap melodrama. Why is it that so many women want to change a fellow. Can't they see that what they like about him is precisely because he is not their husband. If I were ever to get married to any of these women they would hate me within three months. She said she was in love with me, but all it was only lust, and they are very different things,' Walter said, striding about the room. They could hear loud weeping from outside the door.

'But you have to feel sorry for her,' said Godiva in a conciliatory tone, 'After all, she was willing to leave her husband for you.'

'Look here, I can't help if she has these delusions. I tell you, it was kinder in the end to let her know right now that she had no hope of catching me. Would you like her to be moping around for months with some useless hope in what could never be?' Walter said, all in a rush.

'It did seem very cruel, and not at all gentlemanly,' Godiva observed.

'Well, maybe I am not a gentleman, then. In fact, seducing other men's wives isn't a gentlemanly thing to do, but I thought she knew the rules of the game. I would never have even contemplated copulating with her otherwise,' Walter said, bitterly.

'That is a disgusting thing to say!' Godiva said angrily.

'Disgusting, well, possibly, but it's the truth. There is no real love between Agnes and me, nor any real affection for each other. It was supposed to be just sex, dirty animalistic sex, and nothing more. So please don't try to pretend it was anything else. Life isn't a romantic novel, you know,' Walter said bitterly.

'You really are a beast, Walter. So your description of the act works well enough. What a pity that you lack a heart,' Godiva said, disgusted.

'I can only be what I was born to be,' said Walter. He went to his room to change.

'Oh, no. You studied long and hard to be a seducer!' Godiva said loudly, determined to have the last word. He did not deny it.

MONDAY 27TH SEPTEMBER 1909

The Ministry of War was housed in an almost organic growth of government offices established in several old Georgian houses in the area of Whitehall Gardens on the east side of Whitehall, very close to the seat of government. There were approved plans to build new offices to meet the requirements of the twentieth century, and a competition had been won by a young architect. However, building work had not yet begun. Godiva found the block easily enough and checked her story, running it through her mind, rehearsing what she had to say. The bare facts she had gleaned by looking through copies of Hansard, in answers to questions on the subject of oil supply to the navy, asked by Mr Winston Churchill, MP.

Entering the building, she explained her business to the man at the small reception desk. He invited her to sit, and then he used the new internal telephone system to report her arrival to someone in the correct department. She had to wait for several minutes before a heavily built middle aged man in a grey suit and stiff collar came down the stairs with a bouncing step and made his way over to her.

'Miss Williams?' he enquired.

'Yes, that's me,' Godiva agreed.

'I'm Bulliphant, Mr Gurney-Stewart's PPS,' he introduced himself, 'My, my, it is rather unusual to meet a lady journalist. We thought it must be a mistake when we received your request.'

'Well, us ladies seem to be getting just about everywhere in these modern times,' said Godiva, flashing what she hoped was a sly and disarming smile.

'Well, if would like to follow me I will take you up to the office of the junior minister you requested to see,' said the man, as he led her through the over-ground labyrinth, up two flights of stairs and along a maze of narrow corridors with swayback floorboards of stained old oak. They dropped into a walking rhythm and their shoes beat a tattoo on the boards. Eventually they came to an office of faded grandeur and dark-stained wood. There was a number on the door, but it did not seem to follow any system she could recognise in terms of the floor it was on or in relation to the doors around it. She was ushered inside.

'Thank you, Bulliphant,' said a blond young man who bore a strong resemblance to Walter, but without her friend's height and athleticism or the rakish glint of his eye. He had been sitting behind a large desk when she arrived, but stood up on her entry, shook her hand gently and introduced himself as Charles Gurney-Stewart, Minister of Supply at the Ministry of War. He motioned her to take a seat on the other side of his desk.

'Now what is it that you want of me, Miss Williams?' he said. Godiva took out a shorthand notebook and pencil.

'I wanted to ask a few questions concerning the modernising of the navy; specifically, I wanted to know how the supplies of fuel can be accessed throughout the Empire,' she said in a measured tone. Charles thought for some time before replying.

'I'm afraid that I can't comment on government policy, you need to request that information from the Minister. But I must warn you that these matters are not normally given out, just in case the information should prove useful to our enemies, or any potential enemy.'

'Yes, of course I understand that,' said Godiva, 'but the move to the use of oil to fuel ships is common knowledge, and what I was really trying to discover was the administrative steps that have to be taken in order to put the policy into operation. I trust that you think you can talk a little about that, in general terms.'

'Very well, I shall, in, very general terms. Yes, I could say a little about that. The need is to have storage facilities in strategic spots around the globe that the Navy can use.'

'But there needs to be a supply of oil first, does there not?' Godiva asked with a knowing smile.

'Of course, that is the first thing needed,' agreed Charles.

'And there is the new oilfield in Persia, the one discovered last year, as well as the refinery that has been built to turn the raw material into something that can be used on ships,' said Godiva.

'That is common enough knowledge,' said Charles, a little impatiently, 'but please form a question, or I shall not be able to answer you.'

'Well, the question I wished to ask is, do these new facilities require additional security measures?' Godiva enquired, leaning forward in her chair and prepared to write down the answer.

'Yes, but we have such matters very well in hand, and I obviously cannot say more, for reasons of national security,' said Charles, a poker player's blankness of expression on his face.

'Then do you believe that the knowledge of such security measures might be very useful to our enemies?' Godiva continued. Charles had not said anything worthwhile writing down as yet.

'Very useful, I should imagine. But that is a rather interesting question, one which suggests that you have learned something already. Is there anything that I should know about?' Charles in his turn leant forward in his chair.

'Not at present, but I am pursuing certain lines of enquiry at the moment,' Godiva said, guardedly.

'You're not really a journalist, are you?' declared Charles, 'We checked with the publication you claim to represent.'

'I am a freelance writer, but I had to give a publication as reference. They should know my name, though. I have written for them several times over the past year. But I use a man's name as a nom de plume, because readers tend not to take such work from a woman seriously,' Godiva blustered.

'Perhaps we should end this interview now, Miss Williams. I wish you every luck with your career, but I have no wish to continue this conversation. Please leave now,' Charles said with finality. He pressed a button on his desk and Bulliphant came back into the office to escort Godiva out. She had learned very little, other than that Charles was no pushover and that he could not to be easily charmed by a woman's wiles.

◊

In the back room of a book shop on Charing Cross Road two men were browsing among a collection of books concerned with classical architecture. A whispered conversation was taking place between them, long pauses between the spoken sentences.

'What is it you called me here for?' asked the smaller, more strongly built man.

'I have a job for you,' said the taller man, who had a scarred face, 'Only a little job. You have plenty of time to do it before you go on to the main job. If you do it properly, I'll tell you who your real target is.'

'What do you mean by that, Braun?' Asked the shorter man, taking out a book on the architecture of the Parthenon and leafing through it.

'I can tell you who it is that you want to kill, and it won't be very difficult to arrange. I'll give you the name if you do this little job for me,' said Braun.

'Did you know that the Parthenon was built by a man called Kalikrates?' he pronounced the word "Killy-crates".

'That's Kalikrates,' Braun corrected him, 'Now are you willing to take the job on?'

'What do I have to do?' the shorter man asked.

'There is a man who has been bothering one of my associates. I want you to deal with him. Stop him being a nuisance,' said Braun.

'When do you want it done?' asked the shorter man.

'As soon as you can do it. He's not guarded or anything, you should find it easy enough,' Braun reassured.

'I suppose it's in London?' asked the shorter man.

'Not far from here,' said Braun, 'here are the details.' He handed over the sealed envelope with the blue ink message.

'What about my reward?' asked the shorter man.

'Just go to your destination, as we agreed. I'll send you a message when you are there. It concerns another man you would like to meet. Remember that your main task is to keep your eyes and ears open. There is a meeting taking place we want to know about. You must tell us who is there and the detail of any conversations you overhear. Try to keep to your story that you are an engineer, so that they do not become suspicious. How are you getting on with your preparation?' Braun said.

'Alright, I suppose, but it's very different from a boat. There's all sorts of mathematics to get used to. I suppose I can get away with it for a few days. I know the basic workings, but I'm not going to be an expert in three days. They'll find me out soon enough,' said the shorter man.

'The entire job should only take two or three days. After that you are free to go. You should be able to manage that, should you not?' said Braun.

'Well, I'd better hurry up and do this little job for you,' said the shorter man, 'After all, I'm due to go away very shortly.'

'You won't have to tell me whether or not you've succeeded, I'll find out soon enough,' said Braun.

'Do have any more money for me, for my expenses?' asked the shorter man.

'I had thought that you would ask about that,' said Braun with an air of nonchalance, and he handed over another small envelope, 'that should suffice for now'.

'Make sure you pass on that name to me very soon,' said the other.

'Just do your job, and the name will be on its' way to you as soon as I know that you've arrived, and after you've completed this little job in a satisfactory manner,' said Braun.

'Then I look forward to your message, and that is about all we have to say,' said the shorter man with some bitterness. He put the book back on the shelf and strolled out of the room and of the shop. Braun followed after a few minutes.

◊

Sergeant Clift arrived at the flat late that morning and was ushered in by Dorkins. Walter was drinking coffee and reading 'The Times'.

'Welcome, Sergeant,' said Walter, 'Would you like some coffee?'

'No thank you, Sir. This is just a brief call to let you know about your intruder. We've found out who he is, though I won't tell you his name. The thing is, he's not quite what we expected. You see, he's not a criminal, or at least not the sort I recognise. He's actually an actor, though not a successful one. It really is all very curious,' Clift mused.

'But he's still being guarded, isn't he?' Walter inquired.

'Well, in a kind of way, I suppose. You see, Special Branch has taken over and taken him somewhere I don't know about. That got me rather annoyed. I don't like it when an investigation is taken away from me,' said Clift.

'May I inquire as to his health?' Walter asked. Clift drew a breath in through his teeth.

'He'd had some surgery, and apparently was doing quite well. I tried to speak to the surgeon, but he'd been told not to speak to me. I had a word with one of the nurses over a cup of tea. She assured me that the intruder hadn't said a word before he'd been whisked away. What is more, no-one from Special Branch said anything about it to me. That I consider to be the very height of rudeness,' Clift grumbled.

'Well at least he's alive. I'll pass that message on to Miss Williams. It will be a weight off her mind. She was really rather distressed about bashing him like that. She thought that she'd killed him. She's got a kind heart, you know,' said Walter.

'Quite a remarkable young lady, your Miss Williams,' Clift observed, 'She's brave and resourceful. Oh, and another thing, the gun was only loaded with blanks, so you weren't in any real danger, I suppose. It would have made a bit of noise but wouldn't have caused much damage.'

'Yes, that is curious,' said Walter, shaking his head, 'It was just done to frighten me, I suppose. But I won't tell Miss Williams that part, as I've already thanked her for saving my life.'

'What you choose to do in the privacy of your own home is no business of mine, Sir. Well, I must be on my way. But I was just wondering, could you please let me know if you hear anything more about this man's employer. He seems to be a most dangerous man.'

'On that point, Sergeant, I really have to refer you back to our Mr Scrivener,' said Walter, with a rueful smile.

'Another thing that was funny was that this actor chappy had a chitty on him for doing the job, a payment in advance I suppose,' the Sergeant said, frowning.

'Some kind of receipt?' Walter queried, 'how very curious. You'd think they would have more sense than to record such a transaction.'

'The workings of the criminal mind never ceases to amaze me, Sir,' Clift said sadly, 'But in this case, the chitty was from someone with a German name; someone called Braun.'

'Now that really is interesting,' said Walter, thoughtfully. 'Was there anything on this chitty that might allow us to find out who he is?'

'There was an address. It was a postal collection point in a tobacconist's shop. So, without setting a man onto the job, which I am not allowed to do, because of the connection to the Special Branch, I don't suppose that we'll ever find out,' Clift said ruefully.

'Maybe I can find out, or Miss Williams might be able to think of something, I'll leave her a note,' said Walter.

'Just so long as it doesn't get her into any kind of bother,' said Clift with a concerned note in his voice, 'she's been through enough already.'

'Of course I would much rather find out something about Arthur Gregory.' Walter said, grimly.

'Yes, it's a pity that I was warned off,' agreed Clift, 'I'd really like to put him away for several years.'

'As would I, Sergeant, as would I,' Walter agreed, 'And now, I must get ready to go away for a few days. Strictly under orders, you understand.'

'Well, you make sure that you take care of yourself, if you're still mixed up in this business,' said the Sergeant, and he left the flat uttering a few muttered oaths.

Dorkins helped Walter to pack for his trip, packing both evening and country clothes. All in all the clothes and boots and assorted toiletries filled a large trunk. Walter was only visiting for a week. Having organised the packing, Dorkins laid out a set of travelling clothes for Walter, a well tailored tweed jacket, a soft-collared flannel shirt and twill trousers. Walter had, in the meantime, been writing a note to Godiva, detailing what he had learned from Sergeant Clift. For the time being he would have to leave the investigation up to her. After the preparations were complete Walter checked the details of his train ticket with his copy of Bradshaw.

A better servant would have prepared the luggage on the day of departure, but Dorkins was not so reliable as that.

Dorkins had been willing, keen even, to act as Walter's valet for the trip. Walter insisted that he stay to look after Godiva, perhaps travelling up in two days time. Godiva might need his help and advice, as well as his role as a bodyguard. Besides, Walter doubted that Dorkins would be welcome at the meeting which was to take place at Blackleigh Court. As a valet, Dorkins would travel second class, and they would meet up again at the great house, with Dorkins expected to find his own way from Droitwich to the Court. The usual form had to be observed, and the relationship between master and servant made crystal clear for all the world to see.

For now, Walter had an appointment at his Pimlico studio, one which would occupy him for the rest of the afternoon. Alexandra had agreed to model for him, and he had a notion to try his hand at dressing her as a Madonna, with an old nun's habit and a life-size porcelain doll as props. He left a note for Godiva, telling her about the Sergeant's visit.

◊

The man who stood at the threshold of the flat was tall and slim with a nearly full head of greying hair and a full set of side whiskers. Godiva could see that this man was a relative of Walter and invited him in, though still not sure of the relationship. With a deft movement he placed his black silk top hat on the hall table, then placed his fine dove grey gloves inside the hat and rested his silver handled cane against the table. He made his introductions.

'Good afternoon,' he said in clipped tones, 'I am the Duke of Radnor and I am Walter's father.' He regarded Godiva with a penetrating gaze and she felt that she was being considered either as a future daughter-in-law or as a potential mistress.

'You had better come in,' said Godiva, 'and is it 'your grace' for a Duke?' She led him into the living room, seating him on the sofa before continuing. 'I am a friend of Walter, my name is Godiva Williams.'

'I was in London to attend the House of Lords and thought I might come to see my reprobate son and mention the possibility of his gaining some long-overdue useful employment.'

'I'm afraid he's not here at the moment,' said Godiva, 'Can I get you a cup of tea or anything?'

'That would be very pleasant,' said the Duke, 'please have your servant make it'

'Walter's man has the afternoon off, so I shall just have to make it myself.'

The Duke sat bolt upright on the sofa looking round the room and judging the contents. It took Godiva some minutes to boil the kettle and prepare the tea. She found the milk, but no lemon. When she returned she found the Duke examining the books on the main bookshelf. She placed the tray of tea things on the occasional table and he turned to talk to her.

'Do I take it that these are your books?' he asked her.

'They are mostly my books, though Walter may have read them, or some of them. Do you approve of my taste in literature?' she asked.

'You mistake me, my dear young lady, it is just that Walter's taste in books tends more to the sensational and rather less to serious works of politics, science or philosophy, unless his tastes have changed considerably during the last three years,' the Duke said with a small shake of his head.

'How do you take your tea?' Godiva asked.

'With milk, please,' the Duke replied.

Godiva followed the ritual of English tea making, adding the milk before pouring the tea. 'Do you take sugar?' She asked.

'Just one lump please, and a piece of that delicious looking Madeira cake would be very welcome,' said the Duke.

Godiva handed him the cup of tea and passed across the plate with the cake and a napkin.

'Do I take it from your choice of literature that you are a supporter of women's suffrage?' the Duke enquired.

'I prefer to regard myself as a Suffragist rather than a Suffragette,' Godiva said, enthusiastically. 'After all, the word Suffragette was coined as an insult. I am not entirely in favour of violent action. My sympathies used to lie with Millicent Fawcett's NUWSS, but I don't think they will ever change anything. So recently I have taken up with the Pankhursts and the WSPU. Do I take it that you're not a supporter of votes for women?'

'It is not something that I feel passionately about either way. But I do like people with convictions, it seems to indicate some kind of moral fibre,' said the Duke, smiling at Godiva.

Godiva laughed gently. 'But I thought that you were a Conservative. Surely your party is opposed to giving votes to women.'

'My party may object, but as I said, I have no great feelings about it either way. In fact I think on balance that it's probably a good idea. In my experience women are a good deal more conservative, with a small 'c', than men are,' the Duke observed.

Godiva poured herself a cup of tea, black and with two sugars. There was no lemon to add to the cup. 'Did you wish me to pass on a message to Walter?'

'Well, I was thinking of impressing on him the need to earn a living, but if he were to be thinking of marrying you perhaps some new arrangements might be made,' the Duke said with a smile and a brief nod.

'You think that Walter wants to marry me then?' Godiva asked, in some surprise.

'Well, I don't wish to be presumptuous, but given the apparent situation...' he trailed off.

'Ah, yes, I can understand that, but, you see, I am only staying in the spare room for a short while. The thing is that I have no intention of ever marrying Walter. He's my friend and that is all ever I wish him to be. Please understand that I am not cohabiting with him, I am just using the flat while his flatmate is away with the MCC,' Godiva explained.

'What a pity,' said the Duke with regret, 'of all the women I have known him to be associated with, you are the first one who seems to have even a single jot of sense.'

'It is just because I do have some little sense that makes me determined never to marry Walter,' Godiva said with more than a hint of a smile.

The Duke laughed out loud. 'If you ever change your mind, I am sure that you would make me a wonderful daughter-in-law.'

'Well, I'm very flattered,' Godiva declared, and despite herself, she blushed slightly.

'And if you are ever in the vicinity of my estates in Herefordshire you are more than welcome to stay, and I would be most delighted to see you.'

'I might very well take you up on that offer,' said Godiva, genuinely meaning what she said 'If our paths cross again I should be most pleased to resume our acquaintance.'

'There was something else that I wished to say to Walter,' said the Duke, 'concerning a career opportunity for him.'

Godiva considered for a minute before replying. 'I am expecting him back at any time. He just went out to his studio, but he may call in at the gymnasium.'

'Well I think I will give you some indication of what I'm thinking. Recently I had been involved with a company that has discovered significant oil deposits in Persia. I think there are great opportunities in this and it might suit Walter's spirit of adventure to become involved.'

'I have read about the oil deposits in Persia,' said Godiva, wanting to hear more.

'Oh, indeed, we have just discovered some major deposits, just in time too. Y'see, the oil is needed for the Navy. Apparently it's better than coal for powering the ships. And it is vital that we stop the Germans getting a similar supply or prevent us from exploiting it. The way they are developing their own navy is really quite worrying. These new ships they are building are really first rate, you know,' the Duke said, sounding just a little worried.

'But isn't it really the Persian's oil?' Godiva asked innocently.

'Ah, well, we've done a deal with their chieftain, some marauding Riff I dare say, calls himself the Czar or something, and so as long as we can keep him in power he will agree to let us extract the oil. You sound like this expert who works for me. He's always going on about Persia being the seat of all civilization and such rot. But then again he is Danish so what can you expect?' the Duke said with a snort of derision.

'Well it sounds like I may well agree with him to some extent. So who is this Danish person?' Godiva enquired, really wanting to know the answer, but trying to sound as if it were merely a polite question.

'Name of Knudsen, Professor of Geology at Imperial College. He knows all about the rocks and the oil that lies in 'em. I am informed that he is quite well known,' said the Duke, proudly.

'Does he live in London, then?' Godiva asked.

'Yes, he has a place in London somewhere. Must have if he works in Imperial College. Like I said, he's been doing some work for me. In fact, I am trying to raise some funding for some further oil exploration at the moment. And I need to prepare something to make these people want to invest their money,' the Duke confided.

'Is there anything I might be able to do?' Godiva asked, 'I have a science degree and I am very used to preparing my father's works for publication.'

'You know, that sounds like a very good idea. Have a word with this Knudsen feller and get him to give you an idea of what to write. It's no good getting some dried up old academic to write it, he'd never be able to sell anything, and they wouldn't understand what he was on about. And, as I said, Knudsen's Danish, so I don't suppose he can write decent English anyway. Have a go at it and I will pay you the going rate for the right sort of stuff. If you meet him, tell him that I sent you,' the Duke said enthusiastically, 'Just give him my card.' He fished in a pocket and came up with a business card printed on one side. He produced a silver pencil from an inside pocket and wrote something on the back before handing it to Godiva.

'You said he's at Imperial College. I should be able to track him down to his lair easily enough,' said Godiva, exuding an air of confidence.

'Yes, and there's an article about the man in Maxfield's Magazine, this very month. Not that you can mistake the man. He's about six feet tall and seven feet broad, with a beard you could play hide and seek in,' said the Duke.

'Then I'll go out and buy a copy of the magazine. That way I'll know a bit about him when I meet him,' Godiva said, pursing her lips.

'Oh, yes, I suppose you could do that. And I'll send over a package with some details about this oilfield, so you can be a bit more prepared. Now you won't forget to tell Walter about that job, will you?' the Duke said, rising from his seat.

'I shall pass the message on to Walter when he gets back,' Godiva promised.

'That would be most kind of you,' said the Duke with a smile. 'Just tell him to get in touch with me at my club. I shall only be there tonight. Tomorrow I am travelling through France, to Monte Carlo. Of course, if you would care to dine with me, I'm sure we could have a most useful conversation.'

'As I said, I am expecting him back at any time, but you never really know with Walter, he could very well have other appointments.' Godiva's brain was making links between the security services, oil exploration and German spies. It also occurred to her that the Duke might be in the habit of trying to seduce every woman he met, and how this might explain Walter's behaviour towards young women.

◊

There are many back alleyways in London, half-hidden passages that are unlit and which seem to lead to nowhere in particular, though they are the means of getting in and out of lodgings and businesses. In that part of London which still shows in its imprint the town planning of Alfred the Great, such passageways are common and usually without official name, although their colloquial names can be interesting to a passing historian. On a wet night in late September a passing police constable glanced down one of these passages as he made his rounds. There appeared to be a pile of wet clothes on the sodden surface. In the glassy monochrome reflections from the distant street lights the cloth looked to be a dull black. The policeman entered the passageway and prodded the pile with his boot. There was sufficient weight and resistance for him to know that the object on the ground was a body. This constable was equipped with one of the new electric torches, and he shone its beam onto the prostrate form. The body, on examination, was that of a slim young man, lying on his front. The policeman turned him over. The man's face had been beaten to a bloody mess. Both of his arms had been broken below the elbow and projected at odd angles. After checking for a pulse the policeman was able to establish for certain what looked to be obvious, that the young man was dead. But the body was still warm and *rigor mortis* was yet to set in. He had not been dead for very long.

Hurrying back to the entrance to the passageway the policeman gave several sharp blasts of his whistle, urging his fellow coppers to come and assist him. The long, shrill blasts, woke almost all the local residents, and two more constables eventually arrived. One man was sent with a message to fetch a senior detective. In this way the process of investigation was set in motion. The body was conveyed to a local mortuary, and a medical practitioner who was contracted to carry out such duties was called from his bed to perform a post-mortem examination. There was no indication of any gunshots or stab wounds. He had been tortured and then beaten to death. A cloth had been jammed into his mouth to stop any screaming, and his hands had been bound before death, as could be deduced from the ligature marks on his wrists. The rope had been removed before the body had been dumped into the anonymous alleyway.

At the coroner's office the man's pockets were examined to see what the contents were. There was a wallet containing a ten shilling note, a half-crown and two florins. In an inside pocket were several pieces of paper, among which was an old envelope which provided a name and address for the victim. From this they were able to establish that his name was Gordon Temple. Further investigation showed his profession to be that of a chorus-line dancer. On the back of the envelope was a note concerning a meeting at a Lyon's Corner House two days previously. There were two names added to the list, one was that of an Ezekial Dorkins, the other was someone called Walter Mansell-Lacey. A check of the Police records showed that this person was resident in a very expensive flat which belonged to an MCC cricketer, who was also the son of a Moghul ruler in North India, Prince Mehmet Jehar. The records also showed that Lord Walter Mansell-Lacey was the second son of the Duke of Radnor, and had recently been the victim of an aggravated burglary. There was also a note in red ink that any approach to this person should be made via the Special Branch.

◊

That evening Walter dined with his father at White's Club, on the east side of St James's Street. This was the oldest club in London, and being close to royal palaces had attracted a membership of courtiers, gamblers and fashionable young idlers. That had been when it was founded, but by now it was associated with the Conservative Party and ridiculous bets. If you were a Tory or a gambler, or both, you would fit in perfectly.

They were eating in the spacious Coffee Room, where crystal glass chandeliers dangled from a barrel-shaped roof. The tables were spread with spotless white linen and the eating irons were of the finest sliver, without the ridiculous lower middle class invention of the fish knife. The food was traditional and plentiful and good. They went through the menu from potted shrimps to roast pheasant and finished with a figgy pudding. They chatted pleasantly during the meal; serious discussions were likely to ruin the digestion. It was only afterwards, when they had retired to the smoking room and were enjoying their brandy and cigars that the real conversation began.

'I was most impressed by your friend, Miss Williams. She seems a most able and personable young lady,' the Duke began.

'You do realise that her father is Offa Williams. Now I'm quite certain that you haven't read any of his stuff, but in case you hadn't realised, he regards us as the class enemy. Godiva is quite a militant suffragette, and she bears that unfortunate name. All in all, I don't see her mixing easily in the country set. So, if you have any ideas of us getting together, then I should tell you that she would not be seen as an ideal first choice for a wife,' Walter said in a tone which suggested a sense of martyrdom.

'I've just about given up on you finding that kind of wife. Beside's it's not necessary for several reasons. Firstly, Ralph has made the dynastic marriage, so his place is secure when he succeeds me. Ariadne has those ghastly American pretentions, but with the saving grace of being as rich as Croesus! No, what would be better for you is not some poppet who will please the county set, but someone who can further your career in town. Everything is changing and all the old certainties are being challenged. Your Miss Williams represents the future. Us old families have to learn to adapt, to change with the times, otherwise we'll go extinct, like the dinosaurs,' the Duke confided. He took a good amount of brandy and swilled it around his mouth before swallowing, so as to appreciate the taste. Then he drew deep on his cigar.

'Look, I'm a great admirer of Miss Williams, but we are not lovers, and I don't think she'd have me for a husband,' Walter said patiently, 'She came barging into the flat about a week ago after she argued with her father. She has a habit of taking things over. Any alliance with Miss Williams is not a thing to be entered into lightly. She did mention that you had some kind of offer of work for me, so I was wondering what that might be.' He lit a cigarette, sat back in his chair and crossed his legs at the ankles.

'Ah, yes, I did want to have a word with you about that. Through the connection with Ralph's father-in-law I seem to have become involved in the oil business. There's lots of money to be made, great fortunes in fact, but in the financial world you need capital to get started; more capital that I can easily lay my hands on. We've got a lot of land, as you know, but we haven't got huge amounts of ready cash. So I'm setting out a proposal to some stock-market investors. We know the oil is out in Persia, and we know that there's lots of it there. We just need to get it out of the ground, and we need to refine it before it can be used. If this plan succeeds, and I think it stands a jolly good chance of doing so, then I will need someone to run the operation from the Persian end. It occurred to me that you have the necessary wander lust and sense of adventure, so I decided to ask if you were interested,' the Duke said. He looked up and tried to smile reassuringly.

'Can you give me a little time to think about that, Father,' Walter prevaricated, 'I've got some other work on I need to finish first.'

'Oh, not your paintings; you'll never make a living out of that. No, what you need is a proper job; something that can make best use of your talents,' the Duke made an expansive gesture with his hands, spilling some brandy and sending cigar ash onto the arm of his chair.

'Actually, I'm doing a bit of a job for a department of the Navy, and it shouldn't take very long. I'm not just seeking a stay of execution, I really am working,' Walter said persuasively.

'Well, I must admit I'm impressed. So you've gone out and found yourself a job. Quite marvellous,' The Duke said, smiling.

'Actually, they came and found me. And it's only a little job, so I should give you an answer shortly,' Walter admitted.

'I'm off to Monte tomorrow,' the Duke said, 'having a bit of a break after all this organising.'

'Are you taking anyone with you?' Walter asked innocently.

'Oh, no. But I might meet up with someone while I'm there,' the Duke guffawed.

'I'm off myself tomorrow, up to old Randall's place. Doing a bit of shooting and that, and it is connected to the work I'm doing, in a roundabout way. There's someone I've got to see,' Walter said mysteriously, 'Are you going to be in Monte for long?'

'No, no. I've got to be back for some blasted meeting with share-holders in a couple of weeks. So you've got a fortnight's grace to come up with your answer,' The Duke declared, 'and do send my regards to Randall and his family. Still friends with the girls, are you?'

'Of course, we always got on well. They should both be there. Their both married, of course. Caroline's got two children, so far. It should be a jolly time, and I'm looking forward to seeing them,' Walter said, slightly wistfully.

'Good, because you'll need some diversion,' the Duke said loudly, 'you never did enjoy shooting all that much, from what I remember.'

'No, Father, it's not my favourite sport,' Walter said, with a slight sigh, 'I much prefer deer-stalking. That's so much more of a challenge.'

TUESDAY 28TH SEPTEMBER

Godiva took a bus then a tram to Whitechapel Road. She had made a list of all the newsagents in the area as they appeared in the trade directories. Gordon had failed to specify exactly which shop he had talked about, and there were several which seemed suitable. Godiva walked a route which took all of these shops in. As it turned out, there was only one which offered the discrete service of acting as a postal address. This shop was on a side road to the south side of the Pavilion Theatre, away from the main line of shops and close to the poorer housing. The jars and bottles on display were old and dusty, showing that selling tobacco goods was more of a sideline than a main occupation. The shop keeper was of some Levantine descent, surly, suspicious and unsmiling. If he spoke English he didn't let on. Another vital fact Gordon did not know was the box number. When she mentioned that she was looking for a particular box the shop keeper allowed her to run her eyes, at a distance, over the boxes behind the counter. During her examination he stood behind his dusty counter with arms folded. On the third box down on the sixth row Godiva spotted the word "Gregory". It did not take all of her abilities to work out that this was box 63. Taking out a pencil from her notebook she added the box number onto the envelope. Then she handed the envelope, together with a shilling over the counter. The envelope contained a simple note which asked the recipient to reply to G W at her father's address, as he might learn something to his advantage. At such times, Godiva reflected, all you can do is cast your bread upon the water and see what floats back on the tide. This was a proverb which had always bothered her, as her only experience of casting bread upon the water was feeding the ducks on the pond in Highbury Fields.

As she was leaving the shop she saw the unmistakable shape of Professor Knudsen, looking just as he did in the magazine article, coming down the street towards her. He was a massive figure, clad in a grey overcoat with the proportions of a bell-tent. What would the distinguished Dane be doing in this rat-hole she wondered? She was about to approach him, only being stopped by the notion that it was inappropriate as they had not yet been introduced. Instead, she pretended to be doing some window shopping, looking at the stock in a milliners that sold cheap hats to working women. She examined the image of Knudsen reflected in the glass. The Professor went into the same newsagents which she had just come from. He was carrying an envelope, but Godiva could not make out what was written on it. Caution prevented her from following him in.

◊

Godiva had arranged for Walter's tickets to be collected at Paddington Station. To Walter's chagrin, they were third class tickets, but he was sufficiently conscious of his financial situation not to attempt to change them for first class and to travel as he usually did. The train was not too crowded and the standard of the seats was quite good and clean. On the journey to Worcester he entertained himself by flirting with a pair of ladies, the elder chaperoning the younger. There was only a short period when he could really flirt with the younger lady, a pretty but vapid girl. They exchanged words, but he did not find any opportunity to exchange cards.

They came into Worcester Shrub Hill Station on a wide curve on a hill to the North of the city. The tracks had been converted from the wide gauge Brunel had used for the Great Western line to British standard gauge. The result of this is an unnecessarily wide gap between the two lines and a wider than usual bridge between the platforms. As it was, Walter did not have to change platforms, but still had a thirty five minute wait on a drafty platform with swirling rain piercing the line of the roof to splash his boots and luggage.

◊

Godiva was at home in the flat when Sergeant Clift called yet again. He had his overcoat taken from him and hung on a peg in the hallway and was guided into the living room by Dorkins, who afterwards returned to the kitchen to prepare an evening meal. Godiva rose to greet the policeman and sat him in an armchair.

'Is Lord Walter Mansell-Lacey not at home?' Clift asked.

'Walter's gone to the country, Sergeant,' Godiva replied, 'Some kind of shooting party I believe. Is there any reason why you wanted to talk to him?'

'Well, yes, Miss. But it's rather distressing. You see, we found a note with Lord Walter's name and address on it in the pocket of a murdered man. So we were wondering how it came to be there, and I was going to ask your friend.'

'If you don't mind me asking something, Sergeant, who was this murdered man?' Godiva prompted.

'I'm not sure that I should be telling you, Miss, mostly on account of your name being mentioned on a couple of police reports. It seems that you are an active sort of suffragette, and as such you are a suspicious person. Mind you, in the light of what you have already been through, I suppose that it wouldn't do too much harm to tell you. The man's name was Gordon Temple. He was some kind of dancer,' the Sergeant replied.

There was a cry from the direction of the kitchen, and Dorkins burst in.

'What's happened to Gordon?' Dorkins demanded. Clift was initially shocked by this sudden entrance. Then he was angry.

'Have you been listening? I can't abide people eves-dropping, especially servants,' Clift blustered.

'Gordon was a friend of mine. I introduced him to Mr Walter and Miss Williams. That's why he had Mr Walter's name on that note. I gave it to him. It's what Gordon said to Mr Walter and Miss Williams that got him killed. I tried to warn them all about how dangerous he is, but they wouldn't listen,' said Dorkins in a rush.

'Well, then, you'd better sit down and explain yourself a bit more, then,' said the Sergeant, recognising that Dorkins had something important to say. Dorkins swallowed hard, and was trying not to cry as he spoke.

'Gordon's a friend of mine, or, rather, he was, a friend, but not a close one. I knew where he used to work, and when Mr Walter started asking about a certain person, and I knew that Gordon had worked for that person, well, I arranged a meeting in a Lyons Corner House. And Gordon told them what was going on. Someone must have found out, and now Gordon's dead.'

'Excuse me,' said the Sergeant, 'But could you say that again, please.' It was Godiva who made the translation.

'What Dorkins is trying to say is this. Walter and I found out that a man called Gregory was involved in something like blackmail. He runs a sort of club. Dorkins has worked in the theatre and knew who this Gregory was, and also knew Gordon, who had worked at the club. So Dorkins arranged for a meeting between Walter, myself and Gordon Temple. Gordon didn't say very much to us, but he was very worried that if Gregory ever found out he was talking to us, he would get a beating, or worse. And now Gordon is dead. So it seems quite likely that Gregory had something to do with the murder.' She finished her explanation and there was a silence for several seconds.

'You'd better tell me a bit more about this Gregory. I mean, what's his full name, and where is this club of his?' the Sergeant asked.

'Right, Sergeant, his name is Arthur Maundy Gregory, but I don't know the address of the club, though I know his business address,' said Godiva.

'The club is in Paddington,' Dorkins added, 'On South Wharf Road. The place used to be a furniture store.'

'And what was that about blackmail?' Clift asked.

'Mr Gregory runs a club for gentlemen with er, unusual sexual tastes. He blackmails people after they have made use of the services of the club,' Godiva explained. Clift made some notes in a small notebook, using a blunt stub of a pencil.

'And what does this have to do with what Lord Walter is working on?' Clift continued.

'I'm afraid that I can't tell you that, Sergeant,' said Godiva, 'Mainly because I don't know myself. What I will say is that you will probably run up against the Special Branch if you start to investigate him, so don't expect too much.' Dorkins had been sitting in silence, head in hands. He spoke at last.

'God help me, but I'm going to get that bastard Gregory. I don't know how, but nothing is going to stop me. I'm bloody going to get him,' he said.

'Now, now,' said Clift, 'No need for bad language, especially in front of a lady.'

'It's alright, Sergeant. I think that's quite mild, considering what has happened. But, Dorkins, please don't do anything rash. Please come to me before you do anything. I don't want anything to happen to you as well,' said Godiva.

'Yeah, well, you are partly to blame for this. If you hadn't got Gordon to talk, he'd still be alive,' said Dorkins petulantly.

'Yes,' Godiva admitted, 'You may very well be right. Now let me help you, and perhaps between us we can find a way to get to Gregory.'

'Now listen here, both of you,' said Clift, sternly, 'You just leave all this to me, to the Police. We'll get some justice for this Mr Temple. I don't want any stupidity going on concerning this man Gregory. Trust me, I'll deal with it.'

◊

Professor Knudsen's office was on the second floor of the science block of Imperial College. There were obscured glass panels on the side of the office which faced the corridor, but the door was of plain and heavy dark wood. Godiva knocked and was rewarded by a call of 'Enter' from within. She turned the gleaming brass doorknob and entered into a spacious room fitted with bookshelves that rose from floor to ceiling. The spaces on the walls between the bookshelves were covered in colour coded geological maps. There were sufficient hard chairs for the students to receive tuition in groups of up to a dozen. The Professor sat in a wide leather swivel chair behind a large table of some dark wood furnished with the usual paraphernalia of an academic. Besides the full beard he was heavy browed with a broad flat nose. His eyebrows reared up in great tufts and his beard was turning grey around the chin. His lips were full and puffy and only partly covered his large and prominent tobacco stained teeth. He wore a black coat, wing collar and a red and black spotted tie. As she entered he made a point of not standing to greet her.

'Professor Knudsen, I made an appointment to see you,' Godiva started.

'Did you?' the Professor said, 'Remind me of the purpose of your visit'.

'The Duke of Radnor suggested that I see you. He believes you to be the greatest authority on oil exploration in the country.'

'In Europe, certainly, probably in the world,' the Professor interrupted, without undue modesty.

'Well, yes, certainly,' Godiva continued, 'I was hoping that you might be able to help me understand a little about the new discoveries of oil in Persia.'

The Professor stroked his beard while he considered his reply. 'It is not a simple situation, certainly not politically. And as for the geology, you would need some knowledge of science to understand any of it. Do you have a sufficient level of knowledge?'

'I was awarded a degree in Chemistry at the University of Birmingham two years ago. A first, with distinction,' Godiva said with more than a hint of pride.

'I do not personally approve of educating young women to such an intellectual level, especially in the sciences, but given that you seem to have some aptitude in a science it may be possible for me to explain a little to you. Do you know what mineral oil is composed of, or of its derivation?'

'It is formed from the remains of ancient sea organisms, I believe,' Godiva said, trying not to sound annoyed by the nursery school level of the question, 'And it is composed of hydro-carbons.'

'You believe correctly, if in a rather simplistic form. Nevertheless, the deposits are certainly contained in porous rocks which formed on the sea beds of the ancient Earth. These rocks have since been raised to dry land by some geological mechanism. And they are themselves overlain with many layers of rock which were deposited on top of the oil bearing layers at some later date. The oil itself collects in hollows, known as basins. In order to find oil you must find these basins, and drill into them. The oil itself is under pressure due to the weight of the overlying rock and does not even need to be pumped in order to reach the surface, it fact it is under such pressure that it gushes out at a remarkable rate,' the Professor said, still in lecture mode.

'And your work is concerned with identifying where these basins might be?' said Godiva.

'Currently the usual option is to try to find the right types of overlaying rocks and drill down and hope to get lucky by hitting a basin. In almost all cases the drill misses, and drilling such holes is an expensive and time consuming business. My study shows that it is possible to apply certain tests which can produce a much better success rate in discovering where the basins are, and therefore, where the oil is. Using this method allows us to make an educated guess and so save both time and money. This in turn means more oil and more profits for the exploration companies.' Knudsen had stood up during this speech and paced around behind his desk, his hands clasped behind his back.

'I can see the benefits to England of getting this oil,' Godiva mused.

'Have you heard of 'Greek Fire?' Knudsen asked.

'Wasn't that some kind of weapon used by the Byzantines?' Godiva suggested.

'It was a very potent weapon of war. They used it to destroy the Turkish fleets. And we know that the principal ingredient in Greek Fire was crude oil. That and naptha and some volatile addition we don't yet know about. The point is, oil has already played a significant rôle in warfare, in the outcome of a conflict between two major powers. What we do not yet know is what will happen when we let this genie out of the bottle. That is all down to politics. As it was, the Byzantines lost control of the land where the oil was seeping out of the ground, and the Turks never found the recipe. The secret of Greek Fire was lost. The problems occur when one power has a greater supply of oil than the other. This is a new age, and wealth and power will come to depend on who has the most oil. There is no morality when it comes to wealth and power,' Knudsen said, with passion in his voice.

'Right, if I understand this, you believe that there is a major source of oil in Persia, and are concerned about who owns it,' Godiva said.

'Before I answer that question, I need to know why you want to know the results of my studies. There are considerations of commercial and academic interest here,' said Knudsen, guardedly.

'I am preparing a document for the Duke which he hopes will persuade investors to fund some further exploration. And if he can persuade some investors that they are likely to receive a healthy return on their investments, then so much the better.'

'The Duke has kindly funded this sabbatical of mine. It makes me wonder that he hasn't asked me to prepare such a paper myself,' Knudsen queried.

'Well, as you said yourself, this is a complex issue. From what I understand, the Duke wants to explain the possibilities in very plain English. You see, these investor's knowledge of science and geology is very limited. They won't understand anything complicated. You are such a great expert that you might find it difficult to descend to their level of understanding. These investors will only understand a proposition which is presented in the most simplistic of generalizations. I suppose the Duke thinks that it would be an insult to you to ask you to produce this type of work. I hope you understand this is really meant as a compliment to you,' Godiva said. Her answer was followed by a few seconds of silence during which the Professor considered his next statement.

'If I tell you my conclusions it is on the basis that you show me exactly what you intend to print before it is distributed, so that I might correct any basic errors or false claims. I will not allow my work to be misused in that way. You must also agree not to publish anything in the press before my findings are released,' said Knudsen, and he placed the palms of both hands on his desk.

'Of course,' Godiva agreed, 'I should have a first draft ready by the end of next week. And I was wondering if you had some old papers that I might be able to work from.'

'You are welcome to look at my papers, which can be found in the main library. I may find it more difficult to review your work. Unfortunately, Miss Williams, next week I shall be at the Duke's residence in Herefordshire. He has promised me some peace and quiet to allow me to complete this work before I present it to the Royal Society. There are so many interruptions here, such as this one. The Duke himself will be absent from the castle, and there will be a reduced staff, which should allow the quiet that I require. I cannot guarantee to be able to make the necessary corrections to your paper, but I shall attempt to do so if I find that I have the time,' said Knudsen, pompously.

'Then I shall bring the draft to you personally. The Duke has also invited me to come at any time. But I will not be able to stay, as some other business takes me elsewhere, though not far away,' said Godiva.

'Then I shall try to find the time to see you when you come down to Shirl Castle. Good day, Miss Williams.' With this brutally short dismissal the interview was over.

It did not prove too difficult to discover the information contained in the library. There were journals, reports and magazines as well as academic papers. Godiva took copious notes of anything that was relevant, as she was unable to remove the papers as a borrower, not being registered at the College. When Godiva got back to the flat there was a fat package waiting for her from the Duke of Radnor. It contained details of his presentation and included the facts and figures that needed working on.

◊

The train that took Walter to Droitwich Spa was a slow stopper. The car which had been sent to collect him had broken down on the edge of the town and the chauffeur arranged for Walter to get to Blackleigh Court the old-fashioned way by hired pony and trap. He did not arrive at Blackleigh until after dinner time, by which time the chauffeur had made the necessary repairs to Lord Randall's Lanchester and had himself returned. The man with the pony and trap dropped Walter at the front entrance to the Court in a steady, soaking drizzle. The house had a long history, starting out as a medieval hall before becoming a modest gentleman's residence two hundred years previously. After the estate had been bought by a wealthy industrialist the house had expanded in all directions. The new north wing alone was the size of most stately homes, and in its entirety the Court was one of the largest houses in Britain. A footman dashed forward with an umbrella and escorted Walter to the wide portico with Ionic columns where the main entrance was, splashing through the puddles on the drive.

At the door the stately butler, Archer, led him through to the smoking room. Walter protested that he was not dressed for dinner, still being in his damp travelling clothes, but was assured by Archer that he should go straight in. A scatter of middle-aged men in evening dress were visible through the haze of cigar smoke, some seated in armchairs, others in pairs around the fire and around the table with the decanters. Walter was led to Lord Randall who greeted him warmly. Randall was nearly sixty now. He was of middle height and had put on a good deal of weight in middle age. A clipped beard covered his double chin. Randall took Walter to a dour thin man with full but neatly clipped moustaches, wire-rimmed glasses and short dark hair slick with pomade, and made the necessary introductions.

'Major Kell, this is Lord Walter Mansell-Lacey. Walter, this is Major Vernon Kell, who has headed a department of mine at the War Office.'

The men shook hands, Kell's were cold and dry, and his attempted smile was like the brass fittings on a coffin.

'How d'you do?' Walter started.

'Have you known Lord Randall long?' Kell asked abruptly.

'All my life. My father's estates are not far from here, and they are great friends,' Walter replied.

'And your mother is German, I understand.'

'You understand correctly, though she has now returned to her family in Prussia. It was never a happy match, but she did at least provide my father with the required number of sons. After she had done that she decided to go home,' Walter said.

'You speak German?' Kell asked.

'Of course. I was educated in both German and English, and my nanny was German, so I spoke the language from the earliest age.'

'Then I may have a use for you. Y'see I used to run the German section. There is always a demand for young men who can pass for native Germans these days.'

'Why is that? Do you want me to go to Germany?' Walter asked.

'Not me, not my area. But we always need to know what they are up to, even at the embassy, or rather, especially at the embassy. That gentleman over there has more to do with overseas operations. He is Captain Smith-Cumming' He indicated a solidly built man in naval dress uniform standing by the drinks tray. 'I'll introduce you to him later.'

'And the other gentlemen would be...?' Walter asked.

'Over by the fire is Mr John Buchan, who is talking to Lieutenant-General Baden-Powell. Beyond them are Mr Conan Doyle and Mr Somerset Maugham, and over there is Mr William Melville.'

'There seems to be a number of writers of a certain kind of fiction,' Walter observed.

'I have found from experience that there is a particular way of thinking which can make the best use of the available information. It allows the logic of some situations to be understood. Besides, in this new discipline, there needs to be some clear thinking done, so we need to have men about us who can think in creative and unconventional ways,' Kell said, his face close to Walter's.

'Yes, I can see that,' Walter almost agreed, 'But does it help in detail?'

'Ah, but these are very early days, we are taking a wider view at the moment, working out the organization and the best ways to go about doing our business. We won't be talking in any detail here. But I shall now introduce you to Captain Smith-Cumming and he can tell you a little more.' Kell led Walter to Cumming and made the introductions to him and to another man, a Mr Basil Thompson, another writer Walter had heard of.

'But you haven't got a drink yet,' Cumming said, and he poured Walter a generous glass of brandy, 'And do you want a cigar? They really are excellent.'

'Thank you, but I prefer my cigarettes.'

'And have you eaten, my dear fellow?' Cumming said, clapping Walter on the shoulder and spilling some of his brandy.

'I had something on the train,' said Walter.

'Well, I'm sure Archer can fix you up with something afterwards,' said Cummins with a smile.

'To be frank, I'm not all that hungry at the moment. But what I would really like to know is why I was asked to come here for this meeting?' Walter inquired.

'Well, you see, I've been keeping an eye on you, and I believe that you are just the type of man we are after. I must tell you that the business we are involved in is capital sport. My most successful agent in the field, so to speak, is a Mr Riley, who has a great facility for languages and an equal talent in making young ladies fall in love with him. And a woman in love can be influenced, mark my words. If such a woman is secretary to, or a relation of, an important man then a great deal of useful information can be obtained from such a source. By report, you seem to have just the same kind of talent of attracting the amorous attentions of women as Riley does. Now there are several developments in Germany that are worrying and which I intend to find out about. These are in the shipping and arms businesses. And I should also like to keep track of the construction of battleships and submarines in the German Navy shipyards. We need to acquire some technical intelligence that is likely to be of use to us, so that we can make the right responses in return. So what I am proposing is that you become a casual agent for my department. The pay is not wonderful, but it is usually adequate, and if you join up you would be doing a great service to your country, and, as I said, it really is the most capital sport.' Cummins ended this speech by clapping Walter on the shoulder again.

'Well, you've certainly given me something to think about. Would you allow me some time to consider my position?' Walter replied non-commitally.

'Of course, but please be sure to make your answer come in days rather than weeks. We can't hang around forever, and there is plenty of work to do. There is another talent I believe we can benefit from. We have heard about your paintings. I understand that you are a very competent draftsman. A drawing is a good way to include a good deal of useful information in a form that can easily be smuggled out of a hostile country. I once pretended to be a lepidopterist and drew a picture of a butterfly that contained all sorts of information about some naval deployments,' Cummins said, ending with a fruity chuckle.

A hand descended onto Walter's shoulder, and when he turned he found himself gazing into the well-known face of Baden-Powell.

'Please introduce me to this fine looking fellow,' said Powell.

'Yes indeed,' said Cummins, 'This is Lord Walter Mansell-Lacey. Walter, this is Lieutenant-General Baden-Powell.'

'I'm very pleased to meet the hero of Mafeking,' said Walter, wincing internally at such a lame comment.

'Yes, yes,' said Powell, 'But I know of you too. You are a double Oxford blue, if I recall; rugger and rowing.'

'That was some years ago. I'm afraid that I don't do sport at that level these days,' Walter said apologetically.

'That's a pity. Yes, a real pity. I saw the varsity game at Twickenham in '05, and you have genuine talent, I could see that. Speed and strength allied to skill. That's a rare combination. Not the sort of thing you should give up so easily. You should be a full international by now,' Powell said in a considered tone, 'Best open side flanker I've seen in years.'

'I'm rather involved in other occupations, now,' Walter said.

'Yes, Walter is gaining a reputation as an artist, these days,' Cummins interjected.

'But that wouldn't prevent his playing rugby,' Powell protested.

'But it might affect his good looks,' said Cummins.

'What's that?' Powell asked.

'Oh, don't be shocked,' Cummins said, 'I have great plans for Walter here.'

'Did I hear rugby mentioned?' came a baritone Scottish voice from the other side of the room.

'Yes, Doyle,' said Cummins, 'Mr Mansell-Lacey was an Oxford rugby blue.'

'And a rowing blue,' Powell added.

Somehow the conversation turned to boxing, a subject Doyle believed himself to be a expert in. He claimed to have been an amateur international boxer earlier in his life, and went into a detailed description of the stance a boxer should take.

'The best stance to adopt is to place the legs in a 'K' shape, with the left leg bent at about sixty degrees, and the balance on the ball of the left foot. This gives you a strong but flexible base, allowing you to move in all directions, either to avoid a blow, or to deliver one. I saw a demonstration by a professional some years back, and he stood like that. No-one came up from the audience could lay a glove on him'.

'I saw the world title fight last year between Burns and Johnson,' Lord Randall objected, 'And Burns took that stance, but Johnson danced round him, and Burns took quite a beating. He never saw the blows coming, and was never able to turn quickly enough to make an attack. I think your method is fine if the fighters are shoulder to shoulder, but against a mobile opponent, it really is of little or no use'.

'Well,' huffed Doyle, 'It always served me well enough, and I would be willing to demonstrate the skill against anyone here'.

'Johnson, he's that American nigger, ain't he?' Buchan interjected.

'Yes, the world heavyweight champion,' said Lord Randall.

'But he ain't fought the best yet, has he. I mean, if Sullivan or Jeffries were to fight him, he wouldn't have a hope, I mean the feller may have the brawn, and I grant the blacks have that advantage, but he ain't got the brain. Stands to reason, don't it?' said Buchan.

'Oh Johnson's got brains enough,' answered Lord Randall, 'You could see that by the way he fought. He was always one thought and one punch ahead of that Canadian, Burns. And Burns was always considered a clever fighter. I was out in Australia at that time, doing some business in Sydney, so I should know. Johnson's a very clever man in the ring, and he's a better fighter than either Sullivan or Jeffries. He's quick, but he's also patient and skilful, and has a first class fighter's brain. One of them will be forced to fight him now, so we'll see if I'm right'.

'I thought Jeffries had retired,' said Buchan.

'In a manner of speaking,' said Lord Randall, 'But like all fighters, he'll come back if the purse is right'.

'But I still think the proper stance is with the 'K' leg,' Doyle interrupted.

'You used to box at Harrow, didn't you Lacey?' asked Randall.

'Well, yes, Sir,' Walter replied, 'But it wasn't really my sport. I was more interested in rugby and rowing. I didn't continue it at Oxford.'

'But you remember how?' asked Randall.

'I remember some of the principals, but I was never that good at the practice of the art,' replied Walter, failing to mention his weekly work-outs.

'Well, we have some gloves here, so you will be able to help Mr Doyle in his exhibition of pugilism, won't you'.

'If you insist', said Walter, 'But only if Mr Doyle feels up to the task. I do not doubt his skill, but I have the advantage of age'.

'Nonsense,' said Doyle, 'I can still teach you a lesson'.

Servants were called and they moved the chairs around the edge of the smoking room to form a ring, and fetched boxing gloves for the contest. Walter and Doyle were stripped of their jackets, rolled up their sleeves and had the gloves laced onto their hands. The servants withdrew as this was an activity they were not permitted to watch.

The men were a good match in terms of height, and Doyle was still athletic and reasonably slim, but Walter had the physique of a boxer, with broad shoulders and strong arms.

'What do you want me to do, Mr Doyle?' Walter asked.

'Just stand there and try to hit me, of course,' Doyle replied.

Walter stood almost toe to toe with Doyle and aimed a few jabs at him. Doyle was easily able to parry these, or even to sway away from them, chuckling in triumph. Then he launched a straight left at Walter and, as the younger man had not been expecting to defend, the blow caught him flush on the jaw and caused him to step back, shaking his head.

'You see, you see!' said Doyle excitedly, 'It works perfectly'.

'But your opponent wasn't moving,' objected Lord Randall. 'Perhaps you would allow him to box a little more naturally'.

'Of course, of course, it makes no difference to me,' said Doyle, with a trace of contempt.

This time Walter circled around, finding the range with his jabs, with the older man adjusting his stance to meet the angle of attack. Then Walter feinted a move to the left, stepped back to the right and hit Doyle with a fair jab that connected with the side of the older man's head. Doyle growled and aimed several blows back, but Walter was too nimble to be caught by these, and answered the attack by landing a few more light jabs, which only served to incense Doyle further. Doyle aimed a wild uppercut at Walter which might have broken his jaw if it had landed. Walter swayed out of the way and the blow missed by a full foot. In return Walter caught Doyle with a simple left jab to the nose and a straight right that landed square on the older man's solar plexus. He had not used anything like the force he could have generated, but the effect was dramatic as Doyle collapsed gasping on the floor.

'A low blow!' protested Buchan.

'Nonsense!' replied Randall, 'The best body punch I have seen for years'. He looked down at the kneeling form of Doyle. 'Are you alright, old man?'

'Of course I am, Doyle wheezed, 'Just a little winded, that's all'.

'Admit you have been bested, Mr Doyle. Your stance will not do in the modern world,' Randall said in mild triumph.

But Doyle seemed unable to speak much for a further minute. When he was sufficiently recovered he was helped out of the gloves and sat down on a chair. Walter was called over and Doyle insisted on shaking him by the hand.

'Perhaps age has slowed me, Mr Lacey, but I swear that I would have beaten you twenty years ago. However, you proved the better man today'.

'I do not doubt that you would have bested me in your prime,' said Walter, who did, 'And you taught me a good lesson when we were toe to toe'.

'Aye, it still works,' said Doyle with a chuckle.

Lord Randall came over and shook both of their hands. 'A splendid demonstration, gentlemen, and excellent entertainment as well'.

Glasses of brandy were poured for all those in the room, and more cigars were lit. Plans were drawn up for the small shoot that was to take place on the morrow. Then they got down to their proper discussion.

'Have you heard of the case of George Edalji?' Doyle asked.

'Of course,' said Buchan, 'it was in the papers and you wrote a book about it. You got that fellow off the charges, didn't you?'

'You managed to get a degree of justice for him,' Powell said.

'Well, I got him out of prison, but he never got a proper pardon. I got the courts to admit that he never killed those animals; even told them who the real culprit was. But they never admitted that there was an entire lack of evidence that he wrote those letters. And without making it clear that he was completely innocent his name won't be cleared and he can never again practice law. What was sad about the entire case is that the authorities never admitted that they were in the wrong. They had made their minds up as to who was guilty at the very beginning and built the entire case on that.

They never looked at the evidence, never used any kind of logic,' Doyle trailed off.

'And your point is....?' Buchan asked.

'The point is that we must make sure that all our people are logical and open-minded. And that is especially important when you are trying to locate criminals or spies,' Doyle said.

'Yes, you have a point there. That certainly makes sense for the internal services. Mind you, as I see it, what we need for the external service are adventurers and actors and liars. They need to be able to trick or fight their way out of tricky situations and to have a nose for what is important. And, most of all, they need to be able to act independently,' said Cumming.

'I suppose there is a place for the glory boys,' said Kell, 'But that is only if you are playing the short game. What you need to do is to encourage your people to work in their armaments factories, and learn their plans that way. If you take the long view, you will get much better information and the opposition will never know where the information comes from.'

'Well that sounds a bit sneaky to me. Not really the British way,' Buchan complained.

'If we are not sneaky, then the other fellow most certainly will be. You can't rely on foreigners to play the game. You've got to try to think like them,' Cumming said.

'What we need to do is to train our people to weed out the foreign spies. Get their ears tuned in when they hear people asking questions. In order to do that we need to place some of our counter spies into our war industries, and be ready for their spies, said Kell.

'Good God, you mean you want to send in our spies to ferret out their spies!' Buchan said.

'That's all very well, but just how many agents do we need to do that? I mean. Who is going to pay for all these ferrets?' Cumming asked.

'Well, gentlemen, it seems to me that all the points you have made are valid. Now what we need to do is to recruit the right types of agents, and as many as we can afford,' said Doyle.

'I don't want to complain, but when the agencies were set up we were supposed to have equal funding. Even in the past few months that promise has been broken. Now I have considerably less money to work with than Cumming does,' Kell muttered bitterly.

'Now look here, it costs more to recruit and pay agents to work abroad. If you've got some man in a shipyard over here he'll be paid for his work anyway. When an agent is abroad he has to bribe people and generally look wealthy. It wouldn't do to have our agents going round like itinerant tinkers,' Cumming responded.

'I just want enough men to be able to do the job properly. They don't get paid all that well. It's not much fun following people and taking notes. If we are going to do the job properly we need to have enough people on the ground. I mean, Look at that case in the papers, that Sergeant they found in the London Underground. I happen to know that he was at a concentration camp in the South African campaign. It might well be that someone was looking for him for some kind of revenge. We know the man who attacked him was a foreigner. If the resources had been made available to me, I might well have been able to prevent that attack happening. We need to have intelligence officers stationed at the ports to spot foreign spies and to stop them from coming in,' Kell continued.

'So that Sergeant Murphy was a guard at a concentration camp, eh!' Buchan said.

'Not a guard, exactly, he was something to do with supplies,' Kell added.

'You know, I was all in favour of the concentration camps at the time. If they had been administered properly they would have been a good solution,' Doyle mused.

'But they weren't administered properly, were they?' Cumming said, 'What do you think about it, Randall?'

'I don't wish to say much about it. It was notionally part of my duties to look after the section that ran these camps when I was at the ministry. In reality, I had next to nothing to do with either the policy or the administration. But then you knew that, didn't you?' Randall answered.

'If Cumming didn't, then I did,' Kell said.

◊

Dorkins was polishing the brassware around the fireplace, including the rather bent poker when Godiva came in. He muttered a greeting which was less than warm.

'Dorkins, I really need to have a word with you,' she said.

'If it is any more cleaning, then I don't want to do it,' Dorkins protested sulkily.

'No, it's not about that, it's about what happened to Gordon, and what we are going to do about it. I think that if we work together we stand a much better chance of succeeding than if we work alone. Believe it or not, I probably feel as bad about what happened to him as you do,' Godiva said.

'Huh!' Dorkins uttered contemptuously.

'I am so sorry. Really I am. I'm sure if I had been aware of what Gregory was capable of I would have taken greater care to protect Gordon. But it is too late for that now. And I'm not going to talk about justice or anything, because what I want is revenge, pure and simple, and perhaps that is what you want too,' she suggested.

'The thing is, I didn't really like Gordon very much, he wasn't a close friend or anything, and I didn't fancy him, but it was me that persuaded him to talk to you. That's why I feel so guilty. But now that he's dead I feel that I need to do something, only I can't think what,' Dorkins said in a flat tone.

'Look, if there is one thing I am really good at it is planning and plotting. It all comes of being brought up in a socialist household. Nobody plots better than a socialist, especially against other socialists. And I've already got some ideas about what to do. In order to do this I need your help, not in doing any investigating, but in taking messages and passing them on and in using your intelligence to know when something important happens. I know it doesn't sound very grand, but I can't do it without you. I'm going to be very busy over the next few days, and I think I'll need to go away to see Walter's father, and as that is not far from where Walter is staying, I'm going to see him too. I'm sure that there will be some telephone calls to me and probably some letters and callers as well. You know how to use the telephone and I'll leave you the numbers where you can find me. Just in case you need the information, I'll leave the addresses as well, so that you can send me telegrams if you can't use the telephone. I don't know if Walter's father has a telephone in his house. I will leave you enough money to send several telegrams, but I need to stress that you will need to be discrete in what you say in them. You know what I mean, nothing that will attract the attention of anyone who might be taking an interest in what I am doing. It is possible that you might have to be here a little more than usual, just in case anything should happen. I'll go to my bank tomorrow and draw out some money, so that you have plenty, and I have enough to get to Worcestershire and pay for an hotel,' Godiva said, barely pausing for breath. There was a slight pause while Dorkins considered his reply.

'Thank you, Miss. I can see that you are thinking about this. Of course I will be happy to help out. But if I may ask, could you please leave enough money so that I can join Mr Walter if he needs me, or come to see you if there is something I need to tell you that I can't speak about over the phone or in a telegram. I don't think that it will happen, but you never really know what is around the corner.

And you can rely on me to use the telephone and to send the right kind of telegrams. I think I have a pretty good idea about what might be important,' he said proudly.

'I'm sure you do, Dorkins, but what I have learned today is all about why this whole business might be happening, and it's not exactly obviously connected to what happened to poor Gordon. So even if it doesn't seem to have any direct bearing on getting to Gregory, I want you to pass on the information anyway. This is all to do with spies and such stuff, and the Navy. But I don't want to tell you more in case it puts you into any danger.' Godiva continued.

'And I appreciate that, Miss. You can rely on me in this matter. I'll do anything possible to get back at Mr Gregory,' Dorkins said grimly.

'I'm sure we both feel that way,' said Godiva.

WEDNESDAY 29TH SEPTEMBER 1909

Buchan, Powell, Walter and Lord Randall stood watching the construction of the aeroplane. Peters was working with the second chauffeur and two stable boys to position a section of wing which was to be attached to the fuselage. There was a good deal of grumbling and some mild curses being uttered in Worcestershire accents. The wing section, though not heavy, was inclined to twist about a good deal in the strong breeze. Lining the piece up successfully was proving to be a tricky task. Buchan unfolded his shooting stick and then sat down to observe this sport and to smoke a pipe.

'Hey, Randall, how high and fast d'you think this aeroplane of yours can fly?' Buchan asked.

'Well, according to the manufacturer, it should go up to fifteen hundred feet, and fly at over forty eight miles an hour,' Randall replied.

'Y'know,' Buchan mused, puffing on his pipe, 'A thing like that could be very useful in warfare. Whoever was flying it could see exactly where the enemy's positions are, their troop movements and where they have put their artillery. Could make a lot of difference, that could.'

'People at the Ministry of War are thinking on those lines. That's part of the reason I'm having this one built. With a bit of luck, we'll be making our own aeroplanes very soon. That's why I got this one. It has the best engine money can buy and can fly higher and faster than anything else that can get off the ground,' said Randall, with a touch of pride.

'You know, I did suggest that we use balloons for artillery spotting back in South Africa, but the powers in Whitehall seemed to think that they would be an easy target,' Powell said.

'Ah, yes, but an aeroplane would be a fast-moving target and would fly at quite a high altitude. It wouldn't be nearly as easy to hit as a balloon. Any gunner who could hit an aeroplane in flight would deserve a medal in my book,' Randall said with a guffaw.

'It looks a bit tricky to build, mind,' said Buchan.

'Yes, I suppose it is. Well, on reflection, it would have been better to clear out a barn at the home farm and put it in there. I'll certainly do that before winter sets in,' Randall said.

'What gave you the idea to buy one of these machines?' Powell asked.

'In a way I got the idea from Cumming. He learned to fly a couple of years ago.'

'So why isn't he helping you put this thing together?' Buchan asked.

'He wants it to be done as some kind of experiment, I think, so he's not interfering. If I can manage to get this built and working, it means we can transport them anywhere we need them,' Randall answered, stroking his chin.

Walter was looking at the wooden skeleton of the machine that was being built. He could see that it was light but very strong. However, the joints did not appear to be precisely made, either that or damp had swelled the wood, for the wing section stubbornly refused to be fitted to the body, despite some gentle persuasion from a mallet. When one end fitted the other could not be persuaded to fit in the available slot.

'Are there usually problems putting these things together?' Walter asked, 'Or are there some problems with the kit?'

'Ah, well. What happens, you see, is that they build the aeroplane over in France, just to make sure everything fits together and the whole thing is working properly, then they take it apart again and pack it up into giant crates which they send out wherever in the world they have an order. So it is a sort of kit, but it has been put together once,' Randall explained.

'Damned French engineering. Not sure I'd like to trust my life to it,' Buchan muttered.

'Monsieur Bleriot managed to cross the English Channel on an aeroplane that was much less powerful than this,' said Randall, a slightly tetchy note to his voice.

'And I suppose that they are getting better every year,' Walter commented.

'Forget every year, my boy! Every month is more like it, perhaps every week. In a couple of years' time, you will hardly recognise the new flying machines,' Randall said, misty-eyed.

'Going back to what I said,' Buchan started, 'I can see a whole new field of warfare, in the air as well as on the ground and at sea.'

'I'm not sure about that,' Randall said, scratching the side of his nose, 'There are some serious challenges to overcome first, mostly to do with reliability and performance.'

'Well, there seems no limit to human ingenuity if they can get one of these things up in the air in the first place,' said Buchan with an air of wonder.

'If the Boers had one of these things at Ladysmith they'd have known what our real disposition was. They'd have broken into the place within a week,' Powell commented.

'And I for one am very much looking forward to seeing it fly,' Walter said.

'Then you should be a happy man in a few days. I have arranged for a trained pilot to come here tomorrow, to check it out and then to test it,' said Randall with a meaningful nod of his head and a sly smile.

◊

Godiva spread all the documentation she had received from the Duke onto the largest area in the flat, the kitchen table. These included reports from the Anglo-Persian Oil Company. To these she added the papers she had copied from Professor Knudsen's work and some answers to parliamentary questions, together with some reports from The Times newspaper. In order to gain some spatial awareness of the areas involved she had taken down a large modern atlas from the bookshelves and found the towns, ports and areas mentioned. Much of the relevant part of Persia was desert and had very little detail marked. By constant cross-referencing, she was able to see the larger picture of what the oil exploration business was all about. Then she noticed some discrepancies in the compass directions and geographical features mentioned in the APOC reports and those in the Duke's notes, which had been derived from Knudsen. Besides those there were other discrepancies, which concerned the projected output from the currently discovered sources. Knudsen's figures were much lower than the APOC estimates for the oil reserves. In his notes Knudsen specifically urged new areas of exploration to find more oil, and to plan for the shutting down of the current oil wells. This could well be good advice based on new evidence, but the outline geological map which was part of the atlas seemed to indicate that the new areas Knudsen was proposing for exploration were composed of rocks not thought to contain oil. But, maybe, the geological maps were out of date.

A report in The Times concerned the attempt by the Germans to find their own oil in an area to the north of Persia, and the high level of secrecy around what they had found. There was a mention of a Professor Knudsen who had been employed to advise them on which areas were suitable for drilling. By checking the areas mentioned in the newspaper report against the geological map Godiva was able to see that the geology of the area that Knudsen had advised the Germans to try seemed ideal for finding oil. Knudsen was, of course, a Dane, and not a British citizen. There were no reasons why he shouldn't work for the Germans. But the advice he gave seemed to favour the Germans above British interests. Godiva knew that she must ask Knudsen some more questions about this. As he could now be resident at Shirl Castle, the country home of the Duke of Radnor, she decided to take up the Duke's offer and go visiting. She would also use the time to communicate her findings to Walter.

Tommy had spent most of his money and only had sufficient left to pay for a single fare from Frinton to Cambridge. Once there he walked around, searching for a pawnbrokers shop. Such businesses were not to be found on the main thoroughfares, but were located on the back roads near to the colleges, doing business with students who had exhausted their allowances by mid-term. The pawnbroker offered Tommy better terms than he would have received in London, thinking that Tommy was a student, and knowing that such students were likely to redeem their pledges before daring to return home for the Christmas break. The diamond studded tie-pin, signet ring and watch were all of top quality, if of German manufacture, and he was generous with his offer, allowing enough for Tommy to book a thirdd class single to Droitwich, with plenty left over to pay for a room at a local establishment close to Blackleigh Court, the Hundred Inn.

Before he left from Cambridge station he sent a telegram to Charles at his London address just in case he failed to go to Blackleigh Court due to pressure of work. This telegram was dealt with by Charles' PPS who was charged with conveying any such private information to Charles. The name of the PPS was Edward Bulliphant. It was Bulliphant who transcribed the telegram to pass it on to Charles, and sent a copy of the transcription to the owner of a certain gentleman's club in Paddington. The owner of that club contacted his friend Herr Braun at the German Embassy. Herr Braun then sent a message to an agent of his who was working at Blackleigh Court. This telegram was received at Droitwich Post Office, the closest major office to the Court.

The journey which Tommy took from Cambridge to Droitwich involved three changes of trains and some long waits on wind-swept platforms. By chance he happened to find someone going past the Hundred in and was able to hitch a lift on a gig that had been sent to pick up a pair of middle aged sisters who had just come back from holiday and were happy to offer help to this polite and well-spoken young man. He arrived late at the Hundred Inn and had a modest dinner sent up to him in his room. A fellow guest that evening was a single lady called Godiva Williams. They would meet next morning over breakfast.

◊

Walter had found Emily alone in the drawing room. She was seated on the sofa reading Bram Stoker's Dracula. Walter decided that it was time for him to earn his money and so he took a breath and started on his mission.

'Emily,' Walter said, 'I have something rather personal to ask you.'

'What was that, Walter?' Emily said, glancing up at him.

Walter cleared his throat and placed his hands behind his back. 'I said I had something to ask you, and I should warn you, it's a little personal.'

'You already said that, and if you don't mind me saying so, it sounds a little ominous,' said Emily, smiling at him, 'Now you just tell me what is on your mind.'

'Well, it seems that you were seen at a certain London hotel in the company of a foreign gentleman a few weeks ago. Now, there are certain rumours about this gentleman. He is suspected of being some kind of spy for a foreign power. This is sort of official, I need to ask you what happened at that meeting.'

Emily's mouth opened slightly but no words emerged.

'I am sorry to have to ask you about this,' said Walter, 'but it's a matter of National Security, what with Charles being a minister and everything.'

'Oh dear,' Emily managed to say, 'I can assure you that although the meeting you mentioned did occur, nothing improper happened.'

Charles smiled grimly. 'Could you give me a few more details please, Emily. You can start by telling me what this man called himself.'

'He called himself Mr Smith, Schmitt in reality, if you ask me. He was German, I'm sure of it, I know the accent and the bearing, and the funny thing is I had the idea that we might have met before, a long time ago. He said he had something to tell me, something about Charles. It was Smith who decided on the meeting at that hotel. It's called the Palatine.'

'Yes, I know it,' said Walter, 'And unfortunately for you the hotel is often used by adulterous ladies and their beaus. There are all sorts of private investigators who watch who goes in and out.'

'I had no idea,' said Emily, 'it looked to be a nice respectable sort of place.'

'Did you go to a room with him?' said Walter.

'Well, yes, I did, but only so that we could talk in private,' said Emily, 'Nothing at all improper happened. You can't believe I'd do anything improper. I do love Charles, you know.'

'Sorry, Em, but I need to ask this. What was so important that you had go to a hotel bedroom to talk?' said Walter.

'It was all about something that happened to Charles when he was in Germany earlier this year. He went to a spa for a cure. Smith was telling me about something that had to do with a German boy. This boy and Charles were together at Baden-Baden and struck up some kind of friendship. It occurred to me in the way Smith told the story that the boy may have been sent to tempt Charles. So I suppose that they tried tempting him with a woman, and when he didn't take them up on that offer they decided to see if he might prefer men. This boy was very good looking, by all accounts.'

'Did you learn that from Charles?' Walter asked.

'Of course, he told me everything that happened,' Emily agreed.

'So was this Smith or Schmitt person trying to blackmail you by telling you this about Charles?' Water asked.

'Yes, I suppose he was in a way, but if he was really trying to blackmail Charles, surely he would have gone directly to him. In fact I am not exactly sure what he was hoping to achieve. As I said, Charles had already told me about this boy, who goes by the name of Thomas, so I wasn't at all shocked about what I was told. If something had happened I still wouldn't have considered divorcing Charles. It would have been very aggravating if the sory had got out and it led to some kind of scandal, but as I said, there was nothing in the matter, nothing actually happened in Baden-Baden. I always know when Charles is lying to me, and he wasn't then, nor did I sense that he felt ashamed of anything. He told me nothing had happened between him and the boy; that they were just friends, and I believed him.'

'What did Smith want you to do, did he tell you?' Walter asked.

'That was the odd thing, really. He didn't really say, but I had the feeling it was something to do with my father. He kept asking me questions about my father.'

Walter frowned and tried to think of the next question. He decided to keep it simple, 'Why do you think he was asking about your father?'

It was Emily's turn to frown. She considered for a while before answering. 'I think it might have been something to do with his share holdings,' she answered, 'He recently bought lots more shares in some oil companies.'

'Is your father still a major shareholder in Burmah Oil?' Walter asked.

'We never talk about business at home, but as far as I know he is. He has been very busy of late, working with the Admiralty.'

'Well, the Germans would certainly want to know about our naval secrets, but why would they be concerned with his business dealings?' Walter mused.

Emily sighed, 'It's to do with oil for the Navy, you silly goose. You know they found oil in Persia last year.'

'Yes, I know,' said Walter, 'A

nd that makes perfect sense. But it still doesn't explain why Smith was so interested in your father's business interests.'

'He wanted to know about the oil refinery they are building. He was asking about how well the building was going. But I've never taken much interest in father's business, so I couldn't help him anyway. In fact, in seems to have been an entirely wasted attempt to put pressure on me.'

'Did you tell him about coming up to the Court?'

'Oh, he already seemed to know that. He also asked about Father's aeroplane.'

'He does seem to have been taking a funny sort of interest in your father. You said earlier that you thought you recognized this Smith. Do you think you could describe him to me?'

'Yes, I suppose so,' Emily said, and she screwed up her face in the effort of recollection before continuing. 'He was rather distinctive looking, so it isn't that difficult to recall. He's very tall, taller than you by a couple of inches, but he's sort of angular and awkward. He tried to dress as an English gentleman, but he didn't carry himself as he should. He just didn't walk or stand in a English way, and his boots were all wrong. No Englishman would ever wear brown brogues in town. He is very clean shaven, with short dark brown hair, and he has a duelling scar on his right cheek that goes from his left cheekbone almost to his eye. The scar made his face a bit lop-sided, so his left eye looks half-closed. Oh, and he wears gold-rimmed spectacles, which he kept polishing on a blue silk handkerchief that he kept in his top pocket. And he was wearing some kind of cologne, possibly shaving balm, which smelt of cloves.'

'Good grief!' Walter muttered, 'I do believe that you have just described my cousin, Siegfried, to an absolute tee'.

'Yes, of course, that is who it was. He didn't have that scar when I last met him. I was probably only eight or nine at that time. He must have been about twelve. I remember coming over to visit your house, and he was staying there with your aunt.'

'Siegfried always was an unprincipled bounder, even as a child. You know that there is always the possibility that he might try to blackmail you merely for going to that hotel room with him,' said Walter, gravely.

'Well I suppose he could, but I don't think that Charles would be surprised. He expects me to stray. You see, we don't really have any marital relations to speak of. I'm sorry if that's a bit shocking for you,' Emily admitted.

'How long has your marriage been sexless?' Walter enquired tactlessly, after a few seconds of echoing silence.

'It always has been. I am as much a virgin today as the day I was born. And I do want children, I do so very much want to have children,' she said with a sort of grim determination.

Walter was genuinely shocked. He tried to calculate how long Charles and Emily had been married. It must be nearly four years now. And for all of that time the marriage has remained unconsummated. 'You know that you could always get an annulment on those grounds,' he suggested.

'Of course I know that,' Emily retorted, 'But I don't want my marriage annulled. I love Charles and I want to have children with him. I was hoping that maybe he would change, find me attractive.'

'It may not be that bad,' Walter mused, 'Have you ever known him to express any kind of interest in any one else?'

'No, now that you mention it I don't think I have. I don't believe that Charles really has much of a sexual nature. I've never really noticed it, and I don't think it's my fault, as other men seem to find me attractive. Do you find me attractive, Walter?' She glanced down in a modest way.

'Well, I have always liked you, and found you to be a very attractive young woman. But growing up together, I suppose I never really thought of you quite in that way.'

'And yet you seem to have found my sister very attractive,' said Emily, meaningfully.

'As we seem to be having a confessional session, I might as well tell you that she provided me with my first real sexual experience.'

'My word, how old were you when this all happened?'

'I was fourteen. It was that year we all went up to Scotland.'

'Then Caroline would have been seventeen at that time?' Emily suggested.

'She did not seem to be inexperienced, in fact she seemed quite knowledgeable,' Walter answered, realizing that Emily had become the inquisitor.

Emily looked up at Walter, and smiled coyly, 'You know, I have always thought you looked a lot like Charles. You might almost be brothers, although, of course, you are made on a larger scale. When I said that I longed to have a child I really meant it. A woman is supposed to produce a child or two after four years of marriage, and it seems that I cannot rely on Charles to do me the service of providing me with one. The trouble is, if I were to present a child to the world it is better if it looked like Charles. So I was wondering if you might be willing to do me the great honour of fathering a child for me.'

Walter was unable to speak for some seconds. This placed him in a position he was unused to. To cuckold a man you didn't like was a pleasure, almost a duty, but to cuckold a friend, someone he had grown up with seemed morally much more difficult. Also, Emily had been a childhood friend, and he had never really thought of her sexually. For both of these reasons it might prove to be a difficult seduction for him to complete.

Walter attempted to prevaricate. 'This has come as something of a shock. You will have to give me some time to think about it.'

'Please don't think about it for too long,' Emily urged, 'We really should take the opportunity while you and I are both here. And it should be the right time of the month for me to conceive.'

'I shall let you know a little later today. It is not a simple decision for me to make. Perhaps at dinner I will have decided, and can let you know with a nod or a word. Shall we invent a little code?'

Emily considered what code word would do. 'If you do decide to do me the honour, then suggest a game of bridge. And if you should decide against, suggest some other game.'

'Right-oh,' Walter checked, 'It's bridge for yes, and something else for no.'

'Remember that,' Emily said, firmly, 'It means quite a lot to me.'

'I will remember,' said Walter, 'but what if someone wants to play bridge?'

'Oh don't be silly, no-one is going to want to play bridge tonight. All of these men are terribly competitive. None of them will want to play anything as civilized as Bridge,' Emily said, smiling broadly.

'But what if I don't impregnate you tonight, presuming that I do decide to try?' Walter asked rhetorically.

'Then we shall just have to try again I suppose,' Emily said with a smile playing across her lips, 'It would be more convenient if it happened now, but we have to recognise that it might take more than one effort.'

Walter shook his head. 'You know, this sounds awfully cold blooded. I suppose I am more used to the heat of passion. And what about Charles, what would he think? I mean, I thought he was due to get here today. How can we arrange this tryst if he is here?'

'I am perfectly sure that he would be very grateful. He would like to give me a child but is unable to. In a funny way you'll be doing him a favour. And we rarely share a bed anymore. He'll be very tired. He always is. And I think that I shall I tell him for you, after we have done the deed,' Emily said decidedly.

'No, don't do that just yet, I just don't feel right about that, what with him being a lifelong friend and all. And yet I don't want to hide it from him either. In fact I don't don't really know what I feel,' Walter admitted.

'Then do it for me, please Walter. Just do it for me, as a favour.' Emily said, taking his hand and looking into his eyes.

'I'm still going to have to think about it. Mind you, if I do agree, we need to work out the arrangements, I mean, will you come to my room or shall I come to yours?' Walter mused.

'I think it's probably best if I come to you, otherwise the servants are bound to know. The servants always have a good idea about what has been happening, but that can't be helped. Though they probably won't know which woman came your room unless the same woman cleans both rooms or they compare notes. Have you much experience of deflowering virgins?' she added as an afterthought.

'I have deflowered a few, but it seemed impolite to keep an exact score after a certain number.' Walter said, modestly.

'Just as long as you know what to do, the numbers don't really matter,' Emily said with a broad smile.

'Well, until later then,' said Walter, feeling a little dazed, 'And let's hope it all works out.'

'Thank you,' said Emily, and returned to reading her book, as though they had just been discussing the weather.

◊

It took Godiva very little time to pack a Gladstone bag with sufficient clothes, undergarments and toiletries for a visit of three days duration. Putting on a pair of good stout boots which were suitable for a visit to the country and an overcoat and hat which would also do, she picked up her trusty umbrella and walked down the stairs from the flat and out into the street. She took a bus to Paddington Station and bought a ticket for Leominster in Herefordshire, the nearest station to Shirl Castle. She would have to change trains at Hereford.

A thin, clean-shaven man in a low-crowned bowler hat and mud coloured overcoat followed her onto the bus. He was right behind her when she purchased the train ticket and noted her destination in a pocket memo book which he took from an inside pocket. Godiva found a third class compartment occupied by an old lady and an even more elderly gentleman. They were sitting with their backs to the engine, and were the sole occupants. Godiva sat by the window, opposite the elderly couple and placed her bag next to her on the seat to avoid anyone sitting down there. Just before the train pulled out they were joined by a thin man wearing a low-crowned bowler hat. He sat on the same side as Godiva at the other end of the bench seat, her bag positioned between them.

There was a hiss of steam and the train jerked into movement. Godiva put her hand out to stop the bag falling over and noticed that the thin man's left hand lacked the top two joints of the little finger. He was occupied behind a copy of the Daily Mail, but only turned the pages very irregularly, and Godiva suspected that he was not so much reading the paper as using it to hide his face. The old lady offered Godiva a barley sugar, which she accepted, but the man rudely refused the lady's offer of a sweet without lowering the paper.

The train was relatively slow. There was insufficient population in Herefordshire to command a fast train. This one seemed to stop at every cattle shed. And so the journey to Hereford, where she had to change, took almost three hours. The elderly couple left the train at Oxford, and Godiva was thankful that another couple, this time very young, came in and occupied the carriage. By now, Godiva was certain that the thin man was following her. Whether he was representing the group that had murdered Tommy or were a representative of the security services she did not know. Nor could she frame a question which might force him to reveal his true intent with others around. If he was a murderer he would bide his time and lie to her. If he was working for the security services he was unlikely to admit it because that would compromise his mission.

The young couple were lost in each other's company and were paying little attention to anyone or anything else. They brushed fingers together, and were engaged in polite intimacy. All Godiva had separating her from a possible assassin was a Gladstone bag. Luck was with Godiva in that the couple never left the carriage until the train pulled into Hereford, and she was able to push past them, leaving them between herself and the thin man. She almost leapt onto the platform and sprinted for the Ladies Waiting Room, which was fortunately on the same platform. It would be a bold man who would attempt to break in there. Nor was she alone in the waiting room. A stout but active lady of over thirty with frizzy, untidy hair bursting from beneath her hat was sitting on a chair reading a Suffragist magazine. If nothing else, thought Godiva, she would make this lady remember a sister in the struggle for female emancipation. If the assassin killed her she would at least have a witness to her existence.

'Oh, please excuse me, is that the new edition of 'The Suffragette'?' Godiva asked unnecessarily. There was a cover picture of Joan of Arc wearing a tabard displaying the word 'Justice'. The Editor's name was Cristabel Pankhurst.

'Oh, yes,' said the plump lady with a slight nervous laugh, 'I trust that you are a suffragist too.'

'Of course,' said Godiva, 'And I have seen Cristabel Pankhurst speak, and have been introduced to her on one occasion.'

'How marvellous,' said the woman, smiling broadly, showing uneven teeth. 'Is she as splendid in real life as she is in print?'

'Yes, she is really marvellous, quite inspiring,' said Godiva.

'You are lucky, you know. Living out here means that I don't get much chance to see these wonderful ladies. But it is really exciting to meet someone who really knows them. Perhaps I ought to introduce myself. My name is Clarice Edwards,' said the plump lady.

'And I am Godiva Williams,' said Godiva, 'I know it is a silly name, and it makes many people giggle.'

'Absolute nonsense. Lady Godiva was an inspiration. A marvellous lady who fought social injustice,' said Clarice. Godiva looked at her watch to see that the Leominster train was due to arrive in a few minutes.

'Look, I don't mean to be awkward, but I've been receiving some unwanted attention from a man who has been bothering me on the train I came in on. I was wondering if you could see me onto the next train, and stop him coming into the compartment with me,' said Godiva.

'Of course, that sounds really exciting. I'm more than happy to help,' said Clarice, beaming. She stood up, and Godiva could see that she would present a considerable barrier in a train corridor, as she was broad of beam and tall.

'I was wondering if you might be going on the train to Leominster?' said Godiva.

'Absolutely,' said Clarice, 'I'm going on to Shrewsbury, so I have to go through Leominster on my route.

'Look, I'd better describe this man. He's about average height and thin. He's wearing a brownish overcoat and a low-crowned bowler hat. And he's missing the top two joints of the little finger of his left hand,' Godiva said with animation.

'Gosh, and you mean that he's bothering you? Well, I'll soon put a stop to that. We'll travel together and I'll deal with him if he tries to follow you,' Clarice said with grim determination. Godiva thought that she had luckily found a splendid ally. There followed the sound of a train arriving on the near platform. They rose together and walked arm in arm to the train. Godiva could see the thin man waiting in the shadow of a pillar. He entered the train after them and went to the next compartment.

Leominster was the next station, barely ten minutes ride away. Before the train pulled into the station Clarice positioned herself outside of the carriage door of the next compartment and proved an immovable object to the thin man. He swore loudly at her in a boorish manner but was unable to make her move until the train had pulled well out of the station. The social conventions meant that it was not right to push a lady, and besides, she was much bigger than him. Godiva made her way to the Station Hotel, where she had booked a room for the night. There she cancelled her booking and arranged another instead. It would be all too obvious to find her if she stayed at the hotel nearest to the station. No doubt the man would be in communication with his masters at a following station. Paying half her charge for the night won her the favour of the landlord, and she swore him to silence as to where she was going. He was able to direct her to a local firm with a car and driver for hire who were willing to take her to an inn that Walter had mentioned as being near to Blackleigh Court. This was a drive of some fifteen miles, across the county boundary and into Worcestershire. At night this journey would take about an hour.

◊

By the end of morning most of the guests had left, excepting Cumming, Buchan and Doyle, the most clubbable, and Kell who seemed welded to Cumming's side. They were to be replaced later that day by Lady Caroline her husband, Mr Gerald De Vere and their children, and by the Honourable Charles Gurney-Stewart. Along with these visitors would come their respective valets and maids. The Court was a hive of activity for a few hours before their arrival. The servants, especially the chamber maids, dashed around in a blur of activity. They dusted and cleaned and remade the beds with fresh, crisp linen. Fires were made up and scuttles of coal brought up to the rooms. Huge sprays of flowers from the hot houses were set in vases in every room and in the large marble urns on the pillars at the base of the main stairway.

Gerald and Caroline and their children Gerald Arthur and Catherine arrived in an upright 18 hp Lanchester car early in the afternoon and were welcomed back to Caroline's home by a respectful line of servants waiting by the front door and by Lord Randall positioned just inside the door. The chauffeur then drove the car to the rear entrance to unload the luggage. After the welcome ceremony the servants returned to their duties, including carrying the luggage to the various rooms and unpacking the clothes and placing them in wardrobes. This last task was undertaken by Gerald's valet and Caroline's lady's maid. This pair had arrived in the morning in order to prepare the rooms to the satisfaction of their employers.

Walter was not directly involved in the formal greeting, in fact he was riding a nag up the steep slopes of the nearby clock-tower hill at the time, and only saw Caroline and Gerald at a late lunch held in the small dining room. The greetings were polite but warm after having not seen each other for over a year. Caroline had gained a little weight, which was allowed now that she was thirty and the mother of two children, but the more luxuriant bust and hips were emphasised by the corseted narrowness of her waist. She was exquisitely dressed and very handsome. Gerald's hair was receding quite quickly, but it suited his slightly fleshy face and the lack of hair on the top of his head was balanced by the bushy moustache which hung on his upper lip like a yard broom.

The children were fed separately, in the nursery. For lunch there was a magnificent array of chops and steaks, all garnished with vast quantities of potatoes and vegetables. By the standards of the Court this was only a light lunch. Walter was very conscious of his weight and ate abstemiously.

Charles did not arrive until the middle of the afternoon, getting to the Court in time for afternoon tea and cakes. A smaller version of the welcoming ceremony was repeated for his sake. Even before they had finished their tea a telegram arrived for Charles with instructions for him to return to the Ministry immediately to deal with some minor crisis which had arisen. With apologies and handshakes and a chaste kiss for his wife he left with some minimal luggage in Lord Randall's Daimler, heading for the railway station at Worcester Shrub Hill, for the Great Western express back to London. There were stopping trains at nearer stations, but these were much slower than the Daimler at getting to Worcester.

◊

After dinner, and before the ladies retired, Walter suggested a game of bridge. This suggestion was met with a wave of almost complete indifference, and it was decided that a game of billiards would be more entertaining. They organised a competition. Walter managed to defeat Cummins in the first round, but was beaten by the superior tactics of Kell in the next round. After his defeat Walter shared a few brandys with Cumming and listened to some of his store of tall stories. Cumming was an engaging storyteller, with a great collection of tales of derring-do in which he was generally made to look slightly ridiculous whilst being heroic. This helped to pass the evening for Walter until it was time for bed.

◊

Walter waited in his room with a certain sense of dread. He had been sitting by the dressing table trying to read a book, but was unable to take much interest in it. For all his sexually active life he had been anxious not to father children, and used small capote condoms on almost every occasion when conception might take place. These devices were not always satisfactory, but as far as he knew, he had not fathered a child yet, nor had he caught any sexually transmitted disease. It was past midnight when the floorboards creaked slightly in the corridor outside of his room. There was a soft knock at the door. Emily opened the door quietly, and came in without invitation, checking to see that the corridor was empty before closing the door. She was still half dressed, with corset, camisole, petticoat and stockings. Walter was curious as to the covering, having expected her to be changed ready for bed, in a nightdress and dressing gown. He was about to ask about this when Emily put a finger to his lips and then whispered in his ear. 'I want you to undress me, please.' She indicated the lacing on the corset. Walter was well enough used to this task, and loosened the laces slowly and steadily with a certain expertise before Emily shook them free. He then bent down towards her and kissed her gently on the eyelids, cheeks and lips. She returned his kiss, mouth barely parted, breathing quite fast, but seeming as much nervous as excited. He slid his hands down her back and unfastened the strings of her petticoats, which slid to the floor. Emily stepped out of them and kicked them towards the dressing table. She was now in matching lace trimmed camisole and drawers and white silk stockings. Walter eased the strap from her left shoulder and kissed the area of bare skin that was revealed. At this point Emily stopped his hand. Walter thought that she had changed her mind, but was wrong, for she undid the belt of his dressing gown and eased the garment from his shoulders and arms, leaving him in his red silk pyjamas and bedroom slippers. To his relief he found that he was becoming ready for action. It would have been even more embarrassing if he failed to rise to the occasion. Emily lifted her arms above her head, encouraging Walter to lift the camisole away and above her torso.

Her breasts were quite small, with pinky-brown nipples, hardening in the cool air in the room. Before he could play with them she started to unbutton his pyjama top. When it was removed she embraced him, her bare breasts pressing into the bottom of his ribcage. She lifted her face for another kiss, which was duly delivered and returned with more passion this time. She reached a small hand down to the gap in his pyjama trousers and noted his aroused state. Walter unlaced her drawers, which slid to the floor, leaving her wearing only her stockings, which she rolled down and kicked off. He led her to the bed and laid her down, her legs still off the bed, her buttocks on the edge. Undoing the pyjama cord he divested himself of the last of his clothing and kicked off his slippers. After gently parting her thighs he entered the virgin cleft very slowly and gently. Emily had her head raised, trying to see what was happening. Perhaps she was taking notes or maybe she was interested in the mechanics of the operation. She made a soft cry as Walter moved more deeply inside. He gradually increased the pace of his thrusts and was genuinely surprised to find that Emily was coming to orgasm without further prompting. She moaned softly and shook, joining in with the rhythm of his thrusts and they came together in perfect unison. Walter began to withdraw, but Emily put an arm around the small of his back and held him in until his member slipped out after returning to its flaccid state.

She pulled his head down so that she could whisper to him. 'Now I know what Caroline likes so much about sex with you. That was very nice. Thank you for being so gentle.' Then she giggled.

'My dearest Emily, you don't need to thank me at all. Genuinely, it was one of the greatest pleasures of my life. Just a slight word of warning, you may be a little sore in the morning,' Walter warned her.

'If I am, it was all worthwhile. I've heard my girlfriends talk about losing their virginity and being very disappointed with the whole process. I think I must be a very lucky girl, choosing you to do the dreaded deed.' She smiled gently and stroked his head.

'You know, it is just possible that Charles may take more of an interest in you now,' said Walter, 'I had it from one of my ladies. She said that her husband became rather inflamed with passion after he learned of her infidelity; not angry, but aroused by the knowledge.'

'I may tell him, or he may just notice that I am different. We shall see what happens. In the meantime, come into bed with me and hold me for a time.'

Walter obeyed the command. They curled up naked beneath the sheets next to each other, both of them drowsy and satiated. Soon they fell into a deep sleep.

When Walter awoke the next morning Emily was gone, leaving only a depression in the mattress, the rippled folds in the sheet, and a slight hint of perfume to show that she had been present. Walter was missing her already.

THURSDAY 30TH SEPTEMBER 1909

The inn was full and the guests were forced to share tables, as a result of which Godiva found herself seated opposite a slightly built blond man who had some purple bruising around his handsome, slightly feminine face. There were some minutes of uncomfortable silence before a matronly lady bustled to their table and took their breakfast order. The man ordered a hearty meal, heavy on pork products but light on eggs. He had a slight German accent underlying his very correct English. Godiva ordered a more modest and balanced meal that included fruit. As the waitress bustled away Godiva smiled broadly and introduced herself shamelessly.

'Hello, I'm Godiva Williams. Hope you don't mind me introducing myself like this, but it does seem strange us sharing a meal but not talking.'

'My name is Thomas Schmitt,' said the man with an almost imperceptible nod of the head. She could imagine him clicking his heels beneath the table.

'Are you visiting from Germany?' Godiva asked. She was beginning to have an inkling as to who this man was, and what he might be intending to do.

'Yes, and in Germany we are less likely to start a conversation with anyone we have not been properly introduced to,' said Tommy, 'I am sorry if that sounded a little harsh, it is just that I do not fully understand your English manners.'

'No apologies are necessary. It was just me being forward, I'm afraid.' said Godiva, 'Are you here on business?' Tommy considered for some seconds before he replied.

'Yes, I have some business to deal with, some business concerning a friend of mine.'

'Well, I am on a similar errand,' said Godiva, 'My friend is staying at Blackleigh Court, just down the road, and I need to talk to him.'

'An affair of the heart, perhaps?' Tommy asked in a light tone.

'Not really, more something that we have been working on, a kind of joint project, and I need to consult him. He is a guest at the Court, but I have not been invited to the weekend,' Godiva explained.

'So your friend knows Lord Randall?' Tommy asked enthusiastically.

'Yes, that's right. He grew up with Lord Randall's daughters as close friends, and I believe that his father is a great friend of Lord Randall,' Godiva said.

'Then your friend must be an English milord,' said Tommy, a smile crossing his face, 'I too know someone invited to this house party, but it may be more difficult for me to talk to him than it will be for you to talk to your friend. But this business I have is quite important. There is something that I really have to tell him. Now it is my turn to impose on you. It may be that you will be able to help me.'

'Well, perhaps it may be. But I think I would need to know what you want me to do and why it is important before I agree to take any message for you. From what you have just said, I have the feeling that your friend may not wish to talk to you,' Godiva said carefully.

'Yes, of course, that might be true. But what I have to tell to him is very important, and it is also very confidential, very private. And it is more in the nature of a warning, about some people plotting against him. And you are right, he may not wish to see me, but it is vital that I speak to him,' Tommy said, gripping the edge of the table and leaning forward.

'Do you want me to pass a message on to Sir Charles?' Godiva asked in a measured way.

'How did you know who I was talking about?' Tommy asked, a note of panic in his voice.

'I'm sorry, I did not mean to startle you. It's alright, I am working on something which is connected with this matter of yours, but from another perspective. In fact, I think I might know who you are, and how you got to know Charles. My friend was at school with Charles, who was his best friend there. It's a bit of a coincidence, but what my friend and I are working on led us to talk to someone who told us about someone who sounded exactly like you, and about what had happened to you. We heard that you had been beaten up, and I can see the bruises on your face. As it happens, I think that you are very brave to continue doing what you are doing, and you must be a good friend to Charles,' Godiva said reassuringly.

Tommy considered what she had said for a few seconds. 'I do really need to see him in person. If you could persuade him that I have no other choice, that it affects his career, his social standing and his wife. There is something I must explain.'

'Is this about Mr Arthur Gregory?' Godiva guessed, and Tommy winced.

'What do you know about Mr Gregory?' Tommy asked.

'I know that he was responsible for having you beaten up. From what we have worked out he is working for someone in the German embassy. It's that man who was trying to blackmail Lady Emily. I want to know why he is doing it and what his motives are. That is the business that I need to discuss with my friend.' She leaned towards him, trying to encourage a response.

'How do I know that you are not working for Mr Gregory?' Tommy asked. Godiva sighed gently before replying in an urgent, low whisper.

'Would I approach you like that if I was? Surely I would pretend not to know you. As I said, my friend is a lifelong friend of Sir

Charles, and when the British Intelligence found out that there was some kind of plot against him they asked my friend to help, which is why he was sent to Blackleigh Court. I am currently sharing a house with this friend, and I found out enough about what was happening to guess the rest. Between us we have learned some details, including something about you, though we didn't know your name or why you came to England. There is a lot more going on that you do not know about, and I'm not sure that I understand enough about it yet to have a full picture. As for working for Mr Arthur Gregory, do I look like the kind of person who would work with that kind of man?' After that speech Godiva sat back in her chair and let Tommy decide what to do next. There was another silence before he replied, and he indicated with a gesture that he wished her to come nearer before he spoke.

'If you know so much, I might as well tell you what happened to me,' said Tommy with slow deliberation, and in a low voice, 'I met Lord Charles at Baden-Baden last year when he came for the cure. In Germany they know who he is, and who his father-in-law is, so they thought that they could learn much from him. They sent a girl to try to seduce him, a very pretty girl. She may have made it too obvious what she was willing to do, because it did not work. They thought that he might not like women, so they sent me just in case he preferred men. But I know that Sir Charles does not like men in that way. Before I could make that kind of approach to him I had to make friends, and I found him to be a very good man, very honest and kind. I suppose that I fell in love with him, though I know he can never love me in the same way. Now they are trying to ruin him by inventing stories about us. I learned of their plans, and decided to come over to warn him. There was a man at the German embassy, like you said. I never learned his name, but he knew that I was coming here and he is determined to stop me seeing Charles. This man knows Mr Gregory and told him to get rid of me. They had had me beaten and tried to chase me from the country. I pretended to get a ferry from Harwich but I never caught it. I came to Worcestershire when I learned that Sir Charles would be here, when I made a call to his office, pretending to be an old friend. And that is all I know. If you see Sir Charles and he will not see me, or something happens to me, you can tell him what I said, and tell him that I only wish him well.'

'But what could happen to you here?' Godiva asked.

'They have someone working in Lord Randall's house. I know that because I overheard someone talking to Mr Gregory when he first warned me to leave. This man is not English, well, not by the way he spoke, in fact I think he was German. That was just before he had me beaten up. If they find out that I am still in the country and am trying to see Sir Charles, they will kill me. This time it will not be just a beating. They may have guessed that I was coming here, and it will not be difficult to find me, as there are not many German travellers in Worcestershire and I had to hand in my passport when I booked into this hotel,' Tommy said grimly.

'But who is the agent at the Court, do you know?' Godiva asked.

'That I do not know. All I can say is that he must have joined the staff very recently,' Tommy answered.

'If I can find out who it is, I shall make sure that he can do you no harm. And I will plead your case with Sir Charles,' Godiva said definitely.

'But don't tell anyone else. Absolutely no-one,' Tommy insisted.

'I promise you,' Godiva agreed.

◊

At the same time as Godiva sat down with Tommy a telegram arrived for a Mr Peters, who was working assembling an aeroplane for Lord Randall. This message came from someone called Smith and was decidedly cryptic, as telegrams often were, but this was quite a long message. The missive was received by Archer, the butler, who was scandalised that the hired help would be receiving telegrams, especially ones that came to the front door and not to the servant's entrance. He reported his disgust to Lord Randall as his lordship was preparing to go out on a shoot and was about to discuss the final arrangements with the gamekeeper, Mellors, and the domestic staff who were to prepare the catering. Lord Randall was unable to give full attention to Archer's complaint, but made a mental note to have a word with Mr Peters when he had the time.

◊

Godiva put on her walking boots and heavy overcoat and made her way through the village heading towards Blackleigh Court. It was a walk of some two miles, the last third of which was entirely through the grounds of the Court. A persistent drizzle caused droplets of water to form on the waxy wool of her coat, and soaked through her hat, dampening her hair. Mud from puddles splashed onto her boots and the base of her coat and skirt as she walked. The walk was mostly level, slightly downhill at the start, and did not tax her strength, but it was not ideal to arrive at the front entrance of a great country house damp, mud-splashed and in soiled walking boots.

A large motor car, complete with attentive chauffeur stood at the base of the curving flight of Portland stone steps which led to the front entrance. The Chauffeur looked suspiciously at Godiva as she walked past him. There was a man of superior appearance but wearing working clothes talking to the chauffeur, in a conversation that seemed to relate to mechanical matters. As she climbed the steps the front entrance opened and two gentlemen stepped out. One was tall, slim, cold-faced with a bushy moustache and slicked back hair, the other was shorter and had the air of a retired bachelor colonel. He wore a strange hat with four indentations in the crown. Both men tipped their hats to her as they passed as though she were the daughter of a local squire or rector. It was only after they had passed her that that Godiva realized that the second man was Sir Robert Baden Powell, the hero of Mafeking. They climbed into the back of the car.

A middle-aged footman had remained at the door to enquire of her business, which she gave as the car pulled away in a rattle of engine and crunch of gravel.

She was ushered into an ante-room off the hall which had no carpet and so was almost mud-proof while the footman went to look for Walter. Several minutes passed without the servant returning. Some copies of country pursuits magazines graced the table, making the small room feel like a dentist's waiting room. The footman returned sour-faced and without Walter.

'I am afraid that Lord Mansell-Lacey is not in the main part of the house at the moment, Miss. I shall enquire of the outdoor staff to see if if he has gone out shooting,' he said in a voice heavily accented with a nasal Birmingham twang.

'Then I shall wait a little longer,' said Godiva, a little testily.

The footman left again on his errand. She walked around the room trying to find anything which might divert her for a few minutes when a boy of about seven years walked into the room and appraised her appearance without pleasure.

'Hello,' said Godiva, 'who are you?'

'I'm Arthur, but my real name is Gerald, but that's my father's name, so they call me by my second name. Who are you?'

'I'm Godiva, Godiva Williams,' she answered, slightly disconcerted by all the information she had just received.

'That's a funny name. Are you waiting for someone?'

'Yes. I'm waiting for Lord Mansell-Lacey,' said Godiva, 'Do you know him?'

'Yes, his name's Walter, and I call him Uncle Walter, but he's not really a relation. He's painting a picture of Mummy and Aunt Emily,' said the boy.

'Is your Mummy Lady Caroline?' Godiva asked, working out who this child might be.

'Yes, she's my mother, Lady Caroline, but my father doesn't have a title. She gets the title from her father, my grandfather. He's Lord Randall. And Uncle Walter has a title, but I don't,' the boy said wistfully.

'Does it matter that much if you haven't got a title then?' Godiva asked.

'Of course it does. The servants always talk to you differently if they have to use your title. And I suppose that is the same for poor people as well, but I don't know any of them. Are you poor?'

'Not really, my father is quite well off, but he pretends that money isn't important to him,' Godiva said, smiling.

'Well, talking about money is rather vulgar,' said the boy, 'but perhaps it isn't if you haven't got any. And making lots of money is really important.'

This intellectual discussion was brought to an end by the arrival of Walter. He looked a little rumpled and was wiping paint from his hands with a turpentine soaked rag.

'Hello, Arthur, you young scamp,' said Walter, 'What are you doing with Miss Williams?'

'Her name's Godiva,' said Arthur, 'Are you going to marry her, is she pregnant?'

'The answers to those two questions are 'no', and 'no',' said Walter, grinning.

'Why did you ask those questions?' Godiva said, laughing.

'A lady came round to see father, but she saw mama instead. This lady said she was pregnant. I was listening at the door. And she said that Father was, was, responsible, and what was he going to do about it. And Father's already married to Mama, so he couldn't marry her, could he?' said Arthur, 'And Mama gave her some money and she went away.'

'That is quite enough, Arthur, now you go and play while I talk to Miss Williams, and no listening at the door this time!' said Walter. Arthur turned and walked away, head down and hands in his pockets.

'Ah, the delights of the modern family,' said Godiva, smiling grimly.

'Gerald is a bit of a bounder,' said Walter, but he's alright, really.'

'That rather depends on your standards,' said Godiva, 'I mean, at least you are single, but I don't suppose that most of your lady friends are.'

'And I take care not to father too many bastards,' said Walter, thinking back to what had happened the previous night, 'Now, I think we've exhausted the possibilities in that line of conversation. So tell me, what was it that you wanted to talk to me about?'

'Is Sir Charles here?' Godiva asked.

'No, he had to return to London for some reason, just after he got here, poor man. What it must be like to have such responsibility.'

'Oh, dear,' said Godiva, 'I've an urgent message for him from that German boy we found out about. It turns out he was also staying at the Hundred Inn, and I had a good talk with him. Oh, and I think Lord Randall has a spy somewhere here at the Court.'

'What! How did you find that out?' Walter asked.

'From this German boy, Tommy, and he knows the link to Arthur Gregory, though he is a bit sketchy on some points. I think we may be able to get the police onto Gregory if we can get Tommy to talk to them.'

'There is a man here who might be able to help. He's involved with all this spying business. If there is a connection to the Germans, I'm sure he can be relied on to provide some kind of security for this Tommy of yours,' Walter blurted excitedly.

'There is something else, but I promised Tommy that I wouldn't say anything about it except to Sir Charles. I'm not going to break that promise,' Godiva said with nobility.

'Then you are going to have a long wait. Now, look, you've yet to tell me what you came here for,' said Walter, 'What is it that you've uncovered?'

'Oh, that!', said Godiva, 'it's all about the oil for the Navy and the Persian oil fields and the Germans trying to stop us getting a supply of oil. I'm off to your father's place tomorrow morning to see this Danish geologist, Professor Knudsen, who's working for your father preparing something for investors. I've worked most of it out, and I'm just trying to discover the last details. The point is we can make a pretty good guess at why the Germans were trying to blackmail Charles through his wife, and now I know why it didn't work.'

'Right,' Walter said doubtfully, I think that you'd better tell your story to my friend, Captain Mansfield Cumming. He's a bit of an odd fellow, but he knows his job well enough. He's out shooting at the moment, but he'll be back this afternoon.'

'That sounds like a good idea, but I had better get back to the Hundred Inn to reassure Tommy. He won't be very happy when I tell him that Sir Charles has gone back to London,' said Godiva, 'I'll be back a bit later. In the meantime, do you think you can get a message to Charles, telling him that there really is a plot against him?'

'Righty-ho,' Walter agreed. 'I'll send him a telegram as soon as I can. In the meantime I'm rather more concerned that there might be a German spy in our midst. I'll try and rout the man out. Was there any kind of clue as to who it might be?'

'The only thing Tommy said is that it must be someone quite new,' Godiva said.

'In that case I shall have a word with the butler and see who is new to the staff,' Walter said thoughtfully, 'then I'll have a word with my friend in the security service.'

'I had better get back now, and keep an eye on Tommy until you can get someone to look after him.'

Walter returned to his painting, and Godiva walked back through the drizzle to the Hundred Inn.

◊

Godiva asked for Tommy as soon as she had returned to the Hundred Inn, only to be told that he had gone out half an hour before, leaving his bags packed in his room. Shortly before leaving he had been visited by a gentleman of decent appearance, but with some signs of grease stains on his hands and coat. This man had come on a motorcycle from the direction of the Court.

'Was any message left for me by Mr Thomas Schmidtt?' Godiva asked.

'I think there was something,' the landlord said, and he looked behind the desk, rummaging about. 'That's funny, there was definitely an envelope there. It seems to have gone.'

'Did you see him leave?'

'He went out the door with the gentleman with the motorbike, but I didn't see him leave, I had a bill to make out for another guest. The funny thing is that he left his passport behind. I suppose he'll come and collect it later. He looked pretty happy when he left, well, mostly happy and a little bit relieved.'

Godiva had a very bad feeling about what might have happened to Tommy, and now there was no way to tell him that help was almost at hand. She would need to go back to Blackleigh Court and fetch help from Walter and his new friends. She should manage the walk to arrive sometime after lunch.

◊

The shooting had been abandoned that morning. Heavy showers and a high wind were enough to cause the postponement of the day's sport for some hours, and when it continued into the afternoon it was decided to shoot the next day instead. The gentlemen were settled in the study after lunch, reading newspapers when the butler, Archer, entered. He approached Lord Randall and said that the Gamekeeper, Mellors, requested a word with his Lordship concerning the contents of the gun room.

'You mean that a gun has gone missing?' asked Randall.

'No, Sir,' answered Archer, 'Quite the contrary. A gun has appeared that does not belong there'.

'Gentlemen', announced Randall, 'We may have some amusement today after all. We have a mystery to unravel concerning the guns in the gun-room'.

'Has to be more amusing than the news in The Times', said Doyle.

'Yes, let us go and investigate', said Buchan.

The gentlemen folded the papers and trooped down the hallway, past the butler's pantry to the area of the house where the sporting equipment was kept, leaving Cumming and Kell to their private discussions. The gun room door was ajar and Mellors was holding a shotgun, a puzzled look on his grizzled features. The rest of the guns were arranged in the racks with fine, strong chains threaded through the trigger guards keeping them safe and in position.

'So this is the gun in question,' stated Randall.

'Yes, Sir,' answered Mellors, not quite tugging his non-existent forelock.

'Does it belong to any of you, or the other guests?' Randall asked the assembled gentlemen. They all shook their heads.

'And might have one of the servants have brought it in?' Randall asked.

'No, Sir,' replied Mellors, 'There's only me and Archer as has the key to the room. And my key never leaves my person'.

'Tell me, why is there a space for a spare gun?' asked Buchan.

'One of his Lordship's Purdeys has gone back to London to be serviced,' answered Mellors, 'His lordship felt that the action was a little stiffer than it should have been'. He looked affronted by the failure of the gun in his care.

'Let's have a look at this piece', said Randall, taking the gun from the Gamekeeper. He turned it around and examined it 'It is quite a good gun,' said Randall, looking at the stock, 'From a Birmingham maker. Not a top quality one, to be sure, but a very decent piece of work. It was made for a tall man, I would judge, by the position of the left hand grip. I think it should be one of a pair made for some local squire or some such person. It is good and serviceable, without being fancy.' He sniffed the end of the barrels, 'Oh, and it's been fired quite recently'.

'And none of the guests has claimed it, and none of the servants knows about it. The only access is via that door, the cabinets are always kept locked and only Mellors and Archer have keys. It really is a complete mystery', said Buchan.

'If there were one gun missing it would be considered as carelessness or theft. But to have one gun too many is a genuine conundrum. We must consider who put it there and why'. Doyle fingered his moustaches in a thoughtful way. 'Now it seems to me that whoever did it could not have known that there was an empty space in one of the gun cabinets, but somehow came across the weapon, assumed it came from this room and attempted to return it to a place where it never belonged, in an attempt to conceal a theft that did not, in fact, take place. And that itself leads to many more questions, such as where the gun originally came from, and who brought it into the vicinity. This would make a fine plot point for a certain Baker Street detective, but I am damned if I can make head nor tail out of it at the moment'.

'If that were the case, it would require someone to have a copy of the key or be able to pick locks. And, what is more, it would have to be a guest or a servant,' said Randall.

'In my sort of story the villain comes into a room with a gun whenever the plot gets tedious, but this sort of thing would not do for me at all. It is all too confusing and bizarre', said Buchan, 'Yet there must be some reason for it'.

'I think this calls for a decent walk and some good thinking time', said Randall, 'I don't mind braving the weather. After we have all had a think we shall discuss it again at dinner'.

'Good idea', said Doyle, 'A decent walk and a couple of pipe-fulls of some good shag, and I am sure a solution will suggest itself'.

Archer coughed softly. 'If I might suggest, my lord, I shall ask Mr. Peters if he is aware of the gun's provenance.'

'And who might this Mr. Peters be?' Buchan asked.

'He's an expert mechanic. I've brought him over to put together the aeroplane that I just bought,' said Randall.

'He wasn't at dinner,' said Buchan, 'So we haven't met the man.'

'That is because he is a mechanic, not a guest. Mind you, he did receive a telegram today. It was delivered to the front door, and Archer had to take it to him. Damned cheek, if you ask me. Don't know what the world is coming to, a mechanic being served by the butler! The thing put Archer's nose out of joint, I can tell you. By the way, I must really show you the letter of introduction that Peters brought with him. It must have been translated from the French, mind. Bloody awful English, and terribly amusing. Now I think about it, I don't believe that I've told you much about the technical details of the aeroplane.'

'And what kind of thing might this flying machine be?' Doyle asked, with a note in his voice that suggested he was not looking forward to the answer.

'It's a French machine. They make all the best aeroplanes. It's an Antoinette VIII monoplane with a 100 HP V16 engine, with aluminium castings, direct injection and evaporative cooling. It's quite revolutionary,' Lord Randall replied.

'I have absolutely no idea what you are talking about,' said Doyle.

'Who is this pilot you've hired?' Walter inquired.

'Well, I needed a qualified pilot, one who knows this type of aeroplane,' Randall said.

'Answer the question, who might this pilot be, Randall. Is it anyone we might have heard of?' Buchan asked.

'Astonishing as it may seem, it is a lady, and you will probably have heard of her, Miss Dorothy Levitt. She recently undertook training in France on this very type of aeroplane, and I am sure that she will prove to be a more that adequate for the job,' Randall said proudly.

'My word,' said Doyle, 'The fastest girl in the world. I shall very much look forward to making her acquaintance. I have heard several rather interesting stories about her. Didn't know she could fly, aeroplanes, though.'

◊

Walter burst into the study with Godiva close behind. Cumming was seated behind the desk and Kell was pacing the room, his hands behind his back. The reaction of the men to the intruders was somewhat different. Cumming looked up and smiled while Kell turned and glared.

'I'm sorry for interrupting, gentlemen, but there has been a bit of a development,' Walter said.

'It had better be an important development, we have important business to discuss,' Kell said in a curt way.'

'We believe that the Germans have placed a spy here in the house,' Godiva said.

'And who might you be, my dear?' Cumming asked.

'Sorry, we haven't been introduced. I'm Godiva Williams, and I believe that you are Captain Cumming and the other gentlemen is Captain Kell.'

'Well, almost right. Introductions over. Now, kindly explain what you are on about,' Kell said.

'It's a long story, but to cut to the chase, there was a man staying at a nearby inn who was trying to make contact with Sir Charles because he had learnt something about a German plot against him. This man has now disappeared under suspicious circumstances. One of the details he mentioned to Miss Williams is that a spy has been sent to the Court. Given the sensitive nature of the discussions we have been holding, I thought I had better inform you of this straight away,' Walter said.

'Quite right, quite right,' Cumming said.

'But is this informant reliable?' Kell asked.

'Well, I know his life has been threatened and he was badly beaten up for trying to make contact with Sir Charles a week ago. He's not what I would think of as naturally brave, but his actions have been heroic as far as I'm concerned,' Godiva said.

'What is the name of this man?' Kell asked.

'His name is Thomas Schmidtt,' Godiva said.

'German, is he?' Cumming asked.

'Yes, but he is working against them in this matter,' Godiva insisted.

'I'm going to make a telephone call and see what we know about him. In the meantime, do you have any idea as to who the spy in our midst might be?' Kell said.

'All I know is that it is someone who has arrived very recently,' Godiva said.

'Then we will ask the butler and Randall who has come to the house in the last few days,' Cumming said to Kell, 'now you go off and make your telephone call and I will try to find a little more about this matter.'

Kell gave a disgusted little cough and left the room for Lord Randall's study, from where he could make the telephone call in private.

'Right, I think it is time for the long version of this story. Which of you wants to make a start?' Cumming said.

Walter and Godiva glanced at each other and with unsaid agreement Walter began his tale.

'A man in Naval intelligence asked me to sound out Lady Emily about a contact she had made with a known German agent a few weeks ago. That is why I came up here. During the course of investigation I found out about a man who seemed to be working for both British and German intelligence. My manservant knew someone who had worked for this man. We had a meeting with my servant's friend and he told us that the man concerned was a blackmailer and had just had a German boy called Tommy beaten up. Our informant was murdered, probably because he had spoken to us. We didn't know what the plot was at the time, but we do now. There had been a German plot to entrap Sir Charles and blackmail him, and Tommy was the bait. Only Tommy liked Sir Charles much more than he feared his masters and came over to warn Sir Charles about this plot. He came up here to speak to Sir Charles and by coincidence stayed at the same inn as Miss Williams. She recognised him by his description and some things that he said and by the bruises on his face. He asked her to pass a message onto Sir Charles, but, as you know, he returned to London yesterday. By the time she got back to the inn, Tommy had left in the company of a man on a motorcycle. We very much fear that Tommy has been taken by his enemies.'

'Well, that is a very interesting tale. Now, Miss Williams, perhaps you would tell me about your involvement in this story,' Cumming said.

'It started out with me being nosey about what Walter was doing. He tried to keep me out of it, but I can be very determined. Also, I am quite good at research. I managed to trace a booking for a hotel room to the man who had Tommy beaten up. This man had booked the room for the German agent, so we know they are connected. Later I worked out there was also a connection to the Anglo Persian Oil Company. The Germans are trying to stop us getting a reliable oil supply for the Navy. Sir Charles is responsible for that task, which is why they tried to blackmail him. He didn't do anything wrong, so that didn't work. Then they tried to work through Lady Emily, only she wouldn't have any of it. And Lord Randall may also be connected because he is a major shareholder in the oil company, and the Germans wanted to know about his involvement.'

'Well it all sounds positively Byzantine to me. From what you two have just said, I think we ought to go to the inn and try to find out what has happened to friend Tommy. It would probably be better to wait until Colonel Kell gets back. Then we'll go off my motor, mob-handed,' Cumming said.

They did not have long to wait. Kell returned looking rather grim and wasted no time on niceties.

'I've spoken to one of my men about this Thomas Schmidtt, and he is known to be a German agent, more than capable of dissembling. He was probably sent up here to muddy the waters for us, and I think he ran away when Miss Williams spotted him. As for you, Miss Williams, you were not supposed to have anything to do with this matter. You were informed in no uncertain manner that you should leave it alone. Yet you continued to pursue your own private enquiries. I take a very grave view of your interference.'

'Does your man with the information go by the name of Scrivener, by any chance?' Walter enquired.

'I do not have to answer that,' Kell snapped.

'Then Miss Williams actions, and mine by association are to be condemned by an anonymous informant. It suggests some kind of Star Chamber to me.'

'I will have words with you later, Lord Walter.'

'And, no doubt, Mr Scrivener tells you of the value to the intelligence services of Mr Arthur Gregory. But I'll tell you that the only person he works for is himself. He is always open to do work for the highest bidder. He is deeply corrupt and a known liar. If Scrivener believes him then Scrivener is a fool.'

'Keep quiet, you idiot,' Kell hissed between his teeth.

'May I suggest that we go and investigate this matter of the disappearing German boy, if only on the off-chance of it turning out to be important,' Cumming suggested.

'And may I humbly suggest that this is my area of competence. I have decided not to proceed in something useless or counter-productive. You can do what you like,' Kell said coldly.

'In that case, I will see you later. Come along, Miss Williams, Lord Walter,' Cumming said.

The main car was already taken, so Cumming called for the second car, a Vauxhall. Cumming drove himself, in a wild fashion, guided by Godiva to the Hundred Inn.

They trooped in together and found the manager.

'Hello, I believe you have the luggage and passport of a Mr Thomas Schmidtt here. We have come to collect these things,' Cumming said.

'They've already been collected, I'm afraid,' the manager said with a shake of his head.

'Right, I see. Well, who was it that collected them?' Cumming asked.

'It was the same man he left with earlier, so I presumed that it was alright. I hope I haven't done anything wrong. He paid the bill in full, in cash.'

'Could you describe this man to us?' said Walter.

'It was hard to say. He had a long overcoat and a cap pulled down over his face. He was a bit older that you, Sir, I think, but not quite so tall. There didn't seem much to notice about him, really. I hope I didn't do wrong.'

'I'm sure your actions were perfectly reasonable under the circumstances,' Cumming admitted.

'What will Kell make of this?' Godiva asked.

'I'm sure he won't be impressed,' Cumming admitted, 'Look, I've gone out on a limb a bit for you on this, and I do believe you. Let's go into the saloon bar and find a quiet corner where you can tell me a bit more about Tommy and everything.'

'Alright, that sounds like a good idea,' Walter said.

'Do you think I am still safe staying here tonight?' Godiva asked.

'If there really is a spy at the Court, you are probably safer here that coming with us for the night. Just remember to lock the door and don't talk to any strangers,' Cumming suggested.

'I've got to get to Shirl Castle tomorrow,' Godiva said.

'I'll arrange a car to get you there,' Cumming said, 'I'd be interested to know what else you might find out.'

'Send my regards to Mrs Hudson, the housekeeper, will you,' Walter suggested, 'she was very good to me when I was growing up, and to Jackson, the butler.'

'If I meet them, of course I will,' Godiva agreed.

'You know, I've been thinking,' Cumming said meditatively, 'Do you think you could delay going to Shirl Castle by a day. I think I can square this with Kell, and I want to get him involved in this matter. It really is his territory, not mine. Once we've got him on board I'm sure we can proceed at full steam.'

'How will you get him on board?' Walter asked.

'I'll make sure to involve Mr Doyle. Kell is very fond of Mr Doyle's opinions.'

'And what about the spy in our camp?' Walter said.

'That is a problem. What with all the guests coming recently it's a big job to check on all the servants. Archer was quite certain that no new workers have been taken on at the Court recently, so I don't know quite where we stand,' Cumming admitted.

'Maybe Kell will be able to find something out,' Godiva suggested.

'In his present mood, I don't think he'll be too willing to help,' Cumming said.

FRIDAY 1ST OCTOBER 1909

The field of stubble sloped gradually up the incline, steepening as it rose towards the wooded slopes. Beaters were working their way in the less dense woodland to the left of the field where the pheasant pens were, driving the birds across the line of shooters. Walter took no delight in shooting pheasants and had decided to remain at the Court. Gerald, Lord Randall, Buchan, Doyle and Cumming were all standing in a line with twelve bores loaded but broken, waiting for the birds to fly. The men were wearing nearly identical tweed outfits and brown boots, the uniform of the great pheasant hunter. As the pheasants flapped slowly and clumsily past the line of shooters, shotguns were closed, raised and fired. The birds fell from the air like broken kites and were collected by the eager tail-wagging spaniels who were well trained by Mellors. The dead birds were placed into wicker baskets by the deputy gamekeepers before being counted and then sent to the larder. Mellors was keeping score. He was not impressed by the standard of the shooting. Pigeons were a much more difficult target as they flew high and fast, and they really were vermin. Besides, they tasted better than pheasant and it took skill and judgement to shoot them. These pheasants were born in captivity, fed by men to the point where they were completely trusting. Overfed and hardly exercised they could barely fly more than a few yards. But it was not his place to complain. They were the gentlemen, this was their sport and it was his job to ensure that there were birds for them to shoot.

It was the beaters chivvying the birds from cover who came across the body. The corpse lay sprawled across the fragmented remains of a stone hut which had been left as a romantic feature below the woods. The walls of the stone hut nowhere stood more than three feet high and had collapsed entirely on two sides. Moss grew thick and dark green on the tumbled stones, contrasting with the pale grey of the man's suit and the purple-red of the congealing blood which had flowed from his head. The mortal remains were those of a slim man of medium height, neatly dressed as if for the city. His blond hair was streaked with blood from the multiple wounds around his head and most of his face had been blown away by a shotgun blast. The young beater who found him, the fourteen year old son of an estate worker, vomited on the spot at the horror of the sight. Other beaters joined the group around the cadaver and the noise of startled birds fleeing from the wood stopped entirely. The shooters grumbled at the lack of birds to aim at and were taking swigs from hip flasks before another boy was sent to tell them of the grisly discovery. This boy, being a good runner, was given instructions go as fast as he could to the Court and to demand that the police be called. With guns broken and cartridges removed the party gathered around the body.

'Make sure that nobody touches anything until the police have examined the body,' Doyle instructed, 'And try to keep off the surrounding areas as much as you can.' This second instruction was useless as dozens of booted feet had already trampled the entire area.

'I think I might have an idea who this man might be,' Cumming said, grimly, 'and I think Lord Walter should be sent for. It is a great pity that Major Kell had to dash away on that business. His skills would be useful now.'

The boy was sent on his way with the additional instructions.

◊

Walter was continuing with his portrait of Caroline and Emily in a style reminiscent of Augustus John when the commotion caused by the arrival of the boy messenger caused him to lay down his palette and brush and enquire what all the damned noise was about. A minute later a breathless boy requested to speak to him after knocking boldly on the door.

'There's been an accident of some kind,' the boy said.

'What do you mean, an accident?' Walter asked.

'We just found a body near the foot of the hill,' the boy explained, breathless after his run.

'Was it one of our party or a beater?' Caroline asked.

'It's a stranger, not even dressed for the country, your ladyship,' the boy stammered.

'And I am requested to go and look, am I?' Walter said.

'If it please your lordship,' the boy replied.

After putting on an overcoat, a hat and some stout boots, Walter headed with the boy to the scene of the crime. Following the initial shock and thrill of the discovery the shooting party had become less fascinated and more disturbed by the scene. They had retreated some yards distant where they sat listlessly around on their shooting sticks, smoking, and taking fortifying swigs of brandy. After a few minutes they began making occasional observations about the body. The clothes the man wore were not British but the boots were decent enough for town, if not fit for clinging red mud. His hands were smooth and well manicured, so he was not involved in manual labour. The wounds on what remained of his head showed that he had been beaten before being shot, which entirely ruled out suicide. There were old bruises on his face, turned from purple to blue-green. The dew on his clothes suggested that he had been lying there all night, but the clothes were not soaked from the heavy rain which had fallen the previous morning.

'Ah, Walter. Sorry to bring you out on this errand, but I think you might be able to identify this man,' Cumming said.

Walter looked at the man and tried to keep the contents of his stomach under control.

'I'm sorry, but I don't recognise him. But he does fit the description he had of the man who was staying at the Hundred Inn. If it is him, then we never met,' Walter said.

'Well that explains some things,' said Doyle, 'His clothes are mostly clean and neat. He must have been staying somewhere where there were bathrooms. If he was staying at a local inn, then maybe someone from the inn might be able to identify him.'

'I think we have someone who might be able to do just that,' Cumming said.

'Do you mean Miss Williams?' Walter asked.

'Would it be too upsetting for her? If you think so we can always ask the landlord,' Cumming replied.

'What on earth are you two wittering on about?' Randall said.

'A friend of Lord Walter knows the man involved, if it is him,' Cumming replied.

'Well, damn well send for her then, and the landlord as well,' Randall barked out.

'Send the Lanchester round for them, then,' Gerald suggested.

'Good idea, Gerald. Hey, Mellors, send one of your boys to get the chauffeur out of the kitchen and tell him to get the car ready. I think you'd better deal with this, Cumming, as you seem to know what's going on, and take Walter along with you.'

'What about Kell?' Walter asked.

'He had some business to attend to concerning that man they found in the London Underground. He'll be back tomorrow. Besides, we can't go mob handed. He'll get a chance to talk to Miss Williams when he arrives,' Cumming said.

'Come on then.' Walter said, and he started walking back to the Court at a pace which Cumming was unable to match.

'You're not going without us!' Buchan called out and he began the pursuit followed by the other shooters.

◊

Murphy had been awake for three full days before he was capable of speaking to the police. Officers had been stationed to guard him in his hospital bed. On the first day he only gave his details as though he was being questioned as a prisoner of war, just name, rank and serial number. The next day he seemed to be starting to recover his wits and wept at the loss of his leg, and began to make demands for food and beer. Whenever he was asked about what had happened in the store room and how he had got there he became silent, as though the memory were too painful to recollect. On the third he started to make some sense and was able to communicate some details about his ordeal. As the story unfolded, and the description of the stranger was slowly built up, the information which was given out to other agencies brought in a Mr Scrivener, who worked in some undefined role in the Admiralty. Scrivener took off his hat and gloves and laid them neatly in his lap after sitting in a formal pose on the hard wooden chair besides the Sergeant's bed. The Sergeant was dozing fitfully. Scrivener coughed politely to wake him from his slumbers. Murphy shook his head and took in the details of this stranger.

'Sergeant Murphy, I'm Mr Scrivener, and I am here to ask you a few questions, if you able to answer them, that is.'

'Are you from the Police?' Murphy asked.

'Not exactly, more to do with the armed forces, really.'

'Oh, you mean Intelligence. I met some of your sort in South Africa,' said Murphy.

'I'm sorry about the leg,' said Scrivener.

'Huh,' Murphy grunted, 'still, I suppose I ought to be grateful that I'm still alive.'

'Quite so. Now I know what happened to you, or what you told the police, but I need to ask some other questions. Is that alright?'

'You might as well, I'm not exactly doing much at the moment,' Murphy grumbled.

'Very good. Could you start by describing this man. Tell me what he looked like.'

'Like I told the Police, it was quite dark in the pub. But what I do remember is that he was quite tall and sort of well built. His hands were quite rough, and a bit stained, with oil, I think, so he was some kind of working man. He had a cap pulled down, so I don't remember his eyes looked like, but he had curly light brown hair and looked like he'd been out in the sun. His clothes was like the sort you wear going out on a Sunday, sort of smart.'

'Mr Murphy, can you tell me the kind of accent this man had. Did you notice anything when he talked to you?'

'His accent? That's a funny question. Well, he had a foreign accent, but he spoke good English. It was a bit old fashioned, but it was good English,' Murphy replied.

'Could you identify what kind of foreign accent it was?' Scrivener pursued.

'Well,' Murphy considered, 'I recognised that Boer accent, he told me that he was a Boer, and I knew he was from South Africa, but I thought he was an English settler, but there was something else there, American I think.'

'Or Canadian, perhaps?' Scrivener suggested.

'I suppose so, I wouldn't know the difference, myself,' Murphy replied.

'If it was a Canadian accent, then I have a very good idea that I know this particular man, or rather, I know of him, and who his associates are. Thank you very much, Sergeant, you might have given me the piece of information which might allow me to bring this monster to justice.'

'Well, that won't give me my leg back,' Murphy grumbled.

'Quite,' Scrivener agreed, unsure as to what else he could say.

Murphy groaned in pain because he had not been given any painkillers that morning. Scrivener had wanted him to have a clear head during their interview. Now that it was concluded Scrivener asked that Murphy be given a further shot of morphine to deaden the pain of the amputation of his left leg.

◊

'But, my dear Herr Braun, or may I now call you by your real name, Siegfried? I'm not blackmailing you, it is just that you have put some business my way, so I thought we could make this a little less formal, just as I would for a good friend,' said the smooth faced man.

'For some reason, I find that I don't quite believe you,' said the tall, scarred Junkers.

'As I told you, my man swore that he saw young Tommy go onto the Harwich Ferry. If only he had been a sensible boy he would be back home in Germany by now, or somewhere in Holland. Either way he wouldn't be causing you any more trouble.' Gregory cut a cigar, placed it between his lips. He lit a match and waited for the flame to spread before he raised it to the tip of the cigar. 'Unfortunately, for you he managed to get off the ship unobserved. But between us we have managed to track him down again. Your operative has proved very efficient in the past and he should have dealt with Tommy by now. It was fortunate for you that you had your man in the area deal with him.'

'I didn't intend for you to know about him,' said Siegfried.

'Well, I was very impressed with the way he dealt with that inquisitive chorus boy. It was really most professional, so I made some enquiries. I had your man followed and learned quite a bit about him. I put that together with what you told me and it all made sense. Then I discovered that you had sent your Mr Peters to Blackleigh Court. As Tommy had gone there it seemed that you would wish to use Peters to finish this piece of business. I hope you don't mind, but I thought it best that any communication to Mr Peters should come from you. He is, after all, your man and it was up to you to tell him what he should do. If he is anywhere near as efficient as before, then I am sure that you can rely on Tommy's complete silence now,' said Gregory, and he sucked on the cigar again, 'Now, about that payment for my services, if you could pay me a cheque or cash, anything will do. Just to cover my expenses, you understand.'

'It believe was a mistake to put that message in a telegram. We have other ways of communicating with Mr Peters, but this was necessary. I must hope that I have put his mission in jeopardy. The nature of the problem made it urgent,' Siegfried said, 'But, on another matter, having looked at your bill, I must say that you have very high level of expenses. But I suppose I shall have to pay. I will make a request from the Embassy funds. You need not worry, you will get paid.'

'Oh, I'm sure I will. What would you like me to do with those photographs that were taken at my establishment, the ones in which you appear with Mrs Pain?' Gregory enquired, 'On another point, I had a glance at that code that you use. It really is childishly simple to break it. You really ought to choose another.'

'You will pass the negatives, and all the prints to me, as soon as you receive your payment,' said Siegfried firmly.

'Of course,' Gregory confirmed smoothly, 'I have no further use for them.'

'If I find that you have kept any copies, I will make it my business to deal with you personally,' Siegfried snarled.

'No need to be rude, you know that I am a man of my word,' said Gregory, 'And if you act like that I am more likely to keep back a copy in the files of a discrete solicitor, with instructions to pass them on to the Home Office and some of the popular newspapers, just as a form of insurance, should anything happen to me,' said Gregory, with a note of menace in his voice.

'My masters are not likely to regard such evidence with favour. It would ruin me. You can hardly know how much I regret visiting your club,' said Siegfried, sounding like a whipped dog.

'But you did visit, and you did take advantage of the services of Mrs Pain. I have never understood the pleasure some men get when being beaten and abused. But it does provide a very lucrative return for me, and sometimes it pays more than once,' Gregory said nastily.

'Yes, I know that,' Siegfried admitted, 'but I personally feel no shame. It is not as though it is a real perversion, like sodomy. It is just a taste I have, and it harms no-one but me.'

'You don't have to justify your actions to me, but other people may not be so forgiving, so please do not provoke me,' Gregory said.

'I shall not provoke you, and I shall pay you. However, I must have agreement for the payment. The usual procedures must be followed,' Siegfried said with a whining tone in his voice.

'I think I would be happy if the payment were made within the next week,' Gregory said, and he took another puff at his cigar.

◊

Walter, Godiva, Doyle, Cumming, Buchan and Randall were sat around the table in the guest's sitting room at the Hundred Inn. The landlord had been obsequious to the point of absurdity at the presence of the local landowner and so many distinguished gentlemen. He had provided tea and biscuits and stronger drink and ensured that their conversation would be held in private.

'So how does our description of this young man tally with your memory, Miss Williams?' Cumming asked.

'The description is exactly as I remember him, down to the clothes he wore and his boots,' Godiva said, more saddened than surprised at the discovery of the body.

'Then I don't believe that there is any reason to put you though the ordeal of identifying the body. It really is a bit gory,' Cumming said. Several seconds of silence followed.

'I understand that you met the young man we found today,' Doyle said gravely.

'Yes, we had breakfast together yesterday. We had to share a table. He was a very nice boy, and he spoke perfect English. We had a bit of a conversation and when he found I was going to Blackleigh Court he asked me to pass a message on to Sir Charles,' Godiva said steadily.

'What was the message, Miss Williams?' Cumming asked, pouring himself another cup of tea.

Godiva sipped at her tea before answering. 'Well, I promised to keep his secrets, but as he's dead, I don't suppose it matters anymore.' She put her cup and saucer back down on the occasional table. 'He wanted to be thought of as Sir Charles' good friend, and wanted to warn him about a plot against him. I've told Walter and Captain Cumming all about this.'

'Please enlighten us a little, Miss Williams,' Randall said.

'What I found out was that Tommy had been used to entice Sir Charles into a situation where he could be blackmailed. This happened when Sir Charles was at a spa in Germany. The plot didn't work because Sir Charles wasn't interested. What is more, Tommy fell in love with Sir Charles, in a platonic sort of way, and wanted to warn him that the Germans were plotting against him. That's why he came over to England. The German intelligence people found out that Tommy was trying to contact Sir Charles and decided to stop him. So they threatened him and beat him up, and now they seem to have killed him.'

Cumming finished the biscuit he had been nibbling and asked some more questions. 'If it was a German agent who killed Tommy we need to know who he is. If he followed Tommy then he must have stayed somewhere. We'll look at the registers at all the local inns and see if we can find a name we recognise. I'll set Kell onto it. It's much more his line of work.'

'I don't suppose they'll be using their own names, though,' Buchan said.

'Of course not. They wouldn't use their real names, especially if they're German. However, if we've been keeping tabs on them then Kell will almost certainly know the names they generally use,' Cumming said.

'There is another possibility,' Doyle said, stroking his moustache, 'They might have a spy in the camp. I don't need to tell anyone how serious that possibility is, considering the discussions that we have been having this week.'

'Good God!,' Randall spluttered, 'The very idea hardly bears thinking about.'

'Mr Doyle is absolutely correct to raise the idea. I think it very likely from something else Miss Williams told us. We should certainly consider the possibility,' Cumming said.

'Tommy mentioned that he thought the German man at the embassy had put someone in to the house,' Godiva said in a measured way.

'Should Miss Williams be included in this discussion?' Buchan asked.

'Absolutely,' Cumming said, 'After all, she knows more about it than anyone of us.'

'But she doesn't know why we were meeting,' Buchan protested.

'Miss Williams is more than capable of working out what we were up to without any further clues. So please excuse our rudeness, Miss Williams, you are more than welcome to stay,' Cumming said, turning to Godiva.

'Going back to what we were talking about, I hope you're not suggesting that any of my servants are at all suspect. They are all local, and have all been known to us for decades, if not generations,' Randall said, sounding hurt.

'No need to worry about that. I'm sure they're all splendid people. But we still need to do a few checks. Especially if there are any recent arrivals. You can rely on Kell being discrete. He won't upset anyone unnecessarily,' Cumming said reassuringly, but not believing a word he said to them.

'Then I suggest that we return to the Court and give Miss Williams some peace and quiet. I am sorry that we are the bearers of such bad news, Miss Williams,' Randall said.

'Then we can start to find out if there really is a spy in the camp and stop him in his tracks, if he exists,' Buchan said.

◊

The noise of the engine preceded the vehicle by several hundred yards. Alerted by the noise, Walter and Lord Randall made their way to the rear of the Court. A low and elegant green car with a gleaming brass radiator surround pulled into the yard by the garages. It had sprayed gravel from the drive and the braking was unnecessarily dramatic. The driver was a slim young woman in a butcher blue dust coat and matching hat pulled down over her dark, curly hair. When she removed her goggles she revealed dark, liquid eyes. As she climbed out of the car, which had no doors, it was evident to all the men present that she had long and shapely legs. A Pomeranian dog jumped from the passenger seat and ran excitedly around those legs.

'Oh, do be quiet, Dodo,' said the young woman to the dog. It sat by her feet, tongue lolling. Its head swivelled to follow the conversation that followed.

Lord Randall strode over to her and greeted her by kissing a hand that had, until a few seconds before, been covered with a stout leather driving gauntlet.

'Miss Levitt,' said Randall, 'How wonderful to see you. I am so glad that you were able to accept my invitation, and what a wonderful motor car!'

'Thank you, my lord, the car is rather good. Mr Edge wished me to deliver it to you personally. I was hoping to test it on the track at Shelsey Walsh to see how it goes. We've made some changes since last year and it seems to be going faster than ever now,' she said in a breathy voice.

'Of course, of course, you are most welcome to test it. And I understand that you are now qualified to fly aeroplanes.'

'That is the other reason why Mr Edge wanted me to come here. He thinks Mr Napier will be very interested in the engine design of your aeroplane. He is awfully good at designing engines is our Mr Napier. What is more, it is almost exactly the type of aeroplane that I learned to fly in, so I may be of some assistance to you.' She smiled at Lord Randall in a dreamy, wistful and yet calculating way. Walter thought he detected Randall blushing slightly in return. Lord Randall made the introduction.

'Miss Dorothy Levitt, may I present Lord Walter Mansell-Lacey, third son of the Duke of Radnor.'

'I'm honoured to meet you, Miss Levitt,' said Walter.

'Oh, Dorothy, please. And may I call you Walter?'

'Of course,' said Walter, 'I don't really stand on ceremony. And you certainly know how to drive that car.'

'Do you drive, Walter?' she asked.

'No, I've never learned. Perhaps I would if I had a splendid machine like that,' said Walter.

'I would advise that you learn on something a little less powerful,' said Dorothy, 'They can be quite dangerous, these machines, especially when you're racing them.'

'And they cost a great deal of money,' Lord Randall added, 'Mr Selwyn Edge has spent a fortune on the bally things.'

'Well that's true, but he has had a lot of success racing them. I know he is hoping to sell a lot of these very expensive cars, so I am sure that it more than pays for itself,' said Dorothy.

'I shall have to take your word for that, Miss Levitt. In the meantime, I'll have a maid take your things up to your room, and prepare you a bath. I'm sure you'll be needing one after the journey from London,' Randall said.

'I assure you I am quite fresh, but a nice cup of tea would be very welcome,' Dorothy said, flashing another smile.

'That can be arranged most easily,' said Lord Randall and he beckoned to a gardener to run to the house and make the arrangements.

'So you fly aeroplanes as well?' said Walter

'Yes, I went to learn at Châlons Camp, which is near Rheims, this summer. It was the greatest fun.'

'I may learn to drive a car, but I don't think I'll ever try to fly an aeroplane,' said Walter.

'Afraid of heights, are you?' Dorothy asked.

'Not so much afraid of the height as of hitting the ground,' Walter replied, and Dorothy laughed easily at his weak attempt at a joke.

◊

Walter had been half expecting Lady Emily to call when Lady Caroline swooped into the bedroom with the wings of her gauzy negligee floating behind without bothering to knock. She closed and fastened the door behind her. Then she turned to look at Walter with a lascivious smile. Her figure could be clearly seen beneath the translucent silk. Her waist had been compressed into a narrow band since girlhood by tight corseting. Now her figure thickened a little but the waist remained remarkably small. When compared to Godiva's natural shape it looked artificial and rather ugly. It did emphasise her full bust and hips. The swell of her breasts beneath the cloth was clearly visible, but the lined lace band was not transparent. There was a single thin layer of fabric below and the dark stain of untrimmed pubic hair at the joining of her legs was clearly visible.

Her hair was unfastened and flowed in artful curls over her shoulders. Walter had half expected her sister to visit and had anticipated the event with a mixture of anticipation and slight guilt. The possibility of a relationship with Emily made him slightly uncomfortable at the prospect of sex with the elder sister. Caroline put a finger to her lips to indicate that Walter should not talk. She pulled back the covers and slipped into the bed beside him, her negligee parting across her body as she did so. They kissed long and hard.

'Where's Gerald?' Walter asked in hushed tones.

'He wanted to entertain a chambermaid, so I vacated the room for him. Hope you don't mind'. She giggled girlishly.

'That was very generous of you,' said Walter, 'But I have never understood Gerald's obsession with chasing dull, plain maids. After all, he is married to one of the most beautiful women in the country. Mind you, he certainly doesn't waste much time'.

'Gerald can be generous to the maids, and they are pathetically grateful for some little presents he makes. It's probably quite exciting for them too. He's still a very attractive man,' said Caroline.

'If I had a woman like you I certainly wouldn't look elsewhere,' Walter said.

'Well, darling, it's an arrangement that suits us both when I can have an attractive man like you to satisfy me, and Gerald never raises an objection. In fact I know it excites him, thinking about me with other men. And his tastes are really more penny plain that tuppenny coloured. His first experiences were with a maid, and it is where his interests still lie'. She was half sitting now, and he ran the back of his fingers across her cheeks then slid his hand down her neck and onto her breasts.

'Did you want to take off your nightdress?' Walter asked.

'No, I don't want that. Since having children my breasts aren't so firm. I think they are ugly, so I don't want to show them. However, I don't want to get obsessed about that, what about you,' she said, reaching down under the sheets and lifting his nightgown to his waist. 'Well you seem to be ready enough'. She hoisted up her own nightgown and pulled Walter onto her. He started at a slow, gentle pace, gradually increasing the speed as they progressed. He rested his weight on one elbow and reached around to gently stroke her clitoris with the tips of his fingers.

She writhed and bucked, putting a fist against her mouth to stifle the loudest of the noises she was beginning to make. After she came Walter allowed himself to finish. She held him against her chest, his weight pressed hard down against her body, and stroked the nape of his neck.

'My, God, I was looking forward to that. I'd almost forgotten how good you are,' said Caroline, as they separated and she moved across the bed. Moist strands of hair lay across her forehead, the curls unravelling.

'Do you remember that time when I was just fourteen and you were seventeen?' Walter asked.

'Oh, yes,' said Caroline, 'That was very sweet, and you were very willing'.

'What I have always wondered is how you came to learn so much that you could teach me,' Walter said, with a slight shake of the head.

'That is my secret. A woman should always keep some things secret. Whatever I learned, I learned elsewhere. But you really were a very good pupil,' said Caroline. She gave a satisfied sigh and lay her head back on the pillow.

Walter reflected that the memories of Caroline were rather better than the reality. He smiled to think that he had carnal knowledge of both sisters within twenty-four hours. Then he reflected that the act had meant much more with Emily than it had done with Caroline. With Emily he had been her first and only lover. With Caroline, he was just one among many. Could it be that he was falling in love at long last?

SATURDAY 2ND OCTOBER 1909

Walter watched Dorothy leaning over the open bonnet of the Napier car, adjusting some mechanism to her liking. She wore thin brown leather gloves to protect her hands and fingernails from the accumulated oil and dirt. Her neat buttocks were pushed backwards in a suggestive way, their outline visible beneath her butcher blue dustcoat and Walter became somewhat interested. She hummed an indistinct tune as she worked. Her hair was tied back and held by a matching blue mob-cap.

'I would very much like to paint a portrait of you,' said Walter. Dorothy looked up and sideways at him, a few wisps of hair in the way, her eyes half closed in consideration.

'Like this?' she asked, 'And I bet you say the same thing to all sorts of women.'

'Well, I'd rather have you facing me, but the car is very fine, quite sculptural. It would add a good deal of individuality to the portrait,' Walter mused.

'I'm sure you know your own business, but if I am to have my portrait painted, I'd rather have it done away from machinery. Think it perverse if you like, but I hope that there is rather more to me than just a driver,' Dorothy said with a slightly twisted smile.

'Indeed I can believe that,' said Walter, smiling back, 'So how would you like to be painted?'

'I'm not sure that I want to be painted at all. It's never been an ambition of mine. But if I am to have it done, I would prefer that it were done in my very best evening clothes, in some elegant setting,' said Dorothy, a little wistfully.

'If you don't mind me saying so, that sounds a little old fashioned,' Walter commented.

'Then maybe I am just an old fashioned girl. Or maybe I live in an unreal world, the mark of which is how pretty I am and how expensive my dress is, rather than any talent I have,' Dorothy said, with a laugh. Walter laughed lightly in return.

'You really ought to meet a friend of mine. You would have so much in common with her. You could complain about men and the attitudes of society as much as you wish,' said Walter.

'That makes me sound like a Suffragette. But what about this friend of yours? I'm sorry to say this, but you do not strike me as a man who has many women friends. From your words, I should think that you are not enjoying her favours, otherwise your attitude would be rather different,' Dorothy said.

'I really don't want to say much about that,' Walter said, guardedly.

'Oh, come now, I'm sure that you are not at all shy with the ladies,' Dorothy said, and she finished the adjustment she was making. Afterwards she closed the bonnet of the car and removed her gloves. 'Could you help me start the car, please?'

'Right-ho,' said Walter, walking towards the front of the car, 'What do I do?'

'Give the handle a sharp pull clockwise when I ask, and keep your thumbs clear, if you want to keep 'em' Dorothy said. She opened the driver's door, climbed in and set several switches and levers. 'About now would do.' Walter turned the handle, but the engine merely wheezed slightly. Dorothy furrowed her brow and made a few more adjustments.

'Try it again,' she ordered. Walter gave the handle a sharp tug and the engine roared into a rough rhythm, smoke pumping out from the exhaust in acrid clouds. Dorothy made more changes to the controls and the engine started to purr like a contented lion.

'That sounds good,' Walter shouted above the noise of the engine.

'Yes it does, doesn't it?' Dorothy asked rhetorically, 'You know, there is a real art to tuning an engine, and if it doesn't sound right, then it isn't right.'

'Well it sounds good to me. Though I know much more about horses than I do about automobiles,' Walter admitted.

'Well I have to know about automobiles. Driving automobiles is what I do to earn a crust. But what do you do for a living?'

'I paint pictures, and, if I admit it, I'm a gentleman, and gentlemen don't do normal jobs,' Walter explained.

'I used to be a secretary. That's a normal job for a woman, that or mistress. Then Selwyn picked me out because he wanted a pretty face and long legs to show beside his cars. As it turned out, I had a real talent for driving. But I still had to sleep with him in order to get to drive the best cars. You know, darling, you and me, we are quite alike, and I know what you are. You seduce women because you can do it, but you don't much like most of them. I like some men, but when it comes to sexual attraction, the men I like are like you. And it could never work between us. I could never stay with you, nor you with me. Neither of us would have any respect for each other,' said Dorothy, with an air of finality.

'Well, I'll just have to have you as a friendly acquaintance, then,' said Walter, cheerily.

'If you get involved in anything exciting, please think of me and write or telephone. Since I started driving I live for a bit of excitement,' Dorothy purred.

'In that case I think you ought to talk to one of the other guests, Captain Cumming,' Walter said, meaningfully.

'Why's that?' Dorothy asked.

'Because, you might be just the young woman that he is looking for,' Walter laughed.

'I'll consider any reasonable offer,' said Dorothy, returning a smile, 'But I have to go and look at the aeroplane now. I'm not sure that Mr Peters knows enough about engines to get it working properly. I'm not really an absolute expert myself. Still, I'm sure I know a good deal more about high performance engines than our

Mr Peters. In fact. I don't think he's quite the engineer he pretends to be.'

'You may be right,' Walter said thoughtfully, 'I think that he'll be asked a few questions when he's finished his little job. If he isn't a professional engineer, then I'd like to know what he really is.'

◊

Shirl Castle was set on a low hill and was surrounded by extensive parkland. It was approached by a carriage drive of a mile off the road to Leominster. The surface was well maintained and Godiva was not shaken too badly in the Lanchester which conveyed her, but she had to hold onto her hat as it was a blustery day.

There were remnants of a curtain wall and a restored gatehouse to pass through. The main part of the castle had been converted into a family home before the Civil War, and so had escaped the destruction which was visited on so many defendable sites. The rounded towers of weathered red sandstone at the corners were all that remained of the original keep, the interior having metamorphosed into a surprisingly modest sized building, with no more than twelve bedrooms. A small Norman church was situated to the east of the castle, with eighteenth century cupola, clock and box pews for the use of family, guests and, below, the servants. The ancestors of the Mansell-Lacey family had been laid to rest here for centuries. Compared to the size and opulence of Blackleigh Court it seemed to be a modest and approachable house.

The entrance was through an arch in an old tower, ornamented with a portico that had simple Doric columns on either side. It was impressive without being grandiose. A few seconds after she had climbed out of the car and it had driven away she walked boldly up to the front door and yanked at the bell pull. After several long seconds the door was opened by a liveried footman. Godiva explained what her business was and was ushered into the entrance hall, which was panelled with smoke-darkened oak. Portraits of previous Dukes and their ladies and children and dogs were hung at pleasingly random places on the walls. Most of the portraits were very good indeed, though the earlier Dukes looked grim and war-like. Godiva mused that this display of portraiture might explain why Walter had grown up with such a deep love of art.

The footman returned with the Butler, who introduced himself as Jackson. He led Godiva to the library where Professor Knudsen was waiting. This time he rose to greet her and gave a brisk nod of his head while clicking his heels.

'Miss Williams. It is so good to see you again. Please take a seat.' He gestured at one of the library chairs.

'I hope that your work progresses well,' Godiva said, as she sat facing the professor.

'It is almost complete, thank you. It is very peaceful here, with only a small but attentive staff to provide for my needs. Now, do you have that piece of writing you wished me to look at?'

'Yes, indeed. And there was something else that I wished to discuss with you,' Godiva said, trying to formulate a question.

'And what might that be?' Knudsen asked, looking slightly puzzled.

'You mentioned the political situation in Persia, and I wondered if you might explain it further to me,' Godiva said in an innocent tone.

Knudsen laughed curtly. 'The English have installed a corrupt and silly pretender as a king for the Persians. Then they bribed and coerced him into signing away the rights to the oilfield and the site of the oil depot for a miserable pittance. All this they do in the name of the Empire and of the power of the BritishNavy.'

'Then I take it that you do not approve of these actions,' Godiva commented.

'That land is the birthplace of civilization, which to give an exact definition means living in cities. They were the first people to cultivate crops, the first to develop writing, and the first to wage proper war. When we in Europe were living in caves and mud huts painted with woad, they were living in great cities. They may not now be what they once were, but the Persians need to be respected for what they achieved. The arrogance of the modern empire builders is breathtaking. That they should dare to pretend that they are bringing civilization to such a country, which invented the city, when they only wish to exploit the countries for raw materials and for naked power makes me feel rather angry,' Knudsen said in a raised voice, his eyebrows almost dancing.

'And do you include the Germans in that list?' Godiva enquired.

'What empire do the Germans have? Just a strip of arid waste in south west Africa. That the British should so fear them is almost unbelievable. Even the Belgians have more of an empire than the Germans,' Knudsen said with a snort of derision.

'Is that why you passed on all the details of the oil field and the refinery to a German diplomat?' Godiva asked.

'And just what do you mean by that?' Knudsen asked, his bushy eyebrows bristling.

'I know you delivered a package to a Herr Braun, who claims to be a diplomat, but is really a German spy. You used a box in a newsagents in East London. What is more, these seem to be long standing arrangements with Herr Braun to supply him with information. On reflection it seems to me that you are in an ideal position to pass on many of our secrets to the Germans. Do you deny doing it?' Godiva said in a quiet but determined voice.

'Things are always more complicated than they appear at first. If I am to explain to you, I think I need a little air. Will you take a turn around the grounds with me?' Knudsen said, pleasantly.

'By all means,' said Godiva, and they made their way to the front door, where they collected their coats before venturing outside. Knudsen lit his pipe before leaving the shelter of the portico.

They turned a corner in the path by the walled garden, out of direct sight of the house before Knudsen spoke.

'Have you mentioned any of this to the Police?' he asked.

'Yes, or rather I have left a message to be delivered which will arrive this morning, and has probably already been read,' Godiva lied.

'Then it is either very brave, or very foolhardy for you to come here and to confront me like this,' Knudsen said between gritted teeth.

'I thought you would tell me more this way. More than the Police would find out,' Godiva said in an offhand way, 'And besides, I don't think that you will attack me.'

Knudsen made a noise somewhere between a grunt and a cough. He knocked out the ashes from his pipe against the red brick wall, the ashes scattering on the wind and the remaining plug of tobacco glowing as it descended. He then placed the pipe in his overcoat pocket and withdrew a small revolver from the same pocket and levelled it at Godiva's belly.

'Please make your way around this wall, Miss Williams. Unless you can scream extremely loudly and are very lucky you will not be heard. The gardeners are working at the cider press today and there is only a reduced staff in the house.'

'You will be arrested shortly,' said Godiva in a slightly strained tone, 'So I don't think you will gain anything by killing me.'

'Oh, I don't intend killing you, all I intend to do is to keep you out of the way for a little while. Now, tell me, honestly please, just how near are the Police?' Knudsen asked, jabbing the pistol at her and making contact with her bodice.

'There is a meeting of some senior security men at Blackleigh Court. That is less than an hour's drive by car. So you don't have much time.' Godiva blurted out. This was no time for mock heroics.

'Then I have enough time to get away. And if you are not able to tell them what I said, I should have a good start on them,' Knudsen said in a measured tone.

'So you are going to kill me then?' Godiva asked, trying to control the fear in her voice.

'Of course not, not unless you force me to,' said Knudsen in a dismissive way as they reached the corner of the garden, 'Now, please make your way over to the old ice house over there.'

The ice house looked like a partly collapsed brick igloo. It lay close by a steep bank, in the shade of an almost complete double line of ancient chestnut trees. They walked in synchronicity to the structure.

'There is an iron ring on the door. Kindly pull on that, Miss Williams. The handle and hinges are rusty, but have recently been greased, I watched the gardeners do it. It will open easily enough,' Knudsen said, sweetly. He waved the barrel of the pistol in the general direction of the door.

Godiva walked over to the top of the ice house and obeyed the instruction. The trapdoor opened smoothly, though the wet wood was heavy. The smell which rose from the inside was a mixture of damp straw and mould.

'Now, Miss Williams, lower yourself in,' Knudsen instructed.

'But won't I break my legs?' Godiva said, near to panic.

'That is unlikely, Miss Williams. There is a thick mat of straw down there.'

Godiva started to lower herself in gingerly, and had reached the point where she was barely able to support her weight with her hands when Knudsen pushed her hard on the shoulders. She fell though the air and landed with a bump on her backside. She had grazed her elbow quite badly on the frame of the trap door. There may have been plenty of straw, but it was part rotted and it offered less resistance and cushioning that might have been expected.

Godiva may have landed on her buttocks, but it still left her winded and bruised.

'Why are you working for the Germans?' Godiva shouted up, trying to delay her incarceration.

'Because I come from Schlesvig, a part of Denmark which should be in Germany, where it is known as Schleswig. I may have a Danish name, but I have always considered myself to be a German. So the reasons I am doing this now is because I love my country. I am merely being a good German,' Knudsen explained.

'You know you will be captured, don't you?' Godiva shouted up.

'I'm sure I shall be captured eventually, but in the meantime, I shall do as much damage to British interests as I can. Thank you for that information, Miss Williams. It was very kind of you to tell me. You see, I have a colleague at Blackleigh Court at the moment and I need to warn him. I shall get the Duke's chauffeur to take me there. It will be quite a good joke to go to Blackleigh court while the men of your security forces are driving here. Anyway, I am sure that someone will find you in a day or two. You are a brave girl, but you are a little naive and stupid' He closed the hatch door and bolted it shut. Then there was only the muffled sound of the wind and a few stray rays of light creeping in through the cracks in the door. There was no possibility of climbing out.

◊

Lord Randall had received a message from Peters to meet him at the tithe barn to inspect the aeroplane. The machine had been fully assembled and partly tested. Dorothy had helped to tune the engine, though it was still not sounding exactly right, and the finish to the frame looked decidedly rough. When Randall got to the barn it appeared to be deserted. He looked around, and finding no-one there, decided to have a closer look at the aeroplane which was standing outside on the hard surface of Staffordshire blue brick. It was facing the flat field from which the first take-off was to be attempted. The aeroplane looked complete and just about airworthy. The tarpaulins which had protected it during the night had been removed. There was an acrid smell of petrol and hot oil coming from the engine compartment. He walked around the machine, imagining how it would look as it soared in the sky above. He hummed tunelessly as he made this cursory inspection. When he came to the wing struts he twanged the cables, which seemed to be tensioned correctly. The next thing he knew was the sound of approaching feet. Before he could turn around a cloth soaked in chloroform was clamped over his nose and mouth. Within a few seconds he was unconscious.

Peters, with considerable effort, dragged the unconscious man to a hand-cart, lifted the dead weight of the body onto the flat bed of the vehicle and covered it with a blanket. Around the blanket he piled pieces of cloth left over from the covering of the wings and some of the larger wood off-cuts he could find. Pushing the cart in front of him, Peters crossed the cobbled yard and went into a small barn which stood next to the old cow-shed. Peters cleared away the debris from around the prone body and lifted Randall across his shoulder. He then climbed a ladder stair to the small hayloft above. It took a minute for him to regain his breath after this exertion. After tying Randall hand and foot he fixed a piece of cloth across the unconscious man's mouth. Lastly, he piled the hay from the second cutting over Randall's body, hiding him from view. Having completed this part of his work, Peters climbed back down and tidied the hand-cart. He planned to take Randall to a better prison during the evening, when there was less chance of being seen. The clock tower on the hill would be an unlikely place for anyone to search. The motor cycle and sidecar would be his transport. He would lie low until the evening, using his bush-craft in the woods to remain hidden. He had gathered sufficient food and water for a day or two. These items he placed in a knapsack which he had previously hidden in the barn, in a pile of straw by one of the main wooden pillars. The knapsack already held a good knife and a revolver. There was a tile partly missing from the roof of the small barn. Rain water had dripped from there, down the pillar and onto the knapsack in the place it had been hidden. Peters was not used to bush craft in Britain and had failed to wrap the weapons in oil-cloth. The knapsack had been thoroughly soaked and both the knife and the revolver were showing signs of rust.

◊

It was just after eleven in the morning when a large blue Vauxhall car roared up the drive of Blackleigh Court. The driver was in khaki army uniform, with the single stripe of a lance-corporal. Seated in the back was Major Kell, also in full uniform. He got briskly out of the car almost as soon as it stopped, a brown leather attaché case clamped beneath his left arm and swagger stick in his right hand. He took the steps to the front door two at a time, raised his hand to knock at the door, but it was opened before he could strike the mirror-shiny wood. Cumming had opened the door, and he proffered a large hand to be shaken. Kell had to transfer his swagger stick to his left hand before he could provide a right hand to shake. Together they strode into the library and shut the door behind them. Young Gerald Arthur observed the scene from behind a pillar in the entrance hall. He ran to tell Walter about the new arrival.

Walter had just returned from a ride and was leading the horse into the stables where a groom was waiting to unsaddle, water and feed the sweating beast. Young Arthur ran up to Walter and without trying to shout above the sound of shod hooves on the Staffordshire blue brick yard he grabbed Walter's hand and led him, still in riding gear to the library.

'What do you want, Arthur?' Walter asked in hushed tones.

'There's a man come, a soldier, and he looks very important. I think he must have come about that dead man,' Arthur explained, patiently.

'Where is this soldier?' Walter asked.

'He's in the Library with Mr Cumming,' Arthur said.

Thank you, young Arthur. I'll report back to you later. Now, no listening at the door, and I'll bring you some liquorice when I'm done,' Walter said. Arthur stood his ground.

'I don't like liquorice ,' Arthur said.

'Well, what do you like, then?' Walter asked.

'Turkish Delight,' Arthur said, and he ran off.

Walter knocked at the library door. Cumming, opened it a slit, looked out with one eye, nodded and let Walter in.

'Come in, Walter,' said Cumming, 'Major Kell has returned. I've been telling him about what happened. He has a few questions to ask you, and many more for your friend, Miss Williams.'

Walter walked into the room and was met by the unflinching gaze of Kell whose pale eyes were magnified by his wire-rimmed spectacles. He didn't blink.

'What do you know of this Thomas Schmidt man?' Kell asked, chin thrust forward, hands clasped behind his back.

'I came across the name when it was mentioned by a man called Gordon Temple. Temple said that this man, Tommy, had been threatened and beaten up on the orders of someone called Arthur Maundy Gregory. Temple was murdered a couple of days later. I suspect Gregory had something to do with it.' Walter said.

'Why would Gregory do that?' Cumming asked.

'It seems that Schmidt was used by German intelligence in an attempt to blackmail Sir Charles Gurney-Stewart. The Germans thought Charles might be a homosexual, which he isn't. Anyway, this Thomas Schmidt fell for Charles, in a romantic sort of way, and wanted to warn him about the blackmail plot. As to how

Gregory fits into the scheme, I really couldn't tell. My best guess at the moment is that he was working for German intelligence,' Walter explained.

'But why have Schmidt killed?' Kell demanded.

'I suppose, because he could identify the German intelligence officer involved in the plot, Walter said.

'Do you have any idea who this intelligence officer might be?' Kell asked.

'It might be that I do,' said Walter, 'I was asking Lady Emily about the man she talked to at the Palatine Hotel. She gave me a very accurate description. I'm fairly certain the man concerned was my cousin, Siegfried von Braun.'

'I don't know anyone of that name at the German embassy,' Kell said, flatly.

'He's probably using another name,' Cumming added.

'More than likely,' Kell agreed, 'the funny thing is that there is a suspicious character working at the Embassy, and he sometimes uses the name Schmidt. Doesn't look anything like your corpse, though. He's a great thin gangling feller with a duelling scar.'

That's my cousin, Siegfried,' Walter said, impatiently.

'Cousin covers a multitude of possibilities. So what's your exact relationship with this Siegfried von Braun?' Kell asked.

'He's my mother's elder brother's second son,' Walter replied after a few second's thought.

'Where's he come from?'Cumming asked.

'The family is from Brandenburg. They are a big landowning family with some links to the old kings and princes or what-have-you,' said Walter, 'They've got pots of money and are all rabid nationalists,' Walter admitted.

'Let me get this clear,' Kell said, 'This von Braun, calling himself Schmidt is working at the German embassy as a spy. He somehow gets Arthur bloody Gregory to do some dirty work for him. This man, Thomas Schmidt manages to annoy von Braun in some way, and Gregory has him chased away. Now someone has gone and murdered Thomas Schmidt. Look, to save confusion, let's just call him Tommy. So Tommy is murdered here. That means that von Braun or Gregory, possibly, must have had someone come here to do the deed. We need to ask ourselves who that man is, and if he is still here.'

'We've been through this already. All of Lord Randall's servants are to be trusted,' Cumming said.

'Then it must be someone else. Someone who is not a servant,' Kell said.

'The only other people here are guests. I hope you're not suggesting that any of them might have been involved,' Cumming protested.

'So which of the guests are still here, and who has come since I left?' Kell demanded.

'Buchan and Doyle are still here, as is Lady Emily. Lady Caroline and her husband, Gerald and their children arrived two days ago. They brought their servants, but I don't think they can be regarded as serious suspects in this murder. Then there is Miss Dorothy Levitt. She arrived after the body was found, so I don't think it can have been her. That's all, I think,' Cumming said thoughfully.

'No, you've left someone out, said Walter, 'There is the man Peters, the engineer who is putting Lord Randall's aeroplane together.'

'By Jove, you're right. And Peters got a telegram the day before the murder. If he is the man, then the telegram might have been his instructions,' Cumming said enthusiastically.

'I'll go and find him,' said Walter.

'We'll all go in a minute,' said Kell, 'In the meantime I want a word with your friend, Miss Williams. I'm sure she can help fill in some gaps.'

'She went over to my family place, Shirl Castle. It's less than thirty miles from here. She had some business to finish for my father,' said Walter.

'When is she due back? Kell asked.

'I don't know, exactly,' Walter admitted. 'She's not staying here.'

'Dammit! Why did you let her go before I'd spoken to her?' Kell asked, irritably.

'Sorry, old boy. Thought we'd asked all the questions we needed,' Cumming apologised.

'Then I suppose that we had better go and find Peters,' said Kell.

'He should be in the tithe barn in the home farm,' Walter said.

'Lead on, then,' said Kell.

The party of three went through to the back entrance of the house and into the main courtyard. It was a half-mile walk to the home farm from there. Cumming limped badly and had to use a stick.

When they arrived at the tithe barn there was no-one to be found, though the aeroplane looked complete at last. They returned to the Court.

◊

When Lord Randall failed to appear for luncheon there was some comment. He was not the most punctual of men, but he was almost unfailingly courteous, and it was rude not to be present to talk to his guests. After the meal Walter had a question for Caroline and Emily.

'Tell me, what did your father do during the Boer War?' he looked gravely at the sisters in turn.

'He was at the War Office, I think,' Emily replied.

'He had something to do with planning and policy,' Caroline added with more precision, 'Why do you want to know?'

'I'm not sure, really. It's just something nagging at me,' Walter said, his brows furrowed.

'Something about the Boer War, eh?' Cumming said, 'Did you read about that Sergeant they found in the London Underground? He served in the Boer War.'

'Good God!' Kell said, 'Has anyone here spoken to Peters? What would you say his accent was?'

'His accent sounded more like Dutch than Canadian to me,' Dorothy said, 'And you know I've already said that I don't think he's much good as an engineer.'

'Look, it hasn't got into the papers yet, but the man wanted for entombing that sergeant fits the description I have for Peters very nicely, including the accent,' Kell said.

'I don't see what it's got to do with Peters,' Caroline said.

'The Sergeant served in the war. He was at a concentration camp. The man who attacked him wanted revenge for the deaths of his mother and sisters in that camp. Was Lord Randall responsible for the policy on concentration camps?' Kell asked of Caroline.

'Yes, that's right. Charles told me about it. There was some comment about Charles following in his father-in-law's footsteps in the ministry,' Emily said, 'Something about nepotism.'

'I think we'd better organise a search right away for Lord Randall, and for Peters,' Cumming said.

Caroline called for Archer the butler who organised the servants into a search party. Cumming and Kell set out again for the tithe barn. Walter decided to search on horseback. This would allow him to view from a greater height, as well as covering the ground more swiftly. He went to the stables and selected a tall chestnut gelding with a star on its forehead which a groom rapidly saddled for him.

He galloped towards the tithe barn, racing Dorothy, who had taken the Napier car which had been parked at the rear of the house.

Dorothy and Walter arrived first. Walter dismounted and fixed the reins to a chaff cutter which stood beneath the overhang of the roof of the large barn. Dorothy vaulted from the car and ran over to join him. Dodo jumped from the passenger seat and ran in patterns around their legs, barking madly.

'Quiet, Dodo. We've got some work to do,' Dorothy insisted.

Dodo whined and sat, ears back, shaking with excitement.

'Dodo,' Walter said with a sudden flash of inspiration, 'Go find Lord Randall!'

Many generations of breeding had attempted to remove all the behaviour patterns of the wild dog from the Pomeranian, but somewhere within his small body Dodo retained some vestiges of canine instinct. The message took some time to reach his doggy brain, but eventually the hunting behaviour surfaced and he quartered the ground, sniffing and moving his head from side to side, barely above the ground. Next he ran up to the closed door of the small barn and began to scratch at the door. Dorothy opened the door and Dodo charged in. He ran to the base of the stair ladder, raised his head, pointed above and howled. Walter and Dorothy climbed the ladder and found themselves looking at an untidy pile of hay.

'He must be somewhere in the hay!' Walter said, unnecessarily. Both of them bent and moved the top layers away. Within a few minutes Dorothy's hand hit something which felt like fabric. She called Walter over, and together they soon had Lord Randall uncovered. He was just coming round after the chloroform started to wear off. His eyes flicked open. There was a puzzled expression on his face. It was the work of a minute to remove the ropes and the gag and to sit Lord Randall up. He shook his head and stared dazedly around, unable to form words.

Noises outside told them that the others had arrived. Walter called out that Randall had been found and almost ran down the ladder to greet the new arrivals, leaving Dorothy to minister to Randall. Kell and Cumming came in to see for themselves, almost colliding with Walter. Dodo was in a frenzy of excitement, yelping and chasing his tail. Walter reached down to stroke the dog.

'Good boy. Clever boy,' he said to the dog who nipped his hand with blunt, peg-like teeeth. Then he shouted to the new arrivals. 'Hello, you. We've found Randall safe and well, with a little help from our friend Dodo here, who's the hero of the hour. Randall is up the stairs in the hay-loft. He's just coming round now. I think Peters must have used chloroform on him. He was tied up and gagged and hidden under a pile of hay, but, other than that, he seems fine.'

There was a sound of retching from above as Randall's body reacted to the effects of the chloroform. Kell shinned up the ladder to see if he could help.

'Any sign of Peters?' Cumming asked, giving Dodo a thorough stroking. The small dog was positively swaggering around.

'No, I haven't seen hide nor hair of him. I think he might have left,' Walter said.

'I don't think so. It's not the way he works. Remember what he did to that Sergeant down in the underground? No, he intends to come back and finish the job, does our Mr Peters,' said Cumming.

'Are the staff out looking for Peters?' Walter asked.

'Yes, the gamekeeper and the grounds-staff are searching the woods for him. They are getting the beaters involved. They'll find him soon enough,' Cumming said.

'Let's hope so,' Walter said.

Kell and Cumming helped to lower Lord Randall down the stair ladder, and it was obvious that he was now fully conscious, but still very wobbly. He was able to stand, supported by Kell, and he muttered some words of thanks to Walter and to Dodo. Kell and Walter managed to get Lord Randall into the Napier and Dorothy drove him back to the Court. Back at the house Lord Randall was taken to the small sitting room and was set down on a day bed. The family doctor was sent for. Walter mounted the gelding and rode back to the Court at a slow trot. As he approached the main drive he saw another car driving up. This car was familiar. Walter was puzzled at the familiar appearance of the black Renault, until he realised that it was his father's car, and it was being driven by his father's chauffeur. The man in the back was thick-set and bearded and looked nothing like his father. Kicking his horse into a gallop he rode to the front of the house to arrive just as the bearded man was getting out of the car. Walter dismounted and jogged up to the unknown man, who was approaching the steps to the main door. On the way he nodded to the chauffeur who doffed his cap in recognition. The engine was still running.

'Excuse me!' Walter shouted. The man turned to stare at him.

'What?' demanded the bearded man.

'It's just that you have just arrived in my father's car, driven by his chauffeur. From this I must conclude that you have just come from Shirl Castle,' Walter explained.

'That is correct. Now, if you will excuse me I have some urgent business,' the bearded man said. He started to turn again but was interrupted by Walter.

'Are you Professor Knudsen?' Walter asked.

'Yes, I am,' the man agreed in a guarded way.

'A friend of mine was coming to see you today. I was wondering if you had seen her. Her name's Godiva Williams,' Walter said.

'I've never heard of anyone of that name,' Knudsen lied, blushing.

'Oh yes you do! Walter insisted, 'You met her at Imperial College. So why are you lying?' He laid a hand on Knudsen's shoulder.

'Er, yes, I seem to recall the young lady now. But I have not seen her today. Now please let me go. As I said, I have some urgent business to attend to,' Knudsen blustered.

'Who is this urgent business with?' Walter demanded.

'None of your damn business,' Knudsen said and he shook Walter's hand from his shoulder.

'I think it is my business, because, you see, there has been an attack on Lord Randall this very morning. The man who was responsible for the attack is being hunted as we speak,' Walter explained. He was standing right in Knudsen's way.

'I hope Lord Randall was not seriously injured. It was to him I wished to speak,' Knudsen said rapidly.

'He can't talk to you at the moment. Can I help?' Walter asked.

'No, it must be Lord Randall. It is most unfortunate that this has happened. I cannot divulge what I want to say to anyone but Lord Randall. Thank you for your offer, but I cannot talk to anyone else. I hope this fugitive you seek is not dangerous. Where is it that you are hunting for him?' Knudsen said, looking around.

'Over there in the woods,' Walter said, waving his arm to indicate the direction, 'If it is Mr Peters you are referring to.' Knudsen flinched at the mention of the name of Peters.

'Well, as I cannot talk to Lord Randall, I must fetch something from the car for him to read later,' Knudsen said.

Walter watched Knudsen walk to the car and start to speak to the chauffeur. The chauffeur got out of the car and went to look at one of the rear tyres. Knudsen pushed him hard in the back and he fell into the gravel of the driveway. With surprising agility for such a heavy man Knudsen climbed into the driver's seat of the Renault, pushed it into gear and released the handbrake. Walter sprang into the gelding's saddle and set off in pursuit. The car was headed for the edge of the woods away from the direct route to the gatehouse and the gravel of the drive. The horse was initially able to accelerate faster than the car, but had reached top speed as the car continued to accelerate. The wheels cut gouges out of the manicured lawns as Knudsen fought with the steering. The ground was much less even where the lawn ended and he was forced to slow the vehicle to cope with the bumps. This ground did not cause the horse any such problem and Walter began to gain the ground between them at a good rate. There was a hidden ditch, a ha-ha, at the edge of the grassed area. It is a vertical wall on the house side and a sloping ditch on the other side, designed to stop the stock from grazing on the lawns. It was barely visible at ground or standing level until you were very nearly upon it. Knudsen saw the ha-ha at the last moment and attempted to steer away. The narrow wheels of the Renault refused to steer sufficiently and the car lurched over the wall and landed on its' side with sounds of smashing glass and bending metal. Walter's horse leapt the obstacle with ease and landed on the level ground on the other side. Walter wheeled the sweating animal around and dismounted.

Knudsen had knocked his head against the door frame and his scalp was bleeding profusely. Walter ran to the car and tried to drag Knudsen out. The Dane screamed in pain, indicating that he had a broken right arm. The noise of the crash brought a party of beaters out from the woods. They ran over as best they could and helped to haul Knudsen from the car, laying him on the soft moist turf which was lavishly decorated with fresh sheep dung. Meanwhile, the chauffeur had dusted himself off and had raised the alarm at the Court. Cumming was driven up to the scene by Dorothy in the Napier. Kell arrived on a bay mare a few minutes later.

Cumming produced a hip-flask of brandy and used it to revive Knudsen so that he might be questioned. Knudsen coughed slightly at the sting of the brandy in his throat. He sat up, holding a handkerchief to his head with his good hand in an attempt to staunch the flow of blood which was running down his neck and onto his collar. The other arm hung limp by his side.

'Who did you say this fellow is?' Kell asked of Walter.

'His name is Knudsen. He's Danish and a Professor of Geology. He has been staying at my father's place, Shirl Castle, doing some work on the Persian oilfields. My friend, Miss Williams went there this morning to ask him some questions. He denies seeing her, but I know he is lying. When I mentioned Peters' name he got all panicky and tried to drive away,' Walter said, as calmly as he could.

'Is there a telephone at Shirl Castle?' Kell asked in a low voice so that Knudsen could not hear.

'Yes, we had one installed last year. I think I know what you want. I'll call up and see if Miss Williams has been there, and if they saw her leave safely,' Walter said. He mounted the gelding and took a leap back over the ha-ha, which the gelding managed with ease. The gallop to the house only took a minute. The telephone was in the anteroom to the library. Walter jiggled the holder until a female operator came onto the line. He gave the number he wanted. There was some small delay in getting connected, but Walter managed to get through to Jackson the Butler. After brief enquiries Walter learned that Godiva had arrived and seen the Danish gentleman, and that they had gone for a walk in the grounds after this meeting. The Danish gentlemen had mentioned that the lady had left when he asked to use the car, but no-one had seen her leave. Having obtained this information Walter thanked Jackson, replaced the mouthpiece back in its holder, ran out of the house and rode back again to the site of the crashed car. He joined Cumming and Kell in questioning Knudsen.

'What have you done with Miss Williams?' he demanded, grapping the lapels of Knudsen's jacket.

'Nothing. I never saw her,' Knudsen protested.

'Liar. I've just spoken to the Butler and found out that she did come to see you and that you went for a walk in the grounds. No-one saw her after that. What have you done to her?' said Walter, almost spitting out the words.

'I didn't do anything to her,' Knudsen pleaded.

'Just a minute, Lord Walter, I may be able to assist,' Kell said. He leaned over Knudsen and lifted the man's chin so that he could look into the Dane's eyes. 'I imagine that your arm hurts like hell. Now just imagine how much it would hurt if I were to move it a trifle.' He flicked the broken arm with his fingers and the Dane yelped at the pain. 'Now, are you going to answer the question, or do I have to do that again?' Kell asked coldly.

'She's alive and well. I locked her in some building so I could get away safely. I swear I never touched her,' Knudsen said, sobbing and rocking back and forwards.

'That had better be the truth, or I will make it my business to break your other arm. Now tell me why you were coming here, and who it was you came to see?' Kell continued.

'I came to see Peters. I had to tell him that he was about to be found out. He had to get away before he was caught,' Knudsen said.

'What had he come to do?' Kell asked.

'I don't know, they never told me,' Knudsen stammered. Kell flicked the arm once again, bringing a roar of pain from Knudsen. There were tears in his eyes when he spoke again. 'I think he was sent here to spy on some meeting. I don't know the details. He had some personal business as well.'

'Alright, I might believe you. I suppose you ought to see a doctor about that arm. Lucky that one has already been called for Lord Randall,' Kell said.

'What about Peters?' Cumming asked, 'With a diversion like this he's bound to have got away.'

'If Peters' personal business was to kill Randall, then we'd better get back right away,' Kell said decidedly.

'And I need to find out where the Prof here has put Godiva. I'll make another call and send out the search parties,' Walter said. The gelding was getting used to the journey back to the hall by now.

◊

Peters had observed the aftermath of the crash from his hiding place and used the opportunity provided to outflank the beaters and double back to the barn. This was an easy task while those hunting him were engaged in extricating Knudsen from the broken Renault. When he came to the small hay barn he quickly saw that Randall had been rescued. In that case, he decided, his quarry would have been taken to the house. With the disruption caused by the crash many of the servants would be distracted. He should be able to enter the house quite easily and kill Randall before getting away. It wasn't the dramatic ending he had planned, but it would have to do. He loped across to the Court at a steady pace, confident that there would be no-one to see him.

Walter in the meantime had made his second call to Jackson and had instigated the search parties. He gave a description of Godiva to be passed on to the gardeners and gamekeepers. As he was finishing the call the doctor was admitted via the side door in the North wing. Cumbes, the elderly boot-boy, led the doctor to the small drawing room. The footmen had joined the search in the woods and there were few servants about. They passed Walter on the way. Walter had decided to use Randall's Lanchester to get to Shirl Castle, but he needed a driver, and both Randall's chauffeur and Dorothy were back at the site of the crash, along with his father's chauffeur who was grieving at the loss of his own transport. He wandered towards the front door to see if any of these drivers were returning.

Peters saw the doctor arriving, easily identifying him by the bag he carried and guessed the reason for his call. Cumbes had not thought it necessary to lock the door and Peters slipped in without being seen. He followed the doctor at a safe distance, hiding behind a pillar when he saw Walter. As Walter left the main hallway Peters was able to go right up to the door of the small sitting room. He hid in an alcove when Cumbes came out of the door, and he waited a minute while the boot boy returned to his little room. Reaching into the knapsack he retrieved the pistol and unwrapped it from the covering cloth. It felt cold, heavy and damp in his hand. He pulled the hammer of the pistol back and took a deep breath before opening the door. The doctor was standing between him and Randall.

'Get out of the way!' Peters hissed, waving the pistol around. The doctor turned in astonishment and looked at Peters.

'What do you think you are doing?' the doctor said, 'Kindly leave this room, and let me attend to my patient.'

'I told you to get out of the way,' Peters shouted. The doctor did not get out of the way. Peters shot him in the shoulder. The doctor fell down on the floor in a dead faint. Peters walked steadily up to the daybed. He cocked the pistol again and prepared to fire. The rusted chamber of the revolver failed to turn sufficiently to have the bullet line up with the barrel. Randall had sat up, mouth open in horror, unable to speak.

'This is in revenge for my mother and sisters who died in one of the concentration camps you helped to create,' Peters shouted. He raised the pistol and pulled the trigger. There was a metallic click as the hammer came into contact with the mechanism rather than the bullet. Peters swore in frustration and madly checked the revolver to see what was wrong.

Walter had been alerted by the pistol shot and ran back into the house, trying to find the source of the noise. He barged into the small sitting room to find a wild-eyed Peters desperately trying to force the cylinder to move. With a scream of rage and frustration Peters threw the pistol at Walter, who was easily able to duck out of the way. The pistol flew past and shattered a valuable Louis XV mirror. This was to bring some spectacular bad luck to Peters. Shards of silvered glass fell musically to the floor. He saw that Walter was a serious threat and decided on a swift retreat. Running across the room he leapt at and through the closed window. Fragments of glass flew out onto the flowerbeds beyond, shredding the last of the autumnal blooms. After picking himself up, Peters headed around the outside of the house in the direction of the stables. Walter did not attempt to follow directly, and to risk being cut by the glass. Instead he decided to take the shorter route through the house and out the North entrance. Peters, seething with frustration and rage, somehow managed to make a logical decision. He stopped and turned, heading for the front of the house, where there must be vehicles waiting to help in his escape. The only means of transport, however was the gelding which Walter had ridden so much recently. Peters mounted the horse and set out for the Tithe Barn, where his main means of escape lay. Walter had arrived at the stables and saw Peters galloping across to the Home Farm. He would need another mount, and quickly, but none were saddled or ready. There was nothing for it but to pursue Peters on foot. Walter was a sprinter rather than a long-distance runner. He would have to pace himself carefully.

Dorothy had driven back to the front of the court in the Napier where she dropped Kell off. The pair were surprised to see a rider who was not Walter galloping away from them. A short while later they saw Walter's attempt to follow on foot. Dorothy set off to help. She drew up alongside Walter and encouraged him to climb onto the running board on the passenger side of the Napier. As she did so she slowed too much and the engine stalled. It took a minute to get the car restarted.

When they got to the Home Farm they found the main gate closed. It was a strong and solid metal gate, and Dorothy could not risk attempting to drive through it. Walter leapt from the running board and nimbly vaulted the gate. Peters had been priming the engine of the aeroplane and fixing all the controls into the starting position. He tried hard to remember what Dorothy had told him about the sequence required to fire the engine up. Everything was prepared, but he needed the helmet, goggles and gloves which were in the barn. He ran off to fetch them. At the same time Walter was running across the yard.

Walter launched himself at Peters' hips in a full bloodied rugby tackle. A second later Peters and Walter were wrestling on the ground. Peters managed to kick Walter painfully on the shin, causing him to slacken his grip enough for Peters to rise to his feet first. He caught Walter a glancing blow on the chin with his knee as he attempted to rise. Had the blow been square on instead of glancing it would have shattered Walter's jaw, but it only caused him to roll on the ground and somehow stagger to his feet without further mishap. Peters was running once again, and now Walter was winded, pained and slightly dazed. Somehow he broke into a run, and, as though he were attempting to stop a try in the dying seconds of a match, he managed to get into a desperate run with a ten yard gap between himself and the engineer. Peters rounded a corner by the garages with Walter gaining on him with every step, both men breathing heavily. As Walter rounded the corner the top half of a split stable door was opened and flung into his face. Walter collapsed onto the Staffordshire blue brick surface of the yard, already unconscious. Peters kicked him in the ribs, just for luck, and made for the aeroplane.

Dorothy had manoeuvred the Napier around the tight corners of the home farm and into the yard. Seeing Walter lying on the ground she stopped the car, jumped out and ran to him. She went down on her knees to attend to him. His nose was broken and a trickle of blood was coming from the left corner of his mouth. The blood was coming from a minor but painful wound inside his cheek caused by Peters' knee. Dorothy cradled Walter's head in her lap and dabbed the blood away with a grubby cloth she had been using to wipe the car's glasswork.

While this was happening Peters had reached the aeroplane and was preparing for takeoff. It took him three attempts to fire up the engine. He had to swing the propeller then run around and adjust the fuel supply from inside the plane. With the engine running smoothly Peters removed the chocks from under the wheels. This done, the plane began to move under its own power, and Peters had to walk briskly to keep up and then to climb into the cockpit. There was a slight slope down to the flat field which had recently been used as a cricket pitch for the estate workers. The wind was a steady westerly, ideal for takeoff and Peters opened the throttle as far as it would go before making the necessary adjustments to the pitch of the wings. The plane lurched and bounced across the outfield and the cricket square, gaining speed and vibrating in every strut and wire. In a very short time he was airborne, headed west towards the high hills of the Shelseys.

Walter had regained some mild form of consciousness and was looking into the depth of Dorothy Levitt's eyes with a mixture of admiration and confusion. As his wits returned he was able to mutter the simple but effective phrase, 'Stop him!'

Dorothy helped Walter into a sitting position, his back against the garage wall and disappeared around the corner. Within a few seconds she had the mighty Napier re-started and was reversing it into the yard. She caught the edge of the rear left mudguard on a corner of a wall as she turned at full lock. Walter staggered to his feet and had his hands on the passenger door before she could drive off.

'Get in, the, damn you!' Dorothy snarled, and a slightly shaky Walter climbed in as best he could. Dorothy swung the Napier onto the drive, headed for the main road. She turned left at the end of the drive and headed towards the Shelseys, keeping half an eye on the aeroplane. Walter hung on as best he could.

'Look in my bag,' said Dorothy, over the roar of the wind. Walter felt mildly embarrassed at rummaging in a lady's bag, but complied just the same. Near the bottom was a small revolver.

'What have you got a gun for?' Walter shouted above the engine and wind noise.

'Driving alone,' said Dorothy. 'Some men get the wrong idea if they see a young woman without a man. They might try to rob me, or worse. A girl has to protect her honour.'

Though small the gun was heavy, and Walter turned it in his hand to get used to the feel and balance of the weapon. In the distance they could make out the aeroplane. It was trying desperately to gain height, but in the lee of the hill the wind had dropped and the engine was not firing evenly just when it needed to produce maximum power. Much as a buzzard does, the pilot was banking and wheeling, looking for a thermal or a steady wind which would enable the craft to lift sufficiently. Dorothy was driving like a demon without apparent care for her own life or Walter's or anyone else who might be using the road. They passed the Hundred Inn at a fearful pace, startling a local drunk who was attempting to cross the road, and turned a sharp left up the hill in the direction of Bromyard. It was a mark of her skill that neither the turn nor the increasing steepness of the hill caused Dorothy to slacken her pace much. Then, as they crested a false summit, the aeroplane, unable to gain the height needed to clear the hill, veered in their direction. It crossed the road just a few yards ahead and fifty feet above them.

Walter fired the revolver twice in the general direction of the aeroplane, but the combined movements of the two vehicles and the shortness of the barrel of the gun meant that any accuracy achieved was more due to luck than judgement. Perhaps it was a shot, more likely it was due to some mechanical failure or an error by an inexperienced pilot, but suddenly the aeroplane seemed to stall in the air, and the nose fell towards the earth. With a desperate effort Peters turned the sick machine and directed it to a steeply sloping field in which some sheep were grazing. His only alternative would have been to crash into an unforgiving stand of mature beech and oak trees. The aeroplane came to ground with the noise of cracking struts and ripping fabric. The wooden propeller had ripped into the turf and shattered. One of the wheels was torn off, causing the aeroplane to lurch madly and swing around in a tight arc. Dorothy managed to guide the car into the side of the road near a cottage, the slope helping the brakes to work. Only remembering to put the handbrake on at the last second, Dorothy fairly leapt from the car and chased after Walter who was already sprinting across the field, having vaulted over the gate. As he reached the stricken craft Walter approached the stationary wreck cautiously, gun in hand. Peters was groaning in pain, both his legs having been crushed in the crash.

Walter pulled the shattered remains of the cockpit apart with his bare hands. In truth the frame was so shattered that it required little effort. With Dorothy's help he was able to drag Peters from the shattered remains of the aeroplane and lay him on a soft bank of turf. He was groaning feebly. After a few minutes they were joined by Cumming and Doyle, who had driven to the spot in Randall's Lanchester. Doyle remembered his medical training and took charge of the care of the injured man. There seemed no fight left in Peters. He lay on the ground, hardly registering the pain he must have been suffering, and looking glassy-eyed at some distant horizon. Cumming knelt on the ground close to Peters and attempted what was more of a debriefing than an interview.

'Mr Peters, you have failed in the mission you set yourself. Lord Randall is in perfect health. He is a little upset by you trying to kill his doctor, though. You are seriously wounded, but you are lucky. Mr Doyle is a qualified physician and will be able to help you. Having said that, they will almost certainly hang you for several murders and the attempted murder of Lord Randall and his doctor. We know you killed Thomas Schmidt and another man, Gordon Temple. You also illegally imprisoned Sergeant Murphy. We will be putting together a dossier of your movements and those of your associates. As for what you did to ex-Sergeant Murphy and what you tried to do to Lord Randall, well, I understand your motive for revenge. But why did you kill Herr Thomas Schmidt, who was surely no threat to you.'

'I was ordered to do it,' Peters said quietly and slowly.

'Who ordered you?' Cumming asked.

'It was the German, the one from the embassy, that man's cousin,' Peters pointed a finger at Walter.

'Are you going to arrest Siegfried?' Walter asked, having overheard the last remark.

'If we can catch him,' Cumming replied, 'but he'll most likely be on his way out of the country by now. Probably the best we can do is to lodge a formal complaint at the embassy, but they will, of course, deny everything.'

'I don't think he'll be invited back to visit the Castle,' Walter said.

'I'm sorry about the boy,' Peters said in a near whisper, 'I only wanted to take personal revenge, but I needed their help, and that was part of the price they demanded.'

'Were you sent to report on the meeting we had at Blackleigh Court?' Cumming asked in a soft tone.

'That was the main reason I came here. It didn't do much good. Von Braun got the date wrong. By the time I arrived the meeting was already mostly over. There wasn't anything to report back about. He's not a very good spy, is he?' Peters wheezed.

'You know, once we worked out that you had changed your name from the Dutch spelling, "Pieters", you really were quite easy to track. You have helped us, inadvertently, to round up most of von Braun's network of spies,' Cumming said.

'You got the Professor?' Peters asked.

'Oh, yes. He is busy not talking to us at this very moment. But he will talk in time.'

'He's a soft man,' Peters said with a cackle of pained laughter, 'He looks like a Viking, but he squeals like pig. You'll have him talking with no effort at all. He was even worried about some girl asking questions.'

'What girl do you mean?' Cumming asked.

'He means Godiva,' said Walter, 'And the next job for us is to find her. If Knudsen has harmed her in any way I will break his other arm. That's just for starters.'

'I saw the crashed car. He was lucky to have only broken his arm,' Peters said.

'My father is going to be really annoyed when he finds out how Knudsen crashed his car,' Walter said grimly.

'Is that all you care about?' Peters said with a pained laugh.

Walter turned to Dorothy, who had been applying more rouge and powder to her face with the aid of a compact and mirror, trying to undo the weathering caused by the drive.

'Dorothy, could you get me to my father's place, it's about twenty five miles away?' Walter asked.

'Not enough petrol, I'm afraid, said Dorothy, 'the Napier positively drinks the stuff.'

'There's a couple of cans of petrol in the Lanchester,' said Doyle, 'You could use that.' He jogged over to the stately car, which was parked behind the Napier. Dorothy followed him.

Between them they lifted the cans from where they were fixed on the running board, carried then across and half filled the tank of the Napier. Walter had left Peters in the care of Cumming and walked briskly up to join them.

'That's easily enough to get us there,' said Dorothy. She turned to face Walter, 'Will there be any petrol at the Castle?'

'Bound to be,' said Walter, 'There's a big tank of it in the garage. There isn't a decent supply for miles, otherwise.'

'Well come on, then,' Dorothy insisted. She jumped into the driver's seat of the Napier. Walter was getting used to the routine of starting the Napier and it fired up immediately. He climbed into the passenger seat and unfolded his long legs.

'Which way?' Dorothy demanded.

'Towards the start of the hill-climb course,' Walter answered, 'I'll direct you from there.'

Dorothy swung the car left up the last big climb of the hill. They made much steadier progress on this journey, trying to protect the fuel load and to keep the car going. They climbed briefly to the summit of the hill, then made a long twisting descent to the flat land by the edges of the river Teme, which they crossed over on a wide iron bridge. There was a long straight hill shortly afterwards, but the Napier seemed to relish the challenge and roared up at great speed. After the summit of the hill the road became much more winding. They had to avoid a couple of cyclists and a farm cart carrying dung. In very little time they had come to the small market town of Bromyard. From there they turned right onto the serpentine A44 trunk road that could take the traveller all the way from Woodstock to Aberystwyth. At Leominster they had to negotiate the narrow streets before heading north and west to Shirl Castle.

The Napier pulled to a halt by the main entrance with gravel spraying from the wheels. Walter had been thinking of possible hiding places during the drive, working out a list of possible areas to search. A footman was hurrying from the main entrance to see who had come so dramatically into the quiet environs of the Castle. He recognised and greeted Walter and led him to Jackson, the Butler, who had known Walter almost from birth and still spoke to him as though he were seven years old.

'Welcome, Mr Walter, It is very good to see you. We've started the search parties for the young lady who came here earlier. The men were brought back from the cider press and are looking around all the areas at the back of the house. I'm afraid the house is a bit disorganised, and we will need a little time to prepare for you and your guest. May I be so bold as to ask who this young lady is?'

'My chauffeuse, Jackson, Miss Levitt. And it is good to see you, too. May I ask when you last saw the Danish professor? It is rather urgent.'

'He left in the Renault around lunch time, about twelve thirty, I believe, Mr Walter,' Jackson said, 'If you don't mind me mentioning it, Sir, you seem to have damaged your nose.'

'I know that, Jackson. Now, when did you last see the young lady who visited him?' Walter asked.

'Professor Knudsen told me that she had left before he went himself.' Jackson replied.

'And you didn't see her leave?' Walter asked.

'Oh no, Mr Walter. Professor Knudsen told me she had left on urgent business when he asked for the car. I thought it rather curious, because she had arrived in Lord Randall's car only an hour earlier, and that car had left immediately afterwards, so I have to presume that she left on foot.'

'Did you instruct the gardeners to look for her?' Walter asked, getting rather exasperated.

'Of course I did, Mr Walter. I did it just after you telephoned. They were making cider and I had to interrupt them. They looked all around, but they didn't find her.'

'Tell me, when was the last time she was seen, Jackson?' Walter asked.

'Albert, the footman, told me he had seem them going for a walk sometime after eleven o' clock.'

'Which way were they going?' Walter asked.

'I really couldn't say, Mr Walter. I shall ask Albert.'

Albert, it turned out, was the footman who had just greeted Walter. He trotted over as soon as Jackson called his name.

'Albert, kindly tell Mr Walter the direction the Professor took when he went for a walk with the young lady this morning.'

'Well, Mr Jackson, it was in the direction of the walled garden. I was polishing the boots, and I saw them from the boot-room window,' Albert said with a touch of pride.

'Albert,' said Walter, 'you must know that the young lady has gone missing. I want to find her as soon as possible, before it gets dark. Please go and fetch anyone who might be available, cooks, maids, anyone, I know that there aren't many staff here, but find anyone who is. Get them to search all the garden buildings, the sheds, the greenhouses, the store rooms, everywhere. Jackson can you help organise that. I'm going to the gardens now.'

Walter strode away and collected Dorothy from the environs of the car and asked for her help in the search for Godiva. He led her to the walled garden. There were three gardeners who were full-time staff. The Head Gardener, Preece, appeared from a shed where Walter had hidden as a child.

'Mr Walter, Sir. The garden isn't really fit for being looked at in this season,' he protested.

'This isn't an inspection. I want to know if you saw the guest, the professor, or a young lady this morning.'

'We were all working on the cider press this morning, Sir. Then Mr Jackson sent William the stable boy over to tell us to look for this young lady. That was some time ago, and we looked every place we could think, but we didn't find any trace of her. The others have gone for a cup of tea. Would you like me to get them to look a bit further afield, as far as the chestnut walk? If it's important, I'm sure they won't mind being interrupted. I'm sure they'll do the best they can.' Preece replied. By this time some other servants were arriving from the direction of the house. Walter raised his voice to talk to them.

'If you could pay attention,' he called loudly, 'We are looking for a young lady who has gone missing. She is probably in one of the out buildings or store rooms. I want you to look in every place you can think of around the house.'

'How far do you want us to go, Sir?' a bold scullery maid asked.

'Not very far. No more than ten minutes walk from the house.'

'How about the stables?' asked a groom.

'Of course. And the apple store and the hay loft. Anywhere you can think of, including in the house. Organise yourselves into groups looking where you know best,' Walter said.

'What does the young lady look like?' one of the maids asked.

'She is quite tall, with red hair, and she dresses in a rather modern way,' Walter said, 'Any other questions?'

'What about the ice house?' the scullery maid asked.

'Of course,' said Walter, a little irritably, 'look there as well. Now, go to it, before it gets dark.'

There was an excited buzz among the servants. This was the most interesting thing that had happened for months, and was a good opportunity to get away from the tedium of their usual duties. They were about to disperse when Walter remembered another detail.

'The young lady's name is Godiva,' he shouted, 'you may wish to call out her name, in case she can reply.' There was some giggling from the maids at the name being said.

Walter was searching in the tool sheds in the walled garden, which were out of sight from the greenhouses. Everything was neat and orderly, with just a slight covering of soil dust as a reminder that these tools were used in the garden. A tarpaulin covered a small mowing machine, but Godiva was not to be found. A cry came from outside of the garden and the bold scullery maid ran into the garden. Walter walked from the tool shed, dreading what might have been found.

'She's in the ice house,' the maid blurted out.

'Is she alive?' Walter demanded.

'Yes, yes. But she can't get out. We need a rope or something,' the maid almost shouted.

'I'll fetch the long ladder,' Preece said, 'it's behind the greenhouse.'

Walter and the maid ran to the ice house. She had managed to prise the hatch open and Godiva's voice could be heard echoing from within. She was singing a suffragette anthem lustily, appreciating the acoustics of the chamber she had been imprisoned in, and the relief of immanent rescue. Walter leaned over the hatch to see how his friend was.

'Are you alright, old thing?' he asked.

'Mostly fine. A bit bruised, but nothing that won't mend. Can you get a ladder or something, I'd rather like to get out, if you don't mind,' she said.

'There's one on its way,' said Walter. The ladder was carried over by two gardeners just a few seconds later. They were followed by the whole search party, come to see the rescue.

The ladder was lowered down into the chamber, with Godiva being instructed to move out of the way during this process. Within a matter of seconds she was back on the surface, looking a little dirty, but otherwise unharmed. She gave a rough embrace to Walter and patted the nearest gardener on the back.

'Oh, Walter, what's happened to your nose?' she asked, looking at the mis-shapen lump where his once aquiline nose had been.

'I'll tell you all about it in a little while,' Walter said.

'Where's the girl who found me?' she asked. The bold scullery maid, a plain girl with a stained apron, was pushed forward. Godiva shook her warmly by the hand. 'Thank you so very much; I am in your debt. And I shall make sure that you get rewarded for this.'

'Back to your duties, now,' said Jackson, 'The excitement is over.'

The servants returned, grumbling, to their usual tasks, leaving Walter, Dorothy and Godiva standing by the side of the ice house. Walter introduced the two young women to each other. Two independent and attractive women with exceptional skills but very different attitudes to life. When Godiva learned who Dorothy was she became almost gushing. Before long Dorothy was offering to teach Godiva to drive. The trio made their way back to the servant's entrance to the house, from where they were escorted to the small sitting room. Godiva was able to clean up in one of the guest bedrooms. She arrived back in the sitting room a few minutes later to find a sumptuous tea awaiting her. Jackson had made a telephone call to Blackleigh Court, telling Archer the Butler that the missing young lady had been found, safe and well. Walter and Dorothy had waited for Godiva before starting on the food, and they all did good service to the spread of sandwiches, scones and cakes, all washed down with lashings of good strong tea. Their appetites had been sharpened by their adventures and all had missed their lunches. Godiva was most curious to learn what had happened during the day, and how they had managed to find her. They had hardly started telling their stories when they were interrupted by Jackson.

'Very sorry for interrupting, Mr Walter, but there was a telephone call for you which I have answered. It was from two gentlemen who are staying in Blackleigh Court. It was a Mr Kell and a Mr Cumming.

'I'd better call back and let them know all is well,' Walter said. 'In the meantime, could you get some more tea and cakes please, Jackson.'

Certainly, Mr Walter,' Jackson replied.

Walter returned the telephone call and managed to get in touch with Cumming. After telling him of Godiva's recue he enquired after the health of Knudsen and Peters.

'Knudsen's fine, and very talkative,' Cumming's voice crackled over the telephone, 'Peters died shortly after you left. Probably saved the bother of sending him to the gallows.'

'I'm sorry about that. Despite everything, I quite liked the fellow,' Walter said.

'Just to let you know, there was a very interesting telegram in Peters' pocket. They seem to have had some source of information in London. We can talk more about that later. Now, to change the subject, have you had your nose fixed, yet?' Cumming asked.

'Not yet, I'll send out for a doctor now, and hope that no-one shoots him,' Walter said, grimly.

'Then I suggest that you spend the night at the Castle, and all come back together tomorrow morning, refreshed and rested. We'll have a long chat and try to piece together exactly what happened and why,' Cumming said.

'Right. I'll see you tomorrow, then,' Walter said. He put the telephone down and called for Jackson.

'Jackson, please set the maids to making up a couple of rooms. The young ladies will be staying for the night. If you could arrange a bit of dinner, that would be splendid. As you remarked earlier, someone has done something rather nasty to my nose. It is hurting a bit, so fetch a doctor, will you? Oh, and if you know where my father is, I think I'd better get a message to him. Someone has rather bent the Renault. But not to worry, young Pugh wasn't in the car at the time.'

'Certainly, Mr Walter. I'll make all the arrangements. I'm afraid that we don't have a proper dinner arranged, and the cook is on her holidays. I'm sure we'll manage well enough,' Jackson said with a slight nod and he went about his business.

Walter returned to the Drawing Room and continued with his tea.

'Now tell me all about what happened to your nose,' Godiva enquired.

'Well, I had a bit of an accident with a stable door. Actually, we've had quite an exciting time ourselves,' Walter said modestly.

'Yes, Dorothy's been telling me about it,' Godiva confirmed.

'You must tell Godiva what happened in your own words. Just to let her know that I'm not just telling a story,' Dorothy said with a smile.

'Alright, then,' said Walter. He then told what he could remember of the events of the day. Godiva was a suitably receptive audience. She made all the right noises in all the right places. Dorothy filled in the gaps when Walter ran out of words.

'Poor Walter,' Godiva said, 'your nose really is a bit swollen and bent. Let's hope it doesn't ruin your good looks.'

'I think it will make him look even more dashing. There's nothing like an insignificant but visible little war-wound to give a bit of interest to a man's face,' Dorothy said, teasingly.

The doctor arrived at this time and Walter went into the library where the examination of the nose took place.

'You really ought to have had this attended to as soon as you could after the injury happened,' the doctor scolded.

'Well, I've been a little busy since then,' Walter said.

'Let's see what we can do about it. I must warn you that your nose may never look quite the same as it did before. Now, prepare yourself, this may hurt a little,' the doctor warned. He clicked Walter's nose back into approximate position. This act caused Walter more pain than he would have thought possible, but the steady throbbing he had been suffering for some hours was instantly removed. The pain was sharper, and Walter was given a dose of opiate to relieve this symptom. He slept very soundly that night.

Sunday 3rd October 1909

Walter woke late the next morning dulled by the opiate that had helped him to sleep, still feeling as though he had cotton-wool between his ears. It took several cups of strong coffee at breakfast to kick-start his brain. Dorothy and Godiva had breakfasted earlier and were now out on the main drive, with Godiva being given some basic instruction on how to drive a car. She was proving to be an able pupil and Dorothy had allowed her to drive in a straight line up and down the drive at low speed in the Napier. When they returned to the Castle they continued to laugh and talk, walking arm-in-arm into the morning room where Walter was attempting to write a letter to his father, explaining what had happened to his beloved Renault.

There was the sound of a car arriving outside. Dorothy, looking through the window, identified it as Randall's Lanchester. There were two chauffeurs in the front, Randall's man was driving and the Duke's man was beside him, hitching a ride back. In the back of the car were Kell and Cumming.

Randall's man opened the door and stood in a rigid posture of attention while his passengers made their way to the front door. Jackson led the gentlemen into the morning room. Cumming sat in an armchair and looked benignly around the room and at Walter and the young women.

'I hope everyone is feeling rested. We've come to take you back to Blackleigh Court. Miss Williams, you are now formally invited to join us. We have arranged a room for you,' he said.

'I'm afraid that I haven't any suitable clothes with me,' Godiva said.

'Don't worry,' said Dorothy, I've got a few spare dresses, and if they won't do there are another couple of young women who would be happy to help,'

'Yes, I'm sure that Caroline and Emily would be willing to lend you a dress,' Walter said.

Kell had sat on a hard chair. He sat ram-rod straight, and had placed his hat upturned on his lap, with his gloves inside. He looked towards Walter.

'How's the nose, now?' he asked in crisp tones.

'It's still a bit sore,' Walter said, gently touching the swollen bridge of his nose with the index finger of his left hand.

'Had the doctor take a look at it, did you?' Kell continued.

'Yes, he came last night. He clicked it back into place. That hurt like hell.' Walter admitted.

'Just thought I'd mention that you all did brilliantly yesterday. Absolutely top-rate job,' Cumming said.

'It was terrific fun,' Walter said, 'I wouldn't have missed it for the world.' Kell coughed in a slightly disgusted way.

'Thing is, we need to tie up a few loose ends. So we need to talk to all of you. So, if we could make a start, we can get back to Blackleigh Court and begin there,' Cumming urged.

'I'll need to get the Napier back there,' Dorothy said, standing up.

'Of course,' said Kell, 'You can take Miss Williams with you. Lord Walter can ride with us.'

'I'll need to put some more petrol in the tank, first' Dorothy said.

'I'm sure my father wouldn't mind. In fact I know he'd be delighted. I'll get Preece to fill it up now,' Walter said. He went to the door, called for Jackson and gave the necessary instruction.

'Well, I'd better get myself ready,' Dorothy said, leaving the room and going to fetch her bags.

'Me, too,' Godiva agreed, following Dorothy at a trot.

'How's Knudsen doing?' Walter asked.

'Complaining of his treatment. Give me a couple of hours to interrogate him and he'll sing a very different tune,' Kell said, sourly.

'More importantly, how's the doctor?' Walter continued.

'Oh, I'm sure he'll mend, in time,' Cumming said, 'Gave Lord Randall a nasty jolt, mind, seeing him shot like that. His nerves weren't so good at the time.'

'So Randall is mostly alright after all that's happened to him?' Walter asked.

'Randall's not really a man of action. I imagine he'll have a few nightmares. Physically, he's absolutely fine. He's acting a bit frightened at the moment, but I'm sure he'll get over it,' Kell answered.

'Last thing,' Walter said, 'What's happening with my father's Renault? Only I'm writing a letter to my father to let him know what happened to his precious car. Heaven only knows how he's going to react when I tell him.'

'We've had it dragged off to Randall's garages. It might be repairable, but we'll have to get some expert in to look at it. I hope your father is feeling forgiving. After all, it was all in the cause of the Empire,' Cumming explained.

Dorothy and Godiva appeared at the door, dressed in their outdoor clothes. Godiva had her travelling bag with her.

They trooped out of the front door of Shirl Castle and into the two vehicles, bidding their farewells to Jackson, who held the door open for them.

Dorothy set out first, being in the faster car, and the Lanchester followed on at a more leisurely pace.

'I suppose we might as well start the session properly now,' Cumming said to Walter, above the noises of the engine and the rush of the wind.

'What do you mean?' Walter asked.

'We normally do a sort of debrief when someone has done some work. The idea is to find out what happened, what you did, and what we need to do to do it better in the future,' Kell replied, 'But in this case we saw most of it happen.'

'Yes, I thought you knew all about what happened,' Walter said.

'So in this case, we thought we might have a different kind of word with you,' Cumming said.

'The thing is,' Kell started, 'You started doing a simple little job for my department, and ended up doing a very different job for Cumming here.'

'And an excellent job it was, too,' Cumming chipped in.

'Having said that, you didn't exactly fulfil the terms you were hired under. You gave my man Scrivener a few sleepless nights. However, you showed a certain aptitude for seeking the truth, and great determination and drive. Yet, somehow, I doubt that you would be much use to me in the sort of work that I do, which requires a greater degree of discretion than you possess,' Kell continued. Walter looked slightly relieved.

'On the other hand, you gingered things up considerably. That's exactly what I am after. Other people would leave a hornet's nest well alone. You go right up to it and biff it with a stick. The thing is, I need people like you to go around and stir things up a bit. Just the sort of thing to have the opposition chasing their tails. So I want you to come and work for me. It's not terribly well paid, but it is terrific fun. If you'll consider doing it I'll make the arrangements straight away. You'll need a little bit of training, but as far as I'm concerned, you're very nearly the finished article. Well, what do you think of it?' Cumming said.

'You're offering me a job?' Walter queried, almost unable to believe what he was hearing.

'Absolutely. I think you'd make a quite wonderful agent. Perhaps we'll get you some kind of diplomatic cover. Do you think your father would be happy if you were a diplomat?' Cumming said.

'I imagine he would be very happy indeed. He might even restore my allowance. It's not quite what I was supposed to do, but it should do as well as the cavalry. As it would get me out of the country, it should be even more popular with him. Yes, I think on balance he would be very happy,' Walter mused.

'And you'll have to have some kind of military or naval rank,' Kell added.

'That ought to please my father even more,' Walter said with a laugh, 'though I've always tried to avoid being in the Army.'

'Well, that is excellent, really excellent. You can be in the Navy, just like your friend, Scrivener. Now I need to find out where we can sharpen your skills. Do you shoot?' Cumming asked.

'Well, I can shoot well enough, but frankly, I'd rather leave the pheasants and grouse well alone,' Walter said.

'Actually, I meant pistol shooting, and rifle as well. You'll need to be really proficient with guns. It's sometimes necessary to shoot people in our job,' Cumming said.

'I've done some deer stalking, and I'm a pretty useful shot with a rifle, but I don't know anything about pistols. In fact, I'm not very happy with the idea of killing people. I'm not absolutely sure that I could shoot anyone,' Walter mused.

'Just think how it would be if it was a case of shooting someone who is taking pot-shots at you. You'd be amazed how well that concentrates the mind. I'm not asking you to become a full-time assassin, I just want you to be able to look after yourself. In the same sort of line, I want you to learn some tricks of the wrestlers and such people, so you can silence someone without having to use a gun or knife. That really is terribly useful, especially when you are prowling round,' Cumming said in a rapid stream of words.

'Alright, I suppose I could do that. Is there anything else I need to learn?' Walter asked, feeling slightly dazed by the turn of events.

'The last two things are using codes and pick-locks. We can teach you those skills in a trice. You'll need to know how to send a message in code and how to decode messages sent to you. It's also very useful if you can get into closed rooms, and it's not a particularly difficult art. If you prove a really good pupil, we'll show you how to crack a safe. All in all, we'll be setting you up as a most complete criminal. So how would you like to become a thief, a cheat, a liar and a thorough bounder?' Cumming asked, with a slightly cruel grin on his face.

'I'm not really sure, but if it's the same sort of thing as I've already been doing, then I've no doubt that it would suit me splendidly,' Walter replied, smiling.

'We'll have to find some reason for you to be moving around Europe. I believe that you are a bit of an artist, so I suggest we have you working for some art dealership. There are so many powerful men who fancy that they are art collectors. If you could deal with these men, negotiate to sell or buy some pictures, you could get close to the seat of power. Then you could seduce their secretaries or wives and learn the real story in some pillow talk,' Cumming said, grinning at Walter.

'You seem to have a high opinion of my abilities in that line,' Walter said with a wry smile.

'I've seen you operate. You have a genuine talent. It would be a pity to waste that. Right, that's settled then,' Cumming said, and he settled back in his seat.

'Lord Walter, how do you think Miss Williams would react if I were to offer her some employment in my department?' Kell said, turning to Walter.

'I'm not at all sure. She might think it very fine, or she might get on her high horse and absolutely refuse. It all depends on the way you ask her. If you take a tip from me, you'll try to intrigue her with some interesting puzzle for her to solve. That way, she'll do the job first and you can tell her that you're employing her afterwards,' Walter answered, feeling a little disloyal to Godiva.

'Thank you for that. I was wondering what sort of line to take with her. I'm sure we can come up with the right sort of puzzle, if I think about it for a while. Miss Williams has just the right set of skills for me. She's meticulous, steady and has a great nose for trouble. With her in research, I'm sure we'll be able to find us a few foreign agents,' Kell said with a note of determination in his voice.

'Good luck with that, she really can be a little prickly at times. Especially about women's suffrage,' Walter said, with a slight smile.

'I'm well aware of Miss Williams' political beliefs,' Kell said, patiently.

'Don't you think that rather disqualifies her?' Walter asked.

'Not really, because the one factor I didn't mention is that she is extremely discrete,' Kell said, 'Unlike you.'

'Not my strongest point,' Walter agreed, looking down modestly. The car bounced and lurched around a series of corners.

'How about Miss Levitt, what do you think of her?' Cumming asked, changing the subject.

'How do you mean? In what way do I think of her?' Walter asked, puzzled.

'How do you think she'd do as an agent?' Cumming returned.

'I think she is an absolute gem. In fact, I've never met a woman like her. On the other hand, I wouldn't want her getting into any danger,' Walter answered, after a few seconds of consideration.

'But just think of it, she's always dashing around, going to motor races and things. What an absolutely perfect reason for her to be everywhere and to carry little messages. She could do all sorts of useful jobs for us,' Cumming said, enthusiastically, 'in fact I've been considering approaching her for some time now.'

'I'd worry that she has too little sense of danger,' Kell added, thoughtfully.

'Nonsense, she'll do us very well,' Cumming reassured him.

'Do you think you can persuade her to work for you?' Walter asked.

'Just leave it to me!' Cumming said, smugly.

'Well, I understand that her relationship with Mr Selwyn Edge finished recently,' Kell said.

'Even better. That means there's no-one to keep her in England,' Cummings said, rubbing his hands together, 'Though I may have to find her another sponsor.'

They were almost at Blackleigh Court by this time. They continued the rest of the journey in companionable silence, not attempting to talk above the other noises.

Dorothy and Godiva had arrived some ten minutes earlier and had already changed by the time Kell, Walter and Cumming were ushered into the library. Randall was already in the room, a large brandy in his grasp. He offered drinks to the others, but none found alcohol to be necessary. Coffee was sent for.

The gentlemen were joined by Godiva, who arrived at the same time as the coffee. She was a little nervous, as though she was going to a job interview.

'Come in, Miss Williams, and do take a seat,' said Cumming. All the men stood when she opened the door. Godiva sat down in a chair near to the door.

'Sorry to be quite so formal, but I think we need a little privacy here. I've asked Lord Walter to stay in case he can add anything to the story,' Kell said, looking over at Walter.

'There's just a few things we need to sort out, so that we can prepare to do the report. Bit of a bore, but these things must be done,' Cumming said.

'Alright,' Godiva said, 'ask your questions and I'll do my best.' Kell shuffled a pile of papers.

'Firstly, I'd like to know how you made the connection between Professor Knudsen and Siegfried von Braun,' he said with a smile that was meant to be friendly, but looked rather grim.

'Well, it was two things, really. When I was doing some research for the Duke of Radnor, I came across a reference to some work that Professor Knudsen had done for the Germans. The results were very different from the ones he gave to the Duke. That made me rather suspicious. Then I found that the Professor was communicating with someone at the German Embassy using the same postal address as Arthur Gregory used. So I knew there had to be a link there. I already knew that Gregory was doing some work for the Germans, and I was sure he was responsible for the attack on Tommy Schmidt and for sending that man round to threaten Walter,' Godiva answered carefully.

'However, Miss Williams, you still went to question the Professor. That was very foolhardy. Because of what I already knew of you I thought you might try to do something foolish. I had sent a man to keep an eye on you, but you managed to lose him with a very clever piece of improvisation. He's one of our best men, too,' Kell said, his eyes narrowing.

'I'm not sure if you're praising me or telling me off,' Godiva said, 'Either way, it might have helped if you had told me about my shadow. I had to assume that he was one of Arthur Gregory's men or someone sent by the Germans. After what had happened to other people, I was more frightened of your man than I was of the Professor.'

'Before I could tell you I would have had to take you fully into my confidence. The only way I would ever do that is if I had some kind of formal arrangement with you. Now it is entirely possible that I might wish to use you again in some capacity. Your research was quick and accurate, and you are able to make connections between apparently unconnected events and facts. Those are very useful skills. You also displayed hard work, determination and an ability to improvise. I do not hand out plaudits lightly. So when I say that you did an exemplary job you will understand it to be high praise indeed.' Kell said

'Do I understand that you are offering me a job?' Godiva asked in genuine surprise.

'Not exactly, at least not a full-time position. What I would like to propose is that you come in to help when we have a particularly puzzling piece of work. I am prepared to pay you the same as a man in the same work, precisely because you are quite as good as any man we have. So how do you feel about taking up this offer?' Kell asked.

'I'm not sure I can accept. On the practical side, I have other responsibilities. I can't go travelling about all over the place at a moment's notice. Then there is the moral side. You still have to convince me that what you are doing is the best thing to do,' Godiva blurted out.

'Let me answer your questions, then,' Kell said, leaning forward to place his elbows on the table and to steeple his fingers, 'The department I have started is based in London, and there is no foreign travel involved. It is possible that you might have to travel occasionally within Britain, but that would be quite a rare occurrence. As to the morality of what we do, let me just remind you that our entire efforts are geared towards frustrating the plans of foreign spies. We might not be completely blameless in every aspect, but our opponents operate under a very different moral code, one in which lies, deception theft and murder are the common currency. There is no great glory for people like us. We cannot even admit what it is we do. There is no publicity or recognition of the service we devote our lives to.'

'Those are very fine words. What worries me is when you use the services of someone like Arthur Gregory. There is no way you can justify what he did. And the Professor had a certain point when he described what our foreign policy is doing to perfectly innocent peoples,' Godiva said. Kell took a long breath in before replying.

'One of the techniques we use is to find diplomats who are operating as spies and persuade them to spy on their own country instead. If the spy has committed some indiscretion, then we may try to apply a certain amount of pressure with threats or naked blackmail. It is a policy that has worked rather well, so far. That is how we came to make use of the services of Mr Gregory. If he has been working for the Germans, then we will certainly consider never using him again. Please believe me that if you were to work for us you would have no contact with that area of our work. As to foreign policy, I really have no professional opinion on that. Such things come under Major Cumming's *aegis*,' Kell said, with his lips getting increasingly thinner.

'Well, thank you for being so very frank with me. I'm not sure that I can give you an answer immediately. I have such very mixed feelings about the work. Part of me would like the puzzles and the challenge, while another part of me objects most strongly to some of the things you do. Could I give you an answer tomorrow?'

'Certainly, that is perfectly acceptable. I will get in touch with you via Lord Walter. If you decide that you do not want to take up the offer then I must insist that you never mention this meeting or what I have said to anyone. If you decide that you want to work with us you will have to sign a form that says you will never divulge any information about the organisation. Do you agree to that?' Kell asked.

'Yes, of course,' Godiva said with a sigh, 'I'll never breathe a word to anyone.'

'Excellent,' said Cumming, 'now you can stay if you wish or you can leave. You see, I'd like a word with Miss Levitt now. Do you think you could invite her in to see us?'

Godiva stood up, left the room and then returned a minute later accompanied by a puzzled Dorothy Levitt. The pair of young women sat together, Godiva thinking that Dorothy might need moral support among these unscrupulous men.

'Miss Levitt, we have been mightily impressed with your abilities,' Cumming said.

'Thank you, I er, I suppose,' Dorothy said, nervously.

'We are aware of your achievements, and you are quite well known. Are you likely to be competing in some more races and competitions, say next year?'

'That rather depends on Mr Edge. He owns the cars and decides who he wants to race them. It may be that he decides to use another driver. So I can't really give you a complete assurance that I will be driving. Why is it that you are asking me that?' Dorothy said, with a note of confusion in her voice.

'I believe that your, er, relationship with Mr Edge has finished,' Kell said.

'Have you been checking up on me?' Dorothy said, angry now.

'Yes. We thought it best, as we are hoping to employ you. As for finding a car to drive, I'm sure we could help you there,' Cumming said.

'What is it you want me to do?' Dorothy asked in a suspicious tone.

'You go all over Europe and race cars, don't you? And you meet many important and influential people. So we wondered if you might pass on some messages and bring others back to us when you are on your travels,' Cumming suggested.

'Well, I don't see why not. Provided you get me a decent drive and pay me enough,' Dorothy agreed with surprising swiftness, rather taking the wind out of Cumming's sails.

'Oh, er, thank you,' He stammered, 'And I can assure you that it would involve very little or no risk.'

'Oh, I like taking risks. Don't worry about that. It's a great idea. There are always masses of people who come to the races. What could be easier than to hide things in a toolbox or on the car. It would have to fit in with the races, though, or it would look suspicious,' Dorothy said, enthusiastically.

'My thoughts exactly. Welcome on board, Miss Levitt. We can discuss details at my office next week,' Cumming said.

'Well, thank you. Perhaps we can discuss some other work as well. You see, I won't always be a driver, and I really believe that I can offer much more to you than that. If you only use me as a me as a messenger, then you won't be making the best use of me. If you will consider how I can be of service, then I will think of what I can do for you,' Dorothy said. She looked into Cumming's eyes with a determined smile on her face.

'Very well,' Cumming said, 'I will give it serious consideration. It would mean that you would have to take on a new identity, though. You are far too well known to be sent into service as yourself. These things can be arranged and require only minor changes to your appearance. We use a lady who does the stage makeup for some very famous actors and actresses.' He sighed after saying this, then gave a short laugh.

◊

Kell was questioning Knudsen in Lord Randall's office. The Dane was looking dishevelled and defeated. Kell bore an air of quiet triumph.

'Why did you to do this work for the German's?' Kell demanded.

'Because they are not the British,' Knudsen answered, very slowly, as though talking to someone particularly stupid.

'Don't you feel any loyalty to this country, the one where you earned good money, the one that gave you a home?' Kell continued.

'I would have liked to call this country a friend, but it is the actions of the country, it's insatiable greed and it's attitude of superiority to every other country, every other people on the planet which I cannot forgive. You force your beliefs onto everyone else, by using your money and your power and most of all, by using your Navy. So when I got a chance to damage the effectiveness of your Navy, and to hand an advantage to another power, one with which I find myself more sympathetic, I took that chance. There is a war coming, we all know that, and when it comes I want some advantage for your enemies, I want you to lose, so the world will change and Britain will no longer be the top nation,' Knudsen said as though giving a lecture.

'Do you have diplomatic status?' Kell asked.

'You know that I don't,' Knudsen replied.

'That will make things difficult for you,' Kell said, thoughtfully, 'As there are several criminal charges you will be facing, and some even more serious charges concerning your involvement is spying. You are facing a very long prison term.'

'Yes, I know that,' Knudsen said, wincing.

'Mind you, there are prisons and there are prisons. Hard labour can prove very difficult for a middle-aged man who is not used to physical work, while some prisons are much less difficult to survive,' Kell intoned.

'What is it that you want of me,' Knudsen sighed.

'You are willing to do some kind of deal, then?' Kell questioned

'That rather depends on what you are willing to offer me,' Knudsen stated.

'And what we offer you rather depends on what you are willing to tell us,' said Kell, 'And you must realise that you are not of the highest value to us. We cannot make use of your service as the German Intelligence agencies will already be aware that we have caught you. They will not believe anything that you say anymore, in case they come to believe that you are working for us. '

'Yes, I can see that,' Knudsen admitted.

'So the best you can do for us is to tell us exactly what you told to the Germans, and to tell us about your contacts at the German Embassy, and who else you met who might also have been working for the Embassy. If we can root out the entire network, then we will only press lesser charges and your treatment will be much better,' Kell droned. A meaningful silence followed this.

'To start with, I never met or communicated with Peters until today,' said Knudsen.

'Continue,' Kell instructed.

'And look here I've never been a fanatic. If I ever did anything against British interests except to balance things out, just in the interests of natural justice,' Knudsen said.

'Yes, yes, yes, but please don't try to justify yourself any more. Just tell me who your main contact is,' Kell demanded.

'I only knew him as Herr Schmidt. I'm sure that is not his real name,' said Knudsen.

'It isn't,' said Kell, 'Now please describe what he looks like.'

'He's very tall, and I suppose that you could describe him as gaunt. He sometimes wears an eye-glass in his right eye and he has a duelling scar on his left cheek. And he talks with a Prussian accent, very High German, and he has a slight tick at the corner of his mouth,' Knudsen said.

'How old is he? How does he dress? Is there anything else distinctive about him?' Kell fired out the questions.

'Well, I suppose that he is a little over thirty years old. He tries to dress like an English gentleman, but somehow it only makes him look more foreign and strange. As for distinguishing marks, well, he's a very distinctive looking man. But I suppose one thing would be that he has close-cropped hair, which is almost white,' Knudsen answered.

'Well, your description exactly matches a man at the embassy that we are aware of. We will deal with him, probably request that he be moved somewhere else, or possibly a full diplomatic protest, but being a diplomat, we can't directly touch him. Now did you meet anyone else when you were with him?' Kell probed.

'There was an Englishman, but I never knew his name. He barely spoke, but watched. I had the idea that he was some kind of bodyguard. He seems to be employed by Schmidt. He was not too tall, but was well built, like an athlete of some kind, or a wrestler. He looked very tough. But he didn't really have any features that I remember. He was dressed in very plain clothes, and he never stood out in any way. I don't know how to describe him any more than that,' Knudsen concluded.

'And there wasn't anyone else?' Kell persisted.

'No, I never met anyone else,' Knudsen said dully.

'And how did you communicate with Schmidt?' Kell asked, glaring at Knudsen through his thin-rimmed spectacles.

'There was a shop in Whitechapel. It was an address of convenience. If I had anything to tell him I sent a note there, and I called in to see if he had anything to ask of me. But I made sure to burn all the notes I received. It would have been folly to do otherwise,' said Knudsen, eyes cast down.

'Do you have the address of this shop?' Kell asked.

'I'll write it down for you. I have the address committed to memory. But I don't suppose that the owner of the shop knew anything. His business was to keep quiet and just pass the messages on. He wouldn't have dared to open them, and even if he had, they were in a crude kind of code. Schmidt doesn't have much imagination. I'm sure that you could have read the messages easily enough if you had intercepted them,' Knudsen said with a bitter little laugh.

'We did,' said Kell, 'now tell me about this little note we found on you.' He produced a piece of writing paper headed with the crest of the Duke of Radnor from an inside pocket and unfolded it before placing it on the table, facing Knudsen.

'That looks careless, but it was a kind of emergency. I suppose it was the quickest way Schmidt had of getting in contact with Peters. He must have known I would be at the Duke's house and I presume he thought it was safer for me to pass on the information. Someone telephoning Blackleigh Court with a strong German accent, asking for Peters would have looked very suspicious. He should have thought it out better. If he had done he would have sent the message directly, as though it came from the aeroplane company. That would have been quicker and more natural,' Knudsen said. Kell grunted.

'He already tried that before. All he wanted you to do was to warn Peters to leave. He had already sent other instructions to Peters. You are just a dupe in all this. We have copies of the telegrams sent to both you and Peters. We know that you were not the boss of the gang. Von Braun, or Schmidt, as you knew him, was the leader, and Peters was a paid assassin. But he had some private business as well. That was to do with his own history and something Lord Randall was involved with a decade ago,' said Kell.

'That was nothing to do with me,' Knudsen grunted.

'Probably not, but I'm sure we have enough on you to get you sent to prison for a very long time. Prison isn't a very nice place to go at your age,' Kell said in a flat tone.

'Probably not,' Knudsen admitted.

'There is an alternative,' Kell said.

◊

'I think we need to get you cleaned up a bit before dinner,' Dorothy said, glancing at Godiva's wind-blown hair and clothes creased by travel.

'But I didn't bring the right kind of clothes for dining at a country house,' Godiva answered.

'Well, you look about the same size as me, so I ought to be able to find you something suitable,' Dorothy suggested.

They went to Dorothy's room and she produced a variety of clothes from her trunk. Godiva had removed her outer clothing and was washing herself as best she could in the basin in the room with some hot water which had been fetched by a chambermaid. Dorothy looked at Godiva as she washed, considering her waist.

'There may be a problem with most of my clothes, as you don't ever appear to have worn corsets, but I'm sure that I can find something which doesn't have a proper waistline,' Dorothy observed. Godiva turned round to talk to her new acquaintance.

'I'm pleased to say that corsets were never really to be found in my family house. They are all advanced thinkers, and the women all believe in rational dress. My father seems to prefer it, too, so there was no chance of me ever wearing such restrictive garments. And I really don't approve of women distorting their figures just to look fashionable. It can't be good for a woman, especially if she wishes to conceive.'

'But most men prefer a woman to look a certain way, and I've found that it easier to conform to that idea if I want to get on. Until we get the vote we will be entirely dependent on what men think in order to advance in the world. So I shall continue to dress as I do until things change a great deal,' Dorothy said.

'And I shall continue to struggle for women's suffrage so that you can choose another course,' Godiva said with eyes bright for battle.

'Well, even if we do get the vote, I should think that I shall be too old to think about fashionable clothes by that time. And I'm not sure that the world will change so very much even when we do get the vote, at least not in my lifetime, even if I live to be a very old woman, and given my profession, that doesn't seem very likely,' Dorothy said with a sad smile.

'I have to admit that you may very well be right. My father has spent all his life struggling in the cause of socialism, but I know he will never get a tenth of the changes he wants during his lifetime. But getting the vote is just the first stage in our struggle,' Godiva said, 'And, to change the subject, do you have a hairbrush I could use? My hair is in a terrible state.'

'I've got a spare brush in the top drawer over there, and I think that you have very good hair. I really envy you that. I have to spend so much time keeping mine in order. It really is very tiresome if one drives a car, your hair does go all over the place unless it is held rigidly in place,' Dorothy said.

'What I would really find depressing is if, within a few decades after getting the vote, women forgot all about the struggle we went through to get it; if they were to become complacent about the entire business. If that were to happen, then we might as well give up the struggle,' Godiva said with a sigh.

She went to a chest of drawers and removed the spare hairbrush from the indicated drawer before starting to tidy and arrange her hair. Dorothy sat her on a chair and helped to arrange it in a neat and fashionable style. Godiva observed the changes in the mirror and liked what she saw.

'That is very good,' she said, 'I've never considered doing it that way. I suppose it takes another's eye to see it.' She turned her head to admire herself from all angles.

'As long as it's not against your suffragist principals,' Dorothy laughed.

Godiva stood up, walked over to where the clothes were arranged on the bed and selected an outfit which took her fancy. The skirt would not fit around her waist when fastened, but the jacket went down below the hips and covered the area where the skirt would not fasten. Overall, the effect of wearing clothes which she would not normally choose was to transform Godiva into a woman of the type more normally seen in the ranks of higher society.

'How do you find it being in a profession where almost all your competitors are men?' Godiva asked.

'To be perfectly frank with you, I have found a good deal of prejudice, with some races refusing to allow me to compete, but most of the drivers don't take me too seriously, and that suits me very well. If they underestimate my abilities, then it is much easier to beat them at their own game. If I smile sweetly and play the little woman when I speak to them, then I don't challenge their masculinity, and they don't seem to mind me too much. It may sound like I am exploiting my feminine charms, but what is a girl to do when most men, and most women for that matter, think of me as merely a pretty plaything. I know that I can drive better than almost all of the men, and much better than any other woman, but I am much less threatening if I don't get too strident in support of women's rights,' Dorothy explained.

'And what about lovers?' Godiva enquired.

'Well, there is Selwyn, but I need him because he provides the cars for me to drive. I give him lots of publicity in return, and I used to share his bed occasionally. Other than that, I choose discrete young men who don't make too many demands. Your friend, Walter really won't do, not because he is indiscrete, but because he has too high an opinion of himself, and he is too well known. Any arrangement I might make with him would be bound to attract attention, and I can't afford the press making me out to be a scarlet woman, or of Selwyn getting to know,' Dorothy said, 'but that is quite enough about me, what of your sex life?'

'I've had lovers. They were serious men, mostly married. They were men that I admire, but not ones that I would want to marry. To be perfectly frank, I never have enjoyed sex all that much,' Godiva said.

'Why don't you give Walter a go. I hear that he is a very fine lover, and if anyone can give you sexual satisfaction, he will. And it is still possible to be friends as well as lovers, you know,' Dorothy said, smiling.

'I suppose it is because we have had a long relationship not being lovers, and because he doesn't treat his women very well,' Godiva considered.

'Well, I would still encourage you to try him as a lover, and take what you can get. Think of your own pleasure, not his. I really can't see what harm it would do,' said Dorothy, smiling.

'Oh, maybe, I suppose. I shall consider it, but only on my terms, and when I want it to happen,' said Godiva. A dinner gong sounded downstairs.

'Time to go back down, I think,' said Dorothy, and she left the room followed closely by Godiva. The dinner gong was still vibrating as they descended the stairs.

MONDAY 4TH OCTOBER 1909

It was an uneventful trip back up to London. Walter and Godiva shared a compartment on the Worcester train with Kell and Cumming. Cumming kept them entertained with stories of his 'little adventures', as he called them. Kell sat with his briefcase on his knee, examining various papers. He hardly contributed to the conversation at all until they were approaching Oxford. Then he looked up quizzically at Godiva.

'Miss Williams, have you thought any more about my offer, yet?' he asked, baldly.

'Well, I have given your offer a good deal of consideration,' Godiva replied, gripping the handle of her trusty umbrella, 'I suppose that I should like to accept, but I still have some concerns as to certain jobs.'

'Thank you for your guarded acceptance. I will make sure that your views are always considered before offering these jobs to you. We do need to find a way of contacting you at short notice. Perhaps you can consider a way to do that which is convenient to us both,' Kell said, with an uncomfortable attempt at a smile.

'Perhaps I can come and see you a little later in the week,' Godiva said, 'Then we can make the necessary arrangements.'

'Certainly,' Kell agreed, 'I'll just write down the number of my office in of the war department buildings.' He took out a pen and jotted down a number into his memorandum book. Then he tore the page out, folded it in half and handed it to Godiva.

'Agreed,' said Godiva, 'I'll come to see you on Wednesday that's all right.'

'I have an appointment in the morning but the afternoon would be fine,' Kell said, almost getting some animation in his voice.

'The afternoon it is then,' Godiva said firmly.

'Did I tell you about the time I was in Belgrade?' said Cumming, 'I was looking at some naval installations and I was drawing them as parts of a butterfly's wing. If the Austrian police had taken a proper look at they could easily have seen what it was. They must have thought I was a terrible artist.'

'As I'm a competent artist I find that a little worrying,' Walter commented.

'So there I was the sitting on a camp stool with an easel in front of me and a set of coloured inks, trying to pretend that I was looking at a butterfly when all the time I was looking at a dockyard,' Cumming continued.

The train bounced and rattled over a set of points. The briefcase fell from Kells lap and of the papers were scattered over the floor of the compartment. Godiva knelt down to help recover the papers and bumped heads with Kell, causing slight cries of pain and words of concern from Walter and Cumming. Godiva noted that the papers were completed expense claims.

◊

Dorkins was waiting for them when they arrived back at the flat in the middle of the afternoon. He was hopping about excitedly and seemed anxious to speak to them.

'Dorkins, I thought this was your time to be out of the flat,' said Walter with a smile, 'It's very good of you to welcome us back and all that, but I think we are capable of making a cup of tea.'

'I've got some news, Sir, about Mr Gregory. Oh, I'm so glad that you're back. I know where he'll be tomorrow,' Dorkins blurted out.

'Now calm down Dorkins. Just tell us what this is all about,' Godiva said reassuringly.

'I heard it from Fred who was Gordon's flatmate. He works as a waiter at Gregory's, place. He overheard a conversation between Gregory and some German man. There is going to be a meeting at a bookshop in Charing Cross Road tomorrow at eleven o'clock. This means that we can find Gregory and teach him a proper lesson,' said Dorkins.

'Did you hear which bookshop it was,' Godiva said patiently, 'I mean, there are dozens of bookshops in Charing Cross Road. It could be any of them.'

'It's a bookshop called Bindall's or something like that. That's what Gordon's friend heard,' Dorkins said, all in a rush.

'If you could be a bit more sure that's the name of the shop, it would be a great help,' Walter said, patiently.

'Well, that's what it sounded like to him. I would have thought you could find it from that,' Dorkins said, sounding disappointed.

'I'm sure we can,' Godiva said, 'Go and fetch the street directory and we'll look for it now.'

'What if Gregory brings some of his big friends with him?' Dorkins asked anxiously.

'I don't see why he should do that if he is going to a prearranged meeting,' Godiva said considering her words.

Dorkins brought the street and trade directory from the book shelf and Godiva turned to the section on bookshops. There was no entry for Bindall's but there was an entry for Boodalls. Walter gave a small whoop of delight and Godiva grinned broadly.

'You do know that we are going to have to tell Kell about this,' Godiva said quietly.

'Of course,' Walter agreed, 'Perhaps we can send round a note to arrive at eleven o'clock tomorrow morning. By the time Kell's men arrive we should have taken care of our business.'

'Are you sure that there is no danger involved?' Godiva asked with a nervous smile.

'Not entirely,' Walter admitted, 'But I think between myself and Dorkins we can handle anything we are likely to meet. We'll make sure that we have a certain amount of equipment. I have a sword stick.'

'Alright,' Godiva said slyly, 'you go round and see Gregory and I'll go off and tell Kell. Then he shouldn't be able to complain about anything.'

'I'm sure that he'll find something to complain about,' Walter said wryly.

'Just promise me you won't do anything too silly,' Godiva said and she laid her hands on Walter's.

'I promise that Dorkins and I will come back to you safe and sound,' Walter said, smiling at Godiva, then nudging Dorkins in the ribs.

'I've got some knuckle-dusters at home,' Dorkins said, with a hint of pride in his voice.

'Well, bring them along tomorrow,' Walter said, and he clapped Dorkins on the back.

◊

Godiva had a letter from her Father which had arrived since she had gone away. She was standing reading it with her back to the fire.

'What does your Father want?' Walter asked.

'He says he wants me to come back and help him. He's actually offering me a wage this time,' Godiva replied, thoughtfully.

'So are you going back to work for him, then?' Walter enquired.

'I don't think so. Not unless he agrees that women's suffrage is the top political priority and gives me credit for the work I do. I need to have my name in big letters on the front of any book or I'm not collaborating with him. The wage is not the only thing I want. I need some recognition as well. If he wants me to work as his secretary, then I may do that part time, provided he offers me a decent wage, but I won't do any of his thinking or research for him,' Godiva said, her jaw set firm.

'It seems we both have trouble with our Fathers,' Walter mused.

'How do you think your Father will react to the news of your new job?' Godiva asked, looking up at Walter.

'I'm really not sure. I don't suppose it's exactly what he had in mind. If I am working for the foreign office and I can admit that, he might be really pleased. Who knows, he might even restore my allowance.' Walter replied with a wry smile.

'Poor Walter,' Godiva said in mock sympathy, 'Are your tailors still asking for money?'

'The thing is, I'm not even sure when my Father is coming back. He's off in Cannes with his mistress, or one of them. I suppose I could write to him. That would be quite a shock if I did. When I was at Harrow I used to write letters home, but I don't suppose I've sent him a letter in five or six years. We've never exactly hit it off, you know,' Walter said with a sigh.

TUESDAY 5th OCTOBER 1909

Walter and Dorkins had settled themselves behind the dusty window of a bookseller's shop. The shop was across the street, opposite the entrance to Boodles antiquarian bookshop. The shop they were in specialised in books on the subject of art history. While they waited they leafed through the books. Walter was looked at a beautifully illustrated folio on Italian medieval altarpieces, diptychs and triptychs. Dorkins found some illustrations of classical statues and was admiring the muscle definition of the men. So involved did he become that Walter had to nudge him when he saw the awkwardly tall figure of Siegfried entering Boodles.

'He is a tall one, isn't he,' Dorkins remarked loudly and quite unnecessarily. The owner of their shop looked at him through narrowed eyes and indicated that quiet should be observed by raising a finger to his lips.

After a few minutes it was Dorkins' turn to alert Walter to the presence of another arrival. Gregory was sauntering up to the shop. He was the complete dandy in broad-brimmed hat and astrakhan coat. He was wearing spats over his patent leather shoes. In one hand was a silver handled cane and an attaché case was in the other. He was wearing a monocle.

'Good, he's not got any friends with him, at least not as far as I can see,' Walter said in a low voice, knowing that this carried less well than a whisper.

'Time to go,' Dorkins said. They put their books down. Walter told the bookshop owner that he had some business to take care of and would be back to purchase the book in a few minutes.

Dorkins ran across the road, dodging the taxis and the carts. He went into Boodles bookshop and marched sprightly up to the desk where the manager sat.

'I've got a whole shelf-full of books for you from the auction house,' Dorkins said.

'I'm not expecting any consignment today,' said the manager in a soft voice, 'Which auction house do you come from anyway?'

'Stonewaters in the Haymarket,' Dorkins invented, 'Your owner bought a load of beauties. Surprised he didn't tell you.'

'I've never heard of Stonewaters,' the manager said, looking puzzled.

'The load's in the cart, outside,' Dorkins said , and he guided the grey little man out of the shop. When they were outside, Walter approached swiftly. He held up his hand to quieten the manager, then produced two pound notes from his wallet and placed them into the manager's hand.

'We'd like a quiet word with the two gentlemen who have just come into your shop. I'm sure you can find a reason for being away from your station for a few minutes,' Walter said with a wink. The manager opened his mouth as if to answer, then closed it again, thinking that no speech was necessary. He folded the banknotes and placed them in an inside pocket before walking away in the direction of a baker's shop.

Walter and Dorkins entered the bookshop and Walter set the deadlock on from the inside of the door. Then Dorkins turned the sign over to indicate that the shop was closed. Walter checked his sword stick and Dorkins felt in his pocket for the knuckle dusters before they set out into the back of the shop. Both men were wearing rubber-soled shoes, but their footsteps were still noticeably loud on the brown linoleum floor.

There were sounds of a conversation coming from a large side room. The tone of the voices was of hushed excitement from one source and reassurance from the other.

'You must have someone who can find out what has happened!' said the first voice.

'I'm afraid that my agents are almost entirely based in London. I can get men to other cities, but not to the middle of the country,' the other voice answered.

Walter and Dorkins came to a halt outside the door, on the unsighted side of the frame, in order to listen to this conversation.

'But you must know someone who knows someone,' the first voice insisted.

'Even if I did, it might take several days to get an answer back to you. Somehow, I think you need the answers much faster than that,' said the smooth, identifiable voice of Gregory.

'I thought you had contacts with British Intelligence,' said the first man, 'Couldn't you find something out from them?'

'Look, I provide those people with information. If I was to ask them questions they would get suspicious very quickly,' said Gregory.

'I have given you a great deal of money. For that amount of money I expect a bit more help than you seem willing to give. You must appreciate the position that I am in,' said the first man.

At this point Walter tapped Dorkins on the arm and they burst into the room. Gregory had been sitting on a hard chair provided for readers and the other man was standing with his back to a bookshelf facing Gregory. They both jumped up at the intrusion.

'Well, isn't this nice,' said Walter, glaring at the first man, 'Perhaps I ought to make the introductions. This man over here,' he indicated the first man,' is my cousin, Siegfried von Braun, Siegfried, this is my manservant, Dorkins. You, I presume,' he indicated Gregory, 'are Arthur Gregory. My, but this seems like a bad melodrama, so I might as well say it. We meet at last! Well Mr Gregory, this is Dorkins, and you had a friend of his killed.'

'Walter, how dare you presume to introduce me to this lower class fellow!' Siegfried said angrily.

'You haven't introduced yourself, yet,' said Gregory with a sneer.

'Oh, I do so apologise,' Walter said sarcastically, 'You ought to know who is about to hit you. My name is Lord Walter Mansell-Lacey. But you can just plead for mercy.'

'I don't think that you'll hit me,' said Gregory, 'I have powerful friends in British Intelligence. And besides, you don't seem to be armed.' Gregory reached for something in his overcoat, and would have produced a revolver had not Dorkins hit him on the side of the head with a well-aimed copy of Palgraves Golden Treasury. He lurched back with his hand to the left side of his head, but he was quickly alert again. He reached his right hand again to pull out the gun, but Dorkins leapt to the chair and hit him hard on the elbow with a slightly foxed copy of Gibbon's Decline and Fall of the Roman Empire, Volume two. This blow caused Gregory to withdraw his hand from his pocket with a cry of pain. He tried to shake some life back into his stinging, numbed arm.

Siegfried used the distraction caused by this tussle to aim a vicious blow at Walter, but either his aim was not good or Walter's reactions were better. Walter stepped aside, dropped his stick and hit Siegfried with a combination of a straight right to the solar plexus and a left hook to the jaw. Siegfried collapsed in a heap, out for the count.

Gregory realising that Dorkins was both smaller and lighter than he was, jumped out of his chair and charged at him, roaring, trying to force him against a bookshelf. However, Dorkins was too nimble for him and stepped aside, leaving an outstretched foot to trip him. Gregory hit his chin against one of the shelves, biting his tongue badly and having his head jerked back. Dorkins grabbed him by the hair, dragging his head further back, and slapped him twice, very hard, sending the monocle spinning from his eye.

Walter found some strong twine for parcels on one of the shelves. He used the twine to tie Siegfried to a hard chair, using the sword stick blade to cut the string. Then he helped Dorkins to tie Gregory's hands behind his back. The entire confrontation had only taken less than a minute.

Walter gently patted Siegfried on the cheeks in an effort to revive him. The tall German shook his head, and his eyes gradually came into focus. He tried to rise but his bonds were too tight.

'Let me go. Let me go right now. I'm a diplomat . You can't do anything to me,' Siegfried said, spitting out the words in his fury. Walter slapped him much harder.

'I'm going to make an official complaint about you,' Siegfried continued, 'You can't treat me like this.'

'Hand me Gregory's gun, will you please, Dorkins,' Walter commanded in a soft voice. Dorkins handed the weapon over. Walter examined it from every angle.

'Nasty little thing, this. It might go off accidentally and someone could get killed,' Walter said, and he jabbed the barrel of the gun hard into Siegfried's ribs.

'You're nothing but a bully, threatening me when I'm tied up,' Siegfried protested.

'No I'm not,' Walter disagreed, 'a bully likes to pick out a weaker victim and find some way of inflicting pain. Over the past two weeks you and your agents, with the help of Mr Gregory here have done the bullying. Two men are dead and one has had his leg amputated. My colleague, Mr Dorkins, has lost a good friend. I have been threatened with a pistol besides getting my nose badly broken when pursuing a man who had killed twice. My friend was locked in an ice house by another of your agents. I overheard your earlier conversation. You wanted to know what happened to your agents. I can tell you that. Mr Peters is dead. He died following an aeroplane crash. Professor Knudsen has been captured and is now happily telling British Intelligence anything they want to know.'

Dorkins had been rifling through Gregory's attaché case.

'Well, would you believe it. There's some lovely photographs of Siegfried here. Couldn't be clearer. A very professional job, and there's no doubt that it's him. Mind you, it's a very funny composition. He's tied up with some leather straps and there's a large lady threatening to use a whip on him. He does seem a little excited about the prospect,' Dorkins said with malevolent triumph.

'I'm sure your ambassador would be very interested to see those,' Walter said. 'Mind you, I hope you aren't getting too much enjoyment from this situation. The last thing I want to do is to give you any pleasure.' Siegfried grunted.

'What do you want me for?' Gregory said, 'I told you, I've been working with British Intelligence.'

'It seems to me that you have been a bit naughty yourself,' Walter said, grimly, 'And I know it was you who sent a man round to threaten me. I don't know all the details, but I do know that you have been doing some work for my cousin Siegfried here. He's a German spy, so where does that leave you?'

'I wasn't doing his spying for him. I was just providing certain other services at a reasonable price. I was going to tell the people at the Admiralty everything,' Gregory said in a wheedling tone

'You're a piece of excrement, Gregory. Still, you haven't caused me any direct harm. However, my colleague here would like to make a point or two,' Walter said.

'You've had my friends beaten up and blackmailed. You broke one boy's fingers, and you had a friend of mine killed for daring to tell some of your dirty secrets. I'm not going to kill you, but I am going to teach you a lesson,' Dorkins said in a flat tone, 'Do you mind if I borrow your cane, Lord Walter?' Walter handed over the stick, wondering how Dorkins was going to use it. If the blade were used, that would be going too far. Dorkins kept the case closed. Instead he forced Gregory back to the book shelf by poking him in the belly with the ferrule end of the stick. Then he lifted Gregory's bound hands onto the shelf and brought the stick down hard on the outstretched fingers. There was a cracking of bone and a scream of agony from Gregory. He screamed so loud that it was difficult to hear the frantic knocking on the door of the shop.

'Go and let them in, please, Dorkins,' Walter instructed.

A minute later Dorkins returned, leading Scrivener and two policemen.

'What the hell has been going on here?' Scrivener demanded.

'Well, I've caught you a German spy. He's all neatly packaged up and waiting for you. That gentleman over there with the broken fingers,' Walter indicated Gregory, 'He was working for our German friend here. Perhaps I'd better make the introductions . This gangling Teutonic moron is my cousin, Herr Siegfried von Braun. He's based at the German Embassy. Siegfried, this is Commander Henry Scrivener, who works for British counter-intelligence, for whom I have been doing a little job.'

'And these photographs show that the German gentleman was doing something naughty at Mr Gregory's club,' Dorkins added with pride, passing Scrivener the photographs.

'So I suggest that you take our foreign visitor here to some place where he can be properly questioned by our boss,' Walter said.

'Good grief!', Scrivener said, his mouth dropping open. 'Do you really find pleasure in such things?' He shook his head, then he instructed the policeman to untie Siegfried and to place him in the car and guard him closely. Siegfried had a few words to say to Scrivener and Walter before he left.

'You are making a serious error. I am an accredited diplomat. This could lead to a diplomatic incident,' he said to Scrivener before turning to Walter, 'As for you, well, I'll make a promise that I shall see you again. This matter between us isn't finished yet.'

'Ich freue mich schon auf, dass,' Walter said with a short bow.

'Well, Herr von Braun, it seems that you have been engaged in criminal activity. If that is the case it will invalidate any diplomatic privileges you are entitled to,' Scrivener said, officiously as Siegfried was led away.

'Dammit, tell them to let me go,' Gregory protested to Scrivener, 'You know I'm supposed to be working for you.'

'In this case you seem to have been working for the German. If those photographs are genuine, and we can use them against him, it may prove to be just enough to keep you out of prison. If I were you, I should be very contrite and humble, and extremely helpful in all our investigations,' Scrivener said, between gritted teeth. Dorkins grinned broadly at Gregory's discomfiture.

'As for you,' Scrivener said, turning to Walter, 'You not only involve your mistress, you also involve your manservant. Are you stark-staring mad?'

'Well, I'm not working for your department anymore. I've done my job and now I want my payment. I've handed a German spy to you on a plate, together with evidence you can use to blackmail him into working for us. It seems to me that I've done a pretty good job. Perhaps I'm not so bad at this game after all,' Walter said in triumph.

'You really aren't the right person for this kind of work,' Scrivener said, shaking his head.

'Well, pay me my money and get rid of me, then,' said Walter, 'and, by the by, I've got a few expenses to claim for. Shall I come round tomorrow?'

'You know where my office is. I'll pay you off just to get rid of you,' Scrivener said, flatly.

'That's an arrangement which suits me perfectly,' Walter said, laughing.

◊

Back in the flat Walter was recounting the adventures of the day, with Dorkins adding snippets to the story. Godiva decided that it was better to listen. She had fulfilled her part in the adventure by calling on Kell and telling him about the meeting in the bookshop. After telling their story with only a modicum of exaggeration they decided to celebrate with a good lunch. They went to a chop house and ordered large lumps of meat. This was not subtle or sophisticated food but it was plentiful, fresh and well-cooked. The Master of the house, his house-guest and servant sat around a common table in perfect equanimity. The claret served was perfectly acceptable and they became merry after a few bottles. As with all such celebrations a note of wistfulness intruded into their consciousness at the end of the meal. Walter and Godiva returned to the flat, with Dorkins being given the remainder of the day off.

They had only just removed their outdoor clothes when someone rang the bell below. Godiva went down the stairs two at a time and let the visitor in. It was Emily, who asked to talk to Walter. She was led up to the flat and into the sitting room. Walter was surprised to see his friend and paramour and stood up suddenly with a slightly nervous expression on his face.

'Walter, sorry to call in on you like this, but I really need to have a word with you,' Emily said, fiddling with her gloves.

'Tell you what,' Godiva said, smiling, 'I'll make myself scarce while you have your talk.' She went to her room and shut the door.

'Wonderful to see you, though a little unexpected,' Walter said, 'Is there anything I can get you? A cup of tea, perhaps,'

'No, nothing, thank you. I won't be staying all that long. I just had to have a word with you, let you know how things have been,' Emily took a deep breath and gave Walter a nervous smile, 'First thing to say is that as soon as I got back I told Charles about me no longer being a virgin, though I didn't give all the details. It was just as I predicted. He wasn't angry at all; in fact he only seemed relieved. But I wouldn't go so far as to say that he was actually pleased. Then we talked things over for a while, and we went to bed early. Very early, really. Well, not to give the grisly details, everything is just fine now. More than fine, in fact. Everything is just wonderful.'

'I'm very happy for you,' Walter said with a slightly forced smile.

'We are very busy now finding out about each other and what pleases us. I really can't express how wonderful it is. It's so very funny after all this time, but it is wonderful. So, you see, I wanted to thank you for all you did for me, for us really, Charles and me, that is,' Emily said, and she giggled awkwardly.

'No seriously, Emily, it was one of the greatest pleasures of my life. I'm not exaggerating at all. For those few moments I was positively ecstatic,' Walter said with a slightly sad smile, knowing what the next statement from Emily would be about.

'Yes, I enjoyed it too. But now that everything is so good between Charles and me, well, we won't need to do that again. In fact, I wouldn't be able to be unfaithful to Charles. It is just the way I am. So, please forgive me if you expected more, but it must end now. I hope you understand,' Emily said. She held Walter's hand gently, then she stretched up to kiss him on the cheek.

'If you ever need me again, I would be very happy to discuss anything with you,' Walter said.

'Please don't live in hope of that happening,' Emily said, firmly, 'I've got to go now. Thank Godiva for being so discrete. You must both come round to dinner, very soon. I'll send an invitation round in a day or two. Goodbye for now.' She turned away from him and went back out of the flat while Walter remained standing by the fireplace. He should have shown her out, but he was feeling too distraught to move.

Godiva came out of her room when she heard the door close. On seeing the expression on Walter's face she came over and placed a comforting hand on his arm.

'I wasn't listening, but I do have a good idea about what was being said. If you want to talk about it I would be happy to listen,' she said, looking up into his brown eyes, which were slightly moist with emotion.

'For once in my life I have been disappointed in love. I suppose that it is necessary to have your heart broken at some point in your life, but I never thought it would ever happen to me. Well, I shall just have to get used to it, I suppose. I'll throw myself into my work for a while. That should cure it,' Walter said, and he sighed.

'I'm sure that you will be back in the swing in no time,' Godiva reassured him. 'You know, it will make you laugh, but Dorothy was trying to persuade me to have sex with you. I might have done it as well, but if I was to offer now, I would only be seen as a substitute. And you wouldn't want me to take pity on you now, would you?'

'Well, now you mention it, perhaps you would be able to cheer me up,' Walter said with a sad smile.

'Forget it. Absolutely no chance!' Godiva laughed.

'Then I suppose that we shall just have to go on being friends,' Walter said, smiling. He hugged Godiva and gave her a chaste kiss on the forehead.

'There's nothing wrong with friendship,' Godiva said, hugging him back.

'I'll need someone to come back to after I have been on my jaunts,' Walter said, thoughtfully.

'Is that a proposal of marriage?' Godiva asked.

'Forget it. Absolutely no chance!' Walter answered with a laugh.

Author's Note

Walter and Godiva are totally imagined characters, even if I did borrow the name Mansell-Lacey from a village near Hereford. Many other characters who appear in this story really did exist. When the intelligence agencies were set up in 1909 the first directors were Mansfield Smith-Cumming and Vernon Kell. The head of MI6 to this day is known as 'C' from Cumming's lead. I am endebted to Keith Jeffery for his book 'MI6 – The History of the Secret Intelligence Service, 1909 – 1949' for providing some extra background I had not gleaned elsewhere. Various luminaries, including those from the world of literature were invited to comment on the setup and the roles of the various security agencies. These really did include Baden-Powell and Conan-Doyle amongst others.

One of the inspirations in writing this book was when I re-read Buchan's '39 Steps'. Apart from the holes in the plot you could drive a proverbial bus through, I was uncomfortably aware of the xenophobia and racism which appear in a very casual manner in the book. So I put Buchan in as an advisor as well, though he was not well known as an author at the time. If you want more detail of espionage not long after this period, you should read William Somerset-Maugham's book 'Ashenden', which is based on his own experiences. There really were gentleman spies.

During the research period and whilst checking facts during the writing I came across various other characters, such as

Arthur Gregory and Dorothy Levitt. Gregory was later involved in a scandal where he helped David Lloyd George to sell honours for cash. It seems likely that he personally murdered an ex-MP who was trying to expose his activities. He died in Paris in the 30's with a pension provided by the Conservative party, and he was a friend of Alisdair Crowley. If I have slandered him in any way it was in the knowledge that he was not a very nice person, and that he is dead, so he can't sue me. Dorothy Levitt, the fastest girl in the world, was a truly modern woman and an interesting counterpoint to Godiva's type of feminism. Little is known of her activities after 1910, so I felt it to be a fair possibility that she might have worked for the new intelligence agencies. She had a proud and successful record in car-racing, power-boat racing and she learned to fly as described. She raced on the hill-climb course at Shelsey Walsh, which is only a few miles from Great Whitley and is the oldest car racing venue in the world. Cumming was a mad driver, a qualified pilot and raced speedboats, so he might well have known Dorothy.

When I e-publishing an early version of the book, under the title 'Troubled Waters'. I found that I was selling multiple copies to addresses in Switzerland. Someone was keeping an eye on me!

The London locations are based on my vague knowledge of the geography of the city and some personal experience besides the input from my wife who is London born and bred. The descriptions of the clubs and the Admiralty buildings were taken from contemporary sources, but the Palatine Hotel is entirely invented. Shirl Castle is based loosely on Croft Castle in Herefordshire and Blackleigh Court on Great Whitley Court in Worcestershire. The latter was one of the greatest houses in England in its pomp, and was visited several times by the future Edward VII. Both houses are well worth a visit. If you find errors in any of the descriptions of these locations, of contemporary technology or of railway connections of the period I plead guilty, but I did make some effort to keep these reasonable, and it is a work of fiction, not an academic thesis.

Walter and Godiva can be found in the second instalment of their adventures, which takes place in 1910. Various historical characters will appear here as well, including Lenin in exile. This book is to be entitled 'Down in the Flood'. Suffice it to say that the main action is set in Paris in January 1910 and involves revolutionaries, Russian spies, the French security agency and Apache gangsters. I am looking forward to working with Godiva and Walter again in another adventure.

In the meantime, here is the first chapter of 'Down in the Flood' as a taster.

JW

Tuesday 3rd January 1910

Rain squalls were blowing around the Hampshire heath-land making the soldiers shiver. They were dressed only in their PE kit of singlets, shorts and pumps. Walter had been singled out for special treatment by the drill sergeant and was feeling picked on, but not as much as the private who had been selected to act as his target.

'Not right, your bloody lordship. Bite the bastard; gouge his eyes, kick him in the testicles. He's no gentleman, so don't treat him like he is one. Just stop him. Put him out of action,' Sergeant Farmer barked into Walter's face, spraying him with spittle. Walter was breathing heavily from the exertions of his recent action. The soldier who had been volunteered as the target was wearing a heavily padded jacket and lay groaning on his side, having been hit several times, very hard by some of Walter's best body punches.

'I put him down, didn't I?' Walter pointed out.

'I put him down, didn't I, Sergeant,' the sergeant screamed back at him, thin streams of spittle flying from his lips.

'Well I did...... Sergeant,' Walter corrected himself. He wasn't much enjoying this part of his training.

''You too bleedin' posh to talk like a soldier, you great gangly bastard?' the sergeant continued.

'Look, I really don't think I need to be here,' Walter tried to explain.

'Oh, too high and mighty, are we, too good for the likes of us,' Sergeant Farmer said very loudly, a few inches from Walter's face.

'Well, I don't want to put too much emphasis on this, but this is about fitness and self-defence. I'm already fitter and better at self-defence than anyone here, including you, Sergeant,' Walter drawled. The sergeant's face turned purple and he seemed to burst even more blood-vessels in his cheeks.

'You really think you are better than me, do you?' Farmer screamed, 'we'll bloody well see about that. Now you'd better get ready to have your pretty face all bruised you posh bastard!'

'You are welcome to try, Sergeant, but I'd better warn you that I'm a pretty useful boxer. I think I just proved that with what you made me do to young Evans, there,' Walter said in an even tone with the ghost of a smile on his lips.

'What if he had a knife, eh? You wouldn't want to try to punch him then, would you?' the sergeant barked out again. 'Wikins! Get over 'ere with that bleedin' knife.'

A tall, gangling private with ginger hair jogged over with a large knife in his hand and presented himself.

'Right, Mr clever dick Lord fucking almighty, watch this and learn. Wilkins, attack me with that knife!'

Wilkins, the ginger-haired private, winced visibly about being called out, but he raised the knife overhand and lunged clumsily at the sergeant, a grimace of real intent on his face. At the last moment the sergeant stepped sideways and elbowed the hapless Wilkins on the chin. The private dropped the knife, then rolled on the ground, kicking his legs and gurgling.

'Did you see what I did there? Think you could do that?' the sergeant shouted.

'Yes, Sergeant. To both of your questions,' Walter answered.

'Well, see what you can do about this, then,' the sergeant said through gritted teeth. He picked up the knife and advanced slowly towards Walter, knife held underhand, swinging the blade in a figure of eight. Walter retreated in good order until he realised that he was being forced back against a fence. He feinted to move to his left then instantly moved back, stepping inside the swing of the knife, and then hitting the sergeant's upper right arm with the flat of his hand. This stopped Farmer's advance and caused him to wobble slightly. Walter leaned backwards and knocked the sergeant's legs from beneath him with a scything kick. The sergeant went down on his back, his head bouncing on the ground. As he lay winded and stunned Walter scrambled to his feet, then he knelt down hard on the sergeant's groin. The sergeant let out a wheezing groan, and the recruits around all let out a loud cheer, breaking ranks to get a better look at their tormentor's discomfort.

'And that's a couple of acres for you, Sergeant Farmer,' Walter said, getting to his feet. He patted his damp hair down and brushed the worst of the grass and mud from his drill shorts with the flat of his hand.

There was the noise of a galloping horse, with the sound of hooves on wet turf getting louder as it approached. A junior lieutenant in olive drab, apart from gleaming black riding boots, rode up to the straggle of men gathered around the prostrate sergeant.

'Is Lord Walter Mansell-Lacey here?' he asked of no-one in particular.

'That's me,' Walter replied, stepping towards him.

'There's a major wants to see you back at HQ straight away,' the rider said.

'Right-ho, I'll hop along as soon as I can. Got any transport? Walter said, looking round for a vehicle.

''Fraid not,' said the lieutenant.

'Lend me the nag then, will you. Damn sight quicker than walking all the way back,' Walter said, motioning towards the horse.

'Not sure I can do that, my lord. That wasn't what I was asked to do. I was just delivering the message,' said the lieutenant, looking a little anxious.

'You did say it was urgent, didn't you. So use your initiative. Isn't that what you're supposed to do as an officer?'

'Oh, alright then,' the lieutenant reluctantly agreed.

Walter held the bridle for the lieutenant while he dismounted, then lifted himself easily into the saddle.

'Do send my apologies to the sergeant, will you. Explain to him that I was called away,' Walter said with a smile. He turned the horse, a tall black gelding with a white star on its forehead, and rode in the direction of the sprawling mock gothic house which was the unit HQ.

Walter dismounted outside the stables, leaving instructions that the horse should be returned to the young lieutenant as soon as possible. He found a coat with the badges of rank of a captain on a rack. It was two sizes too small for him and far too narrow in the shoulders. He made his way into the house. His shorts and legs were liberally splashed with grey-brown mud.

Walter had to navigate through the corridors of dark oak panelling and up a wide, sweeping staircase to a first-floor room where he had been told the Major was waiting. He rapped loudly on the door.

'Come in,' a voice called out loudly.

Walter pushed the door open and strode into the room. He approached the desk and made a sloppy attempt at a salute, which the Major ignored.

'Forget the salute, but please slouch to attention,' the colonel suggested. He continued to write, his head bowed towards the table. His light brown hair was thinning and the scalp was sunburnt in places, indicating that he had returned only a few weeks ago from a warmer climate.

'You've got a job for me, then,' Walter said, with a slight hint of excitement in his voice. The Major studied Walter's face as if trying to read his thoughts. He was a fleshy man of about fifty years with a moustache like a yard broom

'Colonel Cumming has asked you to do a little job. You've been asked to get ready to travel for a few weeks. You're to go up to London first, as he needs to brief you about the job.'

'Does this job mean working abroad?' Walter asked.

'I believe so,' the Major answered, in a slow and meticulous fashion, 'but, as I said, you need to ask Colonel Cumming about the details.'

'I'd better be on my way, then,' Walter said.

'He's expecting you in two hours. I'll get a driver to take you to the station,' the Major said, 'In the meantime I suggest you put some proper clothing on and return that poor captain's jacket to where you found it, and let us hope that you haven't stretched it beyond use.'

'Yes, Sir,' Walter agreed.

'You should just make it if you take the next train. I'll get my driver to take you to the station now,' the Major said. He pressed a button on his desk. An orderly came smartly in and gave a sharp salute.

'Get my driver to take this gentleman to the station immediately,' the Major ordered.

'What about my things?' Walter asked.

'They're in the car, waiting for you,' the Major said.

'Right; thank you, I suppose,' Walter murmured.

'And surpass expectations,' the Major shouted as Walter left.

*

The offices of newly formed Special Intelligence Services were in a prepossessing building at 64 Victoria Street, which had many turrets and towers in its construction and used more red terracotta brick than good taste allowed for. The office of the joint directors was on the third of seven floors and was cramped and not well designed. To make it even more inconvenient, Colonel Mansfield Smith-Cumming shared his office with Vernon Kell, the head of home security. Cumming's desk had neat piles of papers arranged around a blotter which was edged with green tooled leather. Standing behind Cumming was a small, balding, square-faced man in a dull grey suit and round celluloid collar who studied Walter as he came into the room.

'Ah, Walter, good of you to come so quickly. Not to beat about the bush, I think we might have a little job for you. How's your French?' Cumming said.

'Erm, not bad, I suppose. Not exactly perfect, though,' Walter answered, a little confused.

'That's alright, it will probably be enough. I don't suppose you have any Russian?'

'No, none at all,' Walter admitted, wondering what the job might be.

'That's a pity, but I'm sure you'll muddle through. We want you to do a little job for us in Paris. There are some political exiles out there, revolutionary types and we need to find out what they are doing. This is partly because we think they are organising trouble over here and partly because we need to keep the Russians sweet, as they are on our side, and these revolutionaries certainly want to get rid of the Czar. Think you can manage that?' Cumming asked. The little man winced slightly at this exposition.

'Sorry, but I'm not exactly sure what you want me to do,' Walter said, genuinely puzzled by Cumming's elliptical explanation.

'I want you to seduce the chief revolutionary's mistress and then get her to spill his secrets,' Cummins said with greater precision.

'Well, I'll give it a go. I'll need some more information, before I leave,' Walter said carefully.

'That's where Mr, errr.... Detective Fitch comes in. He's from Special Branch and can give you all the information you need.'

'Don't I need to receive a bit more training on codes and things?' Walter asked

'Oh, don't worry about that. It all takes too long. But what I'm more concerned about is making sure that you're willing to do the dirty on this woman. I want you persuade her to tell us what's going on. You've got to be willing to use her in any way that will work, and have no conscience about it. Think you can manage that?' Cumming said, almost without drawing breath.

'If you ask any of my former lady friends they will tell you that is exactly what I am like,' Walter admitted with a slightly twisted smile.

'Splendid, that's exactly what I wanted to hear. Think you can be ready to leave by tonight?' Cumming asked.

'Yes, I suppose so. Like I said, I was expecting a bit more training first,' Walter answered.

'How is your training going, by the way?' Cumming asked.

'Well, to be perfectly frank, it's no bloody use to me. It isn't exactly what I was expecting, doing PT with a bunch of recruits. I thought it would be about learning secret stuff, like codes and things,' Walter complained.

'Damned if I know why they put you in the charge of a drill sergeant. From all the reports I have received from your instructors you are judged to be lazy, insubordinate and thoroughly arrogant. There's sat there's nothing they can teach you there that you don't already know. We'll be setting up some proper training place next year, so when you come back, we should have something which proves more useful to you. You'll just have to pick it up as you go along in the meantime,' Cumming said.

'I'll pack my bags and be on my way, then,' Walter said, turning to leave.

'Take this gentleman with you. I'm sure he has a great deal to tell you. Best of luck in Paris,' Cumming called out.

'Right-ho,' said Walter. Detective Fitch followed Walter out of the office, staying just behind his shoulder. Walter turned his head to speak.

'What should I call you? I mean, I have to call you something, don't I?'

'You can call me Fitch',' said the man in a slightly squeaky voice, after a few seconds consideration.

'I suppose you are looking for a more discrete place to talk,' Walter commented. Fitch coughed slightly but otherwise didn't reply. He overtook Walter and led him along.

They walked down the corridor, then up a flight of stairs and to the cramped room which was half filled with papers. Sitting behind a small desk was Godiva Williams, Walter's friend and sometime flatmate. The top of the desk was mostly covered by a new Imperial typewriter, He blinked in surprise at seeing her there, and she smiled back at him in a professional way. Fitch carefully shut the door after checking for anyone who might be listening in the corridor.

Godiva was comparing two type-written reports. She was dressed like a respectable typist in an insurance office.

'Oh, hello, Walter. You did well getting here so quickly. As soon as Cumming gave me a time for your arrival I checked it with the trains. I really don't know how he manages to organise his department,' she said, and she smiled up at him.

'Well, I suppose it's a bit different for him. He doesn't need to keep tabs on all those refugees and immigrants like your lot do,' Walter answered. 'Mind you, there are times when we need a bit of organising, which is why they sent me to see you, I suppose.'

'It's very good to see you Walter. I hope the training isn't too painful,' she said with a girlish giggle.

'Not painful for me,' Walter replied with a slightly twisted smile, 'Now, what is it that you wanted to tell me?'

'Oh, do sit down, you're making the place look untidy,' Godiva said.

'Well, I would if there was a chair,' Walter answered.

'Oh, fetch one from out there,' Godiva said, waving a hand in the direction of the door. Walter fetched a small bent wood chair from the outer office and placed himself in an elegant pose in front of the desk, his gloves in his hat on his lap and his feet crossed at the ankles.

'Bloody awful room, isn't it?' said Walter, looking around.

'Better than the accommodation your fellow recruits have,' Fitch said in his reedy voice. He was standing next to Godiva.

'Yes, I suppose so. Now, are you going to tell me exactly what I'm supposed to be doing in Paris?' Walter enquired, looking towards Godiva. It was Fitch who spoke first.

'Like the Colonel said, it's about some political exiles living there. Normally we would just keep an eye on them, and let them quietly rot. However, this lot are a bit different. They have quite a lot of money, which is unusual, and they are a pretty tight group, and we haven't found a way into the group yet. It seems that someone is advising them on how to organise themselves and is also providing them with money. The group that is causing us concern consists of Latvian, but they are co-operating with one Russian group in particular, they call themselves Bolsheviks. Now, Russia's in a bit of a mess at the moment, but we need to keep them on our side. The Czar's a fool, and he's ruled by his wife. She, in her turn is ruled by some rather dubious friends. The whole country could quite easily descend into anarchy. The Czar's an absolutist, and there are lots of aristocrats who are very unhappy. The middle class have been anxious for years. You don't have revolutions without annoying the middle classes. If the money is coming to the Bolsheviks from Russia it would be difficult, but if it is coming from somewhere else, like Germany or Austria, it would be a good deal more serious'.

Godiva spoke next.

'The leader of the Bolsheviks is Vladimir Ulyanov, but he has many other aliases. He runs a newspaper, and when he writes he usually goes by the name of Lenin. He's thirty something years old, and he's Russian, of course. His family are quite middle class, and his father got some kind of gong from their civil service. Mind you, his brother was hung for trying to blow up the Czar, and the whole family is quite radical. He was in internal exile in Siberia, but had to leave Russia after sailing a bit too near the wind. He's been moving around lots of European cities, including London. He writes and edits his own radical newspaper and also produces rabble-rousing pamphlets which advocate the violent overthrow of the government in Russia. Many people think that he is the most influential of the exiled revolutionaries. The thing you need to bear in mind is that the Bolsheviks, unlike the other groups, never want to negotiate or organise a peaceful transfer of power.'

'I thought that you of all people would have a certain amount of sympathy for his aims,' Walter commented, knowing Godiva's socialist sympathies.

'For his aims perhaps, but not for his means. The way he wants to go about bringing reform will leave a lot of innocent people dead. From my moral standpoint, getting people killed is almost universally a bad thing to do,' Godiva answered with a slight grimace. 'As it happens, I have a lot of sympathy for reform in Russia. Did you know that there are almost two thousand topics of conversation that can't legally be mentioned? We had a lot of Russians at our house. My father is very keen on constitutional reform, and he says that in violent revolutions the very worst sort of people rise to power, and I tend to agree with him. This man, Ulyanov has been in London, and I've got all the details of his time here. A lot of the information comes from Detective Fitch, here. Ulyanov's dedication and hard work are really admirable, but he's a miserable man, with no sense of humour or proportion. His stated aim is to increase the happiness of the people of Russia. Trust me when I tell you that if he ever gets any power he will make most of them very miserable.'

'We need this information quite urgently. The Home Office and the Foreign Office are both quite keen to know what's going on so they can work out new policies. Normally SIS wouldn't involve anyone like you, but the Colonel has convinced me that we need someone with your talents. There's a woman who works for the leader of the group. We are just about certain the she is, or was, his mistress. Lately they seem to have disagreed about something and she's none too happy about it. We thought we could use you as bait,' Fitch explained patiently.

'So what's the name of this woman?' Walter asked.

'The woman's called Armand, Inessa Armand, sometimes she calls herself Stephane. She's half French and half English and she was married to a Russian and grew up in Russia. She's thirty four now, but still a bit of a looker. Be careful, mind, she's still a dedicated revolutionary,' Fitch said.

'How do you propose that I introduce myself to her?' Walter asked.

'The idea we are working on is for a couple of toughs to threaten her. You come to her rescue and get to know her as her knight in shining armour. It is essential that you make the rescue look convincing though, as we don't want her to suspect anything. I understand that you will be posing as some kind of artist. That gives you a reason to be in Paris and makes you sound suitably bohemian. If you insist on buying her a coffee or a brandy, just to make sure she's alright it ought to give enough time to get to know her. Perhaps you could tell some story about being involved with the Suffragettes,' Fitch continued.

'Strangely enough, one of my best friends is involved with the women's suffrage movement,' Walter said, half smiling at Godiva, 'I'm not sure about the plan, though. It sounds a bit thin to me.'

'I'm sure we can refine it once you are in Paris. Anyway, I've got all your documents. Can you be ready to leave in a couple of hours?' Godiva said.

'That sounds fine to be. I'd quite like to get back to Paris. There's some old friends I'd like to look up,' Walter said.

'Absolutely not!,' Fitch insisted, 'You will be staying there under an assumed name. We can't have you being recognised while you are in Paris. You will have to keep well away from anyone who is acquainted with you, and any places where you might be known. This isn't a holiday, you know, it's a serious job.'

'Then I take it that I'm not staying in a good hotel,' Walter said with a sigh.

'We have a house near to Ulyanov's apartment on Rue Marie Rose. Somehow I doubt that anyone will recognise you in that district. The good nightclubs and theatres are definitely out of bounds as well,' Fitch said.

'That all sounds rather depressing,' Walter commented.

'The Colonel's going out on a limb for you here. You're not properly trained as yet, so he really shouldn't be sending you. I really hope that we can trust you,' Fitch said in a worried voice, 'now, do you have any questions?'

'Well, quite a lot, actually. I'm going to need a good deal more background information, and what about telling the French security people what I'm doing?' Walter continued.

'I've arranged for you to liaise with the French security agency. Call themselves the Tigers or some such nonsense. One of their people will get in touch once you are in Paris. As for the background, I'll leave that to Miss Williams. She's been working on Ulyanov's case for a little while now. In fact it was her who flagged up the connection between him and the Latvians. Clever girl, Miss Williams,' Fitch said, ending with a short, sharp laugh.

'So, in what way does this man pose a threat to us?' Walter asked.

'He is the spider at the centre of a web of intrigue. There are many groups who rely on him for their planning, and for the money to support their causes. You must remember the Tottenham Outrage about a year ago. There was a policeman and a ten-year old boy killed. Two Latvians tried to rob the wages from a factory. There was a chase, during which the Latvians were shooting all the time. They were eventually cornered and killed. The thing is, they were members of an anarchist group who want independence for Latvia. They needed the money for the group, to build bombs and such. They are far from being the only revolutionary group hiding in England, but mostly these groups are grateful for the shelter we offer. We try to keep tabs on them, or Captain Kell does. Recently, another Latvian group set up, and these ones are linked to our puppet master in Paris. This group is much better organised and funded than the Tottenham people. They pose a threat to our security, and we're sure they are planning more robberies and possibly bomb attacks,' Fitch said.

'So, tell me more about this spy-master in Paris' Walter asked Godiva, half closing his eyes in order to listen better.

'I've been looking at his notes for two weeks now. I started out thinking he had a righteous cause, but a couple of days in, I realized that he had systematically removed any potential rival from his organisation. He is totally obsessed with security, and won't let anyone near him. He lives his life through codes and ciphers. And he's the sort of person who would lay down the life of his friends to save his own reputation. His greatest scorn is reserved for anyone who might wish to negotiate or compromise. Having looked at his books and newspapers I can tell you that his writing is just awful, full of cliché and cant. This man is capable of anything.'

'So I was right. You really don't like him,' Walter said with a smile and a nod.

'What I think about him is not important. The fact is, he supports armed struggle and doesn't care who gets hurt. He encourages all sorts of groups and teaches them how to act as revolutionaries. Some of these groups are active here in England, especially in London, and we expect them to try to raise money by armed robbery,' Godiva continued.

'I thought this Ulyanov man was supplying these groups with money?' Walter questioned.

'Not directly with money, much more with support and training. He's taught a lot of people how to avoid detection and disappear into the background. There is some evidence that he gets them instructed in bomb making and such. There's one man in particular we want to find out about. This one's a Latvian anarchist we know as Peter the Painter. Of course, they all have loads of names. The point is, this Peter the Painter character is very active and is based in London. He used to be a part of Ulyanov's group, but he split away. That's something Ulyanov is not at all keen on, but he might forgive him because he's not a Russian. The thing is, Ulyanov appears quite polite, almost respectable. He even wrote a thank you letter to his landlady when he stayed over here. Also, the policy of the Home Office is to let most of these groups alone, while keeping a watchful eye on them. The thinking is that it is better to let them release their own steam off. If we tried to keep a lid on it the pressure would just build up to an explosion, just like what is happening in Russia. Ulyanov even had a couple of meetings in London for Russian exiles, and we had to use the police to guard them from attack by people stirred up by the reporting in the Daily Mail. Ulyanov know which side his bread is buttered and wouldn't want any attacks to happen here. This Peter the Painter is very different in that he doesn't mind biting the hand that feeds him. He's a very dangerous man, and we know he's already killed several people in his community. If he knew how to build bombs I am certain he wouldn't have any problem setting them off here,' Godiva explained.

'So is Ulyanov sponsoring this Peter man?' Walter asked, struggling to take in the flood of information.

'The service Ulyanov really supplies is expertise, that and the attitude that everything you do is alright, provided it's in the name of the revolution. He tells them how to organise the cells so it is difficult for us to put agents in, and he has other people who can teach them how to build bombs and where to get guns. I told you about the newspaper, but he also produces pamphlets that get delivered to the groups, which tell lurid stories of atrocities. I mean, Russia is in a pretty awful state, but I can't believe some of this stuff,' Godiva continued in an animated way. 'Oh, and that reminds me, be careful, be very careful of the Russian secret service, the Okhrana. If you come across any of them, run a mile. They are particularly vicious.'

'Well, if I spot any of them I'll let you know. Now, tell me, who's doing the translation of all these documents for you?' Walter asked.

'Detective Fitch speaks Russian very well,' Godiva said, nodding towards her colleague, 'and there's a little man we use, but recently I've started learning some Russian myself. I can't speak a word, of course, but I can read it quite well. Anyway, I need to tell you about how Ulyanov's household is set up. He shares a pretty decent apartment with his wife and mother in law. Look, this is stuff you'll need to know by the time you get to Paris. I've got some photos here, and a précis of the notes from the time he was in London.' She pushed a thick sheaf of notes across the desk towards him.

'Ah, a little light reading!' Walter said with a crooked smile.

'Don't worry, you'll have time to read it during your journey,' with a slight smile.

'And when am I supposed to leave?' Walter asked.

'AS I said before, in about two hours,' Godiva replied as she consulted her fob watch.

'Oh, I was hoping to spend an evening in town,' Walter said, sounding a little disappointed, 'Try to catch up with a few friends, perhaps.'

'You'll just have to make new lady friends on the boat train,' Godiva said knowingly. 'I've got your tickets here. And I've a request from 'K' that you go easy on the expenses. We've put some money in an account, but it is a modest amount. There should be enough Francs to be getting along with for a few days and the tickets are there. The details of the account are clear and you can access the money from any Thomas Cook office. Please provide receipts for all of your expenditure, unless you want it taken out of your wages, and remember that the person you are supposed to be hasn't much money. We've booked you into a room not far from Ulyanov's house. The address is in with the other stuff. You'll need to take some of your painting gear with you, enough to travel with.'

'So who am I supposed to be?' Walter askcd, 'and since when did Kell become 'K'?'

'We've got you down as a struggling artist. It's easiest if you keep the name Walter, but from now until you return, your sur-name is Davies. You are the son of the headmaster of a small private school in Sussex. You've quarrelled with your father who refuses to support you while you try to realise your artistic ambitions. It seems quite natural that you would go to Paris, don't you think?' Godiva explained.

'Righty-ho,' said Walter, 'But what about some background on Ulyanov's mistress?'

'Well the details are in the folder, along with some photographs. She's not unattractive, so it shouldn't be too difficult for you to act the part of seducer. Sometimes Ulyanov sends her on missions when he can't turn up, and he has to brief her, so she can provide a good deal of useful information as to who he's been writing to, and what is going on.,' Godiva explained in a slightly testy voice.

'What about the wife?' Walter continued.

'She's a few years older that Ulyanov, and a dedicated revolutionary herself. If she's ever shown any sign of human feelings we have yet to find any evidence. Intellectually she is not in the same league as her husband, but I'm sure she does vital work for him. We think she's a dead loss as a target. She's prepared to live off a little black bread and some water, look after her mother and any whim of Ulyanov and has no fun at all,' Godiva said.

'Is there any more background you need to tell me about?' Walter asked.

'Just a little, I suppose. This is about the Bolsheviks. The word means something like 'the majority of men'. Their main opponents are known as the Mensheviks, or 'the minority of men'. It all came about after a conference. The biggest group got fed up with Ulyanov and left at the end of the evening. Ulyanov then took a vote with mostly his supporters there, and, surprise, surprise, he won it. It was totally unconstitutional of course, but it is typical of the man that he immediately went about shouting about how the vote showed who was the real leader. You'll probably come across some of the Mensheviks along with disillusioned Bolsheviks in Paris. There are a lot more of them than of Ulyanov's people, and they can be found in the cafés and bars, discussing things quite openly. We don't think they're a real problem. Mostly, they are quite reasonable men, and, as I said, Russia really does need a lot of reform. They are the sort of people we can work with, when Russia gets into an even worse state, which it will do. Of course, we can't be seen to be plotting against the Czar, as the Russians are our allies, but just a little reform would go a long way to calming things down there, but their rulers don't want to consider any change,' Godiva said, reeling off the facts like an encyclopaedia.

'I hope this is all in the folder, because I'm sure I haven't taken most of it in,' Walter said, feeling a little overwhelmed.

'Yes, of course. You'll find all that, and plenty more besides in the folder. Please don't flash it about in public. We don't want the French intelligence people, the 2*ieme* Bureau, to know exactly what we know, and they won't tell us everything they know. That's the thing about diplomacy; you need to keep a careful eye on your friends, as well as your enemies. You'll be met by a French intelligence agent when you get to Paris. So don't be too open with the French. Now, I've divided the folder into two sections. At the front are things you can tell this French agent. At the back are the more sensitive papers. That's a much smaller folder. So, for once in your life, Walter, please try to be discrete,' Godiva urged.

'I thought you said I would be dealing with this Tigers mob, now you tell me the French intelligence agency is the 2*ieme* Bureau,' Walter commented.

'Ah, yes,' Godiva started, 'You see the 2*ieme* Bureau is the established agency and they are largely responsible for external intelligence gathering. They don't really have anything to do with counter intelligence. The *Brigades du Tigre* were set up through Clemenceau by the head of Police, Hennion, to combat the criminal gangs, but the Prime Minister has broadened their remit, so they are looking into the activities of foreign political groups and refugees. The other thing is that the 2*ieme* Bureau doesn't trust us British, we are the old enemy, so the Tigers are more likely to co-operate.'

'I'd better get myself ready, then,' Walter said, his head spinning from an excess of information, 'I haven't got much time to get my stuff together before I go to the station. Nice to meet up again, Godiva. Perhaps we can have dinner sometime, after I get back.'

'That would be very nice,' Godiva said, 'but I'm not sure when you'll get back.'

'I'll send you a note when I return,' Walter said. He had realised that his relationship with Godiva was now very different to how it had been. He hoped that outside of work they could get back to being friends. He left after giving Godiva a brotherly kiss on the cheek, shook Fitch by the hand, then hurried outside to get a taxi to his studio in Pimlico, from where he could pick up a set of painting gear suitable for travel. From there he travelled to Victoria Station, to the platform where the train for Dover Marine station would leave.

The ticket he had been given was third class, which was just right for the character he was supposed to be creating, but he had some cash in his pocket and upgraded the ticket to first class for the journey to Dover.

*

A vicious easterly wind was whipping sea-spray around the platforms of Dover Marine station. It stung the eyes of the people who descended from the train at the end of the line. As it dried it would leave white flecks of salt on the dark overcoats of the travellers.

When Walter reached the ticket barrier and the path to the ferry he found the route blocked and a notice informing passengers that the crossing was suspended due to storms. Accommodation was to be provided at a hotel on the harbour front. A charabanc was laid on to transport the passengers the one mile to the hotel. The driver was wrapped in several coats, with a hat, scarf and gloves, but all this did not stop him shivering. As they approached they could see him slapping his arms against his sides to encourage some blood flow.

There were fourteen of them who needed to get into the charabanc, assisted by the railway porters. With their luggage they filled the vehicle. When they were settled in their seats, huddled against the wind and the showers of sleet the bus was encouraged into spluttering life and they were jerked into motion. The street lights were reflected in the glassy surface of the wet road. The surface was tar macadam bonded with granite chips. The quartzite in the stone reflected the light back like cut diamonds. After a very few minutes they arrived at the front of the hotel. This was a white stuccoed structure three stories high which formed part of a crescent which ran along the sea front. Fancy iron work fronted the balconies which faced the harbour. Streaks of rust discoloured the stucco where the iron was embedded into the walls. Their luggage was carried inside by two grumbling porters and dumped in the entrance.

The travellers queued to get their keys at the reception desk. When it came to his turn, Walter decided to pay extra for a room with its own bathroom. He was still feeling the effects of his exertions at the training camp and had mud to wash off. The bath would have to wait for some time, as the dinner gong rang to tell guests to go to the restaurant. Walter only had time to send his luggage to his room and change for dinner before eating.

The meal was not good. It looked appetising enough, but lacked flavour, and was unevenly hot. The wine was cheap, thin and unpleasant, and Walter regretted choosing it. A pint of Bass would have been a much better selection. Across the room he noticed a table at which two women were eating. They were both quite thin, but the younger one had a good bone structure and a certain physical presence. The older woman was severe and mousy, which was an unattractive combination. The younger woman, a girl in reality, gave Walter a small smile, and, when she noticed, the older woman scowled at both the girl and Walter.

*

Walter was taking a leisurely bath in an oversized tub before sleeping. He had just washed his hair and rinsed off the suds by lying down and dipping his head under the water. As he raised his head he heard the outer door of his room being softly opened. In an instant he switched from being relaxed and sleepy to full attention. In sitting up suddenly he slopped some water from the broad rim of the bath onto the floor. After blinking the water from his eyes he fixed his gaze onto the door of the bathroom, which was partly ajar. He placed his hands on the side of the bath and prepared to spring from the tub. Part of a face appeared in the crack of the door, and some minimal pressure caused the door to open inwards. The girl who had been at dinner was looking at him with the same interest and curiosity that he was feeling himself. She was dressed in a respectable dressing gown and ankle slippers. Neither gown or slippers were particularly suited to her slim frame.

'Oh, you're in the bath,' she said, stating the obvious.

'Yes, I'm in the bath,' Walter agreed, wondering where this conversation was leading.

'This is a much nicer room than ours. We have to share a bathroom. It's not very nice having to share with other people, especially if you don't know them,' she continued.

'Is there some reason why you have come into my room; other than to admire it, that is?' Walter asked, feeling more perplexed than anxious.

The girl shuffled into the room and stared down at him as he sat in the bath. Then she giggled. 'Gosh, I've never seen a man with no clothes on before. Well, not a young man, anyway. I think you're very handsome. I hope you don't mind me looking at you like this, only I saw you in the restaurant, and I couldn't help noticing how good looking you were,' she said in staccato phrases.

'Well, thank you for those words of admiration. Look, I'm a little disconcerted by this. I'm sure young ladies aren't supposed to come into the bathrooms of gentlemen, especially if they've not been introduced,' Walter said softly.

'How was I supposed to get introduced to you? I couldn't march up to you in the restaurant, could I? Especially with old Cauldicott guarding me the way she does', the young woman continued, now looking down the length of Walter's torso to his groin.

'So, Miss Cauldicott is your companion. But I still don't know who you are, nor what you're doing in my bathroom,' Walter said, with a small note of impatience in his voice.

'Cauldicott is the dragon of a companion my parents have sent to guard me on the journey. Before we went to bed I put an extra sleeping draft into her warm milk. She won't wake until the morning, so we won't be disturbed.'

'If you won't make the introductions, I'd better help you,' Walter said patiently, 'My name is Walter Davies. I'm an artist.'

'I'm Annabella Aphrodite Saville, and I'm going back to my finishing school after the Christmas break,' said the girl.

'I heard your companion call you Bella in the restaurant,' Walter admitted.

'I hate that name, it's so unromantic,' she said, peevishly, 'that's why I always try to use my full name.'

'And now that I know your name, Miss Annabella Aphrodite Saville, could you please tell me why you came to my room?' Walter asked, now thoroughly amused by the situation.

'Well, I was wondering if you'd like to have sex with me. We talk a lot about sex in the school, and some of the girls boast that they have already lost their virginity, but the men these girls chose were usually unsuitable, you know, quite common types. When I saw you, and noticed that you didn't have anyone with you, I thought you looked just the right sort of man to do the deed. It would mean so much to me if I could arrive back at school with some really juicy event to talk about. My life's mostly pretty boring,' she said.' You don't look much like an artist. You're too clean and not sort of bohemian enough,' she added.

'I am an artist, though. My money mostly comes from my father, and he knows some rich people who buy my paintings. It's easier to sell them if I don't look too scruffy,' Walter explained. 'And how did you know which was my room?'

'I was listening when you were talking to the man at the desk,' she answered.

'I didn't notice you at the time,' Walter admitted, 'Very remiss of me. How old are you, Annabella Aphrodite?'

'I'll be eighteen next month,' said the girl.

'So, you're only seventeen. You really are a very bold girl,' Walter said.

'Shall I go away, or do you want to have sex with me?' the girl asked directly.

'I'll tell you what; you take that dressing gown off and get into the bed and I'll get myself dried off and join you in a minute,' Walter said.

'Do you want me to take my nightdress off as well?' the girl asked.

'That would save a bit of bother later,' Walter agreed.

'Righty-ho,' the girl said. She handed the towel to him, kissing him chastely on the cheek as she leaned forward, and then turned to leave the bathroom. Walter towelled himself dry, dropped the towel onto the damp floor and put on his nightshirt. With a slight smile he reflected that he could hardly be accused of seduction in this case. It should be an amusing way to spend the night. He put on his nightshirt and walked out of the bathroom to join the girl who was waiting for him in the bed, between the cool starched linen sheets.

Lightning Source UK Ltd.
Milton Keynes UK
UKOW03f1153091213

222649UK00006B/46/P